"SLEEK AND NASTY . . . IT'S A BIG, SCARY,
SUSPENSEFUL READ, AND I LOVED EVERY MINUTE OF IT!"
—STEPHEN KING

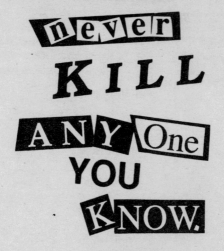

never **KILL** ANY One YOU KNOW.

DON'T MISS
THESE BESTSELLING "LUCAS DAVENPORT" THRILLERS
BY JOHN SANDFORD . . .

SHADOW PREY

"ICE-PICK CHILLS . . . EXCRUCIATINGLY TENSE . . .
A DOUBLE-PUMPED ROUNDHOUSE OF A THRILLER!"
—*KIRKUS*

EYES OF PREY

"ENGROSSING . . . ONE OF THE MOST HORRIBLE VILLAINS
THIS SIDE OF HANNIBAL THE CANNIBAL!"
—*RICHMOND TIMES-DISPATCH*

Berkley Books by John Sandford

RULES OF PREY

JOHN SANDFORD

B

BERKLEY BOOKS, NEW YORK

If you purchased this book without a cover, you should be aware that this book is stolen property. It was reported as "unsold and destroyed" to the publisher, and neither the author nor the publisher has received any payment for this "stripped book."

This is a work of fiction. Names, characters, places, and incidents are either the product of the author's imagination or are used fictitiously, and any resemblance to actual persons, living or dead, business establishments, events, or locales is entirely coincidental.

This Berkley book contains the complete text
of the original hardcover edition. It has been
completely reset in a typeface designed
for easy reading and was printed from new film.

RULES OF PREY

A Berkley Book / published by arrangement with
the author

PRINTING HISTORY
G. P. Putnam's Sons edition / July 1989
Berkley edition / April 1990

All rights reserved.
Copyright © 1989 by John Sandford.
Teaser copyright © 1990 by John Sandford.
This book may not be reproduced in whole or in part,
by mimeograph or any other means, without permission.
For information address: G. P. Putnam's Sons,
a division of Penguin Putnam Inc.,
375 Hudson Street, New York, New York 10014.

The Penguin Putnam Inc. World Wide Web site address is
http://www.penguinputnam.com

ISBN: 0-425-12163-1

BERKLEY®
Berkley Books are published by The Berkley Publishing Group,
a division of Penguin Putnam Inc.,
375 Hudson Street, New York, New York 10014.
BERKLEY and the "B" design
are trademarks belonging to Penguin Putnam Inc.

PRINTED IN THE UNITED STATES OF AMERICA

40 39 38 37 36 35 34 33 32 31

CHAPTER

— 1 —

A rooftop billboard cast a flickering blue light through the studio windows. The light ricocheted off glass and stainless steel: an empty crystal bud vase rimed with dust, a pencil sharpener, a microwave oven, peanut-butter jars filled with drawing pencils, paintbrushes and crayons. An ashtray full of pennies and paper clips. Jars of poster paint. Knives.

A stereo was dimly visible as a collection of rectangular silhouettes on the window ledge. A digital clock punched red electronic minutes into the silence.

The maddog waited in the dark.

He could hear himself breathe. Feel the sweat trickle from the pores of his underarms. Taste the remains of his dinner. Feel the shaven stubble at his groin. Smell the odor of the Chosen's body.

He was never so alive as in the last moments of a long stalk. For some people, for people like his father, it must be like this every minute of every hour: life on a higher plane of existence.

The maddog watched the street. The Chosen was an artist. She had smooth olive skin and liquid brown eyes, tidy breasts and a slender waist. She lived illegally in the warehouse, bathing late at night in the communal rest room down the hall, furtively cooking microwave meals after the building manager left for the day. She slept on a narrow bed in a tiny storage room, beneath an art-deco crucifix, immersed in vapors of turpentine and linseed. She was out now, shopping for microwave dinners. The microwave crap would kill her if he didn't, the maddog thought. He was probably doing her a favor. He smiled.

The artist would be his third kill in the Cities, the fifth of his life.

The first was a ranch girl, riding out of her back pasture toward the wooded limestone hills of East Texas. She wore jeans, a red-and-white-checked shirt, and cowboy boots. She sat high in a western saddle, riding more with her knees and her head than with the reins in her hand. She came straight into him, her single blonde braid bouncing behind.

The maddog carried a rifle, a Remington Model 700 ADL in .270 Winchester. He braced his forearm against a rotting log and took her when she was forty yards out. The single shot penetrated her breastbone and blew her off the horse.

That was a killing of a different kind. She had not been Chosen; she had asked for it. She had said, three years before the killing, in the maddog's hearing, that he had lips like red worms. Like the twisting red worms that you found under river rocks. She said it in the hall of their high school, a cluster of friends standing around her. A few glanced over their shoulders at the maddog, who stood fifteen feet away, alone, as always, pushing his books onto the top shelf of his locker. He gave no sign that he'd overheard. He had been very good at concealment, even in his youngest days, though the ranch girl didn't seem to care one way or another. The maddog was a social nonentity.

But she paid for her careless talk. He held her comment to his breast for three years, knowing his time would come. And it did. She went off the back of the horse, stricken stone-cold dead by a fast-expanding copper-jacketed hunting bullet.

The maddog ran lightly through the woods and across a low stretch of swampy prairie. He dumped the gun beneath a rusting iron culvert where a road crossed the marsh. The culvert would confuse any metal detector used to hunt for the weapon, although the maddog didn't expect a search—it was deer season and the woods were full of maniacs from the cities, armed to the teeth and ready to kill. The season, the weapon cache, had all been determined far in advance. Even as a sophomore in college, the maddog was a planner.

He went to the girl's funeral. Her face was untouched and the top half of the coffin was left open. He sat as close as he could, in his dark suit, watched her face and felt the power rising. His only regret was that she had not known that death was coming, so that she might savor the pain; and that he had not had time to enjoy its passage.

The second killing was the first of the truly Chosen, although he no longer considered it a work of maturity. It was more of . . . an experiment? Yes. In the second killing, he remedied the deficiencies of the first.

She was a hooker. He took her during the spring break of his second year, the crisis year, in law school. The need had long been there, he thought. The intellectual pressure of law school compounded it. And one cool night in Dallas, with a knife, he earned temporary respite on the pale white body of a Mississippi peckerwood girl, come to the city to find her fortune.

The ranch girl's shooting death was lamented as a hunting accident. Her parents grieved and went on to other things. Two years later the maddog saw the girl's mother laughing outside a concert hall.

The Dallas cops dismissed the hooker's execution as a street killing, dope-related. They found Quaaludes in her purse, and that was good enough. All they had was a street name. They put her in a pauper's grave with that name, the wrong name, on the tiny iron plaque that marked the place. She had never seen her sixteenth year.

The two killings had been satisfying, but not fully calculated. The killings in the Cities were different. They were meticulously planned, their tactics based on a professional review of a dozen murder investigations.

The maddog was intelligent. He was a member of the bar. He derived rules.

Never kill anyone you know.

Never have a motive.

Never follow a discernible pattern.

Never carry a weapon after it has been used.
Isolate yourself from random discovery.
Beware of leaving physical evidence.
There were more. He built them into a challenge.

He was mad, of course. And he knew it.

In the best of worlds, he would prefer to be sane. Insanity brought with it a large measure of stress. He had pills now, black ones for high blood pressure, reddish-brown ones to help him sleep. He would prefer to be sane, but you played the hand you were dealt. His father said so. The mark of a man.

So he was mad.

But not quite the way the police thought.

He bound and gagged the women and raped them.

The police considered him a sex freak. A cold freak. He took his time about the killings and the rapes. They believed he talked to his victims, taunted them. He carefully used prophylactics. Lubricated prophylactics. Postmortem vaginal smears on the first two Cities victims produced evidence of the lubricant. Since the cops never found the rubbers, they assumed he took them with him.

Consulting psychiatrists, hired to construct a psychological profile, believed the maddog *feared* women. Possibly the result of a youthful life with a dominant mother, they said, a mother alternately tyrannical and loving, with sexual overtones. Possibly the maddog was afraid of AIDS, and possibly—they talked of endless possibilities—he was essentially homosexual.

Possibly, they said, he might *do something* with the semen he saved in the prophylactics. When the shrinks said that, the cops looked at each other. Do something? Do what? Make Sno-Cones? What?

The psychiatrists were wrong. About all of it.

He did not taunt his victims, he comforted them; helped them to *participate.* He didn't use the rubbers primarily to protect himself from disease, but to protect himself from the police. Semen is evidence, carefully collected, examined, and typed by medical investigators. The maddog knew of a case where a woman was attacked, raped, and killed by one of two panhandlers. Each man accused the other. A semen-typing was pivotal in isolating the killer.

The maddog didn't save the rubbers. He didn't *do something* with them. He flushed them, with their evidentiary load, down his victims' toilets.

Nor was his mother a tyrant.

She had been a small unhappy dark-haired woman who wore calico dresses and wide-brimmed straw hats in the summertime. She died when he was in junior high school. He could barely remember her face, though once, when he was idly going through family boxes, he came across a stack of letters addressed to his father and tied with a ribbon. Without knowing quite why, he sniffed the envelopes and was overwhelmed by the faint, lingering scent of her, a scent like old wild-rose petals and the memories of Easter lilies.

But she was nothing.

She never contributed. Won nothing. Did nothing. She was a drag on his father. His father and his fascinating games, and she was a drag on them. He remembered his father shouting at her once, *I'm working, I'm working, and you will stay out of this room when I am working, I have to concentrate and I cannot do it if you come in here and whine, whine . . .* The fascinating games played in courts and jailhouses.

The maddog was not homosexual. He was attracted only to women. It was the only thing that a man could do, the thing with women. He lusted for them, seeing their death and feeling himself explode as one transcendent moment.

In moments of introspection, the maddog had rooted through his psyche, seeking the genesis of his insanity. He decided that it had not come all at once, but had *grown*. He remembered those lonely weeks of isolation on the ranch with his mother, while his father was in Dallas playing his games. The maddog would work with his .22 rifle, sniping the ground squirrels. If he hit a squirrel just right, hit it in the hindquarters, rolled it away from its hole, it would struggle and chitter and try to claw its way back to the nest, dragging itself with its front paws.

All the other ground squirrels, from adjacent holes, would stand on the hills of sand they'd excavated from their dens and watch. Then he could pick off a second one, and that would bring out more, and then a third, until an entire colony was watching a half-dozen wounded ground squirrels trying to drag themselves back to their nests.

He would wound six or seven, shooting from a prone position, then stand and walk over to the nests and finish them with his pocketknife. Sometimes he skinned them out alive, whipping off their hides while they struggled in his hands. After a while, he began stringing their ears, keeping the string in the loft of a machine shed. At the end of one summer, he h d more than three hundred sets of ears.

He had the first orgasm of his young life as he lay prone on the edge of a hayfield sniping ground squirrels. The long spasm was like death itself. Afterward he unbuttoned his jeans and pulled open the front of his underwear to look at the wet semen stains and he said to himself, "Boy, that did it . . . boy, that did it." He said it over and over, and after that, the passion came more often as he hunted over the ranch.

Suppose, he thought, that it had been different. Suppose that he'd had playmates, girls, and they had gone to play doctor out in one of the sheds. *You show me yours, I'll show you mine*. . . . Would that have made all the difference? He didn't know. By the time he was fourteen, it was too late. His mind had been turned.

A girl lived a mile down the road. She was five or six years older than he. Daughter of a real rancher. She rode by on a hayrack once, her mother towing it with a tractor, the girl wearing a sweat-soaked T-shirt that showed her nipples puckered against the dirty cloth. The maddog was fourteen and felt the stirring of a powerful desire and said aloud, "I would love her and kill her."

He was mad.

When he was in law school he read about other men like himself, fascinated to learn that he was part of a community.

He thought of it as a community, of men who understood the powerful exaltation of that moment of ejaculation and death.

But it was not just the killing. Not anymore. There was now the intellectual thrill.

The maddog had always loved games. The games his father played, the games he played alone in his room. Fantasy games, role-playing games. He was good at chess. He won the high-school chess tournament three years running, though he rarely played against others outside the tournaments.

But there were better games. Like those his father played. But even his father was a surrogate for the real player, the other man at the table, the defendant. The real players were the defendants and the cops. The maddog knew he could never be a cop. But he could still be a player.

And now, in his twenty-seventh year, he was approaching his destiny. He was playing and he was killing, and the joy of the act made his body sing with pleasure.

The *ultimate game*. The *ultimate stakes*.

He bet his life that they could not catch him. And he was winning the lives of women, like poker chips. Men always played for women; that was his theory. They were the winnings in all the best games.

Cops, of course, weren't interested in playing. Cops were notoriously dull.

To help them grasp the concept of the game, he left a rule with each killing. Words carefully snipped from the Minneapolis newspaper, a short phrase stuck with Scotch Magic tape to notebook paper. For the first Cities kill, it was *Never murder anyone you know*.

That puzzled them sorely. He placed the paper on the victim's chest, so there could be no doubt about who had left it there. As an almost jocular afterthought, he signed it: *maddog*.

The second one got *Never have a motive*. With that, they would have known they were dealing with a man of purpose.

Though they must have been sweating bullets, the cops kept the story out of the papers. The maddog yearned for the press. Yearned to watch his legal colleagues follow the course of the investigation in the daily news. To know that they were talking to him, about him, never knowing that he was the One.

It thrilled him. This third collection should do the trick. The cops couldn't suppress the story forever. Police departments normally leaked like colanders. He was surprised they'd kept the secret this long.

This third one would get *Never follow a discernible pattern*. He left the sheet on a loom.

There was a contradiction here, of course. The maddog was an intellectual and he had considered it. He was careful to the point of fanaticism: he would leave no clues. Yet, he deliberately created them. The police and their psychiatrists might deduce certain things about his personality from his choice of words. From the fact that he made rules at all. From the impulse to play.

But there was no help for that.

If *killing* were all that mattered, he didn't doubt that he could do it and get away with it. Dallas had demonstrated that. He could do dozens. Hundreds. Fly to Los Angeles, buy a knife at a discount store, kill a hooker, fly back home the same night. A different city every week. They would never catch him. They would never even *know*.

There was an attraction to the idea, but it was, ultimately, intellectually sterile. He was developing. He wanted the *contest*. Needed it.

The maddog shook his head in the dark and looked down from the high window. Cars hissed by on the wet street. There was a low rumble from I-94, two blocks to the north. Nobody on foot. Nobody carrying bags.

He waited, pacing along the windows, watching the street. Eight minutes, ten minutes. The intensity was growing, the pulsing, the pressure. Where was she? He needed her.

Then he saw her, crossing the street below, her dark hair bobbing in the mercury-vapor lights. She was alone, carrying a single grocery bag. When she passed out of sight directly below him, he moved to the central pillar and stood against it.

The maddog wore jeans, a black T-shirt, latex surgeon's gloves, and a blue silk ski mask. When she was tied to the bed and he had stripped himself, the woman would find that her attacker had shaven: he was as clean of pubic hair as a five-year-old. Not because he was kinky, although it did feel . . . *interesting*. But he had seen a case in which lab specialists recovered a half-dozen pubic hairs from a woman's couch and matched them with samples from the assailant. Got the samples from the assailant with a search warrant. Nice touch. Upheld on appeal.

He shivered. It was chilly. He wished he had worn a jacket. When he left his apartment, the temperature was seventy-five. It must have fallen fifteen degrees since dark. God damn Minnesota.

The maddog was not large or notably athletic. For a brief time in his teens he thought of himself as lean, although his father characterized him as *slight*. Now, he would concede to a mirror, he was puffy. Five feet ten inches tall, curly red hair, the beginnings of a double chin, a roundness to the lower belly . . . lips like red worms. . . .

The elevator was old and intended for freight. It groaned once, twice, and started up. The maddog checked his equipment: The Kotex that he would use as a gag was stuffed in his right hip pocket. The tape that he would use to bind the gag was in his left. The gun was tucked in his belt, under the T-shirt. The pistol was small but ugly: a Smith & Wesson Model 15 revolver. He'd bought it from a man who was about to die and then did. Before he died, when he offered it for sale, the dying man said his wife wanted him to keep it for protection. He asked the maddog not to mention that he had purchased it. It would be their secret.

And that was perfect. Nobody knew he had the gun. If he ever had to use it, it would be untraceable, or traceable only to a dead man.

He took the gun out and held it by his side and thought of the sequence: grab, gun in face, force on floor, slap her with the pistol, kneel on back, pull head back, stuff Kotex in mouth, tape, drag to bed, tape arms to the headboard, feet to baseboard.

Then relax and shift to the knife.

The elevator stopped and the doors opened. The maddog's stomach tightened, a familiar sensation. Pleasant, even. Footsteps. Key in the door. His heart was pounding. Door open. Lights. Door closed. The gun was hot in his hand, the grip rough. The woman passing . . .

The maddog catapulted from his hiding place.

Saw in an instant that she was alone.

Wrapped her up, the gun beside her face.

The grocery bag burst and red-and-white cans of Campbell's soup clattered down the wooden floor like dice, beige-and-red packages of chicken nibbles and microwave lasagna crunched underfoot.

"Scream," he said in his roughest voice, well-practiced with a tape recorder, "and I'll kill you."

Unexpectedly, the woman relaxed against him and the maddog involuntarily relaxed with her. An instant later, the heel of her foot smashed onto his instep. The pain was unbearable and as he opened his mouth to scream, she turned in his arms, ignoring the gun.

"Aaaiii," she said, a low half-scream, half-cry of fear.

Time virtually stopped for them, the seconds fragmenting into minutes. The maddog watched her hand come up and thought she had a gun and felt his own gun hand traveling away from her body, the wrong way, and thought, "No." He realized in the next crystalline fragment of time that she was not holding a gun, but a thin silver cylinder.

She hit him with a blast of Mace and the time stream lurched crazily into fast-forward. He screeched and swatted her with the Smith and lost it at the same time. He swung his other hand and, more from luck than skill, connected with the side of her jaw and she fell and rolled.

The maddog looked for the gun, half-blinded, his hands to his face, his lungs not working as they should—he had asthma, and the Mace was soaking through the ski mask—

and the woman was rolling and coming up with the Mace again and now she was screaming:

"Asshole, asshole . . ."

He kicked at her and missed and she sprayed him again and he kicked again and she stumbled and was rolling and still had the Mace and he couldn't find the gun and he kicked at her again. Lucky again, he connected with her Mace hand and the small can went flying. Blood was pouring from her forehead where it had been raked by the front sight on the pistol, streaming from the ragged cut down over her eyes and mouth, and it was on her teeth and she was screaming:

"Asshole, asshole."

Before he could get back on the attack, she picked up a shiny stainless-steel pipe and swung it at him like a woman who'd spent time in the softball leagues. He fended her off and backed away, still looking for the gun, but it was gone and she was coming and the maddog made the kind of decision he was trained to make.

He ran.

He ran and she ran behind him and hit him once more on the back and he half-stumbled and turned and hit her along the jaw with the bottom of his fist, a weak, ineffective punch, and she bounced away and came back with the pipe, her mouth open, her teeth showing, showering him with saliva and blood as she screamed, and he made it through the door and jerked it shut behind him.

". . . asshole . . ."

Down the hall to the stairs, almost strangling in the mask. She didn't pursue, but stood at the closed door screaming with the most piercing wail he'd ever heard. A door opened somewhere and he continued blindly down the stairs. At the bottom he stripped off the mask and thrust it in his pocket and stepped outside.

Amble, he thought. Stroll.

It was cold. Goddamn Minnesota. It was August and he was freezing. He could hear her screaming. Faintly at first, then louder. The bitch had opened the window. The cops were just across the way. The maddog hunched his shoulders and walked a little more quickly down to his car, slipped inside, and drove away. Halfway back to Minneapolis, still in the grip of mortal fear, shaking with the cold, he remembered that cars have heaters and turned it on.

He was in Minneapolis before he realized he was hurt. Goddamn pipe. Going to have big bruises, he thought, shoulders and back. Bitch. The gun shouldn't be a problem, couldn't be traced.

Christ it hurt.

CHAPTER

— 2 —

The counterman was barricaded behind a wall of skin magazines. Cigarettes, candy bars, and cellophane sacks of cheese balls, taco chips, pork rinds, and other carcinogens protected his flank. Next to the cash register, a rotating stand was hung with white buttons; each button carried a message designed to reflect each individual purchaser's existential motif. *Save the Whales—Harpoon a Fat Chick* was a big seller. So was *No More Mr. Nice Guy—Down on Your Knees, Bitch.*

The counterman wasn't looking at it. He was tired of looking at it. He was peering out the flyspecked front window and shaking his head.

Lucas Davenport ambled out of the depths of the store with a *Daily Racing Form* and laid two dollars and twelve cents on the counter.

"Fuckin' kids," the counterman said to nobody, craning his neck to see further up the street. He heard Lucas' money hit the counter and turned. His basset-hound face tried for a grin and settled for a wrinkle. "How's things?" he wheezed.

"What's going on?" Lucas asked, looking past the counterman into the street.

"Couple of kids on skateboards." The counterman had emphysema and his clogged lungs could manage only short sentences. "Riding behind a bus." Whistle. "If they hit a manhole cover . . ." Suck wind. "They're dead."

Lucas looked again. There were no kids in the street.

"They're gone," the counterman said morosely. He picked up the *Racing Form* and read the first paragraph of the lead article. "You check the sale table?" Wheeze. "Some guy brought in some poems." He pronounced it "pomes."

"Yeah?" Lucas walked around to the side of the counter and checked the ranks of battered books on the table. Huddled between two hardback surveys of twentieth-century literature he found, to his delight, a slim clothbound volume of the poetry of Emily Dickinson. Lucas never went hunting for poetry; never bought anything new. He waited to find it by chance, and surprisingly often did, orphan songs huddled in collections of texts on thermoelectrical engineering or biochemistry.

This *Emily Dickinson* cost one dollar when it was printed in 1958 by an obscure publishing house located on Sixth Avenue in New York City. Thirty years later it cost eighty cents in a University Avenue bookstore in St. Paul.

"So what about this pony?" Gurgle. "This Wabasha Warrior?" The counterman tapped the *Racing Form*. "Bred in Minnesota."

"That's what I think," Lucas said.

"What?"

"Bred in Minnesota. They should whip its ass down to the Alpo factory. Of course, there is a silver lining . . ."

The counterman waited. He didn't have the breath for repartee.

"If Warrior gets any kind of favorite-son action," Lucas said, "it'll push up the odds on the winner."

"That'll be . . ."

"Try Sun and Halfpence. No guarantee, but the numbers are right." Lucas pushed the *Emily Dickinson* across the counter with the eighty-cent sticker price and five cents tax. "Let me get out of the store before you call your book, okay? I don't want to get busted for conspiracy to tout."

"Whatever you say." Suck. "Lieutenant," the counterman said. He tugged his forelock.

Lucas carried the *Emily Dickinson* back to Minneapolis and parked in the public garage across from City Hall. He walked around the wretchedly ugly old pile of liverish granite, across another street, past a reflecting pool, and into the

Hennepin County Government Center. He took an escalator down to the cafeteria, bought a red apple from a vending machine, went back up and out the far side of the building to the lawn. He sat on the grass between the white birch trees in the warm August sunshine and ate the apple and read:

> . . . *but no man moved me till the tide*
> *Went past my simple shoe*
> *And past my apron and my belt*
> *And past my bodice too,*
> *And made as he would eat me up*
> *As wholly as a dew*
> *Upon a dandelion's sleeve*
> *And then I started too.*

Lucas smiled and crunched on the apple. When he looked up, a young dark-haired woman was crossing the plaza, pushing a double baby carriage. The twins were dressed in identical pink wrappings and swayed from side to side as their mother strutted them across the plaza. Mama had large breasts and a small waist and her black hair swung back and forth across her fair cheeks like a silken curtain. She wore a plum-colored skirt and silky beige blouse and she was so beautiful that Lucas smiled again, a wave of pleasure washing through him.

Then another one walked by, in the opposite direction, a blonde with a short punky haircut and a revealing knit dress, tawdry in an engaging way. Lucas watched her walk and sighed with the rhythm of it.

Lucas was dressed in a white tennis shirt, khaki slacks, over-the-calf blue socks, and slip-on deck shoes with long leather ties. He wore the tennis shirt outside his slacks so the gun wouldn't show. He was slender and dark-complexioned, with straight black hair going gray at the temples and a long nose over a crooked smile. One of his central upper incisors had been chipped and he never had it capped. He might have been an Indian except for his blue eyes.

His eyes were warm and forgiving. The warmth was somehow emphasized by the vertical white scar that started at his hairline, ran down to his right eye socket, jumped over the eye, and continued down his cheek to the corner of his mouth. The scar gave him a raffish air, but left behind a touch of innocence, like Errol Flynn in *Captain Blood*. Lucas wished he could tell young women that the scar had come from a broken bottle in a bar fight at Subic Bay, where he had never been, or Bangkok, where he had never been either. The scar had come from a fishing leader that snapped out of a rotting snag on the St. Croix River and he told them so. Some believed him. Most thought he was covering something up, like a bar fight East of Suez.

Though his eyes were warm, his smile betrayed him.

He once went with a woman—a zookeeper, as it happened—to a nightclub in St. Paul where cocaine was dealt to suburban children in the basement bathrooms. In the parking lot outside the club, Lucas encountered Kenny McGuinness, who he thought was in prison.

"Get the fuck away from me, Davenport," McGuinness said, backing off. The parking lot was suddenly electric, everything from gum wrappers to discarded quarter-gram coke baggies springing into needle-sharp focus.

"I didn't know you were out, dickhead," Lucas answered, smiling. The zookeeper was watching, her eyes wide. Lucas leaned toward the other man, hooked two fingers in his shirt pocket, and gently tugged, as though they were old companions trading memories. Lucas whispered hoarsely: "Leave town. Go to Los Angeles. Go to New York. If you don't go away, I'll hurt you."

"I'm on parole, I can't leave the state," McGuinness stammered.

"So go to Duluth. Go to Rochester. You've got a week," Lucas whispered. "Talk to your dad. Talk to your grandma. Talk to your sisters. Then leave."

He turned back to the zookeeper, still smiling, McGuinness apparently forgotten.

"You scared the heck out of me," the woman said when they were inside the club. "What was that all about?"

"Kenny likes young boys. He trades crack for ten-year-old ass."

"Oh." She had heard of such things but believed them only in the way she believed in her own mortality: a faraway possibility not yet requiring examination.

Later, she said, "I didn't like that smile. Your smile. You looked like one of my animals."

Lucas grinned at her. "Oh, yeah? Which one? The lemur?"

She nibbled her lower lip. "I was thinking of a wolverine," she said.

If the chill of his smile sometimes overwhelmed the warmth of his eyes, it didn't happen so frequently as to become a social handicap. Now Lucas watched the punky blonde turn the corner of the Government Center, and just before she stepped from sight, look back at him and grin.

Damn. She had known he was watching. Women always knew. Get up, he thought, go after her. But he didn't. There were so many of them, all good. He sighed and leaned back in the grass and picked up *Emily Dickinson*.

Lucas was a picture of contentment. More than a picture.

A photograph.

The photograph was being taken from the back of an olive-drab van parked across South Seventh Street. Two cops from internal affairs worked in sweaty confinement with tripod-mounted film and video cameras behind one-way glass.

The senior cop was fat. His partner was thin. Other than that, they looked much alike, with brush-cut hair, pink faces, yellow short-sleeved shirts, and double-knit trousers from J. C. Penney. Every few minutes, one of them would look through the 300mm lens. The camera attached to the lens, a Nikon F3, was equipped with a Data Back, which had a battery-operated clock programmed for accuracy through the year 2100. When the cops took their photographs, the precise time and date were burned into the photo frame. If necessary, the photograph would become a legally influential log of the surveillance subject's activities.

Lucas had spotted the pair an hour after the surveillance began, almost two weeks earlier. He didn't know why they were watching, but as soon as he saw them, he stopped talking to his informants, to his friends, to other cops. He was living in a pool of isolation, but didn't know why. He would find out. Inevitably.

In the meantime, he spent as much time as he could in the open, forcing the watchers to hide in their hot, confining wagon, unable to eat, unable to pee. Lucas smiled to himself, the unpleasant smile, the wolverine's smile, put down *Dickinson* and picked up the *Racing Form*.

"You think the motherfucker is going to sit there forever?" asked the fat cop. He squirmed uncomfortably.

"Looks like he's settled in."

"I gotta pee like a Russian racehorse," said the fat one.

"You shouldn't of drank that Coke. It's the caffeine that does it."

"Maybe I could slide out and take a leak . . ."

"If he moves, I gotta follow. If you get left behind, Bendl will get your balls."

"Only if you tell him, asshole."

"I can't drive and take pictures at the same time."

The fat cop squirmed uncomfortably and tried to figure the odds. He should have gone as soon as he saw Lucas settle on the lawn, but he hadn't had to pee so bad then. Now that Lucas might be expected to leave, his bladder felt like a basketball.

"Look at him," he said, peering at Lucas through a pair of binoculars. "He's watching the puss go by. Think that's why we're watching him? Something to do with the puss?"

"I don't know. It's something weird. The way it come down, nobody sayin' shit."

"I heard he's got something on the chief. Lucas does."

"Must have. He doesn't do a thing. Wanders around town in that Porsche and goes out to the track every day."

"His jacket looks good. Commendations and all."

"He got some good busts," the thin cop admitted.

"Lot of them," said the fat man.

"Yeah."

"Killed some guys."

"Five. He's the number-one gunslinger on the force. Nobody else done more than two."

"All good shootings."

"Press loves him. Fuckin' Wyatt Earp."

"Because he's got money," the fat man said authoritatively. "The press loves people with money, rich guys. Never met a reporter who didn't want money."

They thought about reporters for a minute. Reporters were a lot like cops, but with faster mouths.

"How much you think he makes? Davenport?" the fat one asked.

The thin cop pursed his meager lips and considered the question. Salary was a matter of some importance. "With his rank and seniority, he probably takes down forty-two, maybe forty-five from the city," he ventured. "Then the games, I heard when he hits one, he makes like a cool hundred thou, depends on how well it sells."

"That much," said the fat one, marveling. "If I made that much, I'd quit. Buy a restaurant. Maybe a bar, up on one of the lakes."

"Get out," the thin one agreed. They'd had the conversation so often the responses were automatic.

"Wonder why they didn't bust him back to sergeant? I mean, when they pulled him off robbery?"

"I heard he threatened to quit. Said he didn't want to go backwards. They decided they wanted to keep him—he's got sources in every bar and barbershop in town—so they had to leave him with the rank."

"He was a real pain in the butt as a supervisor," said the fat man.

The thin man nodded. "Everybody had to be perfect. Nobody was." The thin man shook his head. "He told me once that it was the worst job he ever had. He knew he was mess-ing up, but he couldn't stop. Some guy would goof off one inch and Davenport would be on him like white on rice.''

They stopped talking for another minute, watching their subject through the one-way glass. ''But not a bad guy, when he's not your boss,'' the fat cop offered, changing direction. Surveillance cops become expert at conversational gambit. ''He gave me one of his games, once. For my kid the computer genius. Had a picture of these aliens, like ten-foot cockroaches, zinging each other with ray guns.''

''Kid like it?'' The thin cop didn't really care. He thought the fat cop's kid was overly protected and maybe even a fairy, though he'd never say so.

''Yeah. Brought it back into the shop and asked him to sign it. Right on the box, Lucas Davenport.''

''Well, the guy's no couch,'' said the thin one. He paused expectantly. A minute later the fat one got it and they started laughing. Laughing doesn't help the bladder. The fat cop squirmed again.

''Listen, I gotta go or I'm gonna pee down my leg,'' he said finally. ''If Davenport takes off for somewhere besides the shop, he'll have to get his car. If you're not here when I get back, I'll run get you outside the ramp.''

''It's your ass,'' said his partner, looking through the long lens. ''He just started the *Racing Form*. You maybe got a few minutes.''

Lucas saw the fat cop slip out of the van and dash into the Pillsbury Building. He grinned to himself. He was tempted to stroll away, knowing the cop in the van would have to follow and strand the fat guy. But it would create complications. He would rather have them where he was sure of them.

When the fat cop got back, four minutes later, the van was still there. His partner glanced over at him and said, ''Nothing.''

Since Lucas hadn't done anything yet, the photos they took had never been developed. If they had been, they would have found that Lucas' middle finger was prominent on most of the slides and they might have decided that he had spotted them. But it didn't matter, since the film would never be developed.

As the fat cop scrambled back into the van and Lucas sprawled on the grass, paging through the poetry again, they were very close to the end of the surveillance.

Lucas was reading a poem called *The Snake*, and the fat man was peering at him through the lens of the Nikon when the maddog killer did another one.

CHAPTER

— 3 —

He had first talked to her a month before, in the records department of the county clerk's office. She had raven-black hair, worn short, and brown eyes. Gold hoop earrings dangled from her delicate earlobes. She wore just a touch of scent and a warm red dress.

"I'd like to see the file on Burhalter-Mentor," she told a clerk. "I don't have the number. It should have been in the last month."

The maddog watched her from the corner of his eye. She was fifteen or twenty years years older than he was. Attractive.

The maddog had not yet gone for the artist. His days were colored with thoughts of her, his nights consumed with images of her face and body. He knew he would take her; the love song had already begun.

But this one was interesting. More than interesting. He felt his awareness expanding, reveled in the play of light through the peach fuzz of her slender forearm. . . . And after the artist, there had to be another.

"Is that a civil filing?" the clerk asked the woman.

"It's a bunch of liens on an apartment complex down by Nokomis. I want to make sure they've been resolved."

"Okay. That's Burkhalter . . . ."

"Burkhalter-Mentor." She spelled it for him and the clerk went back into the file room. She's a real-estate agent, the maddog thought. She felt his attention and glanced at him.

"Are you a real-estate agent?" he asked.

"Yes, I am." Serious, pleasant, professional. Pink lipstick, just a touch.

"I'm new here in Minneapolis," the maddog said, stepping a bit closer. "I'm an attorney with Felsen-Gore. Would you have a couple of seconds to answer a real-estate question?"

"Sure." She was friendly now, interested.

"I've been looking around the lakes, down south of here, Lake of the Isles, Lake Nokomis, like that."

"Oh, it's a very nice neighborhood," she said enthusiastically. She had what plastic surgeons called a full mouth, showing a span of brilliantly white teeth when she smiled. "There are lots of houses on the market right now. It's my specialty area."

"Well, I'm not sure whether I want a condo or a house . . ."

"A house holds its value better."

"Yeah, but you know, I'm single. I don't really want to hassle with a big yard . . ."

"What you really need is a bungalow on a small lot, not much yard. You'd have more space than you would in an apartment, and you could sign up for a lawn service for thirty dollars a month. That'd be cheaper than the maintenance fee on most condos, and you'd maintain resale value."

The maddog got his file and waited until she got a photocopy of the liens. They drifted together along the hall to the elevators and rode down to the first floor.

"Well, hmm, look, in Dallas we had this thing, it was called the multiple list, or something like that?" said the maddog.

"Yes, multiple listing service," she said.

"So if I were to drive around and find a place, I could call you and you could show it to me?"

"Sure, I do it all the time. Let me give you my card."

Jeannie Lewis. He tucked her card into his wallet. As soon as he turned away and stepped out of her physical presence, he saw the artist again, her face and body as she walked through the streets of St. Paul. He hungered for her, and the real-estate agent was almost forgotten. But not quite.

For the next week, he saw the card each time he took his wallet out of his pocket. Jeannie Lewis of the raven hair. A definite candidate.

And then the fiasco.

He woke the next morning, bruised and creaking. He took a half-dozen extra-strength aspirin tablets and carefully twisted to look at his back in the bathroom mirror. The bruises were coming and they would be bad, long black streaks across his back and shoulders.

The obsession with the artist was broken. When he got out of the shower, he saw a strange face in the mirror, floating behind the steamed surface. It had happened before. He reached out and wiped the mirror with a corner of his towel. It was Lewis, smiling at him, engaged in his nudity.

Her office was in the south lake district, in an old storefront with a big window. He drove the neighborhood, looking for a vantage point. He found it on the parking boulevard kitty-corner from Lewis' office. He could sit in his car and watch her through the storefront window as she sat in her cubicle, talking on the telephone. He watched her for a week. Every afternoon but Wednesday she arrived between twelve-thirty and one o'clock, carrying a bag lunch. She ate at her desk as she did paperwork. She rarely went back out before two-thirty. She was stunning. He best liked the way she walked, using her hips in long fluid strides. He dreamt of her at night, of Jeannie Lewis walking nude toward him across the desert grass. . . .

He decided to collect her on a Thursday. He found a nice-looking home on a narrow street in a redeveloping neighborhood six blocks from her office. There were no houses directly across the street from it. The driveway was sunken a few feet into the lawn, and stairs led behind a screen of evergreens to the front door. If he rode with Lewis to the house and she pulled into the driveway, and he got out the passenger side, he would be virtually invisible from the street.

The house itself felt empty. He checked the cross-reference books used by investigators at his office, found the names of the neighbors. He called the first one in the book and got a nosy old man. He explained that he would like to make a direct offer for the house, cutting out the real-estate dealers. Did the neighbor know where the owners were? Why, yes. Arizona. And here's the number; they're not due back until Christmas, and then only for two weeks.

Scouting the neighborhood, the maddog found a small supermarket across from a Standard station a few blocks from the house.

On Thursday, he packed his equipment into the trunk of his car and wore a loose-fitting tweed sport coat with voluminous pockets. He checked to make sure Lewis was in, then drove to the supermarket, parked his car in the busy lot, and called her from a pay phone.

"Jeannie Lewis," she said. Her voice was pleasantly cool.

"Yes, Ms. Lewis?" said the maddog, pronouncing it "miz." His heart was thumping against his ribs. "I ran into you in the clerk of court's office a month ago. We were talking about houses in the lakes area?"

There was a moment's hesitation at the other end of the line and the maddog was afraid she had forgotten him. Then she said, "Oh . . . yes, I think I remember. We went down in the elevator together?"

"Yes, that's me. Listen, to make a long story short, I was cruising the neighborhood down here, looking, and I had car trouble. So I pulled into a gas station and they said it would be a couple hours, they've got to put in a water pump. Anyway, I went out to walk around and I found a very interesting house."

He glanced at the paper in his hand, with the address, and gave it to her. "I wonder if we might set up a time to look at it?"

"Are you still at that Standard station?"

"I'm at a phone booth across the street."

"I'm not doing anything right now and I'm only five minutes away. I could stop at the other realtor's, they're only two minutes from here, pick up the key, and come and get you."

"Well, I don't want to inconvenience you . . ."

"No, no problem. I know that house. It's very well-kept. I'm surprised it hasn't gone yet."

"Well . . ."

"I'll be there in ten minutes."

It took fifteen. He went into the supermarket, bought an ice-cream bar, sat on a bus bench next to the phone booth, and licked the ice cream. When Lewis arrived, driving a brown station wagon, she recognized him at once. He could see her teeth as she smiled at him through the tinted windshield.

"How are you?" she asked as she popped open the passenger-side door. "You're the attorney. I remembered as soon as I saw your face."

"Yes. I really appreciate this. Have I introduced myself? I'm Louis Vullion." The maddog killer pronounced it "Looee Vul-yoan," though his parents had called him "Loo-is Vul-yun," to rhyme with "onion."

"Glad to meet you." And she seemed to be.

The drive to the house took three minutes, the woman pointing out the advantages of the neighborhood. The lakes close enough that he could jog down at night. Far enough away that he wouldn't be bothered by traffic. Schools close enough to enhance the resale value of the house, should he ever wish to sell it. Not so close that kids would be a problem. Enough stability in the housing that neighbors knew each other and strangers in the neighborhood would be noticed.

"The crime rate around here is quite low compared to other neighborhoods in the city," she said. Just then a jet roared low overhead, going in for a landing at Minneapolis-St. Paul International. She didn't mention it.

Vullion didn't mention it either. He listened just enough to nod at the right places. Deeper inside, he was going through his visualization routine. This time, he couldn't mess it up, as he had with the artist.

Oh, yes, he'd assumed the blame for that one; there was no shirking it. He'd erred and he had been lucky to escape.

A one-hundred-thirty-pound woman in good shape could be a formidable opponent. He would not forget that again.

As for Lewis, he couldn't foul it up. Once he attacked, she had to die, because she'd seen his face, she knew who he was. So he'd practiced, as best he could, in his apartment, hitting a basketball hung from a hook in the bathroom door. Like it was a head.

And now he was ready. He'd tucked a gym sock filled with a large Idaho baking potato into his right jacket pocket. The bulge showed, but not much. It could be anything, an appointment book, a bagel. A Kotex pad, the tape, and a pair of latex surgeon's gloves were in his left pocket. He would touch nothing that would take a fingerprint until he had the gloves on. He thought about it, rehearsed it in his mind, and said, "Oh, yes?" at the right spots in Lewis' sales talk.

And as they drove, he felt his awareness expanding; realized, with a tiny touch of distaste, that she probably smoked. There was the slightest odor of nicotine about her.

When they pulled into the driveway, his stomach began to clutch just as it had with the artist and the others. "Nice place from the outside, anyway," he said.

"Wait'll you see inside. They've done a beautiful treatment of the bathrooms."

She led the way to the front door, which was screened from the street by evergreens. The key opened the door, and they pushed in. The house was fully furnished, but the front room had the too-orderly feeling of long-prepared-for absence. The air was still and slightly musty.

"You want to wander around a minute?" Lewis looked up at him.

"Sure." He glanced at the kitchen, strolled through the front room, walked up three stairs to the bedroom level, looked in each room. When he came back down, she was clutching her purse strap in front of her, examining with some interest a crystal lamp on the fireplace mantel.

"How much are they asking?"

"A hundred and five."

He nodded and glanced toward the basement door at the edge of the kitchen.

"Is that the basement?"

"Yes, I believe so."

When she turned toward the door, he took the sock out of his pocket. She took another step toward the basement door. Swinging the sock like a mace, he slammed the Idaho baker into the back of her head, just above her left ear.

The blow knocked her off her feet and Vullion dropped on her back and slammed her again. This one was not like the bitch artist. She was an office worker with no strength in her arms. She moaned once, dazed, and he grabbed the hair on the crown of her head and wrenched her head straight back and shoved in the Kotex. He pulled on his gloves, took the tape from his side pocket, and quickly wrapped her head. As she finally began to struggle against him, he rolled her over, crossed her wrists, and taped them. She was beginning to recover, her eyes half-open now, and he dragged her up the stairs into the first bedroom and threw her on the bed. He taped her arms first, to the headboard, then her legs, apart, to the corner posts of the bed.

He was breathing hard but he could feel the erection pounding at his groin, the excitement building in his throat.

He stepped back and looked down at her. The knife, he thought. Hope there's a good one. He went down to look in the kitchen.

On the bed behind him, Jeannie Lewis moaned.

CHAPTER

— **4** —

The Twin Cities' horse track looks like a Greyhound bus station designed by a pastry chef. The fat cop, no architecture critic, liked it. He sat in the sun with a slice of pepperoni pizza in his lap, a Diet Pepsi in one hand and a portable radio in the other. He took the call on the portable just before the second race.

"Right now?"

"Right now." Even with the interference, the voice was unmistakable and ragged as a bread knife.

The fat cop looked at the thin one.

"Christ, the fuckin' chief. On the *radio*."

"His procedure is fucked." The thin cop was eating the last of a hot dog and had dribbled relish down the front of his sport coat. He brushed at it with an undersize napkin.

"He wants Davenport," said the fat one.

"Something must have happened," said the thin one. They were outside, on the deck. Lucas was on the blacktopped patio below, two sections over. He lazily sprawled over a wooden bench directly in front of the tote board and thirty feet from the dark soil of the track. A pretty woman in cowboy boots sat at the other end of the bench drinking beer from a plastic cup. The two cops went up the aisle to the top of the grandstand, down the staircase, and pushed through a small crowd at the base of the steps.

"Davenport? Lucas?"

Lucas turned, saw them, and smiled. "Hey. How're you doing? Day at the races, huh?"

"The chief wants to talk to you. Like right away." The fat

cop hadn't thought of it until the last minute, but this could be hard to explain.

"They pulled the surveillance?" Lucas asked. His teeth were showing.

"You knew about it?" The fat cop lifted an eyebrow.

"For a while. But I didn't know why." He looked at them expectantly.

The thin cop shrugged. "We don't know either."

"Hey, fuck you, Dick . . ." Lucas stood up with his fists balled, and the thin cop took a step back.

"Honest to Christ, Lucas, we don't know," said the fat one. "It was all hush-hush."

Lucas turned and looked at him. "He said right now?"

"He said right now. And he sounded like he meant it."

Lucas' eyes defocused and he turned toward the track, staring sightlessly across the oval to the six-furlong starting gate. The jockeys were pressing their horses toward the gate and the crowd was starting to drift down the patio to the finish line.

"It's the maddog killer," Lucas said after a moment.

"Yeah," said the fat cop. "It could be."

"Has to be. Goddammit, I don't want that." He thought about it for another few seconds and then suddenly smiled. "You guys got horses for this race?"

The fat cop looked vaguely uneasy. "Uh, I got two bucks on Skybright Avenger."

"Jesus Christ, Bucky," Lucas said in exasperation, "you're risking two dollars to get back two dollars and forty cents if she wins. And she won't."

"Well, I dunno . . ."

"If you don't know how to play . . ." Lucas shook his head. "Look, go put ten bucks on Pembroke Dancer. To win."

The two cops looked at each other.

"Really?" said the thin one. "This is a maiden, you can't know . . ."

"Hey. It's up to you, if you want to bet. And I'm staying for the race."

The two internal-affairs cops looked at each other, looked back at Lucas, then turned and hurried inside to the nearest betting windows. The thin one bet ten dollars. The fat one hesitated, staring into his wallet, licked his lips, took out three tens, licked his lips again, and pushed them across the counter. "Thirty on Pembroke Dancer," he said. "To win."

Lucas was sprawled on the bench again and had started a conversation with the woman in the cowboy boots. When the surveillance cops got back, he moved down toward her but turned to the cops.

"You bet?" he asked.

"Yeah."

"Don't look so nervous, Bucky. It's perfectly legal."

"Yeah, yeah. It ain't that."

"Have you got a horse?" The woman in the cowboy boots leaned forward and looked down the bench at Lucas. She had violet eyes.

"Just a guess," Lucas said lazily.

"Is this, like, a private guess?"

"We've all got a couple of bucks on Pembroke Dancer," Lucas said.

The woman with the violet eyes had a *Racing Form* on the bench beside her, but instead of looking at it, she looked up at the sky and her lips moved silently and then she turned her head and said, "She had a terrific workout at six furlongs. The track was listed as fast but it probably wasn't that good."

"Hmm," said Lucas.

She looked at the tote board for a few seconds and said, "Excuse me, I gotta go powder my nose."

She left, hurrying. The fat cop was still licking his lips and watching the tote board. The odds on Pembroke Dancer were twenty to one. Three other horses, Stripper's Colors, Skybright Avenger, and Tonite Delite, had strong races in the past three weeks. Pembroke Dancer had been shipped in from Arkansas two weeks earlier. In her first race she finished sixth.

"What's the story on this horse?" asked the fat cop.

"A tip from a friend." Lucas gestured over his shoulder

with his thumb, up toward the press box. "One of the handicappers got a call from Vegas. Guy walked into a horse parlor a half-hour ago and bet ten thousand on Pembroke Dancer to win. Somebody knows something."

"Jesus. So why'd he lose his last race so bad?"

"She."

"Huh?"

"She. Dancer's a filly. And I don't know why she lost. Might be anything. Maybe the jock was dragging his feet."

The tote board flickered and the odds on Pembroke Dancer went up to twenty-two to one.

"How much you bet, Lucas?" the fat cop asked.

"It's an exacta. I wheeled Dancer with the other nine horses. A hundred each way, so I have nine hundred riding."

"Jesus." The fat man licked his lips again. He had another twenty in his wallet and thought about it. Across the track, the first of the horses was led into the gate and the fat cop settled back. Thirty was already too much. If he lost it, he'd be lunching on Cheetos for a week.

"So you got anything good?" asked Lucas. "What was this thing about Billy Case and the rookie?"

The fat cop laughed. "Fuckin' Case."

"There was this woman lawyer," said the thin one, "and one day she looks out her office window, which is on the back of an old house that they made into offices. The back of her office looks at the back of the business buildings on the next street over. In fact, it looks right down this walkway between these buildings. At the other end of this walkway there's a fence with a gate in it, like blocking the walkway from the street. So you can't see into the walkway from the street. But you can see into it from this lawyer's office, you know? So anyway, she looks down there, and here's this cop, in full uniform, getting his knob polished by this spade chick.

"So this lawyer's watching and the guy gets off and zips up and he and the spade chick go through this gate in the little fence, back onto the street. This lawyer, she's cool, she thinks maybe they're in love. But the next day, there's two of them, both cops, and the spade chick, and she's polishing both of them. So now the lawyer's pissed. She gets this giant camera from her husband, and the next day, sure enough, they're back with another chick, a white girl this time. So the lawyer takes some pictures and she brings this roll of Kodachrome in to the chief.''

The first of the horses was guided into the back of the gate and locked. The woman with the violet eyes got back and settled at the end of the bench. The thin cop rambled on. ''So the chief sends it down to the lab,'' he said, ''and they're only like the best pictures anybody ever took of a knob-job. I could of sold them for ten bucks apiece. So the chief and the prosecutors decide there's some problem with the chain of evidence and we wind up in this lawyer's office with a video unit. Sure enough, here they come. But this time they got both the spade chick and the white chick. This is like in Cinemascope or something. Panavision.''

''So what's going to happen?'' Lucas asked.

The fat one shrugged. ''They're gone.''

''How much time did they have in?''

''Case had six years, but I don't give a shit. He had a bad jacket. We think he and a security guard was boosting stereos and CD players out of a Sears warehouse a few months back. But I feel sorry for the rookie. Case told him this was how it's done on the street. Gettin' knob-jobs in alleyways.''

Lucas shook his head.

''Right on the street, in daylight,'' said the fat cop.

The last horse was pushed into the back of the gate, locked, and there was a second-long pause before the gate banged open and the announcer called ''They're all in line . . . and they're off, Pembroke Dancer breaks on the outside, followed by . . .''

Dancer ran away from the pack, two lengths going into the turn, four lengths at the bottom of the stretch, eight lengths crossing the wire.

''Holy shit,'' the fat cop said reverently. ''I won six hundred bucks.''

Lucas stood up. ''I'm going,'' he said. He was staring at

the tote board, calculating. When he was satisfied, he turned to the other two. ''You coming behind? I'll drive slow.''

''No, no, we're all done,'' said the fat cop. ''Thanks, Lucas.''

''You ought to quit now,'' said Lucas. ''The rest of these races are junk. You can't figure them. And, Bucky?''

''Yeah?'' The fat cop looked up from his winning ticket.

''You won't forget to tell the IRS about the six hundred?''

''Of course not,'' the cop said, offended. Lucas grinned and walked away and the fat cop muttered, ''In a pig's eye.'' He looked at his ticket again and then noticed that the woman with the violet eyes was hurrying after Lucas. She caught him just before he got inside, and the fat cop saw Lucas grin as they walked together into the building.

''Look at this,'' he said to the thin cop. But the thin cop was looking at the tote board and his lips were moving quietly. The fat cop looked at his partner and said, ''What?''

The thin cop put up a hand to hold off the question, his lips still moving. Then they stopped and he turned and looked after Lucas.

''What?'' said the fat cop, looking in the same direction. Lucas and the woman with the violet eyes had disappeared.

''I don't know much about this horse-race bullshit,'' said the thin cop, ''but if I'm reading the tote board right, this exacta payoff, Davenport took down twenty-two thousand, two hundred and fifty bucks.''

The office of the chief of police was on the first floor of City Hall, in a corner. Windows dominated the two walls that faced the street. The other two walls were covered with framed photographs, some in color, some in black and white, stretching back in time to the forties. Daniel with his family. With the last six Minnesota governors. With five of the last six senators. With a long and anonymous chain of faces that all looked vaguely the same, faces that took up space at chicken dinners for major politicians. Directly behind the chief was the shield of the Minneapolis Police Department and a plaque honoring cops who had been killed in the line of duty.

Lucas sprawled in the leather chair that sat squarely in front of the chief's desk. He was surprised, though he tried not to show it. It had been a while since anything surprised him, other than women.

"Pissed off?" Quentin Daniel leaned over his glass desktop, watching Lucas. Daniel looked so much like a police chief that a number of former political enemies, who were now doing something else, made the mistake of thinking he got the job on his face. They were wrong.

"Yeah. Pissed off. Mostly just surprised." Lucas did not particularly like Daniel, but thought he might be the smartest man on the force. He would have been surprised—again—to know that the chief thought precisely the same about him.

Daniel half-turned toward the windows, his head cocked, still watching.

"You can see why," he said.

"You thought I did it?"

"A couple of people in homicide thought you were worth looking at," said Daniel.

"You better start at the beginning," Lucas said.

Daniel nodded, pushed his chair away from his desk, stood up, and wandered to a wall of photographs. He inspected the face of Hubert Humphrey as though he were looking for new blemishes.

"Two weeks ago, our man made a run at a St. Paul woman, an artist named Carla Ruiz," he said as he continued his inspection of Humphrey's face. "She managed to fight him off. When St. Paul got there, the sergeant in charge found her looking at a note. It was one of these rules he's leaving behind."

"I haven't heard a thing about this Ruiz," Lucas said.

The chief turned and drifted back to his chair, no hurry, his hands in his pockets. "Yeah. Well, this sergeant's a smart guy and he knew about the notes in the first two killings. He called the head of St. Paul homicide and they put a lid on it. The only people who know are the St. Paul chief and his chief of homicide, the two uniforms who took the call, a couple of people in homicide here, and me. And the artist. And now you. And every swingin' dick has been told that if this leaks, there'll be some new foot beats out at the land-fill.''

"So how'd it point to me?'' Lucas asked.

"It didn't. Not right away. But our man dropped his gun during the fight with the artist lady. The first thing we did was print it and run it. No prints—checked everything, including the shells. We had better luck on the ownership. We ran it down in ten minutes. It went from the factory to a gun store down on Hennepin Avenue, and from there to a guy named David L. Losse—''

"Our David L. Losse?''

"You remember the case?''

"Shot his son, said it was an accident? Thought somebody was breaking into the house?''

"That's him. He fell on a manslaughter, though it was probably a straight-out murder. He got six years, he'll serve four. But there's still an appeal floating around. Because of the appeal, the evidence was supposedly up in the property room. We went up and looked. The gun is gone. Or it was gone, until the killer dropped it.''

"Shit.'' Things had disappeared from the property room before. Five grams of cocaine became four. Twenty bondage magazines became fifteen. As far as Lucas knew, this was the first time a gun had gone missing.

"You had access to the evidence room a couple of times. During the Ryerson case and during that hassle over the Chicago burglary gang. We cross-referenced everything we had from the killings and the witness. Times, places, the artist's description. We could eliminate as suspects all the women who had access to the room. We could eliminate cops who were confirmed on-duty when the killings took place. People have been killed or attacked in all three shifts . . . Anyway, we got it down to your name, basically. You're the right size. Nobody ever knows where you're at. You're a games freak and this guy is apparently playing some kind of game. And the gun came out of the property room. I never really thought you were the one, but . . . you see how it went down.''

"Yeah, I see," Lucas said sourly. "Thanks a lot."

"Hey, what would you have done?" Daniel asked defensively.

"Okay."

"Now we know you're clean," the chief said. He leaned back in his chair, stretched, and crossed his legs. " 'Cause our man did another one. Four to six hours ago. We figure it was just about the time you were sitting out on the lawn eating that apple.''

Lucas nodded. "Where's this one?"

"Down by Lake Nokomis. Just west of the lake, up in those hills.''

"Can you contain it?"

"No." Daniel shook his head. "This is three. If we tried to contain it, we'd be leaking like a rusty faucet by tomorrow afternoon. That'd cause more trouble than if we go out front with it. I've already called a press conference for nine o'clock tonight. That'll give the TV stations time to make the ten-o'clock news. I want you to be here. I'll outline the killings, appeal for help, all that. And I'm assigning you to the case, full-time.''

"I don't want it," said Lucas. "Homicide bores me. You walk around all day talking to civilians who don't know anything. There are other guys do it better. And I got a lot of stuff going on this crack business. I got a half-dozen guys picked out—''

"Yeah, yeah, yeah, that's absolutely fuckin' wonderful, but the media is going to hang us all by our balls if we don't get this freak," Daniel said, cutting Lucas off in mid-sentence. "You remember back a few years when those two women got killed in the parking ramps? Like two, three weeks apart, different guys? Pure coincidence? You remember how the media went out of their minds? You remember how the TV stations were having seminars on self-defense? How they had reports every night on progress? You remember all that?''

"Yeah." It had been a nightmare.

"This is going to be worse. Those guys in the parking ramps, we grabbed one the same day, we got the other one a couple days after he did it. We still got hysteria. This guy, he's killed three, attacked another one, raped them and stabbed them, and he's still on the loose."

Lucas nodded and rubbed his jaw with his fingertips. "You're right. They'll go berserk," he admitted.

"Guaranteed. This doesn't happen in the Twin Cities. So fuck the crack. I want you on this thing. You'll work by yourself, homicide will work parallel. The media'll like that. They think you're some kind of fuckin' genius."

"What does homicide think about me working on it?" Lucas asked.

"A couple of guys will be moaning about it, because they always do, but they'll go along. Besides, I don't care what they think. Their asses aren't on the line. Mine is. I come up for new term next year and I don't need this sitting on my back," Daniel said.

"I've got full access?"

"I talked to Lester. He'll cooperate. He really will." Lucas nodded. Frank Lester was the deputy chief for investigations and a former head of robbery-homicide.

"I'll want to talk to this artist," Lucas said.

Daniel nodded. "The woman doesn't have a pot to piss in. We had to get her a phone two days after she was attacked. Just in case the guy comes back after her. Here's her number and address." He handed Lucas a slip of paper.

Lucas tucked the slip in his pants pocket. "They're processing this Nokomis killing now?"

"Yeah."

"I better get down there." He stood and started for the door, stopped and half-turned. "You really didn't think I did it?"

Daniel shook his head. "I've seen you around women. I didn't think you could do that to them. But I had to know for sure."

Lucas started to turn away again, but Daniel stopped him. "And, Davenport?"

"Yeah?"

"Be here for the press conference, okay? Dress just like that, the tennis shirt and the khakis. You got any jeans? Jeans might be better. Those whatdaya call them, acid jeans?"

"I could change on the way back. I got some stone-washed."

"Whatever. You know how that TV puss goes for the street-cop routine. What's your title again?"

"Office of Special Intelligence."

The chief snapped his fingers, nodded, and scrawled "OSI" on his desk pad. "See you at nine," he said.

Jeannie Lewis lay on the narrow bed with her hands bound up over her head, where they were taped to the headboard. A look of inexpressible agony held her face, her mouth locked open by the Kotex pad stuffed between her jaws, her eyes rolled so far back that nothing but the whites could be seen beneath the half-closed lids. Her back was arched from the pressure of the bonds, the nipples of her small breasts pointing left and right, nearly white in death. Her ankles were bound to the opposite corners at the foot of the bed, but she had managed to roll her thin legs inward, a final effort to protect herself. The knife still protruded from the top of her abdomen, just below the sternum, its handle almost flat against her stomach. It had been slipped in at an acute angle, to more directly penetrate the heart without complications of bone or muscle.

"Pushed it in and wiggled it," said the assistant medical examiner. "We can tell more after the autopsy, but that's what it looks like. Just a little entry slit, but a lot of damage around the heart."

"Professional?" asked Lucas. "A doctor?"

"I wouldn't go that far. I don't want to mislead you. But it's somebody who knows what he's doing. He knows where the heart is. We want to leave the knife in place until we get downtown and take some pictures, X rays, but from the look of the handle, I'd say it's about the most efficient knife for the work. Narrow point, sharp, rigid blade, fairly thin. It'd slip right in.''

Lucas stepped over to the bed and looked at the knife handle. It was smooth, unfinished wood. ''County Cork Cutlery'' was branded on the wood.

''County Cork Cutlery?''

''Forget it. There's a whole drawer full of it, out in the kitchen.''

''So he got it here.''

''I think so. I did the first woman he killed, Lucy What's-her-name. He did her with a plastic-handled knife, nothing like this one.''

''Where's the note?''

''In the baggie, over on the chest of drawers. We're sending it to the lab, see if they can print it.''

Lucas stepped over to the chest and looked at the note. Common notebook paper. Even if there were six pads of it in a suspect's home, it would prove nothing. The words were cut from a newspaper and fastened to the paper with Scotch tape: *Never carry a weapon after it has been used.*

''He lives by those rules,'' the medical examiner said. ''He didn't even pull the knife out, much less carry it anywhere.''

''Note looks clean.''

''Well, not quite. Hang on a second,'' the medical examiner said. He peeled off the plastic gloves he was wearing, replaced them with a thinner pair of surgeon's gloves, opened the baggie, and slipped the note halfway out.

''See this kind of funny half-circle under the tape?''

''Yeah. Print?''

''We think so, but if you look, you can see there's no print. But it's sharply defined. So I think—'' he wiggled his fingers at Lucas—''that he was wearing surgeon's gloves.''

''That says doctor again.''

''It could. It could also say nurse, or orderly, or technician. And since you can buy the things at hardware stores, it could be a hardware dealer. Whoever he is, I think he wears gloves even when he's sitting at home making these notes.

So now we know something else: he's a smart little cock-sucker.''

"Okay. Good. Thanks, Bill.''

The medical examiner eased the note back in the bag. "Can we take her?'' he asked, tilting his head at Lewis' body.

"Fine with me, if homicide's finished.'' A homicide cop named Swanson was sitting at a table in the kitchen, eating a Big Mac, fries, and a malt. Lucas stepped into the doorway of the bedroom and called across to him. "I'm done. Can they take her?''

"Take her,'' Swanson said around a mouthful of fries.

The medical examiner supervised the movement, with Swanson ambling over to watch. They pulled the bag over her head, carefully avoiding the knife, and lifted her onto a gurney.

Like a sack of sand, Lucas thought.

"Nothin' under her?'' asked Swanson.

"Not a thing,'' said the medical examiner. They all looked at the sheets for a moment; then the medical examiner nod-ded at his assistants and they pushed the gurney out the bed-room door.

"Lab's coming through with a vacuum. They haven't printed the furniture yet,'' Swanson said. What he meant was: Don't touch anything. Lucas grinned. "They'll take the sheets down for analysis.''

"I don't see any stains.''

"Naw, they're clean. I don't think there's any hair, either. Took a close look, but she didn't have any broken fingernails, didn't look like anything balled up underneath them, no skin or blood.''

"Shit.''

"Yeah.''

"I want to poke around out here a little. Anything criti-cal?''

"There's the potato . . .''

"Potato?''

"Potato in a sock. It's out in the living room.'' Lucas followed him into the living room, and Swanson used his foot to point under a piano bench. There was an ordinary argyle sock with a lump in one end.

"We think he hit her on the head with it," Swanson said. "First cop in saw it, peeked inside, then left it for the lab."

"Why do you think he hit her with it?" Lucas asked.

"Because that's what a potato in a sock is for," Swanson said. "Or, at least, it used to be."

"What?" Lucas was puzzled.

"It's probably before your time," Swanson said. "It used to be, years ago, guys would go up to Loring Park to roll the queers or down Washington Avenue to roll the winos. They'd carry a potato with them. Nothing illegal about a potato. But you put one in a sock, you got a hell of a blackjack. And it's soft, so if you're careful, you don't crack anybody's skull. You don't wind up with a dead body on your hands, everybody looking for you."

"So how'd the maddog know about it? He's gay?"

Swanson shrugged. "Could be. Or could be a cop. Lots of old street cops would know about using a potato."

"That doesn't sound right," Lucas said. "I never heard of an *old* serial killer. If they're going to do it, they start young. Teens, twenties, maybe thirties."

Swanson looked him over carefully. "You gonna detect on this one?" he asked.

"That's the idea," Lucas said. "You got a problem?"

"Not me. You're the only guy I ever met who detected anything. I have a feeling we're gonna need it this time."

"So what do the other homicide guys think?"

"There a couple new guys think you're butting in. Most of the old guys, they know a shit storm's about to hit. They just want to get it over with. You won't have no trouble."

"I appreciate that," Lucas said. Swanson nodded and wandered away.

Lewis had been found in the back bedroom by another real-estate agent. She'd had a midafternoon appointment, and when she didn't show up, the other agent got worried and went looking for her. When Lucas had arrived, pushing through the gloomy circle of neighbors who waited beside the house and on the lawns across the street, Swanson briefed him on Lewis' background.

"Just trying to sell the house," he concluded.

"Where are the owners?"

"They're a couple of old folks. The neighbors said they're down in Phoenix. They bought a place down there and are trying to sell this one."

"Anybody gone out to Lewis' house yet?"

"Oh, yeah, Nance and Shaw. Nothing there. Neighbors said she was a nice lady. Into gardening, had a big garden out back of her house. Her old man worked for 3M, died of a heart attack five or six years ago. She went to work on her own, was starting to do pretty good. That's what the neighbors say."

"Boyfriends?"

"Somebody. A neighbor woman supposedly knows him, but she hasn't been home and we don't know where she is. Another neighbor thinks he's some kind of professor or something over at the university. We're checking. And we're doing all the usual, talking to neighbors about anybody they saw coming or going."

"Look in the garage?"

"Yeah. No car."

"So what do you think?"

Swanson shrugged. "What I think is, he calls her up and says he wants to look at a house, he'll meet her somewhere. He tells her something that makes her think he's okay and they ride down here, go inside. He does her, drives her car out, dumps it, and walks. We're looking for the car."

"Anybody checking her calendars at her office?"

"Yeah, we called, but her boss says there's nothing on her desk. He said she carried an appointment book with her. We found it and all it says is, 'Twelve-forty-five.' We think that might be the time she met him."

"Where's her purse?"

"Over by the front door."

Now, wandering around the house, Lucas saw the purse

again and stooped next to it. A corner of Lewis' billfold was protruding and he eased it out and snapped it open. Money. Forty dollars and change. Credit cards. Business cards. Lucas pulled out a sheaf of plastic see-through picture envelopes and flipped through them. None of the pictures looked particularly new. Looking around, he saw Swanson standing by the bedroom door talking to someone out of sight. He slipped one of the photos out of its envelope. Lewis was shown standing on a lawn with another woman, both holding some kind of a plaque. Lucas closed the wallet, slid it back in the purse, and put the photograph in his pocket.

It was cold when he left the murder scene. He got a nylon jacket from his car, pulled it on, and sat in the driver's seat for a moment, watching the bystanders. Nobody out of place. He hadn't really thought there would be.

On the way back to the station, he crossed the river into St. Paul, stopped at his house, changed into jeans, and traded the nylon jacket for a blue linen sport coat. He thought about it for a few seconds, then took a small .25-caliber automatic pistol and an ankle holster from a hideout shelf in his desk, strapped it to his right ankle, and pulled the jean leg down to cover it.

The television remote-broadcast trucks were stacked up outside City Hall when Lucas got back to police headquarters. He parked in the garage across the street, again marveled at the implacable ugliness of City Hall. He went in the back doors and down to his office.

When he'd been removed from the robbery detail, administration had to find a place to put him. His rank required some kind of office. Lucas found it himself, a storage room with a steel door on the basement level. The janitors cleaned it out and painted a number on the door. There was no other indication of who occupied the office. Lucas liked it that way. He unlocked it, went inside, and dialed Carla Ruiz' phone number.

"This is Carla." She had a pleasantly husky voice.

"My name is Lucas Davenport. I'm a lieutenant with the Minneapolis Police Department," he said. "I need to interview you. The sooner the better."

"Jeez, I can't tonight . . ."

"We've had another killing."

"Oh, no. Who was it?"

"A real-estate saleslady over here in Minneapolis. The whole thing will be on the ten-o'clock news."

"I don't have a TV."

"Well, look, how about tomorrow? How about if I stopped around at one o'clock?"

"That'd be fine. God, that's awful about this other woman."

"Yeah. See you tomorrow?"

"How'll I know you?"

"I'll have a rose in my teeth," he said. "And a gold badge."

The briefing room was jammed with equipment, cables, swearing technicians, and bored cops. Cameramen negotiated lighting arrangements, print reporters flopped on the folding chairs and gossiped or doodled in their notebooks, television reporters hustled around looking for scraps of information or rumor that would give them an edge on the competition. A dozen microphones were clipped to the podium at the front of the room, while the tripod-mounted cameras were arrayed in a semicircle at the rear. A harried janitor fixed a broken standard that supported an American flag. Another tried to squeeze a few more folding chairs between the podium and the cameras. Lucas stood in the doorway a moment, spotted an empty chair near the back, and took a step toward it. A hand hooked his coat sleeve from behind.

He looked down at Annie McGowan. Channel Eight. Dark hair, blue eyes, upturned nose. Wide, mobile mouth. World-class legs. Wonderful diction. Brains of an oyster.

Lucas smiled.

"What's going on, Lucas?" she whispered, standing close, holding his arm.

"Chief'll be here in five minutes."

"We've got a newsbreak in four minutes. I would be *very* grateful if I knew what was going on in time to call it in," she said. She smiled coyly and nodded at the cables going out the door. The press conference was being fed directly to her newsroom.

Lucas glanced around. Nobody was paying any particular attention to them. He tilted his head toward the door and they eased outside.

"If you mention my name, I'll be in trouble," he whispered. "This is a personal two-way arrangement between you and me."

She colored and said, "Deal."

"We've got a serial killer. He killed his third victim today. Rapes them and then stabs them to death. The first one was about six weeks ago, then another one a month ago. All of them in Minneapolis. We've been keeping it quiet, hoping to catch him, but now we've decided we have to go public."

"Oh, God," she said. She turned and half-ran down the hallway toward the exit, following the cables.

"What'd you tell that bitch?" Jennifer Carey materialized from the crowd. She'd been watching them. A tall blonde with a full lower lip and green eyes, she had a degree in economics from Stanford and a master's in journalism from Columbia. She worked for TV3.

"Nothing," Lucas said. Best to take a hard line.

"Bull. We've got a newsbreak in . . ." She looked at her watch. "Two and a half minutes. If she beats me, I don't know what I'll do, but I'm very smart and you'll be very, very sorry."

Lucas glanced around again. "Okay," he said, pointing a finger at her, "but I owed her one. If you tell her I leaked this to you too, you'll never get another word out of me."

"You're on," she said. "What is it?"

Late that night, Jennifer Carey lay facedown on Lucas' bed and watched him undress, watched him unstrap the hideout gun.

"Do you ever use that thing, or do you wear it to impress women?" she asked.

"Too uncomfortable for that," Lucas lied. Jennifer sometimes made him nervous. He felt she was looking inside his head. "It comes in handy. I mean, if you're buying some toot from a guy, you can't be packing a gun. They figure you for a cop or maybe some kind of nutso rip-off psychotic, and they won't serve, won't deal. But if you got a hideout in a weird place and you need it, you can have it in their face before they know what you're doing."

"Doesn't sound like Minneapolis."

"There are some bad folks around. Anytime you get that much money . . ." He peeled off his socks and stood up in his shorts. "Shower?"

"Yeah. I guess." She rolled over slowly and got off the bed and followed him into the bathroom. The print pattern from the bedspread was impressed on her belly and thighs.

"You could've brought McGowan home, you know," she said as he turned on the water and adjusted it.

"She's been coming on to me a little," Lucas agreed.

"So why not? It's not like you're bored by the new stuff."

"She's dumb." Lucas splashed hot water on her back and followed it with a squirt of liquid bath soap from a plastic bottle. He began rubbing it across her back and butt.

"That's never stopped you before," she said.

Lucas kept scrubbing. "You know some of the women I've taken out. Tell me a dumb one."

Jennifer thought it over. "I don't know them all," she said finally.

"You know enough of them to see the pattern," he said. "I don't go out with dummies."

"So talk to me like a smart person, Lucas. Did this killer torture these women before he killed them? Daniel was pretty evasive. Do you think he knows them? How does he pick them?"

Lucas turned her around and pressed his index finger across her lips.

"Jennifer, don't pump me, okay? If you catch me off guard

and I blurt something out and you use it, I could be in deep trouble.''

She eyed him speculatively, the water bouncing off his chest, his mild blue eyes darkened with an edge of wariness.

''I wouldn't use it before I told you,'' she said. ''But you never blurt anything out. Not that you didn't plan to blurt out. You're a tricky son of a bitch, Davenport. I've known you for three years and I still can't tell when you're lying. And you play more goddamn roles than anyone I've ever met. I don't even think you know when you're doing it anymore.''

''You should have been a shrink,'' he said, shaking his head ruefully. He cut the water off and pushed open the shower door. ''Hand me that big towel. I'll dry your legs for you.''

A half-hour later, Jennifer said hoarsely, ''Sometimes it gets very close to pain.''

''That's the trick,'' Lucas said. ''Not going over the line.''

''You come so close,'' she said. ''You must have gone over it a lot before you figured out where to stop.''

Two hours later, Lucas' eyes clicked open in the dark. Somebody was watching. He thought about it. The ankle gun was in the desk . . . Then Jennifer poked him, and he realized where it was coming from.

''What?'' he whispered.

''You awake?''

''I am now.''

''I've got a question.'' She hesitated. ''Do you like me more than the others or are we all just meat?''

''Oh, Jesus,'' he groaned.

''Say.''

''You know I do. Like you better. I can prove it.''

''How?''

''Your toothbrush? It's the only one in the bathroom cabinet besides mine.''

There was a moment of silence and then she snuggled up on his arm. ''Okay,'' she said. ''Go to sleep.''

CHAPTER

— 5 —

For the first twenty rings he hoped it would stop. He got out of bed on the twenty-first and picked up the receiver on the twenty-fifth.

"What?" he snarled. The house was cold and he was naked, goose bumps erupting on the backs of his arms, his back, and his legs.

"This is Linda," said a prim voice. "Chief Daniel has called a meeting for eight o'clock sharp and you're to be there."

" 'Kay."

"Would you repeat that, Lucas?"

"Eight o'clock in the chief's office."

"That's correct. Have a good morning." She was gone. Lucas stood looking at the receiver for a moment, dropped it onto the hook, yawned, and wandered back to the bedroom.

The clock on the dresser said seven-fifteen. He reached over to Jennifer, swatted her on the bare butt, and said, "I gotta get out of here."

"Okay," she mumbled.

Still naked, Lucas padded back down the hallway to the living room, opened the front door a crack, made sure nobody was around, popped the screen door, and got the paper off the porch. In the kitchen, he shook some Cheerios into a bowl, poured on milk, and unfolded the paper.

The maddog led the front page, a double-deck headline just below the *Pioneer Press* nameplate. The story was straightforward and accurate as far as it went, with no men-

tion of the Ruiz woman. The chief hadn't talked about sur-
vivors. Had lied, in fact—had said the only known attacks by
the killer were the three that produced deaths. Nor had he
mentioned the notes.

There was a short, separate story about Lucas' involve-
ment in the investigation. He would work independently of
homicide, but parallel. Controversial. Killed five men in line
of duty. Commendations. Well-known game inventor. Only
cop in Minnesota who drove a Porsche to work.

Lucas finished the story and the Cheerios at the same time,
yawned again, and headed down to the bathroom. Jennifer
was staring at herself in the medicine-cabinet mirror and
turned her head when he came in.

"Men have it easy when it comes to looks, you know?"

"Right."

"I'm serious." She turned back to the mirror and stuck
her tongue out. "If anybody at the station saw me like this,
they'd freak out. Makeup all over my face. My hair looks like
the Wolf Man's. My ass hurts. I don't know . . ."

"Yeah, well, let me in there, I have to shave."

She lifted an arm and looked at the dark stubble in her
armpit. "So do I," she said morosely.

Lucas was ten minutes late for the meeting. Daniel frowned
when he walked in, and pointed at the empty chair. Frank
Lester, the deputy chief for investigations, sat directly opposite him. The other six chairs were occupied by robbery-
homicide detectives, including the overweight head of the
homicide division, Lyle Wullfolk, and his rail-thin assistant,
Harmon Anderson.

"We're working out a schedule," Daniel said. "We figure
at least one guy ought to know everything that's going on.
Lyle's got his division to run, so it's gonna be Harmon here."

Daniel nodded at the assistant chief of homicide. Anderson
was picking his teeth with a red plastic toothpick. He stopped
just long enough to nod back. "A pleasure," he grunted.

"He won't be running you, Lucas, you'll be on your own,"

Daniel said. "If you need to know something, Harmon'll tell you if we got it."

"How'd it go with the media this morning?" Lucas asked.

"They're all over the place. Like lice. They wanted me on the morning show but I told them I had this meeting. So then they wanted to shoot the meeting. I told them to go fuck themselves."

"The mayor was on," said Wullfolk. "He said we had some leads we're working on and he'd expect to get the guy in the next couple of weeks."

"Fuckin' idiot," said Anderson.

"Easy for you to say," Daniel said gloomily. "You're civil service."

"You got some ink," said Anderson, squinting at Lucas.

Lucas nodded and changed the subject. "What about the weapon from the property room?"

Anderson stopped picking his teeth. "We run a list," he said. "We got thirty-four people, cops and civilians, who might of took it. There are probably a few more we don't know about. Found out the fucking janitors go in there all the time. I think they're smoking some of the evidence. Everybody says he's clean, of course. We got IAD looking into it."

"I want to talk to them, the thirty-four people," Lucas said. "All at once. In a group. Get the union guy in here too."

"For what?" Wullfolk asked.

"I'll tell them that I want to know what happened to the gun, and the guy that tells me, I won't turn him in. And that the chief will call off the IAD investigation and nothing more'll happen. I'm going to tell them that if nobody talks to me, we'll go ahead with the shoo-flies and sooner or later we'll find out who it is and then we'll prosecute the son of a bitch on accessory-to-murder and throw his ass in Stillwater."

Anderson shook his head. "I wouldn't buy it, if I was the guy."

"You got a convincer?" asked Daniel.

Lucas nodded. "I think so. I'll outline how the interrogation will go and I'll tell them that I won't read them their rights or anything else, so even if they are prosecuted, the whole thing would be entrapment and the case would be thrown out. I think we could build it so the guy would buy it."

Anderson and Daniel looked at each other, and Anderson shrugged. "It's worth a try. It could get us something fast. I'll set something up for late afternoon. Try to get as many as I can. Four o'clock?"

"Good," Lucas said.

"We've set up a data base in my office, we got a girl typing everything in and printing it out. Everybody working it gets a notebook with every piece of paper we develop, every interview," Anderson said. "We'll go over everything we know about these people. If there's a connection or a pattern, we'll find it. Everybody's supposed to read the files every night. When you see something, tell me. We'll put it in the file."

"What do we have so far?" asked Lucas.

Anderson shook his head. "Not much. Personal data, some loose patterns, that sorta shit. Number one was Lucy Bell, a waitress, nineteen years old. Number two was a housewife, Shirley Morris, thirty-six. Number three was the artist that fought him off, Carla Ruiz. She's thirty-two. Number four was this real-estate woman Lewis, forty-six. One was married, the other three were not. One of the other three, the artist, is divorced. The real-estate woman was a widow. The waitress was a rock-'n'-roller, a punk. The real-estate lady went to classical-music concerts with her boyfriend. It goes like that. The only pattern seems to be that they're all women."

Everybody thought about it for a minute.

"What's the interval between murders?" asked Lucas.

"The first one, Bell, was July 14, then Morris was on August 2, nineteen days between them; then the next was Ruiz on August 17, fifteen days after Morris; then Lewis on August 31, fourteen days later," said Anderson.

"Getting shorter," said one of the cops.

"Yeah. That's a tendency with sadistic killers, if he is one," said Wullfolk.

"If they start coming faster, he'll be doing them off the top of his head, not so careful-like," said another of the cops.

"We don't know that. He may be picking them out six months ahead of time. He may have a whole file of them," Anderson said.

"Any other pattern to the days?" asked Lucas.

"That's one thing, they're all during the week. A Thursday, a Tuesday, a Wednesday, and another Wednesday. No weekends."

"Not much of a pattern," Daniel said.

"Anything about the women?" asked Lucas. "All tall? All got big tits? What?"

"They're all good-looking. That's my judgment, but I think it's right. All have dark hair, three of them black—the Bell girl, who dyed hers black, Ruiz, and Lewis. Morris' hair was dark brown."

"Huh. Half the women in town have blonde hair, or blondish," said one of the other detectives. "That might be something."

"There are all kinds of possibilities in this stuff, but we gotta be careful, because there's also coincidence to think about. Anyway, look for those patterns. I'll make a special list of patterns," Anderson said. "Bring in your notebooks every afternoon and I'll give you updates. Read them."

"What about the lab, they sittin' on their thumbs, or what?" asked Wullfolk.

"They're doing everything they can. They're running down the tape he used to bind them, they're sifting through the crap they picked up with the vacuum, they're looking at everything for prints. They haven't come up with much."

"If any of these notebooks get to the media, there are going to be some bodies twisting in the wind," said Daniel. "Everybody understand?"

The cops all nodded at once.

"I don't doubt that we're going to spring some leaks," Daniel said. "But nobody, *nobody* is to say anything about the notes the killer is leaving behind. If I find somebody leaks to the media on these notes, I'll find the son of a bitch and fire him. We've been holding it close to our chests, and it's going to stay that way.''

"We need a surefire identifier that the public doesn't know about,'' Anderson explained. "They knew they had the Son of Sam when they looked through the window of his apartment and saw some notes like the ones he'd been sending to the cops and the media.''

"There's going to be a lot of pressure,'' Daniel said. "On all of us. I'll try to keep it off your backs, but if this asshole gets one or two more, there'll be reporters who want to talk to the individual detectives. We're going to put that off as long as we can. If we get to the point where we've got to do it, we'll get the attorney in to advise you on what to say and what not to say. Every interview gets cleared through this office in advance. Okay? Everybody understand?''

The heads bobbed again.

"Okay. Let's do it,'' he said. "Lucas, hang around a minute.''

When the rest of the cops had shuffled out, Daniel pushed the door shut.

"You're our pipeline to the media, feeding out the unofficial stuff we need in the papers. You drop what we need on one of the papers and maybe one TV station as a deep source, and when the others come in for confirmation, I'll catch that. Okay?''

"Yeah. I'm a source for people at both papers and all the TV stations. The biggest problem will be keeping them from figuring out I'm sourcing all of them.''

"So work something out. You're good at working things out. But we need the back door into the media. It's the only way they'll believe us.''

"I'd just as soon not lie to anybody,'' Lucas said.

"We'll cross that bridge when we come to it. But if you gotta burn somebody, you burn him. This is too heavy to fool around with.''

"Okay.''

"You got an interview with that artist?"

"Yeah. This afternoon." Lucas looked at his watch. "I've got to close down my net and get back here by four. I better get moving."

Daniel nodded. "I got a real bad feeling about this one. Homicide won't catch the guy unless we get real lucky. I'm looking for help, Davenport. Find this son of a bitch."

Lucas spent the rest of the morning on the street, moving from bars to pay phones to newsstands and barbershops. He talked to a half-dozen dope dealers ranging in age from fourteen to sixty-four, and three of their customers. He spoke to two bookies and an elderly couple who ran a convenience mail drop and an illegal switchboard, several security guards, one crooked cop, a Sioux warrior, and a wino who, he suspected, had killed two people who deserved it. The message was the same for all of them: I will be gone, but, I trust, not forgotten, because I will be back.

Freezing the net worried him. He thought of his street people as a garden that needed constant cultivation—money, threats, immunity, even friendship—lest the weeds of temptation begin to sprout.

At noon Lucas called Anderson and was told that the meeting had been set.

"Four o'clock?"

"Yeah."

"I'll see you before that. Talk it over."

"Okay."

He ate lunch at a McDonald's on University Avenue, sharing it with a junkie who nodded and nodded and finally fell asleep in his french fries. Lucas left him slumped over the table. The pimple-faced teenager behind the counter watched the bum with the half-hung eyes of a sixteen-year-old who had already seen everything and was willing to leave it alone.

Ruiz' warehouse studio was ten minutes away, a shabby brick cube with industrial-style windows that looked like dirty checkerboards. The only elevator was designed for freight and was driven by another teenager, this one with a complexion as vacant as his eyes and a boombox the size of a coffee table. Lucas rode the elevator up five stories, found Ruiz' door, and rapped on it. Carla Ruiz looked out at him over the door chain and he showed her the gold shield.

"Where's the rose?" she asked. Lucas had the shield in one hand and a briefcase in the other.

"Hey, I forgot. Supposed to be in my teeth, right?" Lucas grinned at her. She smiled back a small smile and unhooked the chain.

"I'm a mess," she said as she opened the door. She had an oval face and brilliant white teeth to go with her dark eyes and shoulder-length black hair. She was wearing a loose peasant blouse over a bright Mexican skirt. The gun-sight gash on her forehead was still healing, an angry red weal around the ragged black line of the cut. Bruises around her eyes and on one side of her face had faded from black-and-blue to a greenish yellow.

Lucas stepped inside and pocketed the shield. As she closed the door he looked closely at her face, reaching out with an index finger to turn her chin up.

"They're okay," he said. "Once they turn yellow, they're on the way out. Another week and they'll be gone."

"The cut won't be."

"Look at this," Lucas said, tracing the scar line down his forehead and across his eye socket. "When it happened, this wire fishing leader was buried right in my face. Now all that's left is the line. Yours will be thinner. With some bangs, nobody'll ever see it."

Suddenly aware of how close they were standing, Ruiz stepped back and then walked around him into the studio.

"I've been interviewed about six times," she said, touching the cut on her forehead. "I think I'm talked out."

"That's okay," said Lucas. "I don't work quite like the other guys. My questions will be a little different."

"I read about you in the paper," she said. "The story said you've killed five people."

Lucas shrugged. "It's not that I wanted to."

"It seems like a lot. My ex-husband's father was a policeman. He never shot his gun at anybody in his whole career."

"What can I tell you?" Lucas said. "I've been working in areas where it happens. If you work mostly in burglary or homicide, you can go a whole career without ever firing your gun. If you work in dope or vice, it's different."

"Okay."

She pulled a dinette chair out from a table and gestured at it, and sat on the other side. "What do you want to know?"

"Do you feel safe?" he asked as he put his briefcase on the table and opened it.

"I don't know. They say he got in by slipping the locks, so the landlord put on all new locks. The policeman who was here said they're good. And they gave me a phone and I have a special alarm code for 911. I just say 'Carla' and the cops are supposed to come running. The station is just across the street. Everybody in the building knows what happened and everybody's looking for strangers. But you know . . . I don't feel all that safe."

"I don't think he'll come back," Lucas said.

"That's what the other cops, uh, the other policemen said," she said.

"You can call us cops," Lucas said.

"Okay." She smiled again and he marveled at her even white teeth. She wasn't pretty, exactly, but she was extraordinarily attractive. "It's just that I'm the only witness. That scares me. I hardly go out anymore."

"We think he's a real freak," said Lucas. "A freak-freak, different from other freaks. He seems to be smart. He's careful. He doesn't seem to be running out of control. We don't think he'll come back because that would put him at risk."

"He seemed crazy to me," Ruiz said.

"So talk about it. What did he do when he first came after you?" Lucas asked. He thumbed through his copy of her interviews with St. Paul and Minneapolis homicide detectives. "How did it work? What did he say?"

For forty-five minutes he carefully led her through each moment of the attack, back and forth until every split second was covered. He watched her face as she relived it. Finally she stopped him.

"I can't do this much more," she said. "I was having nightmares. I don't want them to come back."

"I don't want them to either, but I wanted to get you back there, living through it. Now I want you to do one more thing. Come here."

He closed his briefcase and handed it to her. "These are your groceries. Start at the door and walk past the pillar."

"I don't—"

"Do it," Lucas barked.

She walked slowly back to the door and then turned, her arms wrapped around the briefcase. Lucas stepped behind the pillar.

"Now walk past. Don't look at me," he said.

She walked past and Lucas jumped from behind the pillar and wrapped an arm around her throat.

"Uhhh . . ."

"Do I smell like him? Do I?"

He eased up on his arm. "No."

"What? What'd he smell like?"

She turned into him, his arm still over her shoulder. "I don't . . . he had cologne of some kind."

"Did he smell like sweat? Perspiration? Were his clothes clean or did they stink?"

"No. Like after-shave, maybe."

"Was he as big as I am? Was he strong?" He pulled her tight against his chest and she dropped the briefcase and turned into him, beginning to struggle. He let her struggle for a moment and then she suddenly relaxed. Lucas tightened his grip further.

"Shit," she said and she fought and he let her go, and she turned into him, her eyes wide and angry. "Don't do that. Stay away." She was on the edge of fear.

"Was he stronger?"

"No. He was softer. His hands were soft. And when I relaxed, he relaxed. That's when I stamped on his instep."

"Where'd you learn that?"

"From my ex-husband's father. He taught me some self-defense things."

"Come here."

"No."

"Come here, goddammit."

She reluctantly stepped forward, afraid, her face pale. Lucas turned her again and put his arm around her neck without tightening it.

"Now, when he had you, he said something about not screaming or he'd kill you. Did he sound like this?" And Lucas tightened his grip and pulled her high, almost off her feet, and said hoarsely, "Scream and I'll kill you."

Ruiz struggled again and Lucas said, "Think," and let her go, pushing her away. He walked away until he was near the door. Ruiz had her hands at her throat, her eyes wide.

"New Mexico," she said.

"What?" Lucas felt a spark.

"I think he might be from New Mexico. It never occurred to me until now, but he *didn't* sound quite like people up here. It wasn't the words. It's not an accent. It's almost, like, a *feeling*. I don't think you'd even notice it, if you weren't thinking about it. But it was like back home."

"You're from New Mexico?"

"Yes. Originally. I've been up here six years."

"Okay. And you said he smelled like cologne. Good cologne?"

"I don't know, just cologne. I wouldn't know the difference."

"Could it have been hair oil?"

"No, I don't think so. I think it was cologne. It was light."

"But he didn't stink? Like he was unwashed?"

"No."

"He was wearing a T-shirt. You said he was white. How white?"

"Really white. Whiter than you. I mean, I'm kind of brown, you're tan-white, he was real white."

"No tan?"

"No. I don't think so. That's not my impression. He was

wearing those gloves and I remember that his skin was almost as white as the gloves were.''

"You said when you were talking to the St. Paul police that he was wearing athletic shoes. Do you know what kind?''

"No. He just knocked me down and I was getting up and I remember the shoes and the little bubble thing on the side . . .'' She stopped and frowned. "I didn't tell the other officers about the bubble thing.''

"What kind of bubble thing?''

"Those transparent bubble things, where you can look inside the shoe soles?''

"Yeah. I know. Do you go down to St. Paul Center much?''

"Sometimes,'' she said.

"If you've got the time, walk over this afternoon and look at the shoes, see if there's anything like it. Okay?''

"Sure. Jeez, I didn't think . . .''

Lucas took out his badge case, extracted a business card, and handed it to her. "Call me and let me know.''

They talked for another ten minutes, but there was nothing more. Lucas made a few final notes on a steno pad and tossed the pad and the investigation notebook back in his briefcase.

"You scared me,'' Ruiz said as Lucas closed the case.

"I want to catch this guy,'' Lucas said. "I figured there might be something you wouldn't remember unless you walked through it again.''

"I'll have nightmares.''

"Maybe not. Even the worst ones fade after a while. I won't apologize, considering the situation.''

"I know.'' She plucked at the seam of her skirt. "It's just . . .''

"Yeah, I know. Listen, I've got to make a call, okay?''

"Sure.'' She walked back to a stool next to a loom and sat on it, her hands resting between her legs. She was subdued, almost depressed. Lucas watched her as he dialed the information operator, got the number for St. Anne's College, hung up, and redialed the new number.

"Think about something else entirely," he said to her across the room.

"I try, but I can't," she said. "I just keep going over it in my head. My God, he was right in here . . ."

Lucas held up a hand to stop her for a moment. "Psychology department. . . . Thanks. . . . Sister Mary Joseph. . . . Tell her Detective Lieutenant Lucas Davenport . . ." He glanced at Carla again. She was staring fixedly out the window.

"Hello? Lucas?"

"Elle, I've got to talk to you."

"About the maddog?" she asked.

"Yeah."

"I was halfway expecting you to call. When do you want to come?"

"I'm in St. Paul now. I've got to be over in Minneapolis for a meeting at four, I was hoping you could squeeze me in now."

"If you come right this minute, we can walk down to the ice-cream store. I've got a faculty meeting in forty-five minutes."

"I'll see you in front of Fat Albert Hall in ten minutes."

Lucas dropped the phone back on the hook.

"You going to be okay?" he asked as he headed for the door. "I was a little rough . . ."

"Yes." She continued to stare out the window and he paused with his hand on the bolt.

"Will you check downtown for me? About those shoes?"

"Sure." She sighed and turned toward him. "I've got to get out of here. If you can wait a minute, I'll get my purse. You can walk me out of the building."

She was ready in a moment and they rode the old elevator down to the first floor. The elevator operator had plugged a set of headphones into his boombox, but the sound of heavy metal leaked out around the edges.

"That shit can sterilize you," Lucas said. The operator didn't respond, his head continuing to bob with the pounding beat of the music.

"This elevator guy . . ." Lucas said when they got off the elevator. There was a question in his voice.

"No chance," Carla said. "Randy's so burned out that he can barely find the right floors. He could never organize an actual attack on somebody."

"All right." He held the door for her and she stepped out on the sidewalk.

"It's nice to be out," she said. "The sunshine feels great." Lucas' car was parked a block toward Town Center and they strolled together along the sidewalk.

"Listen," she said when he stopped beside the Porsche. "I get over to Minneapolis once a week or so. I show in a gallery over there. If I stopped in some morning, could you let me know how things are going? I'd call first."

"Sure. I'm in the basement of the old City Hall. You just leave your car—"

"I know where you are," she said. "I'll see you. And I'll call you this afternoon, about the shoes."

She walked off down the sidewalk and Lucas got in the car and started it. He watched her through the windshield for a moment and she looked back and smiled.

"Hmph," he grunted. He rolled down the street until he was beside her, pulled over, and rolled down the passenger-side window.

"Forget something?" she asked, leaning over the window.

"What kind of music do you listen to?"

"What?" She seemed confused.

"Do you like rock?"

"Sure."

"Want to go see Aerosmith tomorrow night? With me? Get you out of your apartment?"

"Oh. Well. Okay. What time?" She wasn't smiling but she was definitely interested.

"Pick you up at six. We'll get something to eat."

"Sure," she said. "See you." She waved and stepped back from the car. Lucas made an illegal U-turn and headed back toward the Interstate. As he pulled away, he glanced in his rearview mirror and saw her looking after him. It was silly, but he thought he felt their eyes touch.

Sister Mary Joseph had grown up as Elle Kruger on the near north side of Minneapolis, a block from the house where Lucas was born. They started grade school the same autumn, their mothers walking them down the cracked sidewalks together, past the tall green hedges and through the red brick arches of St. Agnes Elementary. Elle still ran through Lucas' dreams. She was a lovely slender blonde girl, the most popular kid in the class with both the pupils and the teachers, the fastest runner on the playground. At the blackboard, she regularly thrashed the class in multiplication races. Lucas usually finished second. In the spelldowns, it was Lucas who won, Elle who finished second.

Lucas left St. Agnes halfway through fifth grade, after the death of his father. He and his mother moved down to the south side and Lucas started at public school. Later, at a hockey tournament, he was warming up, swinging down the ice, and he stopped on the opponents' side of the rink to adjust his skates. She was there in the crowd, with a group of girls from Holy Spirit High. She had not seen him, or not recognized him in his hockey gear. He stood transfixed, appalled.

It had been six years. Other girls, gawky as she had been beautiful, had blossomed. Elle had not. Her face was pitted and scarred by acne. Her cheeks, her forehead, her chin were crossed with fiery red lines of infection. The small part of her face free of scarring was as coarse as sandpaper from attempts at treatment.

Lucas skated away, around the rink toward the home bench, Elle's face bobbing in his mind. A few minutes later, the players for the two teams were introduced and he skated out to center ice, his name booming from the public-address system, unable *not* to look, and found her grave eyes following him.

After the match he was clumping toward the tunnel to the locker rooms when he saw her standing on the other side of the barricade. When their eyes met her hand came up and fluttered at him and he stopped and reached across the barrier and took her hand and said, "Can you wait for me? Twenty minutes, outside?"

"Yes."

He drove her home after a tour of southern and western Minneapolis. They talked as they had when they were children, laughing in the dark car. At her house, she hopped out and ran up to the porch. The light came on, and her father stepped out.

"Dad, do you remember Lucas Davenport, he used to live down the street?"

"Sure, how are you, son?" her father said. There was a sad edge to his voice. He asked Lucas in and he sat for another half-hour, talking to Elle's parents, before he left.

As he walked out to the curb, she called him from her bedroom window on the second floor of the house, her head backlit against the flowered wallpaper.

"Lucas?"

"Yeah?"

"Please don't come back," she said, and shut the window.

He heard from her next a year and a half later, a week before graduation. She called to tell him that she was entering a convent.

"Are you sure?"

"Yes. I have a vocation."

Years later, and two days after Lucas had killed his first man as a police officer, she called him. She was a shrink of sorts, she said. Could she help? No, not really, but he would like to see her. He took her to the ice-cream shop. Professor of psychology, she said. Fascinating. Watching minds work.

Did she have a vocation? Lucas wondered. Or was it her face, the cross that she bore? He couldn't ask, but when they left the shop she took his arm and smiled and said, "I have a vocation, Lucas."

A year later, he sold his first game and it was a hit. The *Star-Tribune* did a feature story about it and she called him again. She was a game player, she said. There was a games group at the college that regularly got together . . .

After that, he saw her virtually every week. Elle and another nun, a grocer and a bookie, both from St. Paul, a defense attorney from Minneapolis, and a student or two from St. Anne's or the University of Minnesota made up a regular war-gaming group. They met in the gym, played in an old unused room off what had been a girls' locker room. They furnished the room with a half-dozen chairs, a Ping-Pong table for the gaming maps, a used overhead light donated by a pool parlor, and a bad stereo that Lucas got on the street.

They met on Thursdays. They were currently working through Lucas' grandest creation, a replay of the Battle of Gettysburg that he would never be able to sell commercially. It was simply too complex. He'd had to program a portable computer to figure results.

Elle was General Lee.

Lucas parked the Porsche just down the hill from Albertus Magnus Hall and walked through the falling leaves up the hill toward the entrance. As he reached the bottom of the steps, she came out. The face was the same; so were the eyes, grave and gray, but always with a spark of humor.

"He can't stop," she told him as they strolled down the sidewalk. "The maddog falls into a category that cop shrinks call the sadistic killer. He's doing it for the pleasure of it. He's not hearing commands from God, he's not being ordered by voices. He's driven, all right, but he's not insane in the sense that he's out of control. He is very much in control, in the conventional sense of the word. He is aware of what he's doing and what the penalties are. He makes plans and provides for contingencies. He may be quite intelligent."

"How does he pick his victims?"

She shrugged. "Could be a completely adventitious encounter. Maybe he uses the phone book. But most likely he sees them personally, and whether he realizes it or not, he's probably picking a type. There may well have been an encounter of some kind when he was young, with his mother, with a female friend of his mother's . . . somebody whose sexual identity has become fixed in his mind.''

''These women are small and dark—dark hair, dark eyes. One is a Mexican-American . . .''

''Exactly. So when he encounters one of these types, she somehow becomes fixed in his mind. Why it's that particular one, when there are so many possibilities, I just don't know. In any case, after he's chosen her, he can't escape her. His fantasies are built around her. He becomes obsessive. Eventually . . . he goes after her. Acts out the fantasies.''

At the ice-cream parlor, she ordered her usual, a hot-fudge with a maraschino cherry. A few of the customers glanced curiously at them, the nun in her black habit, the tall, well-dressed male who was so obviously her friend. They ignored the passing attention.

''How long would it take him to fix on a particular woman? Would it be an instantaneous thing?''

''Could be. More likely, though, it would be some kind of encounter. An exposure, a conversation. He might make some kind of assessment of her vulnerability. Remember, this may be a very intelligent man. Eventually, though, it goes beyond his control. She becomes fixed in his mind, and he can no more escape her image than she can escape his attack.''

''Jesus. Uh, sorry.''

She smiled at him. ''You just didn't get enough of it, you know? If you'd stayed at St. Agnes for another two, three years, who knows? Maybe it'd be Father Davenport.''

Lucas laughed. ''That's a hair-raising thought,'' he said. ''Can you see me running the little ankle-biters through First Communion?''

''Yes,'' she said. ''In fact, I can.''

The phone was ringing when Lucas got back to his office. It was Carla. She thought the shoes on the maddog were the Nike Air model, but she was not sure which variation.

''But the bubble thing on the sole is right. There wasn't anything else like it,'' she said.

''Thanks, Carla. See you tomorrow.''

Lucas spent ten minutes calling discount shoe stores, getting prices, and then walked up the stairs to the homicide office. Anderson was sitting in his cubbyhole, looking at papers.

"Am I set on the meeting?" Lucas asked.

"Yep. Just about everybody will be there," Anderson said. He was a shabby man, too thin, with nicotine-stained teeth and small porcine eyes. His necktie was too wide and usually ended in the middle of his stomach, eight inches above his belt. His grammar was bad and his breath often smelled of sausage. None of it meant much to his colleagues. Anderson had a better homicide-clearance rate than any other man in the department. On his own time he wrote law-enforcement computer-management programs that sold across the country. "There'll be four missing, but they're pretty marginal anyway. You can talk to them later if you want."

"What about the union?"

"We cooled them out. The union guy will give a statement before you talk."

"That sounds good," Lucas said. He took out his notebook. "I've got some stuff I want to get in the data base."

"Okay." Anderson swiveled in his chair and punched up his IBM. "Go ahead."

"He's very light-complexioned, which means he's probably blond or sandy-haired. Probably an office worker or a clerk of some kind, maybe a professional, and reasonably well-off. May have been born in the Southwest. New Mexico, like that. Arizona. Texas. May have moved up here fairly recently."

Anderson punched it into the computer and when he was done, looked up with a frown. "Jesus, Davenport, where'd you get this?"

"Talking to Ruiz. They're guesses, but I think they're good. Now. Have somebody go around to the post offices and pull the change-of-address forms for anybody coming in from those areas. Add Oklahoma. Everybody who moved into the seven-county metro area from those places."

"There could be hundreds of them."

"Yeah, but we can eliminate a lot of them right off the bat. Too old, female, black, blue-collar, originally from here and moving back . . . Besides, hundreds are better than millions, which is what we got now. Once we get a list, we might be able to cross-reference against some other lists, if we get any more."

Anderson pursed his lips and then nodded. "I'll do it," he said. "We got nothing else."

They met in the same room where the press conference had been held the night before, thirty-odd cops and civilians, an assistant city attorney, three union officials. They stopped talking when Lucas entered the room.

"All right," he said, standing at the front. "This is serious. We want the union to talk first."

One of the union men stood, cleared his throat, looked at a piece of paper, folded it, and stuck it back in his coat pocket.

"Normally, the union would object to what's going to happen here. But we talked it over with the chief and I guess we've got no complaint. Not at this point. Nobody is being accused of anything. Nobody's going to be forced to do anything. We think for the good of the force that everybody ought to hear what Davenport's going to say."

He sat down and the cops looked back at Lucas.

"What I'm going to say is this," Lucas said, scanning the crowd. "Somebody took a piece out of the property room. It was a Smith, Model 15. From the David L. Losse box. You remember the Losse case, it was the guy who lit up his kid? Said it was an accident? Went down on manslaughter?" Several heads nodded.

"Anyway, it was probably somebody in this room who took it. Most of the people with access are here. Now, that gun was used by this maddog killer. We want to know how he got it. We don't think anybody here is the maddog. But somebody here, somehow, got this gun out to him."

Several cops started to speak at the same time, but Lucas put up his hand and silenced them.

"Wait a minute. Listen to the rest of it. There might be any number of reasons somebody thought it was a good idea to take the piece. It's a good gun and maybe somebody needed a backup piece. Or a piece for his wife, for home protection, and it got stolen. Whatever. The maddog gets his hands on it. We're looking for the connection.

"Now, the chief is going to put IAD on it and they're going to be talking to every one of you. They're not going to do anything else until they find out what happened."

Lucas paused and looked around the room again.

"*Unless,*" he said. "Unless somebody comes forward and tells me what happened. I give you these guarantees. First, I don't tell anybody else. I don't cooperate with IAD. And once we know, well, the chief admits there'd be no reason to really push the investigation. We got better things to do than chase some guy who took a gun."

Lucas pointed at the assistant city attorney. "Tell them about the punishment ruling."

The attorney stepped toward the center of the room and cleared his throat. "Before the chief can discipline a man, he has to give specific cause. We've ruled if the cause is alleged criminal wrongdoing, he has to provide the same proof as he would in court. He is not allowed to punish on a lesser standard. In other words, he can't say, 'Joe Smith, you're demoted because you committed theft.' He has to prove the theft to the same standards as he would in court—actually, for practical purposes, he has to get a conviction."

Lucas took over again.

"What I'm saying is, you call me, tell me where to meet you. Bring a lawyer if you want. I'll refuse to read you your rights. I'll admit to entrapment. I'll do anything reasonable that would kill my testimony in court. That way, even if I talked, you couldn't be punished. And I won't talk.

"You guys know me. I won't burn you. And we've got to catch this guy. I'm passing out my card, I've written my home phone number on the back. I want everyone to put the card in his pocket, so the guy who needs it won't be out there by himself. I'll be home all night." He handed a stack of business cards to a cop in the front row, who took one, divided the rest in half, and passed them in two directions.

"Tell them the rest of it, Davenport," said the union man.

"Yeah, the rest of it," said Lucas. "If nobody talks to me, we push the IAD investigation and we push the murder investigation. Sooner or later we'll identify the guy who took the gun. And if we have to do it that way . . ."

He tried to pick out each face in the room before he said it: ". . . we'll find a felony to hang on it. We'll put somebody in Stillwater."

An angry buzz spread through the group.

"Hey, fuck it," Lucas said, raising his voice over the noise. "This guy's butchered three women in the worst way you could do it. Go ask homicide if you want the details. But d n't give me any brotherhood shit. I don't like this any better than you guys. But I need to know about that piece."

Anderson caught him in the hall after the meeting.

"What do you think?"

Lucas nodded down the hallway, where a half-dozen of his cards littered the floor.

"Most of them kept the cards. I've got nothing to do but go home and wait."

CHAPTER

— 6 —

Bats flicked through his head, bats with razor-edged wings that cut like fire. Monsters. Kill factor low, but they were virtually transparent, like sheets of broken glass, and almost impossible to see at night in the thorn brush outside the dark castle . . .

Lucas looked up at the clock. Eleven-forty. Damn. If the cop who took the gun was planning to call, he should have done it. Lucas looked at the phone, willing it to ring.

It rang. He nearly fell off his drawing stool in surprise.

"Yes?"

"Lucas? This is Jennifer."

"Hey. I'm expecting a call. I need the line open."

"I got a tip from a friend," Jennifer said. "He says there was a survivor. Somebody who fought off the killer. I want to know who it was."

"Who told you this bullshit?"

"Don't play with me, Lucas. I got it solid. She's some kind of Chicana or something."

Lucas hesitated and realized a split second later that his hesitation had given it away. "Listen, Jennifer, you got it, but I'm asking you not to use it. Talk to the chief first."

"Look. It's a hell of a story. If somebody else gets onto it and breaks it, I'd feel like an idiot."

":It's yours, okay? If we have to break her out, we'll get you in first. But the thing is, we don't want the killer to start thinking about her again. We don't want to challenge him."

"C'mon, Lucas . . ."

"Listen, Jennifer. You listening?"

"Yeah."

"If you use this before you talk to the chief, I'll find some way to fuck with you. I'll tell every TV station in the world how you fed the name and address of an innocent woman to a maddog killer and made her a target for murder and rape. I'll put you right in the middle of the controversy, and that means you'll lose your piece of it. You'll be doing dog-sled stories out of Brainerd."

"I heard he hit her in her apartment, so he already knows—"

"Sure. And after about a week of argument, that'd probably come out too. In the meantime, the local feminists would be doing a tap dance on your face and you wouldn't be able to get a job anywhere east of the Soviet Union."

"So fuck you, Lucas. When can I talk to Daniel?"

"What time you want him?"

"Nine o'clock tomorrow morning."

"I'll call him right now. You be down there at nine."

He dropped the phone in its cradle, looked at it for a second, picked it up, and dialed Daniel's home phone. The chief's wife answered and a moment later put Daniel on the phone.

"You got him?" He sounded like he was talking around a bagel.

"Yeah, right," Lucas said dryly. "Go stand on the curb in front of your office and I'll drop him off in twenty minutes. If I'm late, don't worry, I'll be along. Just wait there on the curb."

The chief chewed for a minute, then said, "Pretty fuckin' funny, Davenport. What do you want?"

"Jennifer Carey just called. Somebody told her about Ruiz."

"Shit. Wasn't you, was it?"

"No."

"Somebody told me you were puttin' the pork to the young lady."

"Jesus Christ . . ."

"Okay, okay. Sorry. So what do you think?"

"I shut her mouth for the time being. She's coming down to your office to see you tomorrow. Nine o'clock. I'd like to hold her off Ruiz for at least a couple of days. But if somebody tipped her, it's going to get out."

"So?"

"So when she sees you tomorrow, tell her to hold off a couple of days and then we'll set up an interview for her, if Ruiz will go along. Then, if Ruiz is willing to go along, we'll set up an interview for six o'clock in the evening and let Jennifer tape it for the late news. While I'm over there with her, you can call a press conference for eight o'clock or eight-thirty. Then I bring Ruiz over, we let the press yell at her for twenty minutes or so, and they get tape for ten o'clock."

"Carey'll be pissed if we burn her."

"I'll handle that. I'll tell *her* that you wouldn't go for an exclusive break, but she's the only TV station with a personal interview. The other stations will have nothing but press-conference stuff. Then we'll tell the *other* stations that Carey had a clean tip, had us against the wall, but because you're their friend, you decided to go with a press conference. That way, everybody owes us."

"How about the papers? They're out of it."

"We let them sit in on the interview with Carey so they can drop in long profiles. They won't publish until the next morning anyway, so Jennifer still gets the break. I'll feed it to the two papers as special treatment from you. I'll let them know that the even-handedness could change if we start having trouble with them."

"Okay. So tomorrow morning I'll see Carey at nine o'clock, put her off, maybe feed her a tidbit. We can work all the rest out later, in detail."

"See you tomorrow."

"Don't forget the meeting."

When he got off the phone, Lucas rubbed his eyes and bent over the drawing table again. He read penciled numbers from a list on a yellow legal pad, cranking them through an electronic desk calculator. A near-empty coffee cup sat at the top of the table. He took a sip of the oily remnant and grimaced.

Lucas wrote games. Role-playing fantasies, Civil War historical reconstructions, combat simulations from World War II, Korea, Vietnam, Stalingrad, Battle of the Bulge, Taipan, the Punch Bowl, Bloody Ridge, Dien Bien Phu, Tet.

The games were marketed through a New York publisher who would take all he could create, usually two a year. His latest was a role-playing fantasy adventure. They were the best moneymakers but the least intrinsically interesting.

He looked at the clock again. Twelve-ten. He walked over to the sound system, picked out a compact disc, slipped it in the player, and went back to the numbers as Eric Clapton started on "I Shot the Sheriff."

The fantasy game's story line was complicated. An American armored platoon was fighting in the Middle East at some unspecified time in the near future. The platoon got word that a tactical nuke was headed toward it and dug in the best it could.

At the instant of expected detonation, there was an intolerable flash and the platoon found itself—complete with M3 tanks—in Everwhen, a land of water and fens and giant oaks. Where magic worked and soulless fairies danced in the night.

The whole thing tended to give Lucas a headache. Every fantasy game in the world, he thought, had a bunch of computer freaks with swords wandering around Poe-esque landscapes with red-haired freckled beauties with large breasts.

But it was money; and he had a responsibility to the prepubescent intellectuals who might someday buy his masterpiece, the Grove of Trees. He thought about Grove for a minute, the Gettysburg game he was perfecting in the weekly bouts at St. Anne's. Grove required an IBM computer and a separate, dedicated game room, along with teams of players. It took two nights just to set up the pieces. As a game it was impractical and unwieldy. But fascinating.

He tapped the pencil against his teeth and stared sightlessly over the drawing table. On the fifth night of the game, Jeb

Stuart was still out of touch with Lee, riding far to the east around the Union army that was slowly crawling north toward Gettysburg. That had happened in the actual conflict, but this time, in the game, Stuart—in the person of the St. Paul grocer—was moving more aggressively to close the gap and could reach Gettysburg in time to scout the good ground south of town.

In the meantime, Lee's order of battle had been shuffled. As he closed through the mountains toward Gettysburg, Pickett's division was in the lead and was hunting for bear. Even if Reynolds—a university student—got there ahead of Stuart, and Reynolds managed to stay alive, as he hadn't in the original fight, Pickett's aggressiveness might push him aside and allow the Confederates to take the hills at the end of Cemetery Ridge or even the entire ridge. If he did, then the gathering Union forces would have to choose between an offensive battle or retreating on Washington. . . .

Lucas sighed and wrenched his mind back to Everwhen, which was, naturally, under attack by the forces of evil. The armored platoon had been called in by a good wizard who planned to introduce a new element to what had been a losing war: technology. Once signed up with the forces for good, the armored platoon would march on the cloud-veiled castle of the Evil One.

The story was not particularly original. Working the details into a logical game was an ordeal.

Like the M3 tanks. Where did they get fuel and repairs? Magic. How did the platoon acquire magical talents? By valiant deeds. Save a virgin from a dragon and the magic quotient goes up. If the dragon kicks your ass, it goes down.

The creatures of Everwhen were a troublesome problem. They had to be dangerous, interesting, and reasonably original. They also had to be exotic, but familiar enough to be comprehensible. The best ones were morphologically related to familiar earth creatures: lizards, snakes, rats, spiders. Lucas spent dozens of winter evenings sitting in his leather chair in the den, a yellow pad on his lap, dreaming them up.

The slicers were one of them. A slicer was a cross between

a bat and a razor-edged plate of glass. Slicers attacked at night, slashing their targets to pieces. They were too stupid to be affected by magic, but were easy enough to kill with the right technology. Like shotguns.

But how would you even see them? Okay. Like bats, they used a kind of sonar. With the right magic, the platoon's radios could be tuned to it. Could you get them all? Maybe. But if not, there were hit points to be worked out. So many hit points, and a character died. Lucas had to take care not to kill off the characters too easily. The players wouldn't stand for it. Nor could the game be too simple. It was a matter of walking the line, of luring the players deeper and deeper into the carefully crafted scenarios.

He worked hunched over the drawing table in a pool of light created by the drafting lamp, hammering out the numbers, drinking coffee. When Clapton started on ''Lay Down, Sally'' he got up and did a neatly coordinated solo dance around the chair. Then he sat down, worked for fifteen seconds, and was back up with ''Willie and the Hand Jive.'' He danced in the dark room by himself, watching the song time counting down on the digital CD clock. When ''Hand Jive'' ended, he sat down again, called up a file on his IBM, read out the specs, and went back to the numbers after an almost unconscious glance at the clock. Twelve-fifteen.

Lucas lived in a three-bedroom ranch home, stone and cedar, across Mississippi Boulevard and a hundred feet above the river. When the leaves were off the trees in the fall and winter, he could see the lights of Minneapolis from his living room.

It was a big house. At first, he worried that it was too big, that he should buy a condominium. Something over by the lakes, where he could watch the singles out jogging, skating, sailing.

But he bought the house and never regretted it. He paid $120,000 for it, cash, in 1980. Now it was worth twice that. And in the back of his head, as he pushed into his thirties and contemplated the prospect of forty, he still thought of children and a place for them.

Besides, as it turned out, he quickly filled up the space. A beat-up Ford four-wheel-drive joined the five-year-old Porsche in the garage. The family room became a small gym, with free weights and a heavy bag, and a wooden floor where he did kata, the formal exercises of karate.

The den was converted to a library, with sixteen hundred novels and nonfiction works and another two hundred small volumes of poetry. A deep leather chair with a hassock for his feet, and a good light, were the main furnishings. For those times when reading didn't appeal, he'd built in a twenty-five-inch color television, videotape player, and sound system.

Tools, laundry appliances, and outdoor sports gear were stored in the basement, along with a sophisticated reloading bench and a firearms locker. The locker was actually a turn-of-the-century bank safe. An expert cracksman could open it in twenty minutes, but Lucas didn't expect any expert cracksmen to visit his basement. A snatch-and-run burglar wouldn't have a chance against the old box.

Lucas owned thirteen guns. His daily working weapon was a nine-millimeter Heckler & Koch P7 with a thirteen-shot clip. He also carried, on occasion, a nine-millimeter Beretta 92F. Those, and the small ankle gun, were kept on a concealed shelf in his workroom desk.

The basement locker contained two Colt .45 Gold Cups, both further customized by a Texas gunsmith for combat target competition, and three .22's, including a Ruger Mark II with a five-and-a-half-inch bull barrel, a Browning International Medalist, and the only nonautomatic, a bolt-action Anschutz Exemplar.

In the bottom of the locker, carefully oiled, wrapped, and packaged, were four pistols he'd picked up on the job. Street guns, untraceable to anyone in particular. The last weapon, also kept in the locker, was a Browning Citori over-and-under twenty-gauge shotgun, the upland version. He used it for hunting.

Of the rest of the house, the two smaller bedrooms actually had beds in them.

The master bedroom became his workroom, with a drawing table, drafting instruments, and the IBM. There were two walls of books on weapons and armies—on Alexander and Napoleon and Lee and Hitler and Mao, details of Bronze Age spears and Russian tanks and science-fiction fantasies that discussed seeker-killer shells, rail guns, plasma rifles, and nova bombs. Ideas that he would weave into the net of a game. The slicers flitted through Lucas' mind like splinters as he worked over the drawing table, hammering out the numbers.

When the phone rang, he jumped. It seldom rang; few people had the number. Thirty-odd more this evening, he thought, laying his pencil on the table. He glanced at the clock: twelve-twenty-two. He stepped across the room, turned down the CD player, started the tape recorder he'd attached to the receiver, and picked up the extension.

"Yes?"

"Davenport?" A man's voice. Middle-aged, or a little past it.

"Yeah."

"You taping this?" Vaguely familiar. He knew this man.

"No."

"How do I know that?"

"You don't. What can I tell you?"

There was a pause; then the voice said, "I took the Smith, but I want to talk to you about it face-to-face."

"Let's do it now," said Lucas. "This is a very heavy situation."

"The deal is like you said this afternoon?"

"That's right," Lucas said. "It won't go any further. No comebacks."

There was a pause; then, "You know that taco joint across I-94 from Martin Luther College?"

"Yeah?"

"Twenty minutes. And, goddammit, you come alone, you hear?"

Lucas made it in eighteen. The restaurant parking lot was empty. Inside, a lone diner stared out a window as he nursed a cup of coffee over the cardboard remains of his meal. An employee was mopping the floor and turned to watch Lucas come in. The countergirl, probably a student from the university, smiled warily.

"Give me a Diet Coke," Lucas said.

"Anything else?" Still wary. Lucas realized that in his leather bomber jacket, jeans, and boots, with a day-old beard, he might look threatening.

"Yeah. Relax. I'm a cop." He grinned, took the badge case out of his shirt pocket, and showed it to her, and she smiled back.

"We've had some problems here," she said.

"Holdup?"

"Last month and the month before. Four months ago it was twice. There are some bikers around."

When the cop came in, Lucas recognized him instantly. Gray-haired, wearing a lightweight beige jacket and brown slacks. Roe, he thought. Harold Roe. Longtime cop. Must be near retirement.

Roe looked around, stopped at the counter, got a coffee, and walked over.

"You it?" Lucas asked.

"You wearing a wire?"

"No."

"If you are, you're entrapping me."

"I admit it. If I am, I'm entrapping you. But I'm not."

"Read me my rights."

"Nope."

"Hmph. You know, this is all horseshit," Roe said, taking a sip of his coffee. "If they put you on the witness stand, you might tell a whole 'nother story."

"Won't be any witness stand, Harry. I could walk out of here right now, go to Daniel, say 'Harry Roe is the man,' and the IAD would put together a case in three days. You know how it goes, once they got a starting point."

"Yeah." Roe looked around wearily and shook his head. "Jesus, I hate this."

"So tell me."

"Not much to tell. I figured that piece was cold. Never show up in a million years. There was this guy down the block, Larry Rice was his name, I grew up with him. He was a maintenance man for the city. I used to see him around City Hall all the time. You probably seen him yourself. Heavyset guy with a limp, always wore one of those striped train-engineer hats."

"Yeah, I remember him."

"Anyway, he was dying of some kind of cancer, little bit by little bit. It was working its way up his body. First he couldn't walk, then he couldn't control his bowels, like that. His wife was working and he was at home. One day these neighborhood punks came in and took the TV and stereo right out from in front of him. He had this wheelchair, but he couldn't fight them. He couldn't identify them, either, because they were wearing paper sacks on their heads. . . . Assholes is who they were."

"So you got him the gun?"

"Well, his wife came over after this happened, and asked my wife if I had an extra gun. I didn't. I'm no gun freak— sorry, I know you're into guns, but I'm not."

"That's okay."

"So I went up there to the property room and I knew about the gun because I worked on the case. I figured there was no way in hell it would ever be needed for anything."

"And you took it."

Roe took a sip of his coffee. "Yep."

"So this Rice guy . . ."

"He's dead. Two months ago."

"Shit. How about his wife?"

"She's still out there. After the meeting this afternoon, I went over and asked her about the gun. She said she didn't know where it was. She looked, but it was gone. She said the last couple of weeks before he died, Larry sold a whole bunch of personal stuff to get money for her. He was afraid he wouldn't leave anything. She said when he died, he left about a thousand bucks behind."

"She doesn't know who got the gun?"

"No. I asked her how he sold the stuff and she said he just sold it to people he knew, friends and so on. He had a little sign in the window, she said, but he didn't advertise it or nothing. People might see the sign walking by on the sidewalk, but that was all." Roe passed a slip of paper across the table. "I told her you'd want to see her. Here's her address."

"Thanks." Lucas drained the last of his Coke.

"Now what?" asked Roe.

"Now nothing. If you've been telling the truth."

"It's the truth," Roe said levelly. "I feel like a piece of shit."

"Yeah, it's a bummer. It won't go any further than this table, though I suppose if we ever need Mrs. Rice to testify, somebody could figure it out. But it won't come to anything."

"Thanks, man. I owe you."

Roe left first, relieved to get away. Lucas watched his car pull out of the parking lot, then got up and strolled past the counter.

"You mind if I make a comment?" he asked the countergirl.

"No, go ahead." She smiled politely.

"You're too pretty to be working in this place. I'm not hustling you, I'm just telling you. You're an attraction. If you stay here, sooner or later you're going to catch some bad news."

"I need the money," she said, her face tense and serious.

"You don't need it that bad," he said.

"I have two more years at the university, one year for my bachelor's and nine more months for my master's."

Lucas shook his head. "If I knew your parents, I'd call them. But I don't. So I'm just telling you. Get out of here. Or get on the day shift."

He turned and started away.

"Thanks," she called after him. But he knew she wouldn't

do anything about it. He stepped outside, considered the problem for a minute, and went back in.

"How many tacos could you rip off without anyone knowing about it? I mean, every night. A couple of dozen?"

"Why?"

"If you gave a cup of coffee and a free taco to every patrol cop who came in, say, from ten o'clock at night to six in the morning, you'd have cops around, or arriving or leaving, most of the night. It'd give you some cover."

She looked interested. "We wouldn't have hundreds of cops or anything, would we?"

"No. On a heavy night, maybe twenty or thirty."

"Shoot," she said cheerfully. "The owner has trouble keeping people working here. He's kind of desperate. I don't think I'd have to steal them. I think he'd say okay."

Lucas took out a business card and handed it to her. "This is my office phone. Call me tomorrow. If the boss says okay, I'll get the word out about the free coffee and tacos. I'll tell both towns, you'll have cops coming in from all over the place."

"I'll call tomorrow," she said. "Thanks really a lot."

Lucas nodded and turned away. If it worked out, he'd have another source on the street.

When Lucas designed his games, he laid them out on sheets of heavy white drawing paper, twenty-two by thirty inches, so he could draw the logical connections between the elements. The visual representation helped him to avoid the inconsistencies that drew sophomorically scathing letters from teenage gamers.

Back at the house, he got four sheets of paper, carried them to the spare bedroom, and pinned them to the wall with push-pins. With a wide-tip felt pen he wrote the name of one victim at the top of each sheet: Bell, Morris, Ruiz, Lewis. Beneath the names, he wrote the dates, and under the dates, what he hoped were relevant personal characteristics of the victims.

When he finished, he lay back on the bed, propped his

head on a pillow, and looked at the wall charts. Nothing came. He got up, put up a fifth one, and wrote "Maddog" at the top of it. Under that he wrote:

Well-off: Wears Nike Airs. Clean clothes. Cologne.
    Convinced real-estate saleswoman that he could
    afford expensive home.
May be new to area: Has accent, wore T-shirt on
    August night.
May be from Southwest: Ruiz recognized accent.
Office job: Soft hands & body, arms white. Not a
    fighter.
Fair skin: Arms very pale. Probably blond.
Sex freak? Game player? Both? Neither?
Intelligent. Leaves no clues. Wears gloves even when
    preparing notes, loading shells in pistol.

He thought a moment and added. "Knew Larry Rice?"
He peered at the list, and reached out and underlined "real-estate saleswoman" and "Knew Larry Rice?"

If he was new to the area, maybe he really was looking for a house, and met Lewis that way. It would be worth checking area real-estate offices.

And he might have known Larry Rice. But that worked against the proposition that he was new to the area—if Rice had been dying of cancer, that would presumably take some time, and he wouldn't be making many friends along the way.

A hospital? A doctor in a hospital? It was a possibility. It would account for the maddog's delicate touch with the knife. And a doctor would have the soft hands and body, and would be well-off. And doctors, especially new ones, were mobile. All of these women could have been to a doctor. . . .

He walked back to the library and took down a volume on the history of crime and paged through it. Doctors as murderers had a whole section of their own.

Dr. William Palmer of England killed at least six and maybe a dozen people for their money in the mid-nineteenth century. Dr. Thomas Cream killed half a dozen women with botched abortions and poison in Canada, the U.S., and England; Dr. Bennett Hyde killed at least three in Kansas City; Dr. Marcel Petiot murdered at least sixty-three Jews whom he had promised to smuggle out of Nazi-occupied France; Dr. Robert Clements of England killed his four wives before he was caught. The "torture doctor" of Chicago, who had studied medicine but never quite became a doctor, killed as many as two hundred young women who had been attracted to the city by the 1893 World's Fair. The worst of the bunch, of course, were the Nazis. Medical men associated with the death camps had killed thousands.

The list of doctors who had killed only one or two was lengthy, including several celebrated cases in the United States since the 1950's.

Lucas shut the book, thought about it, and looked at his watch. Two-thirty. Far too late to call. He paced and looked at his watch again. Fuck it. He went into the workroom, got his briefcase with Carla Ruiz' phone number, and called. She answered on the seventh ring.

"Hello?" Half-asleep.

"Carla? Ruiz?"

"Yes?" Still sleepy, but suspicious now.

"This is Lucas . . . the detective. I'm sorry to wake you up, but I'm sitting here looking at some stuff and I need to ask you a question. Okay? Are you awake?"

"Uh, yes."

"When was the last time you saw a doctor and where was it?"

"Uh, gee . . ." There was a long silence. "A couple of years ago, I guess. A woman at the clinic over on the west side."

"You're sure that was the last? No visits to hospitals, nothing like that?"

"No."

"How about with a friend, just stopping by, visiting?"

"No. Nothing like that. I don't think I've been in a hospital since, well, my mother died, fifteen years ago."

"Know any doctors socially?"

"A few come to the gallery, I guess. I don't really know any personally. I mean, I've talked to some at openings and so on."

"Okay. Look, go on back to bed. I'll talk to you tomorrow. And thanks."

He dropped the phone back on the hook. "Shit," he said aloud. It was possible, but a long shot. He made a mental note to check the gallery for regular patrons who were doctors. But it didn't sound good.

He looked at the charts for a few more minutes, yawned, turned out the light, and headed for his bedroom. The guy was smart. Nuts, but smart. A player? Maybe.

Maybe a player.

CHAPTER

— 7 —

Lucas edged into the briefing room, late again.

"Where the fuck you been?" Daniel asked angrily.

"Up late," Lucas said.

"Sit down." Daniel looked around the room. A half-dozen detectives peered into their working notebooks. "To sum up, what we got is about three hundred pages of reports that don't mean diddly-squat. Am I wrong? Somebody tell me I'm wrong."

Harmon Anderson shook his head. "I don't see anything. Not yet. It might be in there, but I don't see it."

"What about this stuff that you got, Lucas?" asked one of the detectives. "Is it reliable?"

Lucas shrugged. "Yeah, I think so. There're a lot of guesses in there, but I think they're pretty good."

"So what?" said Daniel. "So we're looking for a medium-sized white guy who works in an office. That cuts it down to a half-million guys, not including St. Paul."

"Who recently moved up here from the Southwest," said Lucas. "That cuts out another 499,000 guys."

"But that could be bullshit. Probably is," Daniel snorted.

"We might know a little more in a couple of hours," Lucas said. Daniel raised an eyebrow. "The gun guy called last night. I know where the gun went."

"Well, Jesus!" Daniel exploded.

Lucas shook his head. "Don't get your hopes up." He explained how the gun got to Larry Rice and that Rice was dead. "His wife told my man that she doesn't know where the pistol went. Probably sold. Could have been stolen, I suppose.''

''Okay, but it's something,'' said Daniel. ''He had the gun for what, six months? And he probably sold it to somebody he knew.''

Daniel pointed at Anderson. ''Your best man. Best interrogator. Put him on her. We squeeze every goddamned drop out of her. Everybody her old man saw in the last six months. She must know most of them. The killer should be on the list.''

''I'm talking to her this afternoon,'' Lucas said, looking at Anderson. ''One o'clock. Your man could meet me there, we'll go in together.''

''So are we going to get the name of the guy who took the piece?'' asked Daniel.

Lucas shook his head. ''No. I swore. You could probably break it out of Rice, if you want, but you really don't want to know. He was doing a kindness. He's a pretty good guy.''

Daniel looked at him for a minute and nodded. ''Okay. But if it becomes relevant . . .''

''You might be able to break it out of Rice,'' Lucas repeated. ''You won't get it from me.''

There was a moment of silence; then Daniel let it go. ''We've got another problem,'' he said. ''Somebody fed a story to Jennifer Carey that we have an attack survivor. I'm going to talk to her in ten minutes and try to put her off. Anybody know anything about who tipped her off?''

Nobody answered.

''We can't have this,'' Daniel said.

One of the detectives cleared his throat. ''I might, uh, have an idea about that.''

''What?''

''She shot that documentary on St. Paul cops, the one that ran on PBS? She's got sources over there you wouldn't believe.''

''Okay. Maybe that's it. So now, we don't talk to St. Paul cops any more than we have to. Be polite, but . . .'' He groped for a word. "Reserved." He looked around. "Anything else?"

Lucas opened his notebook and looked at a short list on the back page.

"I'd like to find out about doctors. Did any of these women see the same guy? Ruiz' doctor is a woman, but there may be a few male docs going through her gallery. She could have been picked up there, and we ought to check."

"We can check that," said Anderson.

"How about those change-of-address cards?"

"That's a problem," Anderson said. "We called the post office and they don't have cards for incoming people. Only people moving out. So if we want to check change-of-addresses for people coming to the Cities, we'd have to take the Cities and all the suburb names and go to every post office in the Southwest and check them."

"They're not computerized?"

"Nope. It's done at the local post offices."

"Dammit." Lucas looked at the chief. "What'd it take to check all the major cities down there, ten guys for three weeks? Something like that?"

"Three months is more like it," said Anderson. "I looked in the phone book and there are about eighty post-office branches just in the Minneapolis area, and that doesn't include St. Paul and the St. Paul suburbs. So then I looked at a map and the major cities we'd have to check, and I figure maybe two thousand post offices to cover just the bigger cities. And at each one, we'd have to check for all the different cities and suburbs up here. We'd be lucky if a guy could do three or four a day, even with good cooperation from the post offices."

"Maybe we could work through the post office," Daniel suggested. "Get a list of all the post offices, work out some kind of form they could fill out, and mail it to them. Explain how important it is, call all these places to make sure they're doing it . . . ."

"If we did it that way, we could maybe do it with a couple, three guys full-time," said Anderson.

"They wouldn't have to be cops," Daniel said. "Work up a form and I'll talk to the post office. I'll send a couple of clerks over there to handle it."

"Driver's licenses," said one of the detectives.

"What?"

"If he just moved in, he probably had to get a new driver's license. They make you surrender your old one when you move in. The Public Safety people over at the state should have a record."

"Good," said Daniel. "We need that kind of thinking. Check that."

The detective nodded.

"Anything else?" he asked. "Lucas?"

Lucas shook his head.

"All right," said Daniel, "let's do it."

"Detective Davenport."

Lucas turned and saw her walking down the hall, Carla Ruiz, a smile on her face.

"Hi. What are you doing over here?"

She wrinkled her nose. "Divorce stuff. When I moved out of the house, my ex-husband was supposed to sell it and give me half the money. He never sold it and we're trying to get him moving."

"Unpleasant."

"Yeah. It just drags things out. I've been over here a half-dozen times. I'm tired of it."

"Got time for a cup of coffee?" Lucas asked, tilting his head toward the cafeteria.

"Ah, no, I guess not." She glanced at her watch. "I've got to be in the judge's chambers in twelve minutes."

"I'll walk you down to my corner," Lucas said. They fell in together and started toward the tunnel that led to the county courthouse. "Sorry about that weird call last night."

"That's okay. This morning I almost thought it was a dream. Did it help?"

"Oh, I guess. I was thinking maybe a doctor did it. Maybe

all the women had the same doctor or something. You just about eliminated that possibility.''

"Bet that made you happy,'' she said, smiling again.

"It's early,'' he said. They walked along for a minute and Lucas said, "We might have a problem. Involving you.''

"Oh?'' She was suddenly serious.

"One of the television stations got a tip about you. A reporter, Jennifer Carey, is in talking to the chief right now. She wants an interview.''

"Is he going to give her my name?''

"No. He's going to put her off, but it can't hold up. Carey's got good sources over in St. Paul. Sooner or later, she'll find out, and she'll harass the hell out of you.''

"So what do we do?''

"We've been thinking it might be better to give her an interview and then give the rest of the stations a press conference with you. Get it over with. That way, we can control it. You won't have people hitting you by surprise.''

She thought it over, her face downcast.

"I don't trust those people. Especially TV.''

"Carey's about the best of them,'' Lucas said. "She's a friend of mine, to tell you the truth. I didn't tell her about you, though. I don't know where she got the information. Maybe from St. Paul.''

"Would she really be okay?''

"She'd probably do the most sensitive job. After it was done, we'd get you out of town for a few days. When everything cooled off, you could slide back in quietly and probably be okay.''

"Can I think about it?'' Carla asked.

"Sure. The chief will probably call you about it.''

"If I went out of town, would the city pay? It's not like I'm rich.''

"I don't know. You could ask the chief. Or if you want to, you can stay in my cabin. I've got a place on a lake up north, in Wisconsin. It's a pretty place, quiet, out-of-the-way.''

"That might be okay,'' she said. "Let me think.''

"Sure.''

There was a long moment of silence which Lucas broke by asking, "So how long have you been divorced?"

"Almost three years. He's a photographer. He's not a bad guy. He even has some talent, but he doesn't use it. He doesn't do anything. He just sits around. Other people work, he sits. One of the reasons I'm so anxious to get the money out of the house is that it was my money."

"Ah. Good reason."

"I'm looking forward to Aerosmith tonight," she said, "I mean, if it's still on."

"Sure it's on," Lucas said. He stopped at a branching corridor. "I turn here. See you at six?"

"Yes. And I'll think about the TV thing." She walked on, half-turned to wave, and kept going. Nice, he thought as he watched her go.

Mary Rice was not very bright. She sat slumped on a kitchen chair, looking nervously at Lucas and Harrison Sloan, the second detective assigned to talk to her. Sloan had the ingratiating manner of a vacuum-cleaner salesman.

"It's very essentially important that we get a complete list from you," he purred, scooting his chair an inch closer to Rice's. He looked like a gynecologist on an afternoon soap opera, Lucas decided. "We would like to get a calendar or something, so we could figure out week by week and day by day who your husband saw."

"I won't tell you the man who gave me the gun," she said, her lower lip quivering.

"That's okay. I talked to him last night and that's all worked out," Lucas assured her. "We do need to know everybody else."

"There aren't very many. I mean, we never had a lot of friends, and then one or two of them died. When Larry got his cancer, some of the others stopped coming around. Larry had to wear this bag come out of his side, you know . . ."

"Yeah," said Lucas, wincing.

"There'll still be quite a few people," said Sloan. "Mailmen, neighbors, any doctors or medical people who came here . . ."

"There was only a nurse," she said.

"But those are the kind of people we're looking for."

Lucas listened for a few more minutes as Sloan worked to relax her, then broke in.

"I have to leave," he told Rice. "Detective Sloan will stay and chat with you, but I have a couple of quick questions. Okay?" He smiled at her and she glanced at Sloan and then back and nodded.

"I'm looking for a white man, probably about my size, probably works in an office somewhere. He might have an accent, kind of southwestern. Kind of cowboy. Probably well-to-do. Does that jog anything in your memory? Do you remember anybody like that?"

She frowned and looked down at her hands, at Sloan, and then around the kitchen. Finally she looked back at Lucas and said, "I don't remember anyone like that. All our friends are white. There haven't been any colored people in here. Nobody with a lot of money that I know of."

"Okay," Lucas said, an impatient edge to his voice.

"I'm trying to remember," she said defensively.

"That's okay," Lucas said. "Did your husband have people here that you didn't know about?"

"Well, he put a sign in the window for some things he wanted to sell. He had some of those little doll things he brought back from the war against the Japs. Those little carvings? Somebody bought those. He got five hundred dollars for fifteen of them. They were real cute things. Like little pigs and rats, all curled around."

"You don't know who that was, who bought them?"

"Oh, I think so. I got some kind of receipt somewhere." She looked vaguely around the kitchen again.

"Did you ever see the man who bought them?"

"No, no, but I think he was older. You know, Larry's age. I got that idea."

"Okay. Try to find that receipt and give it to Detective Sloan. Was there anybody else?"

"The mailman would stop and talk, he's a younger fellow, maybe forty. And a young fellow came out from the welfare. We weren't on welfare," she said hastily, "but we had some medical assistance coming . . ."

"Sure," said Lucas. "Listen, I'm going to run. We appreciate any cooperation you can give Detective Sloan."

Lucas went out through the kitchen door, let it close behind him, and walked down the steps. As he passed the kitchen window he heard Rice say, ". . . don't like that fellow so much. He makes me nervous."

"Quite a few people would agree with you, Mrs. Rice," Sloan said soothingly. "Can I call you Mary? Detective Davenport is . . ."

"Pushy," said Rice.

"Lot of people would agree with you, Mary. Look, I really hope we can work together to catch this killer . . ."

Lucas smiled and walked out to his car, opened the door, looked inside for a moment, then shut it and walked back to the house.

Inside, Sloan and Rice were looking at a steno pad on which Sloan had written a short list of names. They both looked up when Lucas came back in.

"Could I use your telephone?" Lucas asked.

"Yes, it's right . . ." She pointed at the wall.

Lucas looked in his notebook, dialed and got Carla Ruiz on the second ring.

"This is Lucas. How many times were you in the courthouse on the divorce?"

"Oh, four or five. Why?"

"How about before you were attacked? Right before, or when?"

"Let me go get my purse. I keep an organizer . . ."

He heard the receiver land on the table and looked over at Rice.

"Mrs. Rice, this guy from welfare. Did you have to go down to the county courthouse to see him, or did he come out here, or what?"

"No, no, Larry was disabled when we found out he could

get some medical, so this fellow came out here. He came out twice. Nice boy. But I think Larry knew him from before, from work.''

''That's a county job. I thought your husband worked for the City of Minneapolis.''

''Well, he did, but you know, people go back and forth all the time, between City Hall and the courthouse. Larry's job, he knew everybody. Every time something went wrong, they called him because he could fix anything. He used to see . . . the police officer who gave us the gun down in the cafeteria.''

Ruiz was back on the line.

''I was over there three weeks and four weeks before,'' she said.

''Before you were attacked.''

''Yes.''

''Thanks. Listen, see you at six, but try to remember everybody you saw in the courthouse, okay?''

''Got something?'' asked Sloan when Lucas hung up the phone.

''I don't know. You got the phone number where this Lewis woman worked, the real-estate office?''

''Yeah, I think so.'' Sloan got out his project notebook, ran down the list, and gave Lucas the number. He dialed and got the office manager and explained what he wanted.

''. . . So did she go down there?''

''Oh, sure, all the time. Once a week. She carried a lot of the paperwork for us.''

''So she would have been down there before she was killed?''

''Sure. You people have her desk calendars, but she hadn't taken any vacation in the couple of months before she died, so I'm sure she was down there.''

''Thanks,'' Lucas said.

''Well?'' said Sloan.

''I don't know,'' Lucas said. ''Two of the women were in the courthouse shortly before they were attacked. Even the woman from St. Paul, and it wouldn't be that common for somebody from St. Paul to be over in the Hennepin County courthouse. And Mr. Rice was there all the time. It would be a hell of a coincidence.''

"One of the other women, this Bell, the waitress-punker, was busted out at Target on Lake Street for shoplifting. It wasn't all that long ago. I remember that from our notebooks," Sloan said. "I bet she went to court down there. I don't know about the Morris woman."

"I'll run Morris," Lucas said. "It could be something."

"I got her house number, maybe her husband's there," Sloan said. He flipped open his notebook and read out the number as Lucas dialed. Lucas let it ring twenty times without an answer, and hung up.

"I'll get him later," Lucas said.

"Want me to check on this welfare guy?"

"You might take a look at him," Lucas said. He turned to Rice. "Did the welfare worker have an accent of any kind? Even a little one?"

"No, not that I remember. I know he's from here in Minnesota, he told me that."

"Damn," said Lucas.

"Could be a Svenska," said Sloan. "You get some of those Swedes and Germans from out in central Minnesota, they still got an accent. Maybe this Ruiz heard the accent and thought it was something like southwestern."

"It's worth a look," Lucas said.

At the office, he called Anderson and got Morris' husband's office. He answered on the first ring.

"Yes, she did," he said. "It must of been about a month before . . . Anyway, she used to work out at a health club on Hennepin Avenue, and about once a week she'd get a parking ticket. She'd just throw it in her glove compartment and forget about it. She must have had ten or fifteen of them. Then she got a notice that they were going to issue a warrant for her arrest unless she came down and paid and cleared this court order. So she went down there. It took most of a day to get everything cleared up."

"Was that the only time she was down there?"

"Well, recently. She might have been other times, but I don't know of any."

When he finished with Morris, Lucas called the clerk of court and checked on Lucy Bell's appearance date on the shoplifting charge. May 27. He looked at a calendar. A Friday, a little more than a month before she was killed.

So they had all been in the courthouse. The gun had come from City Hall, through a guy who hung around the courthouse. Lucas walked down the hall to Anderson's office.

"So what does it mean?" Anderson asked. "He's picking them up right here?"

"Picking them out, maybe," Lucas said. "Three of them were involved in courts and would have court files. Our man could be researching them through that."

"I'll check on who pulled the files," Anderson said.

"Do that."

"So what do you think?" Anderson asked.

"It was too easy," Lucas said. "This cat don't fall that easy."

Aerosmith was fine. Lucas sat back in his seat, watching with amusement as Carla bounced up and down with the music, turning to him, laughing, reaching a fist overhead with the other fifteen thousand screaming fans to shake it at the stage. . . . .

She asked him up for coffee.

"That's the most fun I've had since . . . I don't know, a long time," she said as she put two cups of water in the microwave.

Lucas was prowling the studio, looking at her fiber work. "How long have you been doing this?" he asked.

"Five, six years. I painted first, then got into sculpture, and then kind of drifted into this. My grandmother had a loom, I've known about weaving since I was a kid."

"How about this sculpture?" he asked, gesturing at the squidlike hangings.

"I don't know. I think they were mostly an effort to catch a trend, you know? They seemed okay at the time, but now

I think I was playing games with myself. It's all kind of derivative. I'm pretty much back to straight weaving now.''

"Tough racket. Art, I mean."

"That isn't the half of it, brother," she said. The microwave beeped and she took the cups out, dumped a spoon of instant gourmet coffee into each cup, and stirred.

"Cinnamon coffee," she said, handing him a cup.

He took a sip. "Hot. Good, though."

"I wanted to ask you something," she said.

"Go."

"I was thinking I did pretty well when I fought this guy off," she said.

"You did."

"But I'm still scared. I know what you said the other night, about him not coming back. But I was lucky the first time. He wasn't ready for me. If he comes back, I might not be so lucky."

"So?"

"I'm wondering about a gun."

He thought about it for a minute, then nodded.

"It's worth thinking about," he said. "Most people, I'd say no. When most people buy a gun, they instantly become its most likely victim. The next-most-likely victims are the spouse and kids. Then the neighbors. But you don't have a spouse or kids and you're not likely to get in a brawl with your neighbors. And I think you're probably cool enough to use one right."

"So I ought to get one?"

"I can't tell you that. If you do, you'd be the most likely victim, at least statistically. But with some people, statistics are nonsense. If you're not the type of person to have stupid accidents, if you're not careless, if you're not suicidal or think a gun's a toy, then you might want to get one. There is a chance that this guy will come back. You're the only living witness to an attack."

"I'd want to know what to get," Carla said. She took a sip of coffee. "I couldn't spend too much. And I'd want some help learning to use it."

"I could loan you one, if you like, just until we get the guy," Lucas said. "Let me see your hand. Hold it up."

She held her hand up, fingers spread, palm toward him. He pressed his palm against hers and looked at the length of his finger overlap.

"Small hands," he said. "I've got an older Charter Arms .38 special that ought to fit just about right. And we can get some semiwadcutter loads so you don't get too much penetration and kill all your neighbors if you have to use it."

"What?"

"Your walls here are plaster and lath," Lucas explained. He leaned back and rapped on a wall, and little crumbs of plaster dropped off. "If you use too powerful a round, you'll punch one long hole through the whole building. And anybody standing in the way."

"I didn't think of that." She looked worried.

"We'll fix you up. You live about a hundred yards from the St. Paul police indoor range. I shoot over there in competition. I could probably fix it to give you a few lessons."

"Let me sleep on it," she said. "But I think so."

When he was leaving, she closed the door except for a tiny crack and said as he started down the hall, "Hey, Davenport?"

He stopped. "Yes?"

"Are you ever going to ask me out again?"

"Sure. If you're willing to put up with me."

"I'm willing," she said, and eased the door closed. Lucas whistled on his way to the elevator, and she leaned against the door, listening to the sound of him and smiling to herself.

Late that night, Lucas lay in the spare bedroom and looked at the charts pinned to the wall. After a while he stood and wrote at the bottom of the killer's chart, "Hangs around courthouse."

CHAPTER

— 8 —

He was delighted by the newspapers.

He knew he shouldn't save them. If a cop saw them . . .
But then, if a cop saw them, here in his apartment, it would
be too late. They would know. And how could he not save
them? The inch-high letters were a joy to the soul.

The *Star-Tribune* had SERIAL KILLER SLAYS 3 CITIES
WOMEN. The *Pioneer Press* was bigger and better: SERIAL
KILLER STALKS TWIN CITIES WOMEN. He liked the word
"stalks." It reflected a sense of a continuing process, rather
than a historical one; and work that was planned, instead of
random.

Purely by chance, on the night the story broke, he saw a
nine-o'clock newsbreak promoting it. The station's top reporter, a tall blonde in a trench coat, rapped the harsh word
"murder" into a microphone set up outside City Hall. An
hour later, he taped TV3's ten-o'clock news report, which
replayed key parts of the press conference with the chief of
police.

The conference was chaotic. The chief was terse, straightforward. So were the first few questions. Then somebody
raised his voice, cutting off a question from another reporter,
and the whole conference reeled out of control. At the end,
newspaper photographers were standing on chairs in front of
the television, firing their strobes at the chief and the half-
dozen other cops in the room.

It took his breath away. He watched the tape a half-dozen
times, considering every nuance. If only they'd run the whole
press conference, he thought; that would be the responsible

thing. After thinking about it for a moment or two, he called the station. The lines were busy and it took twenty minutes to get through. When he finally did, the operator put him on hold for a moment, then came back to tell him there were no plans "at the present time" to run the entire conference.

"Might that change?" he asked.

"I don't know," she said. She sounded harassed. "It might. About a million people are calling. You oughta check the *Good-Morning Show* tomorrow. If they decide to run it, they'll say then."

When he got off the phone, the maddog got down on his knees with the VCR instructions and figured out how to program the time controls. He'd want to tape all the major newscasts from now on.

Before he went to bed, he watched the tape one last time, the part with Lucas Davenport. Davenport had been shown in a brief cut, sitting cross-legged in a folding chair. He was wearing jeans and an expensive-looking sport coat. Called the smartest detective on the police force. Working independently.

He got up early for the *Good-Morning Show*, but there was nothing but a rehash of the news from the night before. Later, when he was reading the morning papers, he found a short sidebar on Lucas Davenport in the St. Paul paper, with a small photograph. Killed five people? A *games* inventor? Wonderful. The maddog examined the photo closely. A cruel jawline, he decided. A hard man.

The maddog could barely work during the day, impatiently rushing through the stack of routine real-estate and probate files on the desk before him. He spent a few more minutes with two minor criminal cases he was also handling, but finally pushed those aside as well. The criminal cases were his favorites, but he didn't get many of them. The maddog was recognized in the firm as an expert researcher; but it was already being said that he would not work well before a jury. There was something . . . wrong about him. Nobody said it publicly, but it was understood.

The maddog lived alone near the University of Minnesota, in one of four apartments in a turn-of-the-century house that had been modernized and converted to town houses. He rushed home after work, hurrying to catch the six-o'clock news. There was no more hard information, but TV3 had news crews out all over the city getting reaction from people in the street. The people in the street said they weren't scared, that the police would get him.

A cop in a squad car revealed that he signed himself "maddog," and the newscasters picked it up. The maddog liked it.

After the news, he spent an hour cleaning and squaring his meticulously neat apartment. He usually watched television at night or rental movies on his VCR. That night he couldn't sit still. Eventually he went downtown, from bar to bar, cruising the crowds. He saw a James Dean-wannabe at a fashionable disco, a young man with long black hair and wide shoulders, a T-shirt under a black leather jacket, a cruel smile. He was talking to a girl in a short white dress that showed her legs all the way to her crotch and from the top down almost to her nipples.

You think he's dangerous, he thought of the woman, *but it's all a charade. I'm the dangerous one. You don't even see me in my sport coat and necktie, but I'm the one. I'm the One.*

It was time to begin again. Time to begin looking. The need would begin to work on him. He knew the pattern now. In ten days or two weeks, it would be unbearable.

So far he had taken a salesgirl, a housewife, a real-estate agent. How about one out of the pattern? One that would really mess with the cops' minds? A hooker, like in Dallas? No need to hurry, but it was a thought.

He was drifting along, deep in thought, when a voice called his name.

"Hey, Louie. Louie. Over here."

He turned. Bethany Jankalo, God help him. One of the associates. Tall, blonde, slightly buck-toothed. Loud. And, he'd been told, eminently available. She was on the arm of a professorial type, who stood tall, sucked a pipe, and looked at the maddog with disdain.

"We're going to the *Mélange* opening," Jankalo brayed. She had a wide mouth and was wearing fluorescent pink lipstick. "Come on. It's a lot of laughs."

Jesus, he thought, and she's an attorney.

But he fell in with them, Jankalo running her mouth, her escort sucking his pipe, which appeared to be empty and made slurping sounds as he worked it. Together they walked down a block, to a gallery in a gray brick building. There was a small crowd on the walk outside. Jankalo led the way through, using her shoulders like a linebacker. Inside, middle-aged professionals carried plastic glasses of white wine through the gallery while staring blankly at the canvases that lined the eggshell-white walls.

"Who dropped the pizza?" Jankalo laughed as she looked at the first piece. Her escort winced. "What a bunch of shit."

Some of it was not.

The maddog did not know about art; wasn't interested in it. On the walls of his office, he had two duck prints, taken from the annual federal waterfowl stamps. He'd been told they were good investments.

But now his eyes were opened. Most of the work was, indeed, very bad. But Larson Deiree did riveting nudes posed against bizarre situational backdrops. Their contorted bodies caught in explicitly sexual offerings, the recipients of the offers, men in overcoats and broadbrimmed hats and wing-tip shoes, their faces averted, shown as alienated strangers. Power transactions; the women as unequivocal prizes. The maddog was fascinated.

"Have a wine and a cracker, Louie," Jankalo said, handing him a glass of pale yellow fluid and a stack of poker-chip-size crackers.

"Sort of like 'I argued before the Supreme Court in my Living Bra,' huh?" she asked, looking at the Deiree painting behind him.

"I . . ." The maddog groped for words.

''You what?'' Jankalo said. ''You like that?''

''Well . . .''

''Louie, you're a pervert,'' she said, her voice so loud it was virtually a shout. The maddog glanced around. Nobody was paying any attention. ''That's my kind of man.''

''I like it. It makes an argument,'' the maddog said. He surprised himself. He didn't think in those terms.

''Oh, bullshit, Louie,'' Jankalo shouted. ''He's just hanging some snatch out there to hype the sales.''

The maddog turned away.

''Louie . . .''

He thought about killing her. All in an instant, he thought about it.

It would have a certain artistic spontaneity to it. It would, in a way, follow the maxim that he not establish a pattern, because it would not be calculated and planned. And it would be amusing. Jankalo, he didn't doubt, would largely cooperate, right up to the moment the knife went in. He felt a stirring in his groin.

''Louie, you can be such an asshole,'' Jankalo said, and walked away. She had said, *Louie, you're a pervert . . . my kind of man.* An offer? If so, he'd let it dangle too long. She was headed back to her professor. The maddog was not good in social situations. He took a bite of cracker and looked around, straight into the eyes of Carla Ruiz.

He looked away.

He did not want to catch her eye. The maddog believed that eye contact was telling: that she might look him in the eye and suddenly *know.* They had, after all, shared a considerable intimacy.

He maneuvered so that he could watch her from angles, past others. The cut on her forehead looked bad, the bruises going yellow. The maddog was still badly bruised himself, green streaks on his back and one arm.

Maybe he should come back on her.

No. That would violate too many rules. And the need to do her had passed.

But it was tempting; for revenge, if nothing else, like the farmgirl he'd blown off the horse. The thought of killing made him tingle, pulled at him, like a nicotine addict who had gone too long between cigarettes.

The need would grow. Better start doing research Monday. At the latest.

CHAPTER
— 9 —

Jennifer Carey was staring at him in the dark again.

"What?" he asked.

"What, what?"

"You're staring at me."

"How do you know I'm staring? You're looking the other way," she said.

"I can feel it." Lucas lifted his head until he could see her. She was sitting up, looking down at him. The thin autumn blanket had fallen around her hips and the flickering candle gave her skin a warm pink glow.

"I'm thirty-three," she said.

"Oh, God," he groaned into his pillow.

"I'm taking a leave of absence from reporting. I'll work half-time, producing. Do some free-lance writing."

"You can starve that way," Lucas said.

"I've got money saved." Her voice was level, almost somber. "I've been working since I was twenty-one. I've got that fund from my folks. And I'll still be half-time with the station. I'll be okay."

"What's this about?"

"It's about the old biological clock," she said. "I've decided to have a baby."

Lucas didn't say anything, didn't move. She grinned. "Ah, the nervous bachelor, already scouting escape routes."

There was another long moment of silence. "That's not it," he said finally. "It's just kind of sudden. I mean, I really like you. Are you bailing out? Should I be asking who the lucky guy is?"

"Nope. See, I figured you might not be interested in co-operating with my little plan. On the other hand, from my point of view, it's not that often you meet a guy who is intelligent, physically acceptable, heterosexual, *and* available. I decided I'd have to take things in my own hands, if you know what I mean."

Lucas was on his back staring at the ceiling. Looking down at him, she saw his stomach muscles tighten, and his chest lifted off the bed as though he were levitating, his head coming up, eyes wide.

"Jennifer . . ."

"Yeah. I'm pregnant."

He flopped back on the pillow.

"Oh."

She laughed. "You can be one of the funniest men I know."

"Why is that?"

"I tried to figure out what you'd say when I told you. I thought of everything except 'Oh.' "

He sat up again, his face deeply serious. "We ought to get married. Like tomorrow. I can fix the blood tests—"

She laughed again. "Yo. Davenport. Wake up. I'm not getting married."

"What?"

"Just a few minutes ago you said you liked me, not loved me. For one thing. Besides, I don't want to marry you."

"Jennifer . . ."

"Listen, Lucas. I'm touched by the offer. I wasn't sure you'd make it. And you'd make a wonderful father. But you'd make an awful husband and I couldn't put up with that."

"Jennifer . . ."

"I thought it out."

"What about me, goddammit?" he said. He threw off the blanket and knelt over her, his heavy fists in tight balls, and she dropped flat, suddenly, for the first time afraid of him. "It's my kid too. Right? I mean, it *is* mine?"

"Yes."

"And I don't want my kid being a little fuckin' bastard."

"So what are you going to do, beat me into marriage?"

He looked down at his balled fists and suddenly relaxed. "No, of course not," he said softly. He flopped down beside her.

"Look. I'm going to have the kid," she said. "If you don't want anyone to know he's yours, that's okay. If you don't mind, I'd love to have you around to help. I'll be here in the Cities. I assume you will be too."

"Yeah."

"So we'll really be together."

"No. Not sharing a bed every night. Look, I'm going to tell you. I'm going to spend the next nine months—"

"Seven months."

"—seven months trying to convince you to marry me. If you won't, what would you say about moving in here?"

"Lucas, this house is a men's club. You've got everything but spittoons."

"Listen, I'll tell you what . . ."

"Lucas, we've got months to figure out the exact arrangements. And right now I feel kind of horny again. Something about your reaction. It was much nicer than I expected."

A few minutes later she said, "Lucas, you're not paying attention."

And a few minutes after that she gave up. "It's like trying to make love with a rope. A short rope. No offense."

He didn't laugh. He said, "Jesus Christ, I'm going to have a kid." And then he reached over and placed a hand on her stomach. "I've always wanted a kid. Maybe two or three." He looked at her. "You don't think it could be twins, do you?"

The next morning, Jennifer was peering at herself in the mirror over the bathroom sink and Lucas stopped by the door and looked at her.

"Doesn't show," he said.

"In a month it will," she said. She turned her face to him. "I want the interview with that Chicana chick."

"The chief—"

"I don't care about the chief. I got some more background on her, and I'll go with what I've got unless you set something up. Tonight, tomorrow."

"I'll check."

She looked back in the mirror and stuck her tongue out. "This is going to be weird," she said.

The shower was running when Lucas finished dressing. He hurried in to the kitchen telephone, found Carla's phone number in his pocket directory, and dialed. The shower stopped just as the phone was answered.

"Carla? This is Lucas."

"Yes, hi. What's going on?"

"We're getting some fierce pressure for an interview with you. The woman from TV3, Jennifer Carey, has a leak somewhere. She knows some things about you and it's only a matter of time before somebody tracks you down. It might be better if we went ahead and gave her an interview while we can control things a bit."

There was a moment of silence.

"Okay. If you think so."

"It'll be in the afternoon or early evening. I'll get back to you."

"Should I pack a suitcase?"

"Oh . . . yeah. You want me to go to the chief for a hotel, or you want to try the cabin?"

"How about the cabin? I like the lakes."

"Pack a bag. We'll go up tonight."

Lucas hung up and redialed, calling Daniel on his direct line.

"Linda? I need to talk to the chief."

"He's pretty busy, Lucas. Let me ask."

"Jennifer Carey says she's going with the story about the survivor."

"Hang on."

Jennifer walked down the hall, rubbing her wet hair with a bath towel, and got a bagel out of the refrigerator.

Lucas covered the phone's mouthpiece with the palm of his hand. "Something's happening," he said.

She stopped chewing. "What?"

"I don't know."

Jennifer pulled out a kitchen chair and lowered herself into it as Linda came back on the line. "I'm switching you in," the secretary said.

Daniel was on a second later. "Lucas? I was about to call. You better get down here."

"What's happening?"

"Sloan interviewed this Rice woman about the gun?"

"Yeah, I was there for some of it."

"She mentioned a welfare guy. Sloan put that with your idea that he picks his victims in the courthouse and did some checking. This welfare guy fits a lot of the profile. He's gay. He's in the right age and size slot. And listen to this: he's into art. Sloan was greasing one of the women from the welfare office, got her talking about Smithe, and she was saying what a waste this guy is. Big, good-looking, but she said she went to an opening and saw him there with his boyfriend. Sloan checked with the Ruiz woman. She was at the opening. It was a week before she was hit."

"Damn." Lucas thought for a moment. "I don't know."

"What?"

"Hang on a second. Jennifer Carey is sitting here." Lucas put his hand over the mouthpiece again. "Go on back to the bathroom and shut the door."

"Hey . . ."

"Don't give me any trouble, Jennifer, please? This is a private conversation. We'll have to work out some rules, but right now . . ."

"All right." She stood and flounced out of the room and down the hall, and he heard the door close behind her.

He took his hand off the mouthpiece.

"I sent her back to the bathroom. She's pissed . . . There, the door closed. I'll tell you what, chief, it seems awfully easy. The guy is too smart to be caught that quick. And a week is a pretty short time to check her out."

"Sure, but we only caught him through a freak accident. He didn't plan to lose the gun."

"Then why didn't the brass have prints on them? He used gloves to load the son of a bitch."

"Sure, but I bet he didn't know where the gun came from— that we could trace it. And he is gay. All the shrinks say he will be."

Lucas thought about it. "That's a point," he admitted. "Okay. It sounds like he's worth a check."

"We don't want to fuck up. I think we're going to want you to . . . develop some intelligence on him."

"Okay." Daniel wanted him to bag the guy's house. "Listen, Carey wants to talk with Ruiz. I think I should set it up. It'll keep her off this other thing."

"What does Ruiz think?"

"She seems to be willing. Or I could talk her into it. We could set it up just the way we talked about. That'd keep all the newsies busy while we work on Smithe."

"Do it. And get down here. We're going to meet at ten."

"Come on out," he hollered. He stepped into the hallway and noticed the bathroom door was open. He walked swiftly to the bedroom and pushed the door open. Jennifer was screwing the mouthpiece back on the phone.

"I needed one more minute," she said. It wasn't an apology.

"Goddammit, Jennifer," Lucas said in exasperation.

"I don't take orders about news stuff. Not from cops," she said, tightening the mouthpiece and replacing it on the receiver.

"We gotta work something out," he said, hands on his hips. "What'd you hear?"

"You've got a suspect. He's gay. That's all. And about Ruiz."

"You can't use it."

"Don't tell me—"

"You might think that listening on my private line is something that a real hard news broad would do, but your lawyers wouldn't think it's so cute. Or the station, after they thought about it. The state news council might have a few words about it too. And to tell you the truth, I kind of think this gay guy might not be the right one. If he's not, and you constructively identify him, he'll be the new owner of the station after the libel suit.''

"I'll think about it.''

"Jennifer, if we're going to have a kid together, we can't play mind games anymore. I've got to trust you. On the cases I'm working on, you only use what I say is okay.''

"I don't make that kind of deal.''

"You better start or we're going to have trouble. We'll both be sitting around afraid to talk to each other. Besides, it only applies to the cases I'm working on.''

She thought it over. "We'll figure something out,'' she said noncommittally. "I won't cover for you. If I come up with a tip from another source, I'll use it.''

"Okay.''

"It won't be so much of a problem when I start producing,'' Jennifer said. "I'll be concentrating on longer-range stuff. Not police stuff.''

"That'd be better for both of us. But what about this thing? Will you hold off for now?''

"What about this Ruiz woman?''

"I already called her, while you were in the shower. She says she'll do it. We should be able to set something up for tonight. You heard Daniel, he says to go ahead.''

Jennifer thought it over and finally nodded. "Okay. Deal. I'll hold off on the suspect as long as you promise that I get the first break. If there's a break.''

"I promise you'll share it.''

"God damn, Lucas . . .''

"Jennifer . . .''

"This is going to be hard,'' she said. "Okay. For now. I'll give you notice if I think I have to change my mind.''

He nodded. ".I'll call Ruiz again and set up a specific time.''

"The guy's name is Jimmy Smithe,'' Anderson told him as they walked down the hall to the meeting room. "I pulled his personnel file out of the computers and ran it against the psychological profile the shrinks put together and the information we developed. There are some matches.''

''How about misses?'' Lucas asked. ''Does he come from the Southwest?''

''No. As far as I can tell, he was born and raised here in Minnesota, went to the University of Michigan, worked in Detroit for a while, spent some time in New York, and came back here to take a job in welfare.''

''You run his sheet?''

''Nothing serious. When he was seventeen the Stillwater cops gave him a ticket for possession of a small amount of marijuana.''

''What's his rep with welfare?''

''Sloan says it's pretty good. Smithe is gay, all right, doesn't hide it, but he doesn't flaunt it either. He's smart. He gets along with other people in his department, including the guys. He's up for a promotion to supervisor.''

''I don't know, man. He doesn't sound tight enough.''

''He's there physically. And we can put him with two people.''

When Lucas and Anderson arrived, Daniel was talking to the other eight cops in the room.

''I don't want the word to get out of this group,'' he said. ''We've got to take a close look at this guy without anybody knowing.''

He poked a heavy finger at Sloan.

''You hit the neighborhood. Tell them it's a security investigation for a job offer with the department. If we need to back it up, I'll come up with some bullshit about a liaison officer between police and the gay community on AIDS and other problems. What the police can do to help, sensitivity training, all that. They ought to buy it.''

''Okay.'' Sloan nodded.

''Actually, that's not a bad idea,'' Lucas said.

''We've got enough gays of our own without going outside," Daniel said. He poked a finger at Anderson. "Find out everything you can and cross-check it with the other victims. We've got him with Ruiz. See if we can match up somewhere else.

"Now, you guys," he said to the other six detectives, "are going to watch every move he makes. Two guys all the time, round the clock. Overtime, no problem. You see an eighty-year-old society lady getting gang-banged, you call it in and forget it. You never take your eyes off this motherfucker. You got that? Smithe is the *only* priority. And I want fifteen-minute checks on location. Call it into Anderson during the day, the duty officer at night."

"My husband's going to love this," one of the women cops muttered.

"Fuck your husband," said Daniel.

"I'd like to," said the cop, "but people keep putting me on nights."

When the meeting broke, he asked Lucas to stay behind.

"You got the Ruiz thing fixed?"

"Yeah. I talked to her just before I came in. We'll do it tonight, at her place. Six o'clock. She's willing, if it'll help, and it'll cool out Carey."

"I hope your dick isn't getting you in trouble with that woman."

"It's under control," Lucas said. "I'll tip the papers and the TV people that you'll be calling a press conference. And I'll talk to the papers about doing their interviews at the same time Carey does hers. We'll be back over here for the press conference at nine. Afterward, I'm going to head up to my cabin for a couple of days. I've got some time coming."

"Jesus, this isn't such a good time for a vacation."

"I've got things covered. I'll leave my number with the shift commander if you need me."

"Okay, but tonight prep Ruiz for making some kind of appeal for cooperation, will you? You know the stuff." Daniel leaned back in his chair, put one foot on his desk, looked at his wall of photographs, and changed the subject. "You know what we need."

"Yeah."

"I'll tell Anderson to give you location checks. We already know he lives alone. It's a little house down by Lake Harriet."

"Not far from where Lewis worked. The real-estate woman."

"We thought of that," Daniel said. "He didn't buy the house from her agency, though."

"Look. Don't get too far out front on this thing, okay? I mean you personally," Lucas said. "If there's a leak to the press, tell them that you're looking at a guy, but you think it's thin."

"You don't believe it?"

"I've got a bad feeling."

"Can you get something going this afternoon? That might tell us something."

"I'll give it a shot."

Nobody said anything about a bag job.

From his office, Lucas called the newspapers and television stations and tipped friends that Daniel would be calling a press conference. He talked separately to assignment editors from both papers and suggested that they keep a soft-touch reporter around late, that there'd be a good next-day story breaking around six o'clock.

That done, he got Smithe's address and phone number from Anderson and found the house on a city map. He knew the neighborhood. He thought about it for a minute, pursing his lips, then opened the bottom drawer of his desk, reached far into the back, and found the lock rake. It was battery-operated, roughly the same shape but only half the size of an electric drill, with two prongs sticking out where the drill bit would have been. One prong was bent, the other straight. Lucas unscrewed the butt cap, reversed the batteries into working position, and squeezed the trigger. The picks rattled for a second and he released the pressure and sighed.

• • •

Smithe's house was tan stucco with a postage-stamp lawn. Fifteen-foot-tall junipers flanked the concrete steps that led to the front door. There were only occasional people on the quiet streets around the house. Lucas cruised by twice, then drove out to a street phone.

"Anderson."

"This is Davenport. Where's Smithe?"

"Just had a call. He's at his desk."

"Thanks."

Next he dialed Smithe's number and let it ring. After the thirtieth ring he took a pair of wire cutters from the glove compartment, looked around, nipped off the receiver, and dropped it on the floor of the car. If the receiver was gone, there was little chance that a passerby would manually disconnect the phone.

The Porsche was too noticeable to park outside Smithe's house. Lucas dropped it a block away and walked down the street, the pick in his jacket pocket. A kid was pedaling a bike along the street and Lucas slowed and let him pass. At Smithe's house he turned in and walked straight up to the steps without looking around.

He could hear the phone ringing from the porch. The lock was an original, from a door that was probably installed in the fifties. The pick took it out in less than a minute. Lucas pushed the door open with his knuckles and stuck his head inside.

"Here, boy," he called. He whistled. Nothing. He stepped inside and pushed the door shut.

The house was still and smelled faintly of some chemical. What? Wood polish? Wax. Lucas cruised quickly through the ground floor on a preliminary survey, stopping only to lift the ringing phone, silencing it.

The living room was sparsely but tastefully furnished with an overstuffed couch-and-chair set and a teardrop glass coffee table from the fifties. The kitchen was a pleasant, sunny room with yellow tiles and a half-dozen plants perched on the counter near the window. There was a bathroom with a cast-iron tub, a small bedroom with a double bed pushed into a corner, an empty chest of drawers, and a desk and chair, apparently used as an office and a guest bedroom. He checked the drawers in the desk and found bills, financial statements, and copies of income-tax returns.

The master bedroom had been converted into a media room, with a set of five-foot-tall speakers and a twenty-seven-inch television facing a long, comfortable couch. One wall of the media room was lined with photos. Smithe stood next to a smiling older couple that Lucas assumed were his parents. Another photo showed him with two other men, all showing a strong family resemblance, probably his brothers; they were dressed in high-school wrestling uniforms, flexing their biceps for the camera. There was a picture of Smithe throwing hay off a rack with his father. Smithe with a diploma. Smithe with a male friend on the streets of New York, arms wrapped around each other's waists.

Where's the bedroom? Lucas went down the hall, found the stairs going up. The bedroom ran the whole length of the house and featured a king-size bed still rumpled from the night before. Jeans, underwear, and other pieces of clothing were scattered around on chairs. A bookcase held a few books, mostly science fiction, and a small selection of gay skin magazines. Lucas looked at the chest of drawers. Keys, cologne, a money clip with the insignia of Ducks Unlimited, a small jewelry box, a photo of Smithe with another man, both bare from the waist up, arms around each other's shoulders.

Lucas pulled open the top drawer. Prophylactics. Two boxes, one of lubricated, the other nonlubricated, both boxes about half-empty. He took one of the lubricated variety and dropped it in his pocket. Ran through the rest of the drawers: a bundle of letters from a man named Rich, fastened together with a rubber band. Lucas looked at two: chatty letters from an ex-lover. No threats, no recriminations.

Checked the closet. Athletic shoes, five pairs. Adidas, Adidas, Adidas, Adidas, and Adidas. No Nike Airs. Down the stairs, into the bathroom. The medicine chest had four bottles of prescription drugs: two penicillin, one of them expired, a weak painkiller, a tiny bottle of ophthalmological ointment.

Through the kitchen, the basement stairs, and down. Basement unfinished. A gun rack with three shotguns. The back room: weights. A full set, with an elaborate weight bench. Pictures of weight lifters in full grease, pumped and flexed. A handmade exercise chart, with checks next to the days of the week when each exercise was completed. He didn't miss often.

Back out to the main room. A chest of drawers. More guns? Lucas ran through it, nothing but tools. Up the stairs, through the living room. Two nice drawings, both in charcoal, nudes of long sinuous women. Glanced at the watch: in nine minutes now.

Into the office. Pulled out drawers. Financial records, letters. Nothing interesting. Brought up IBM computer. Loaded Word Perfect. Loaded files disks. Letters, business correspondence. Smithe worked at home. Nothing like a diary.

Last check. Looked at the photos in the media room again. Happy, Lucas thought. That was what he looked like.

Checked watch. Seventeen minutes. And out.

He stopped at Daniel's office.

"What?" Daniel looked harassed.

Lucas dipped into his pocket, took out the packaged ring of the prophylactic, tossed it on the desk. Daniel looked down without touching it, then back up.

" 'Share,' " he read from the pack. He looked up at Lucas. "The notebooks have a list that the lab made up, the rubbers that use the kind of lubricant they found in the women."

"Yeah."

"This one on it?"

"Yeah."

"God damn. We got anything we can make a warrant with?"

"It'd be thin."

Daniel reached out and pushed an intercom button.

"Linda, get Detective Sloan for me. Detective Anderson down in homicide should be able to reach him. I want to talk to him right away."

He took his finger off the button and looked at Lucas. "Any problems out there?"

"No."

"I don't want you on TV for the next few days. Stay out of sight at this press conference just in case somebody saw you on the street."

"Okay. But I got in clean."

"Christ, if this is the guy, we're going to look good. Out in Los Angeles they can chase these guys for years, and some of them they never catch." Daniel ran his fingers through his hair. "It's gotta be him."

"Don't think like that," Lucas said urgently. "Think cool. When we pick somebody up, the media's going to go berserk. If it's not him, you'll be dangling from a tree limb. By your balls. Especially with the gay politics around here."

"All right, all right," Daniel said unhappily. He swung one hand in the air as though brushing away gnats. The phone rang and he snatched it up.

"Yeah. We've been waiting." He looked at Lucas and mouthed "Sloan." "Did you ever check that list of houses Lewis sold? . . . Yeah. How many? . . . What about dates? . . . Huh. Okay. Stay with that, pick up any more you can find. Talk to her boyfriend, see what bars they went to, any that we might cross with Smithe. . . . Yeah. We might be going for a warrant. . . . What? . . . Wait a minute."

Daniel looked up at Lucas.

"Sloan says the garbage pickup is tomorrow. He wants to know if he should grab the garbage if Smithe brings any out."

"Good idea. It's not protected; we don't need a warrant. If we find anything in it, that could build the warrant for us."

Daniel nodded and went back to the phone. "Grab the garbage, okay. And good work. . . . Yeah." He slammed the phone back on the hook.

"Lewis sold a house the next block over. Seven weeks before she was killed."

"Oh, boy, I don't know—"

"Wait, listen. Sloan's been talking to people out there. Smithe is a jogger and he jogs down that same block almost every summer evening. Right past the house she sold."

"That's weak."

"Lucas, if we get one more thing, anything, I'm going in for a warrant. We've got Laushaus on the bench, he'd give us a warrant to search the governor's underwear. With the governor in it."

"It's not getting the warrant I'm worried about. I'm worried about the reaction."

"I'll handle it. We'll be careful."

Lucas shook his head. "I don't know. I've got a feeling that everybody's starting to run in one direction." He glanced at his watch. "I've got to make some calls on the Ruiz interview. Take it easy, huh?"

Lucas talked to an assignment editor at the *Pioneer Press:*

"Wally? Lucas Davenport."

"Hey, Lucas, how's the hammer hangin'?"

"Wonderful expression, Wally. Where'd you hear that?"

"I thought the pigs talked like that. Excuse me, I meant cops. Just trying to be friendly."

"Right. You got one of your hacks who can meet me on the front porch of the St. Paul cop shop, say about six o'clock?"

"What's up?"

"Well, to tell you the truth, we got a survivor from a maddog attack and we're going public."

"Whoa. Hold on."

There was a series of muffled exclamations on the other end of the line, then a new voice, female. Denise Ring, the city editor.

"Lucas, this is Denise. Where'd this woman come from?"

"Hey, Denise. How's the hammer hangin'?"

"What?"

"Wally just asked me how the hammer was hangin'. I thought it was newspaper talk."

"Fuck you, Lucas. And fuck Wally. What's with this survivor?"

"We got one. We held back, because we needed to talk to her a lot. But Jennifer Carey found out about it—"

"From you?"

"No. I don't know where she heard it. St. Paul cops, I think."

"You're sleeping with her."

"Jesus Christ, does everybody read my mail?"

"Everybody knows. I mean, we figured it was just a matter of time. She was the last available woman in town. It was either her or you'd have to start dating out-state."

"Look, Denise, you want this story or what?"

"Yeah. Don't get excited."

"Jennifer said she was going public, whether we cooperated or not, so we talked to the survivor and she said she'd be willing to make an appeal. Jennifer wanted it exclusive, but Daniel said no. Said to call you and the *Star-Tribune*, so that's what I'm doing."

"Six o'clock? Cammeretta will be there. How about art?"

"Send a photographer. Jennifer will have a camera."

"Is that what this press conference is about at nine?"

"Yeah. The survivor'll be talking in public to the other stations, but you and TV3 and the *Strib* will have the exclusive stuff from the six-o'clock meeting."

"Not exclusive for us. Jennifer will have it first."

"But not as much—"

"And the *Strib* will be there with us."

"But I'm sure you'll do it better."

"We always do," Ring said. "Okay. Six o'clock. What'd you say her name was?"

Lucas laughed. "Susan B. Anthony. Wait. Maybe I got that wrong. I'll know for sure at six."

"See you then," Ring said.

Lucas tapped the cut-off button, redialed the *Star-Tribune*, gave the assignment editor the same story, and then called Carla.

"You'll be there, right?" She sounded worried.

"Yeah. I'll come over about five and we'll talk about what you want to say. Then when it's time, I'll walk over to the station and get them. That'll be about six. It'll be Jennifer Carey from TV3, a cameraman, two newspaper reporters, and two newspaper photographers. I know all of them and they're pretty good people. We'll break it off about seven. Then we'll go out for something to eat and come over here to Minneapolis for the press conference. We can talk about that on the way over."

"Okay. I'm going to do my hair. What else?"

"Wear a plain blouse. Not yellow. Light blue would be good if you've got one. Jeans are fine. Stay away from the makeup. Just a touch of lipstick. Jennifer's pretty good. You'll do fine."

"I'm Jennifer Carey. How are you?"

"I'm fine. I see you on the news . . ."

Lucas watched them talk as Jennifer's cameraman, the two newspaper reporters, and the two photographers looked curiously around the studio. Jennifer was watching Carla's face closely, gauging her reactions, smiling, encouraging her to talk.

"Okay, listen, guys," Jennifer said finally, turning to the newspaper people. "Why don't we do it this way. I need camera time, so why don't we have Carla tell her story for you guys and we'll film that, and you can get your pictures. That'll let Carla get what she wants to say in mind. Then we'll do our interview."

"I'll want to stay around for your interview," said the *Star-Tribune* reporter. The *Pioneer Press* reporter nodded.

"No problem, but no breaking in."

Lucas watched as the two newspaper reporters extracted the story from Carla. She relaxed under the friendly attention, becoming almost ebullient as she told how the killer had fled for his life. After fifteen minutes Lucas called for a time-out.

"We've got to make the press conference at nine o'clock," he said to Jennifer. "You better get started."

"We'd like to get you to walk through it, just show us where the guy grabbed you, and what happened from there. Use it for the art, the pictures," said one of the newspaper photographers.

Carla re-created it, starting from the door, a mime of a woman carrying groceries and then suddenly attacked. As she walked about, becoming increasingly animated, the photographers danced around her, their strobes flickering like lightning.

When they were done, Jennifer led her through it again, acting the part of the attacker. When that was done, the two women sat and chatted, the cameraman taking frontal and reverse shots of both, with facial close-ups.

"Okay. Is there anything we missed?" asked Jennifer. She glanced at her watch.

"I don't think so," said Carla.

"We all done, guys?" she asked the other reporters. They both nodded.

"Okay, I'm shutting it down," Lucas said. "Nobody gets back in for a last word. If you think of anything you *must* have, get it from your guys at the press conference. Okay? Everybody cool?"

He ushered them out five minutes later.

"What do you think?" he asked Carla after they were gone.

"It was interesting," she said, her eyes bright.

"Yeah, well, the press conference will be different. Lots of very quick questions, maybe nasty. Don't mention this interview or the other stations will go crazy. By the time they see TV3, we want you out of sight."

On the way to the press conference, Carla said, "How long have you known Jennifer Carey?"

He glanced across at her. "Years. Why?"

"She stood in your space. And you didn't notice. That usually means . . . intimacy at some level."

"We've been friends for a long time," Lucas said neutrally.

"Have you slept with her?"

"We don't know each other well enough to talk about that kind of thing," he said.

"Sounds like a big *yes* to me," she said.

"Jesus."

"Hmm."

The press conference was short, loud, and finally nasty. The chief spoke after Carla.

"Do you have any suspects?" one reporter shouted.

"We are checking all leads—"

"That means no," the reporter shouted.

"No, it doesn't," Daniel said. Lucas winced.

"Then you *do* have a suspect," a woman called.

"I didn't say that."

"You want to tell us what you're saying? In short words?"

An hour after the press conference, whipping north along I-35 in Lucas' Porsche, Carla was still hyper.

"So you'll have tapes of Jennifer's interview?"

"Yeah, the recorder's set. You can look at them when you get back."

"It sure went downhill after the chief called that guy a jerk," Carla said.

Lucas laughed. "I loved it. The guy *was* a jerk. But it chilled out Daniel, too. That's good. He'll be more careful."

"And you're not going to tell me about the suspect?"

"Nope."

It was a three-hour drive to Lucas' cabin. They stopped at a general store to stock up on groceries and Lucas chatted with the owner for a minute about fishing. "Two large last week," the owner said.

"How big?"

"Henning, the doctor, the row-troller? He got one forty-eight and a half inches off the big island in those weeds. He figured thirty-two pounds. Then some guy on the other side of the lake, tourist from Chicago, I think he was fishing out of Wilson's, took a twenty-eight-pounder.''

"Henning release it?''

"Yeah. He says he's not keeping anything unless there's a chance it'll go forty.''

"Could be a long wait. There aren't that many guys in the North Woods with a forty-pound musky on the wall.''

"It's beautiful,'' Carla said, looking out at the lake.

"Doesn't hurt to have the moon out there. It's almost embarrassing. It looks like a beer ad.''

"It's beautiful,'' she repeated. She turned back into the cabin.

"Which bedroom should I take?'' He pointed her back to the corner.

"The big one. Might as well take it, since I won't be here. There's a bike in the garage, it's a half-mile out to the general store, three miles into town. There's a boat down at the dock. You ever run an outboard?''

"Sure. I used to go north with my husband every summer. One thing he could do was fish.''

"There are a half-dozen rods in a rack on the porch and a couple of tackle boxes under the glider, if you want to try some fishing. If you go off the point out there, around the edges of the weed bed, you'll pick up some northern.''

"Okay. You going back right now?''

"In a little while. I'll stick the food in the refrigerator and then I'm going to have a beer and sit out on the porch for a while.''

"I'm going to get changed, take a shower,'' Carla said.

Lucas sat on the glider and kept it gently swinging, his feet flexing against the low window ledge below the screen. The nights were getting cool and there was just enough wind to bring in the scent and the sound of the pines. A raccoon crossed through the yard light of a neighboring cabin, heading back toward the garbage cans. From the other way, a few lots down the lake, a woman laughed and there was a splash. From the cabin behind him, the shower stopped running. A few minutes later, Carla came out on the porch.

"You want another beer?"

"Mmm. Yeah. One more."

"I'm going to have one."

She was wearing a pink cotton robe and rubber shower shoes. She brought back a Schmidt and handed it to him, sat next to him on the glider, and curled her legs beneath her. Her hair was wet and the drops of water glistened like diamonds in the indirect light from the windows.

"A little cool now," she said. "You ever come up here in winter?"

"I come up here every chance I get. I come up in the winter and ski, cross-country. There are trails all over the place. You can ski for miles."

"Sounds great."

"You're invited," Lucas said promptly.

As they talked he could feel the warmth coming off her, from the shower.

"Are you getting cold?"

"Not yet. Maybe in a few minutes. Right now it feels fresh." She turned and leaned backward, her head on his shoulder. "It doesn't seem like a cop ought to have a place like this. I mean, a drug-and-vice guy with a Porsche."

"Doctor's orders. I got so I was doing nothing but work," he said. He eased an arm behind her shoulder. "I'd be on the street all day and sometimes half the night, then I'd go home and work on my games. I'd get so cranked I couldn't sleep even when I was so tired I couldn't walk. So I went in to see the doc. I thought I ought to get some legal downers and he said what I really needed was a place not to work. I never work up here. I mean, never money-work. I chop wood, fix the garage, work on the dock, all that. But I don't money-work."

"Guess what?" Carla said.

"What?"

"I don't have a goddamn thing on under this robe." She giggled a beer giggle.

"Jeez. Absolutely buck naked, huh?"

"Yep. I figured, why not?"

"So can I consider this an official pass?"

"Would you rather not?"

"No, no, no no no." He leaned forward and kissed her on the jaw just below her ear. "I was desperately figuring my chances. I'd been such a nice guy all along, it seemed sort of crass to suddenly start hustling."

"That's why I decided to come on to you," she said. "Because you weren't rushing me like some guys."

Much later in the night, she said, "I've got to sleep. I'm really starting to feel the day."

"Just one thing," he said in the dark. "When we went through that routine up in your apartment the first time I interviewed you, you said the guy who jumped you felt softer than me. You still think that?"

She was silent for a moment, then said, "Yes. I have this distinct impression that he was a little . . . not porky, but fleshy. Like there was fat under there and that he wasn't terribly muscular. I mean, he was a lot stronger than I am, but I only weigh a little over a hundred pounds. I don't think he's a tough guy."

"Shit."

"Does that mean something?"

"Maybe. I'm afraid it might."

Early the next morning Lucas walked out to his car, fished under the seat, and retrieved a Charter Arms .38 special revolver in a black nylon holster and two boxes of shells. He carried them back to the house.

"What's that?" Carla asked when he brought it in.

"A pistol. You thought you might need one."

"Hmm." Carla closed one eye and squinted at him with the other. "You brought it up with you, but didn't bring it out last night. That suggests you expected to stay over."

"A subject which does not merit further exploration," Lucas declared with a grin. "Get your shoes on. We've got to take a hike."

They went into the woods across the road from Lucas' cabin, followed a narrow jump-across stream that eventually became a long damp spot, then turned into a gully that led into the base of a steep hill. They came out on a grassy plateau facing a sandy cutbank.

"We'll shoot into the cutbank," Lucas said. "We'll start at ten feet and move back to twenty."

"Why so close?"

"Because if you're any further away, you ought to run or yell for help. Shooting is for close-up desperation," Lucas said. He looked around and nodded toward a downed log. "Let's go talk about it for a minute."

They sat on the log and Lucas pulled the pistol apart, demonstrated the function of each piece and how to load and unload it. He was clicking the brass shells into the cylinder when they heard a chattering overhead. Lucas looked up and saw the red squirrel.

"Okay," he whispered. "Now, watch this."

He pivoted slowly on the log and lifted the weapon toward the squirrel.

"What are you going to do?"

"Show you what a thirty-eight will do to real meat," Lucas said, his eyes fixed on the squirrel. The animal was half-hidden behind a thick limb on a red pine but occasionally exposed its entire body.

"Why? Why are you going to kill it?" Carla's eyes were wide, her face pale.

"You just don't know what a bullet will do until you see it. Gotta stick your fingers in the wounds. Like Doubting Thomas, you know?"

"Hey, don't," she commanded. "Come on, Lucas."

Lucas pointed the weapon at the squirrel, both eyes open, waiting.

"Hit the little sucker right between the eyes, never feel a thing . . ."

"Lucas . . ." Her voice was up and she clutched at his gun arm, dragging it down. She was horrified.

"You look horrified."

"Jesus Christ, the squirrel didn't do anything . . ."

"You feel scared?"

She dropped her arm and turned cold. "Is this some kind of lesson?"

"Yeah," Lucas said, turning away from the squirrel. "Hold on to that feeling you had. You felt that way for a squirrel. Now think about unloading a thirty-eight into a human being."

"Jesus, Lucas . . ."

"You hit a guy in the chest, not through the heart, but just in the chest and you'll blow up his lungs and he'll lie there snorting out this bright red blood with little bubbles in it and usually his eyes look like they're made out of wax and sometimes he rocks back and forth and he's dying and there's not a thing that anybody can do about it, except maybe God—"

"I don't want the gun," she said suddenly.

Lucas held the weapon up in front of his face. "They're awful things," he said. "But there's one thing that's even more awful."

"What's that?"

"When you're the squirrel."

He gave her the basics of close-in shooting, firing at crude man-size figures drawn in the sand of the cutbank. After thirty rounds she began hitting the figures regularly. At fifty, she developed a flinch and began to spray shots.

"You're jerking the gun," Lucas told her.

She fired again, jerking the gun. "No I'm not."

"I can see it."

"I can't."

Lucas swung the cylinder out, emptied it, put three shells in random chambers, and handed the pistol back to her.

"Shoot another round."

She fired another shot, jerking the weapon, missing.

"Again."

This time the hammer hit an empty chamber and there was no shot, but she jerked the pistol out of line.

"That's called a flinch," Lucas said.

They worked for another hour, stopping every few minutes to talk about safety, about concealment of the gun in her studio, about combat shooting.

"It takes a lot to make a really good shot," Lucas told her as she looked at the weapon in her hand. "We're not trying to teach you that. What you've got to do is learn to hit that target reliably at ten feet and at twenty feet. That shouldn't be a problem. If you ever get in a situation where you need to shoot somebody, point the gun and keep pulling the trigger until it stops shooting. Forget about rules or excessive violence or any of that. Just keep pulling."

They fired ninety-five of the hundred rounds before Lucas called a halt and handed her the weapon, loaded with the last five rounds.

"So now you'll have a loaded gun around the house," he said, handing it to her. "You carry it back, put it where you think best. You'll find that it's kind of a burden. It's the knowledge that there's a piece of Death in the house."

"I'll need more practice," she said simply, hefting the pistol.

"I've got another three hundred rounds in the car. Come out here every day, shoot twenty-five to fifty rounds. Check yourself for flinching. Get used to it."

"Now that I've got it, it makes me more nervous than I thought it would," Carla said as they walked back to the cabin. "But at the same time . . ."

"What?"

"It feels kind of good in my hand," she said. "It's like a paintbrush or something."

"Guns are great tools," Lucas said. "Incredibly efficient. Very precise. They're a pleasure to use, like a Leica or a Porsche. A pleasure in their own right. It's too bad that to fulfill their purpose, you've got to kill somebody."

"That's a nice thought," Carla said.

Lucas shrugged. "Samurai swords are the same way.

They're works of art that are complete only when they're killing. It's nothing new in the world.''

As they crossed the road back to the cabin, she asked, "You've got to go?"

"Yeah. I've got a game."

"I don't understand that," she said. "The games."

"Neither do I," Lucas said, laughing.

He took his time driving back to the Twin Cities, enjoying the countryside, resolutely not thinking about the maddog. He arrived after six, checked Anderson's office, found that he had gone home for the evening.

"Sloan's still out somewhere," the shift commander said. "But nobody's told me to look for anything special."

Lucas left, changed clothes at home, stopped at a Grand Avenue restaurant in St. Paul, ate, and loafed over to St. Anne's.

"Ah, here's Longstreet, slow as usual," Elle said. Even as General Robert E. Lee she wore her full habit, crisp and dark in the lights of the game room. A second nun, who wore conventional street dress and played the role of General George Pickett, was flipping through a stack of movement sheets. The attorney, Major General George Gordon Meade, commander in chief of the Union armies, and the bookie, cavalry commander General John Buford, were studying their position on the map. A university student, who played General John Reynolds in the game, was punching data into the computer. He looked up and nodded when Lucas came in. The grocer, Jeb Stuart, had not yet arrived.

"Talking game-wise," the bookie said to Lucas, "you've got to do something about Stuart. Maybe take him out as a playable character. He keeps getting loose, and when he gets word to Lee, it changes everything."

Lucas relaxed and started arguing. He was in his place. The grocer arrived ten minutes later, apologizing for his tardiness, and they started. The battle went badly for the Union. Stuart was getting scouts back to the main force, so Lee knew the bluecoats were coming. He concentrated on Gettysburg more quickly than had happened in historical fact, and Pickett's division—marching first instead of last—brushed aside Buford's cavalry, pressed through the town, and captured Culp's Hill and the north end of Cemetery Ridge.

They left it there. Late that evening, as they sat around the table talking over the day's moves, the attorney brought up the maddog.

"What's happening with this guy?" he asked.

"You looking for a client?" asked Lucas.

"Not unless he's got some major bucks," the attorney said. "This is the kind of case that will stink up the whole state. But it's interesting. It could be a hard case for you to make, actually, unless you catch him in the act. But the guy who gets him off . . . he's going to smell like a buzzard."

"Some of the people playing *this* game have noticed a buzzardlike odor," the grocer said. He was feeling expansive. He was rehabilitating old J.E.B. Stuart, making him a hero again.

The lawyer rolled his eyes. "So what's happening?" he asked Lucas. "You gonna catch him?"

"Not much progress," Lucas said, peeling a chunk of cold pizza out of a greasy box. "What do you do with a fruitcake? There's no way to track him. His mind doesn't work like an ordinary crook's. He's not doing it for money. He's not doing it for dope, or revenge, or impulsively. He's doing it for pleasure. He's taking his time. It might not be quite at random—we've found a few patterns—but for practical purposes, they don't help much. Like the fact that he attacks dark-haired women. That's maybe only thirty or forty percent of the women in the Cities, which sounds pretty good until you think about it. When you think about it, you realize that even if you eliminate the old women and the children, you're talking about, what, a quarter-million dark-haired possibilities?"

The bookie and the grocer nodded. The other nun and the student chewed pizza. Elle, who had been fingering the long string of rosary beads that swung by her side, said, "Maybe you could bring him in to you."

Lucas looked at her. "How?"

"I don't know He fixates on people and we know the type. But if you put out a female decoy, how would you know he'd even see her? That's the problem. If you could get a decoy next to him, maybe you could pull him into an attack that you're watching."

"You've got a nasty mind, Sister," the bookie said.

"It's a nasty problem," she answered. "But . . ."

"What?" The lawyer was looking at her with a small smile on his face.

"Interesting," she said.

CHAPTER
— 10 —

"Daniel's hunting for you." Anderson looked harassed, teasing his thinning blond hair as he stepped through Lucas' office doorway. Lucas had just arrived and stood rattling his keys in his fist.

"Something break?"

"We might go for a warrant."

"On Smithe?"

"Yeah. Sloan spent the night going through his garbage. Found some wrappers from rubbers that use the same kind of lubricant they found in the women. And they found a bunch of invitations to art shows. The betting is, he *knows* this Ruiz chick."

"I'll talk to the chief."

"Where have you been?" Daniel asked.

"My cabin. I ditched Ruiz up there," Lucas said.

Daniel snapped his fingers, remembering. "That's right. Dammit. I didn't know she was going with you. How come your cabin?"

Lucas shrugged. "She would only give the interview if we could get her away afterward. This seemed simpler than trying to get the city to keep her in a hotel."

Daniel's eyes narrowed; then he gave Lucas a tiny nod. "So what is it, three hours up there?"

"Yeah."

"Okay. We're going to turn you back around. We want you to show her a photo spread, see if she can pick out Smithe. Take the chopper up."

"Anderson said you're going for a warrant," Lucas said.

"Maybe. Once we knew what we were looking for, we had Sloan go through the garbage scrap by scrap. Sure enough, he found some wrappers from those Share rubbers. So we got him with Rice, we know he's been at the same art shows as Ruiz, and he very well might have seen Lewis. Then this punk chick, she hung out at the clubs off Hennepin, mixing it up with the gays on the streets, he could have bumped into her there. And we got the lubricant, and the opportunity to meet them here in the courthouse. And he's gay. Depending on what you get, we could go for it. We've got Laushaus ready to sign whatever we need."

"We could find twenty guys who fit the same pattern."

"What's your problem with this, Davenport?" Daniel asked in exasperation. "You've taken guys down on one-tenth of what we got."

"Sure. But I knew I was right. This time we might be wrong. All we've got is the easy stuff, and nothing else. I think he's a workout freak; Ruiz said the attacker was soft. This guy's a native Minnesotan; Ruiz said he has a southwestern accent. Ruiz says the guy wears Nike Air shoes; he didn't have any Nike Airs in his closet. Eight pairs of shoes, but no Nike Airs."

"There's the rubber."

"That's the only thing, and that's not definitive."

"He knows guns."

"Not handguns. There wasn't a handgun in the place."

"Listen, just get up there with the pictures," Daniel said. "They've got a package for you down at the lab."

"Will you make the call on the warrant? Or you going to let homicide do it?"

"I've been pretty deep in this," Daniel said. "I wouldn't want to shove the responsibility off on somebody else."

"Let homicide make the call," Lucas urged. "They'll do what you want, but you'll be able to change your mind if there's a problem. And something else. Maybe you ought to suggest that they keep the warrant in their pocket. Ask the guy to come in, get him a lawyer, tell him that you have the warrant, and then if he can come up with anything that cools the case, you just pitch the warrant and shake his hand.''

"He might not go for that."

"Man, I'm getting real bad vibes from this thing.''

"We got people being killed,'' Daniel said. "What if we're right and we just let it go and he gets another one?''

"Put a heavier net around him. If he tries, we've got him.''

"What if he waits for three weeks? Have you seen the television? It's like the Ayatollah and the hostages. 'Day Fifteen of the Maddog's Reign of Terror.' That'll be next.''

"Goddammit, chief . . .''

Daniel waved him off. "I'll think about it. You get up there and show the mugs to Ruiz. Call back and tell us what she says.''

Lucas tried to call Carla from the station and from the airport, but there was no answer.

"Get her?'' asked the pilot.

"No. I'll find her when we get up there.''

The chopper cut the travel time to the cabin to less than an hour, sweeping across the high-colored hardwood forests and the transition zone into the deep green of the North Woods. The pilot dropped the aircraft beside a road intersection three hundred yards out from the cabin, and he and Lucas walked in with the manila envelopes full of photos. Carla was waiting by the back porch.

"I was out in the boat and I heard the helicopter. I couldn't think of anybody else that it might be for. What happened?'' She looked curiously from one to the other.

"We want you to look at some pictures,'' Lucas said as they went inside. He gestured at the pilot. "This is Tony Rubella. He's the helicopter pilot but he's also a cop. I'm going to record the interview.''

Lucas put his tape recorder on the table, said a few test words, ran the cassette back, and listened until he was satisfied that it was working. Then he started it again and read in the time, date, and place.

"Conducting the interview is Lucas Davenport, lieutenant,

Minneapolis Police Department, with Officer Anthony Rubella, Minneapolis Police Department. Interviewee is Miss Carla Ruiz of St. Paul. Carla Ruiz is well-known to Officer Davenport as the victim of an attack in her residence by a man believed to have committed a series of murders in the city of Minneapolis. We will show Ruiz a photo array of twelve men and ask if she recognizes any of them.''

Lucas dumped a dozen photographs on the table, all of young men, all shot on the street, all vaguely similar in appearance, size, and dress. Eleven of them were cops or police-department clerical personnel. The twelfth was Smithe. Lucas arranged them in a single row and Carla leaned over them and studied the faces.

"I know this guy for sure," she said, tapping one of the cop photos. "He's a cop. He works off-duty as a security guy at that grocery store at the bottom of Nicollet."

"Okay," Lucas said for the recorder. "Miss Ruiz has identified one photo as a man she knows and she says she believes he is a police officer. Our data indicate that he is a police officer. I am asking Miss Ruiz to turn the photograph over, to mark it with the capital letter A, and to sign her name and put the date below it. Miss Ruiz, will you do that now?''

Carla signed the photo and went back to the display. "This guy looks familiar," she said, tapping the photo of Smithe. "I've seen him on the art scene, you know, openings, parties, that sort of thing. I don't know why, but I've got it in my head that he's gay. I think I might have been introduced to him."

"Okay. Are you sure about him?"

"Pretty sure."

"Okay. Miss Ruiz has just identified the photograph of Jimmy Smithe. I will ask Miss Ruiz to mark that photograph on the back with a capital letter B and sign her name and the date."

Carla signed the second photo and Lucas asked her to look at the photo spread again.

"I don't see anybody else," she said finally.

"I am now showing Miss Ruiz seven additional photographs of Jimmy Smithe and asking her if she confirms her identification of him in the random spread."

Carla looked at the second group of photos and nodded.

"Yes. I know him."

"Miss Ruiz has confirmed that she knows the suspect, Jimmy Smithe. She has also added details, such as she believes him to be homosexual and that he frequents art galleries and that she may have been introduced to him. Miss Ruiz, does anything else come to mind about Mr. Smithe?"

"No, no, I really don't know him. I remember him because he's handsome and I got the impression that he's intelligent."

"Okay. Anything else?"

"No."

"Okay. That concludes the interview. Thank you, Miss Ruiz." He punched the button on the tape, ran it back, listened to it, then took the cassette out of the recorder, put it back in its protective box, and slipped it into his pocket.

"Now what?" Carla asked.

"I've got to use the phone," Lucas said. He went straight through to the chief.

"Davenport? What?"

"She knows him," Lucas said. "Picked him out with no problem."

"We're going to take him."

"Listen. Do it my way?"

"I don't know if we can, Lucas. The media's got a smell of it."

"Who?"

"Don Kennedy from TV3."

"Shit." Kennedy and Jennifer were professional bedmates. "Okay. I'll be back in an hour and a half. When are you taking him?"

"We were waiting for your call. We've got a couple guys here and we'll get the surveillance people. He's working at his desk over in the county building. We're just going to walk over and get him."

"Who made the call? To make the bust?"

There was a pause. Then, "Lester."

"Outstanding. Stay with that."

Daniel hung up and Lucas turned to Rubella. "Get the chopper cranked up. We've got to get back in a hurry."

When Rubella was gone, he took Carla's hands.

"They've got a case against this guy, but I don't like it. I think they're making a mistake. So just sit tight, okay? Watch the evening news. I'll call every night. I'll try to get back up here in a couple of days, if things cool down."

"Okay," she said. "Be careful." He kissed her on the lips and jogged down the dusty track after Rubella.

The flight back to the Cities and the drive from the airport took two hours. Anderson was sitting at his desk, his feet up, staring distractedly at a wall calendar when Lucas arrived.

"Where've you got him?" Lucas asked.

"Down in interrogation."

"His lawyer in there?"

"Yeah. That could be a problem."

"Why's that?"

" 'Cause it's that asshole McCarthy," Anderson said.

"God damn." Lucas ran his hands through his hair. "The usual bull?"

"Yeah. The little dickhead."

"I'm going down there."

"Chief's down there."

"We're not getting anything out of him." Daniel was leaning on the wall outside the interrogation room. "That prick McCarthy won't let him say a word."

"He smells a good one," Lucas said. "If this goes to trial and he gets Smithe off, he can quit the county and make some real money in private practice."

"So what're you going to do?" Daniel asked.

"I'm going to be a good guy. A real good guy. And I'm going to get mad and read off McCarthy."

"Not too much. You could jeopardize what we got."

"Just plant a seed of doubt."

Daniel shrugged. "You can try."

Lucas took off his jacket, loosened his tie and mussed his hair, took a deep breath, and went through the door at a jog. The interrogators, the lawyer, and Smithe were seated around a table and looked up, startled.

"Jesus. Sorry. I was afraid I'd miss you," Lucas said. He looked down at McCarthy. "Hello, Del. You handling this one, I guess?"

"Does the pope shit in the woods?" McCarthy was a short man in a lumpy brown suit. His dishwater-blond hair swelled out of his head in an Afro, and muttonchops swept down the sides of his square face. "Is a bear a Catholic?"

"Right." Lucas looked at the interrogators. "I've been cleared by Daniel. You mind if I ask a few?"

"Go ahead, we ain't gettin' anywhere," said the senior cop, swirling an oily slick of cold coffee in a Styrofoam cup.

Lucas nodded and turned to Smithe. "I'll tell you up front. I was one of the people who questioned the survivor of the third attack. I don't think you did it."

"Is this the good-guy routine, Davenport?" asked McCarthy, tipping his chair back and grinning in amusement.

"No. It's not." He pointed a finger at Smithe. "That was the first thing I wanted to tell you. The second thing is, I'm going to talk for a while. At some point, McCarthy here might tell you to stop listening. You better not—"

"Now, wait a minute," McCarthy said, bringing the chair legs down with a bang.

Lucas overrode him. "—because how can it hurt just to listen, if you're not admitting anything? And your lawyer's priorities are not necessarily the same as yours."

McCarthy stood up. "That's it. I'm calling it off."

"I want to hear him," Smithe said suddenly.

"I'm advising you—"

"I want to hear him," Smithe said. He tipped his head at McCarthy while watching Lucas. "Why aren't his priorities the same as mine?"

"I don't want to impeach the counselor's personal ethics," Lucas said, "but if this goes to trial, it'll be one of the big trials of the decade. We just don't have serial killers here in Minnesota. If he gets you off, he'll have made his name. You, on the other hand, will be completely destroyed, no matter what happens. It's too bad, but that's the way it works. You've been around a courthouse long enough to know what I'm talking about."

"That's enough," said McCarthy. "You're prejudicing the case."

"No I'm not. I'm just prejudicing your job in it. And I won't mention that again. I'm just—"

McCarthy stepped between Lucas and Smithe, his back to Lucas, and leaned toward Smithe. "Listen. If you don't want me to represent you, that's fine. But I'm telling you as your lawyer, right now, you don't want to talk—"

"I want to listen. That's all," Smithe said. "You can sit here and listen with me or you can take a hike and I'll get another attorney."

McCarthy stood back and shook his head. "I warned you."

Lucas moved around to where Smithe could see him again.

"If you've got an alibi, especially a good alibi, for any of the times of the killings, you better bring it out now," Lucas said urgently. "That's my message. If you've got an alibi, you could let us go to trial and maybe humiliate us, but you'd have a hard time working again. There'd always be a question. And there'd always be a record. You get stopped by a highway patrolman in New York and he calls in to the National Crime Information Center, he'll get back a sheet that says you were once arrested for serial murder. And then there's the other possibility."

"What?"

"That you'll be convicted even if you're innocent. There's always a chance that even with a good alibi, the jury'd find you guilty. It happens. You know it. The jury figures, what the hell, if he wasn't guilty, the cops wouldn't have arrested him. McCarthy here can tell you that."

Smithe tipped his head toward McCarthy again. "He told

me that as soon as I started dealing in alibis, you'd have guys out on the street trying to knock them down."

Lucas leaned on the interrogation table. "He's absolutely right. We would. And if we can't, I guarantee you'd be back on the street and nothing happens. Nothing. You haven't been booked yet. You never would be. Right now, we've got a good enough case to pick you up, maybe take it to trial. I don't know what these guys have been telling you, but I can tell you that we can put you with two of the victims and a third guy who is critical to the case, and there's some physical evidence. But a good alibi would knock the stuffing out of it."

Smithe went pale. "There can't be. Physical evidence. I mean . . ."

"You don't know what it is," Lucas said. "But we have it. Now. I suggest you and Mr. McCarthy go whisper in the hallway for a couple of minutes and come back."

"Yeah, we'll do that," McCarthy said.

They were back in five minutes.

"We're done talking," McCarthy announced, looking satisfied with himself.

Lucas looked at Smithe. "You're making a bad mistake."

"He said—" Smithe started, but McCarthy grabbed him by the arm and shook his head no.

"You're playing the weak sister," McCarthy said to Lucas. "From what you've said, there're only two possibilities: You've got no case and you're desperate to make one. In which case you won't book him. Or you've got a case, in which case you'll book him no matter what we say and use what he says against him."

"McCarthy, a fellow out in the hall called you a dickhead," Lucas said wearily. "He was right. You can't even see the third possibility, which is why we're all sweating bullets."

"Which is?"

"Which is we got a good case that feels bad to a few of us. We just want to *know*. We've got pretty close to exact times on two of the attacks, real close on a third. If Mr.

Smithe was out of town, if he was talking to clients, if he was in the office all day, he'd be in the clear. How can it hurt to tell us now, before we book—''

''You're just afraid to book because of what will happen if you're wrong.''

''Goddamn right. The department will look like shit. And Smithe, not incidentally, will take it right in the shorts, no offense.''

''Now, what the fuck does that mean?''

''He knows I'm gay,'' Smithe said.

''That's a prejudicial remark if I ever—''

''Fuck it,'' said one of the interrogators. ''I don't want to hear any more.''

He stalked out of the room and a minute later Daniel stepped in.

''No deal?'' he asked Lucas.

Lucas shrugged.

''No deal,'' said McCarthy.

''Take him upstairs and book him,'' Daniel told the remaining interrogator.

''Wait a minute,'' said Smithe.

''Book him,'' Daniel snarled. He stormed out of the room.

''Good work, McCarthy, you just built your client a cross,'' Lucas said.

McCarthy showed his teeth in what wasn't quite a smile. ''Go piss up a rope,'' he said. They left in a group—Smithe, McCarthy, and the interrogation cop. As they went, the cop turned to Lucas.

''You know the difference between a skunk dead on the highway and a lawyer dead on the highway?''

''No, what?''

McCarthy turned his head.

''There's skid marks in front of the skunk,'' the cop said. Lucas laughed and McCarthy bared his teeth again.

''Look at them down there, like lice on a dog,'' Anderson said gloomily, exploring his gums with a ragged plastic toothpick. On the street below, television cameramen, reporters, and technicians were swarming around the remote-broadcast trucks parked outside City Hall.

"Yeah. Looks like Lester is going to have a full house," Lucas said. Jennifer's head bobbed through the swarm, headed toward the entry below them. "Got to run," Lucas said.

He caught her just inside the entrance, dragged her protesting through the halls to his office, pushed her into the desk chair, and closed the door.

"You tipped Kennedy about the gay. You told me you wouldn't."

"I didn't tip him, Lucas, honest to Christ."

"Bullshit, bullshit, bullshit," Lucas stormed. "You guys have washed each other's hands before, I've seen you do it. As soon as Daniel told me that Kennedy had the tip, I knew it was from you."

"So what are you going to do about it, Lucas? Huh?" She was angry now. "This is what I do for a living. It's not a fuckin' hobby."

"Great goddamn way to make a living."

"Better than renting yourself out as a stormtrooper."

Lucas put his fists on his hips and leaned close to her face. She didn't back off even a fraction of an inch. "You know what you did to get a break on a story? You pushed the department into booking an innocent man, which will probably kill the guy. He's in the welfare department surrounded by women and they'll never trust him again, no matter what anybody says. He's a suspect, all right, but I don't think he did it. I was trying to get them to go easy, but your fuckin' tip pushed them into picking him up."

"If they don't think he did it, they shouldn't pick him up."

Lucas slapped himself on the forehead. "Jesus. You think all the questions are easy? Smithe might be guilty. He might not be guilty. I might be wrong about him, and if I am and if I talked the department into letting him go, he might go right back on the street and butcher some other woman. But I might be right and we're destroying the guy, while the real killer is planning to rip somebody else. All we needed was a little time, and you snooped on a private conversation out of my house.''

''And?''

Lucas turned cool. ''I've got to make some basic decisions about whether to talk to you at all.''

''I didn't really need to hear that phone call at your place,'' Jennifer said. ''I would have gotten it anyway. I've got sources here you wouldn't believe. I don't need you, Lucas. I might just tell you to go fuck yourself.''

''I'll take the risk. I can't put up with spying. I am considering—considering—calling a lawyer and having him call your general manager to tell him how you got the information and threatening to file suit against the station for theft of proprietary information.''

''Lucas—''

''Get out of here.''

''Lucas . . .'' She suddenly burst into tears and Lucas backed a few steps away.

''I'm sorry,'' he said, miserably. ''I just can't . . . Jennifer . . . stop that, goddammit.''

''God, I'm a wreck, my makeup. I can't do this press conference. . . . God . . . can I use your phone?'' She poked at her face with a tissue. ''I want to call the station, tell them to let Kathy Lettice take it. God, I'm such a mess . . .''

''Jesus, stop crying, use the phone,'' Lucas said desperately.

Still sniffling, she picked up the phone and dialed. When it was answered, her voice suddenly cleared. ''Don? Jen. The guy's name is Smithe and he works for welfare—''

''Goddammit, Jennifer!'' Lucas shouted. He grabbed the phone, twisted it out of her hand, and slammed it on the hook.

''I cry good, don't I?'' she asked with a grin, and she was out the door.

''Davenport, Davenport,'' Daniel moaned. He gripped handfuls of hair on the side of his head as he watched Jennifer finish the broadcast.

". . . called by some the smartest man in the department, told me personally that he did not believe that Smithe is guilty of the spectacular murders and that he fears the premature arrest could destroy Smithe's burgeoning career with the welfare department . . ."

"Burgeoning career? TV people shouldn't be allowed to use big words," Lucas muttered.

"So now what?" Daniel asked angrily. "How in the hell could you do this?"

"I didn't know I was," Lucas said mildly. "I thought we were having a personal conversation."

"I told you that your dick was going to get you in trouble with that woman," Daniel said. "What the hell am I going to tell Lester? He's been out there in front of the cameras making his case and you're talking to this puss behind his back. You cut his legs out from under him. He'll be after your head."

"Tell him you're suspending me. What's bad? Two weeks? Then I'll appeal to the civil-service board. Even if the board okays the suspension, it'll be months from now. We should be able to put it off until this thing is settled, one way or another."

"Okay. That might do it." Daniel nodded and then laughed unpleasantly, shaking his head. "Christ, I'm glad that wasn't me getting grilled. You better get out of here before Lester arrives or we'll be busting him for assault."

At two o'clock in the morning the telephone rang. Lucas looked up from the drawing table where he was working on Everwhen, reached over, and picked it up.

"Hello?"

"Still mad?" Jennifer asked.

"You bitch. Daniel's suspending me. I'm giving interviews to everybody except you guys, you can go suck—"

"Nasty, nasty—"

He slammed the receiver back on the hook. A moment later the phone rang again. He watched it like a cobra, then picked it up, unable to resist.

"I'm coming over," she said, and hung up. Lucas reached for it, to call her, to tell her not to come, but stopped with his hand on the receiver.

Jennifer wore a black leather jacket, jeans, black boots, and driving gloves. Her Japanese two-seater squatted in the driveway like red-metal muscle. Lucas opened the inner door and nodded at her through the glass of the storm door.

"Can I come in?" she asked. She was wearing gold-wire-rimmed glasses instead of her contacts. Her eyes looked large and liquid behind the lenses.

"Sure," he said awkwardly, fumbling with the latch. "You look like a heavy-metal queen."

"Thanks loads."

"That was a compliment."

She glanced at him, looking for sarcasm, found none, peeled off the jacket, and drifted toward the couch in the living room.

"You want a coffee?" Lucas asked as he closed the door.

"No, thanks."

"Beer?"

"No, I'm fine. Go ahead, if you want."

"Maybe a beer." When he got back, Jennifer was leaning back on a love seat, her knee up on the adjacent seat. Lucas sat on the couch opposite her, looking at her over a marble-topped coffee table.

"So what?" he said, gesturing with the beer bottle.

"I'm very tired," she said simply.

"Of the story? The maddog? Me?"

"Life, I think," Jennifer said sadly. "The baby was maybe an attempt to get back."

"Jesus."

"That little scene with you today . . . God, I don't know. I try to put a good face on it, you know? Gotta be quick, gotta be tough, gotta smile when the heavy stuff comes down. Can't let anybody push you. Sometimes I feel like . . . you remember that little Chevrolet I had, that little Nova, that I wrecked, before I bought the Z?"

"Yeah?"

"That's how my chest feels sometimes. All caved in. Like everything is still hard, but all bent up. Crunched, crumbled."

"Cops get like that."

"Not really. I don't think so."

"Look, you show me a guy on the street for ten or fifteen years—"

She held up a hand, stopped him. "I'm not saying it's not tough and you don't get burned out. Awful stuff happens to cops. But there are slow times. You can take some time. I never have time. If things get slow, for Christ's sake, I've got to *invent* stuff. You show me a slow day, where a cop might cruise through it, and I'll show you a day when Jennifer Carey is out interviewing some little girl who got her face burned off two months ago or two years ago because we had to have something by six P.M., or else. And we don't have time to think about it. We just do it. If we're wrong, we pay later. Do now, pay later. What's worse, there aren't any rules. You don't find out until later if you're right or wrong. Sometimes you never find out. And what's right one day is wrong the next."

She stopped talking and Lucas took a swig of beer and watched her. "You know what you need?" he said finally.

"What? A good fuck?" she asked sarcastically.

"I wasn't going to say that."

"Then what?"

"What you need is to leave the job for a while, get married, move in here."

"You think being a housewife is going to fix things?" She looked almost amused.

"I didn't say housewife. You said housewife. I was going to suggest that you move in here and not do a fuckin' thing. Take a class. Think things over. Take a trip to Paris before the kid gets here. Something. That argument this afternoon, those fake tears, my God, that's so tough it's not human."

"The tears weren't fake," she said. "The alibi was, afterward. I was thinking, I couldn't break down and cry on the job. Then I got home, and I thought, why not? I mean, I'm not stupid. You gave me that little lecture about Smithe, you think I don't know I might have hurt him? I admit it. I might have hurt him. But I'm not sure. I'm—"

"But look at what you're putting yourself through the wringer for. You got the name out to Kennedy, and for what? A ten-minute lead on the other reporters? Christ . . ."

"I know, I know all that. That's why I'm over here. I'm screwed up. I don't know that I'm wrong, but I'm not sure that I'm right. I'm living in murk and I can't stop."

Lucas shook his head. "I don't know what to do."

"Well." She took her leg off the love seat. "Could you come over and sit next to me for a minute?"

"Um . . ." Lucas stood up, walked around the table, and sat down next to her.

"Put your arm up around my shoulder."

He put his arm around her shoulder and she snuggled her face into his chest.

"You ready for this?" she asked in an oddly high-pitched, squeaky voice.

He tried to pull back and look down at her, but she clung to him. "Ready for what?"

She pressed her face against him even more firmly, and after a few seconds, began to weep.

No sex, she said later. Just sleep. He was almost asleep when she said quietly, "I'm glad you're the daddy."

CHAPTER

— 11 —

Louis Vullion did not laugh.

Home late the night of the announcement, he neglected to look at his videotapes and learned of the arrest the next morning in the *Star-Tribune*.

"This is not right," he said, transfixed in the middle of his living room. He was wearing pajamas and leather slippers. A shock of hair stood straight up from his head, still mussed from the night.

"This is *not right*," he hissed. He balled up the paper and hurled it into the kitchen.

"These people are idiots," the maddog screamed.

He turned to the tapes and watched the announcement unfold, his rage growing. Then the face of Jennifer Carey, with her statement that the game inventor, the lieutenant, Lucas Davenport, disagreed, thought they had the wrong man.

"Yes," he said. "Yes."

He ran the tape back and played it again. "Yes."

"I should call him," he said to himself. He glanced at the clock. "No hurry. I should think about it," he said.

Don't make a mistake now. Could this be a ploy? Was the gamesman setting him up? No. That simply wasn't possible. The game was free-form, but there were *some* rules; Davenport, or the other cops—whoever—wouldn't dare permit this man, this gay, to be crucified as part of a ploy. But why was he arrested? Except for the gamesman, Davenport, the police seemed confident that they had a case. How could this mistake happen?

"So stupid," the maddog said to the eggshell-white walls. "They are so fucking dumb."

He couldn't think of anything else. He sat at his desk and stared blindly at the papers there, until his shared secretary asked if he was feeling unwell.

"Yes, a little, I guess; something I ate, I think," he told her. "I've got the Barin arraignment and then I think I'll take the rest of the work home. Something closer to the, ah, facilities."

Barin was a teenage twit who had drunk too much and had driven his car into a crowd of people waiting on a corner to cross a street. Nobody had been killed, but several had been hospitalized. Barin's driver's license had been suspended before the latest accident, also for drunken driving, and he had served two days in jail for the last offense.

This time, it was more serious. The state was in the throes of an antidrinking campaign. Several heretofore sacred cows, for whom the fix would have routinely been applied only a year before, had already done jail time.

And Barin was an obnoxious little prick attached to a large and foul mouth. His father, unfortunately, owned a computer-hardware company that paid a substantial retainer to the maddog's firm. The father wanted the boy to get off.

But the boy was doomed. The maddog knew it. So did the rest of the firm, which was why the maddog had been allowed to handle the trial. Barin would serve three to six months and possibly more. The maddog would not be blamed. There was nothing to be done. The senior partners were patiently explaining that to the father, and the maddog, already indemnified against failure, secretly hoped the judge would sock the little asshole away for a year.

The arraignment was the last of the morning. The maddog arrived early and slipped onto a back bench in the courtroom. The judge was looking down at a young girl in jeans and a white blouse.

"How old are you, Miss Brown?"

"Eighteen, judge."

The judge sighed. "Miss Brown, if you are sixteen, I would be distinctly surprised."

"No, sir, I'm eighteen, three weeks past—"

"Be quiet, Miss Brown." The judge thumbed through the charge papers as the prosecuting and defense attorneys sat patiently behind their tables. The girl had large doe-eyes, very beautiful, but her face was touched with acne and her long brown hair hung limply around her narrow shoulders. Her eyes were her best point, the maddog decided. They were frightened but knowing. The maddog watched her as she stood shifting from foot to foot, casting sideways glances at her public defender.

The judge looked over at the prosecutor. "One prior, same deal?"

"Same deal, Your Honor. Eight months ago. She's been home since then, but her mother threw her out again. The caseworker says her mom's deep into the coke."

"What are you going to do if I let you out, Miss Brown?" the judge asked.

"Well, I've made up with my mom and I think I'm going to earn some money so I can go to college next quarter. I want to major in physical therapy."

The judge looked down at his papers and the maddog thought he might be trying to hide a smile. Eventually he lifted his head, sighed again, and looked at the public defender, who shrugged.

"Child protection?" the judge asked the prosecutor.

"They sent her to a foster home the last time, but the foster mother wouldn't have her after a couple of days," he said.

The judge shook his head and went back to reading the papers.

She was quite a sensual thing in her own way, the maddog decided, watching her nervously lick her lips. A natural victim, the kind who would trigger an attack by a wolf.

The judge at last decided that nothing could be done. He fined her one hundred and fifty dollars on a guilty plea to soliciting for prostitution.

Barin, the twit, showed up just as the case was being disposed. An hour later, when the maddog walked back to the clerk's office, the Heather Brown file was in the return basket. He slipped it out and read through it, noted that she was picked up on South Hennepin. Heather Brown's real name was Gloria Ammundsen. She had been on the street for a year or more. The maddog noted with interest in a narrative section that she had offered the arresting officer a variety of entertainments, including bondage and water sports.

The maddog took his extra work home, but couldn't get anything done. He made a quick supper—sliced ham, fruit, a half-squash. Still agitated, he went out to his car and drove downtown, parked, and walked. Through Loring Park, where the gays cruised and broke and rebroke in their small groups. Over to Hennepin Avenue, and south, away from town. Punks on the street, watching him pass. One kid with a mohawk and dirty black jacket, unconscious on a pile of discarded carpet outside a drugstore. Skinheads with swastikas tattooed on their scalps. Suburban kids hanging out, trying to look tough with cigarettes and black makeup.

A few hookers. Not too obvious, not flagging down cars, but there along the streets for anyone who needed their services.

He looked at them carefully, walking by. All young. Thirteen, fourteen, fifteen, he thought. Fewer sixteen, even fewer eighteen. Very few older. The older ones were the quick-blow-job-in-the-doorway sort, dregs so battered by the street, so unable to get inside, to a sauna, a back room, that they were little more than wet, mindless warm spots in the night, open to any sort of abuse that happened along.

He spotted Heather Brown outside a fast-food restaurant. Most of the hookers were blonde, either natural or bottle. Heather, with her dark hair, reminded him of . . . Who? He didn't know, though it seemed a shadow was back there in his memory. In the night, away from the fluorescent lights of the courtroom, she was prettier.

Except for her eyes. Her eyes had been alive in the courtroom. Out here they had the thousand-yard stare found in battle-fatigue cases. She wore a black blouse, a thigh-length black leather skirt, open-toed high heels, and carried an oversize black bag. Her body, her face, *said* something to him. Her *look* called to him.

"Whoa," she said as he approached and slowed down. "What's happening?"

"Just out for a stroll," he said pleasantly.

"Nice night for it, officer." Her green eye shadow had been applied with a trowel.

The maddog smiled. "I'm not a cop. In fact, I won't even try to pick you up. Who knows, *you* might be. A cop, I mean."

"Oh, sure," she said, cocking a hip so her short skirt rode up.

"Have a good one," he said.

"Ships passing in the night," she said, already looking down the street past him.

"But if I were to come back some night, do you usually go out for your walks around here?"

She turned and looked at him again, the spark of interest rekindled. "Sure," she said. "This is kind of my territory."

"You got a place where we could go?"

"What for?" she asked cautiously.

"Probably a half-'n'-half, if it doesn't cost more than fifty. Or maybe you'd know something more exciting."

She brightened up. He'd made the offer, mentioned a specific act and money, so he wasn't a cop.

"No problem, honey. I know all kinds of ways to turn a boy on. I'm here most every night but Thursday, when my man takes me out. And Sunday, 'cause there's no action."

"Fine. Maybe in a night or two, huh? And you got a place we can go?"

"You got the cash, I got the crash," she said.

"What's your name?"

She had to think about it for a minute. "Heather," she said finally.

• • •

"You are making a mistake," the maddog said. He paced the living room. "It's got to be a mistake."

But it was tantalizing. He looked at the personnel directory on the table. Davenport, Lucas. The number. It would be a mistake, but how? Get him at home, late at night, he'd be off guard. No automatic tape to record the voice.

He thought about it and finally wrote the number on a piece of paper, went back out to the car, drove a mile to a phone booth, and dialed. The phone at the other end rang once. It was answered by a baritone voice, absolutely clear. No sleep in it.

"Detective Davenport?"

"Yeah. Who's this?"

"An informant. I saw the story on television last night, your dissent from the actions of your superiors, and I want you to know this: you're absolutely right about the maddog killer. The gay man is not him. *The gay is not him.* Do you get that?"

"Who is this?"

"I'm not going to tell you that, obviously, but I know that you have arrested the wrong man. If you ask him about leaving the notes, he won't know about them, will he? He won't know that you should never kill anyone you know. Never have a motive. Never follow a discernible pattern. You should do something to remedy this miscarriage or I'm afraid that you will be severely embarrassed. The maddog will demonstrate this man's innocence sometime in the near future. Did you get all that, lieutenant? I hope so, because it's all I have to say. Good-bye."

"Wait—"

The maddog hung up, hurried to his car, and drove away. In a block he started to giggle with the excitement of it. He hadn't anticipated the surge of joy, but it was there, as though he'd survived a personal combat. And he had, in a way. He had touched the face of the enemy.

CHAPTER
— 12 —

Lucas was sitting at the drafting table, a printout of the rules for Everwhen on the tabletop. He rubbed his late-night beard, thinking. The notes. The guy knew the notes. And the accent was there, and it was right. Barely perceptible, but it was there. Texas. New Mexico.

He picked up the phone and dialed Daniel.

"It's Davenport."

The chief was unconscious. "Davenport? You know what time it is?"

Lucas glanced at his watch. "Yeah. It's twelve minutes after two in the morning."

"What the fuck?"

"The maddog just called me."

"What?" Daniel's voice suddenly cleared.

"He quoted the notes to me. He had the accent. He sounded real."

"Shit." There was a five-second pause. "What'd he say?"

Lucas repeated the conversation.

"And he sounded real?"

"He sounded real. More than that. He sounded pissed off. He'd seen Jennifer's piece, about how I didn't think Smithe did it. He wants me to set things straight. Man, he wants the *credit*."

There was a long silence. "Chief?"

Daniel moaned. "So now we got Smithe in jail and the maddog is about to rip another one."

"We've got to start backing away from Smithe. Go butter up the public defender tomorrow. McCarthy is sucked on

Smithe's neck like a lamprey. If we can get him off, maybe we can talk some sense to the guy about giving us an alibi. If he does—if he gives us anything—we can turn him loose.''

"If he doesn't?''

"I don't know. Keep trying to work something out. But if the guy who called me is real, and I'd bet my left nut on it, then I suspect Smithe will come up with something. He's had some time in Hennepin County now, and you know that place.''

"Okay. Let's do it that way. God, the first appearance was fourteen hours ago, and we're already doing a two-step. I'll talk to the PD tomorrow and see if there's a deal somewhere. You stop at homicide in the morning and make a statement on the phone call. The preliminary hearing is Monday? If we're going to move, we ought to do it before then. Or the maddog may do it for us. That'd be a real turd in the punch bowl, wouldn't it?''

"The guy usually hits at midweek,'' Lucas said. "This is Thursday morning. If he follows the pattern, he'll do it tonight or wait until next week.''

"He said 'the near future' on the phone?''

"Yeah. It doesn't sound like he was ready to go. But then, he could be . . . dissembling.''

"Good word.''

"He started it. I'm sitting here trying to remember the exact words he used, and he used some good ones. 'Dissent' and 'miscarriage.' Maybe some more. He's a smart guy. He's had some education.''

"Glad to hear it,'' Daniel said wearily. "Fuck it. I'll talk to you tomorrow.''

When he got off the phone, Lucas couldn't focus on the game and finally left it. He wandered out to the kitchen, got a beer from the refrigerator, and turned out the light. As the light went out, a yellow-and-white rectangle caught his eye and it meant something. He took a step down the hallway, frowned, stepped back, and turned on the light. It was the cover on the phone book.

"Where'd he get my number?'' Lucas asked aloud.

Lucas was unlisted.

"The goddamn office directory. It has to be."

He picked up the phone and dialed Daniel again, but the line was busy. He put the phone back on the hook, paced for one minute by his watch, and dialed again.

"What, what?" The chief was snarling now.

"It's Davenport again. Just had an ugly thought."

"Might as well tell me," Daniel said in vexation. "It'll add color to my nightmares."

"Remember back when you had me under surveillance? Thought it might be a cop, and you had a couple of reasons?"

"Yeah."

"This just occurred to me. The guy called me at home. The only place my number is listed is in the office directory. And that Carla identified one of the pictures she had seen as a cop . . ."

"Uh-oh." There was another long silence; then, "Lucas, go to bed. I got Anderson out of the sack to tell him about the call. I'll call him again and tell him about this. We can figure something out tomorrow."

"We'd look like idiots if Carla fingered the guy in our lineup and we ignored it."

"We'd look worse than that. We'd look like criminal conspirators."

The phone rang again and Lucas cracked his eyelids. Light. Must be morning. He looked at the clock. Eight-thirty.

"Hello, Linda," he said as he picked up the phone.

"How'd you know it was me, Lucas?"

"Because I have a feeling the shit hit the fan."

"The chief wants to see you now. He says to dress dignified but get down here quick."

Daniel and Anderson were huddled over the chief's desk when Lucas arrived. Lester was sitting in a corner, reading a file.

"What's happened?"

"We don't know," Daniel said. "But the minute I walked in the door, the phone rang. It was the public defender. Smithe wants to talk to *you*."

"Great. Did you say anything about the call last night?"

"Not a thing. But if he's ready to alibi, maybe we can find a way to dump the whole thing on McCarthy . . . something along the lines of Smithe decided to cooperate and with his cooperation we were able to eliminate him as a suspect. We could come out smelling like a rose."

"If we can eliminate him," Anderson said.

"What about this cop?" Lucas asked "The one Carla picked out?"

"I came down last night after the chief called," Anderson said. "I pulled the rosters. He was on duty when Ruiz was attacked, with a partner, up in the northwest. I talked to his partner and he confirms they were up there. They took a half-dozen calls around the time of the attack. We went back and checked the tapes, and he's on them."

"So he's clear," said Lucas.

"Thank Christ for small favors," Daniel said. "You better haul ass over to the detention center and talk to Smithe. They're waiting for you."

McCarthy and Smithe waited in a small interrogation room. The decor was simple, being designed to repel bodily fluids. McCarthy was smoking and Smithe sat nervously on a padded waiting-room chair, rubbing his hands, staring at his feet.

"I don't like this and I'm writing a memorandum to the effect," McCarthy spat as Lucas walked in.

"Yeah, yeah." He looked at Smithe. "Could I ask you to stand up for a minute?"

"Wait a minute. We wanted to talk—" McCarthy started, but Smithe waved him down and stood up.

"I hate this place," he said. "This place is worse than I could have imagined."

"Actually, it's a pretty good jail," Lucas said mildly.

"That's what they tell me," Smithe said despondently. "Why am I standing up?"

"Flex your pecs and stomach for me."

"What?"

"Flex your pecs and stomach. And brace yourself."

Smithe looked puzzled, but dropped his shoulders and flexed. Lucas reached out with his fingers spread and pushed hard on Smithe's chest, then dropped his hand and pushed on his stomach. The underlying muscles felt like boards.

"You work out?"

"Yeah, quite a bit."

"What's this about?" McCarthy asked.

"The woman who survived. The killer grabbed her from behind, wrapped her up. She said he felt kind of thick and soft."

"That's not me," Smithe said, suddenly more confident. "Here, you turn around."

Lucas turned and Smithe stepped behind him and wrapped him up. "Get loose," Smithe said.

Lucas started to struggle and twist. He had enough weight to move Smithe around the floor in a tight, controlled dance, but the encircling arms felt almost machinelike. Try as he might, he couldn't break loose.

"Okay," Lucas said, breathing hard.

Smithe released him. "If I had her, she wouldn't get loose," Smithe said confidently. "Does that prove anything?"

"To me it does," Lucas said. "It wouldn't convince a lot of other people."

"I saw that thing on television, about you believing me," Smithe said. "And I can't handle this jail. I decided to take a chance on you. I have an alibi. In fact, I've got two of them."

"We could do all of this at the preliminary," McCarthy said.

"That's four days away," Smithe said sharply. He turned to Lucas. "If my alibis are good, how soon do I get out?"

Lucas shrugged. "If they're good and we can check them, we could have you out of here this afternoon."

"All right," Smithe said suddenly. "Mr. McCarthy

brought my calendar in. On the day Lewis was attacked, that afternoon, I was doing in-service training. Started at nine o'clock in the morning and went straight through to five. There were ten people in the class. We all ate lunch together. That wasn't long ago, so they'll remember.

"And on the day Shirley Morris was killed, the housewife? I got on a plane for New York at seven o'clock that morning. I have the plane tickets and a friend took me out to the airport, saw me get on the plane. I've got hotel bills from New York, they have the check-in time on them. Morris was killed in the afternoon, and I checked in during the afternoon. I bet they'll remember me, too, because when I went up to my room with the bellhop, he pulled back my sheet and there was a rat under it and the guy freaked out. I freaked out. This is supposed to be a nice hotel. I went down to the desk and they gave me a new room, but I bet they remember that rat. You can check it with phone calls. And Mr. McCarthy has the bills and plane tickets at his office."

"You should have told us," Lucas said.

"I was scared. Mr. McCarthy said . . ." They both turned and looked at McCarthy.

"It was too much all at once. You were grilling him, everybody was running around yelling, we had to cool out or we could make a mistake," McCarthy said.

"Well, we sure made a mistake doing it this way," Smithe said. "My family knew I was gay, my parents and my brothers and sisters and a few friends back home, but most people in my high school didn't, most of the people around the home place . . ."

He suddenly sat down and started to sob. "Now they all know. You know how hard it'll be to go back to the farm? My home?"

McCarthy stood up and kicked his chair.

In the lobby of the detention center, Lucas stopped at a phone and made a single call.

"Lucas Davenport," he said. "Can you meet me someplace discreet? Quickly?"

"Sure," she said. "Name the place."

He named a used-book store on the north side of the loop. When she arrived, he thought how out-of-place she looked. With her perfect hair and faultless makeup, she wandered through the stacks like Alice in Wonderland, stunned by the presence of so many baffling artifacts. Annie McGowan. Pride of Channel Eight, the Now Report.

"Lucas," she whispered when she saw him.

"Annie." He stepped toward her and she reached out with both hands, as though she expected Lucas to take her in his arms. He instead took her hands and pulled her close to his chest.

"What I'm going to tell you now must be kept a secret. You must give me journalistic immunity or I can't tell you," he said, glancing back over his shoulder. *Introduction to Method Acting 1043, two credits.*

"Yes, of course," she blurted. Her breath smelled like cinnamon and spice.

"This gay fellow arrested for the maddog murders? He didn't do it," Lucas whispered. "He has two excellent alibis that are being checked out even as we speak. He should be released late this afternoon. No one, but no one, knows this outside the police department, except you. If you wait until three-thirty or so, you can probably catch his attorney—you know McCarthy, the public defender?"

"Yes, I know him," she said breathlessly.

"You can catch him outside the detention center, signing Smithe out. Better stake the place out around three o'clock. I don't think it could happen earlier than that."

"Oh, Lucas, this is enormous."

"Yeah. If you can keep it exclusive. And I'll give you another tip, but this also has to come from 'an informed source.' "

"What?"

"These women were supposedly raped, but nobody ever found any semen. They think the killer may be using some kind of . . . foreign object because he's impotent."

"Oh, jeez. Poor guy."

"Uh, yeah."

"What kind of object?"

"Uh, well, we don't know exactly."

"You mean like one of those huge rubber cocks?" The words came tripping out of her perfect mouth so incongruously that Lucas felt his chin drop.

"Uh, well, we don't know. Something. Anyway, if you handle this right and protect me, I'll have more exclusive tips for you. But right now I've got to get out of here. We can't be seen together."

"Not yet, anyway," she said. She turned to go, and then stepped back.

"Listen, when you call me at the station, they'll know who my source is if you keep leaving your name. I mean, if you can't get me."

"Yeah?"

"So maybe we should use a code name."

"Good idea," Lucas said, dumbfounded. He took a card from his wallet, wrote his home phone number on the back of it. "You can call me at the office or at home. I'll be one place or the other when I call you. When I call, I'll say 'Message for McGowan: Call Red Horse.'"

"Red Horse," she whispered, her lips moving as she memorized the phrase. "Red Horse. Like the horse in chess?"

More like the fish, the red horse sucker, Lucas thought. McGowan stepped forward another step and kissed him on the lips, then with a flash of black eyes and fashionable wool coat was gone down the stacks.

The store owner, an unromantic fat man who collected early editions of Mark Twain's *Life on the Mississippi*, appeared in the dim aisle and said, "Jesus, Lucas, what're you doing back there, squeezin' the weasel?"

Lucas stopped at Daniel's office and outlined Smithe's alibis. Together they went to the homicide division and outlined them to Lester and Anderson.

"I want everybody off everything else, I want this checked right now," Daniel said. "You can start by going over to the welfare office, see about this in-service training. That'll give us a quick read. Then look at these tickets, make a few calls. If it all checks, and I bet it will, we'll set up a meeting with the prosecutor's office. For like one o'clock, two o'clock. Decide what to do.''

"You mean drop the charges," Lester said.

"Yeah. Probably."

"The press'll eat us alive," Anderson said.

"Not if we play it right. We tell them that Davenport was the only guy Smithe would trust, told him the stories, Davenport came to us, and we realized our mistake."

"Sounds like a lead balloon to me," Lester said.

"It's all we got," Daniel said. "It's better than having McCarthy shove it down our throats."

"Christ." Lester's face was gray. "I made the call. They're going to be all over me. The fuckin' TV."

"Could be worse," Daniel said philosophically.

"How?"

"Could be me."

Lucas and Anderson started laughing, then Daniel, and finally Lester smiled.

"Yeah, that'd be un-fuckin'-thinkable," Lester said.

Lucas spent the rest of the morning in his office, talking to contacts around the Cities. Nothing much was moving. There were rumors that somebody had been killed at a high-stakes poker game on the northeast side, but he'd heard a similar rumor three weeks earlier and it was beginning to sound apocryphal. Several hundred Visa blanks had hit the Cities and were working through the discount stores and shopping centers; some heavy-hitting retailers were upset and were talking to the mayor. There was a rumor about guns, automatic weapons going out-country through landing strips in the Red River Valley. That was a weird one and needed checking. And a strip-joint owner complained that a neighboring bar was putting on young talent: "It ain't fair, these girls ain't old enough to have hair on their pussy. Nobody else is gettin' any business, everybody's down at Frankie's." Lucas told him he'd look into it.

• • •

"It all checks," Daniel said. "We faxed a photo out to New York, had the cops run it over to the hotel, and the bellhop remembers him and remembers the rat. He couldn't remember the exact date, but he remembers the week it was in. It's the right week."

"How about the in-service?"

"Checks out. That's the clincher, because there isn't any question about it. As soon as we asked the question, word was all over welfare that we fucked up. It'll be all over the courthouse by tonight."

"And?"

"We've got a meeting with the prosecutor and the public defender at two o'clock," Daniel said. "We're going to recommend that all charges be dismissed. We'll have a press conference this evening."

"He's going to sue our butts," Anderson said.

"We'll ask for a waiver," Daniel said.

"No chance," said Lucas. "The guy is freaked." He looked at the chief. "I don't think I ought to show at the press conference."

"That might be best."

"If anybody asks, you can tell them I'm on vacation. I'm going to take a couple of days off and go up north."

Lucas left City Hall at three and wandered down to the detention center, stopping only to pick up a box of popcorn. Annie McGowan and a cameraman were outside the center, waiting. Lucas sat on a bus bench a block away, and a half-hour later saw McCarthy walk out of the center with Smithe right behind. They were with two older people, a man and a woman, whom Lucas recognized as Smithe's parents from the photos in his house. McGowan was on them in a flash, and after a bit of milling around, they apparently agreed to a brief on-camera interview. Lucas balled up the empty popcorn bag, tossed it under the bench, and smiled.

• • •

"Press conference at seven," Anderson said, spotting Lucas in the hall.

"I've got something going tonight," Lucas said. "And I'm trying to hide out for a while."

Before leaving, he made arrangements for backup with the patrol division and headed home in time for the six-o'clock news. McGowan looked wonderful as she delivered her scoop. After two minutes of videotaped interview outside the detention center, the cameras cut back to McGowan in the studio.

"Now Report Eight has also learned that police believe the real killer is sexually impotent and the women may actually have been raped using some kind of blunt object because he is incapable of raping them himself."

She turned to the anchorman and smiled. "Fred?"

"Thanks for that exclusive report, Annie . . ."

Lucas turned to Channel Four. The last story of the broadcast was a recap of McGowan's, obviously stolen: "We have just learned that Jimmy Smithe, who was arrested in the investigation of the multiple murders of three Twin Cities women, has been released and that police apparently now believe him to be innocent of the crimes . . ."

Jennifer was on the phone five minutes later.

"Lucas, did you feed her that?"

"Feed who what?" Lucas asked innocently.

"Feed McGowan the Smithe release?"

"Has he been released?"

"You jerk, you better be wearing your steel jockstrap the next time I'm over, because I'm bringing a knife."

Late that evening, he cruised Lake Street in an unmarked departmental pool car, watching the night walkers, the drinkers, the hookers, looking for any one of a dozen faces. He found one just before ten.

"Harold. Get in the car."

"Aw, lieutenant . . ."

"Get in the fuckin' car, Harold." Harold, a dealer in free-market pharmaceuticals, got in the car.

"Harold, you owe me," Lucas said. Harold weighed a hundred and thirty pounds and was lost in his olive-drab field jacket.

"What do y' want, man?" he whined. "I haven't been talking to anybody . . ."

"What I want is for you to go into Frankie's and do some light drinking. On me. But light. Wine, beer. I don't want you hammered."

"What's the bad part?" Harold asked, suddenly looking perkier.

"They're going to put some young puss up on the bar. Real young. When they do, I want you to walk out and tell me. I'll be up the block. You come out as soon as she starts, hear? Not two minutes later, just as soon as she starts." He handed Harold a ten.

"Ten? You want me to stay in there drinkin' on ten?" he complained.

Lucas gripped the front of Harold's field jacket and shook him once. "Listen, Harold, you're lucky I don't charge you for the privilege, okay? Now, get your lame ass in there or I'm going to rip your fuckin' face off."

"Jesus, lieutenant . . ." Harold got out, and Lucas slumped in the seat, watching the passersby. Most were drinking or already drunk. A few drug cases walked by. A pimp and one of his string; Lucas knew him, and put his head down further, his hand up to block a view of his face. The pimp never looked toward him. A pusher, a pusher, a fat-faced boy who might just have come in from the country, and a drunk salesman. He watched the parade for a half-hour before Harold eased up to the car.

"There's one on and she's real young," he whispered.

"Okay. Take off." Harold vanished. Lucas used the radio to make a prearranged call for patrol backup, pulled on a tweed shooting hat and a pair of windowpane glasses, got out of the car, locked it, and headed down the street to Frankie's.

Frankie's smelled of old beer and cheap wine. The front room, next to the street, was empty except for two unhappy-looking women sitting across from each other in a red leatherette booth. The bartender was wiping glasses and casually watched Lucas pick his way through the empty tables to the entry arch into the back room.

The back room was jammed, thirty or forty men and a half-dozen women in a cloud of cigarette smoke, clapping to the rock music that poured out of a jukebox. The girl was dancing on the bar, stripped down to a tiny brassiere and a pair of translucent blue underpants. Lucas shouldered his way through the crowd and spotted Frankie himself behind the bar, pushing out plastic glasses of beer as fast as the tap would pour them. Lucas tilted his head up at the girl. Eleven? Twelve? She did a bump and reached behind her back with one hand, her teeth biting her lower lip in a semiprofessional grin. She was feeding off the crowd's enthusiasm. With another bump, she popped the brassiere and slowly peeled it off, carefully covering her tiny breasts with her forearms as she did it. After a few more bumps she tossed the brassiere behind the bar and switched into a new dance, her exposed breasts bobbing in the flashing ceiling lights.

"Bottoms, bottoms, bottoms," the crowd was chanting, and the girl hooked her thumbs in the top of the pants and after coyly pulling them down an inch here and an inch there, turning, bending, peering out between her legs, she stood and slid them off, her back to the audience, and then turned to finish the dance.

And the bartender from the front screamed, "There're cops outside."

"Take off," yelled Frankie. As the crowd broke for the two doors, he reached up and grabbed the nude girl by the ankle. Lucas lurched forward and got his gun out, his elbows on the bar, and poked the muzzle of the weapon into Frankie's cheek.

"Don't make me have an accident, Frank," he said. "This weapon has a very light trigger pull." Frankie froze. Three uniformed cops ran in from the front, pressing customers to the wall as they passed. A dozen Zip loc bags of cocaine and crack hit the floor. Lucas looked up at the girl. "Get down," he said.

She leaned over and carefully spat in his face.

• • •

"So what happened to her?" Carla asked.

They sat on the edge of the dock, their feet hanging over the water. It was an hour before sunset and they had just walked down to the dock from the firing range in the woods. The afternoon was cool and quiet, the violet hue of the sky reflected in the water. Three hundred feet out, a musky fisherman was working a surface lure around the edges of a submerged island. The water was as flat as a tabletop and they could hear the paddle-wheel chop-chop-chop of the lure as the fisherman retrieved it.

"We dropped her off with child protection," Lucas said. "They'll try to figure out who her parents are, get her back there. Two weeks from now she'll run away again and start hooking or dancing or whatever. At her age, it's the only kind of job she can get."

"What about Frankie?"

"We wrote him up for everything we could think of. We'll get him on some of them, felonies. He'll do some time, lose his liquor license."

"Good. They ought to . . . I don't know. A twelve-year-old."

Lucas shrugged. "The average age of the hookers out on the street is probably fourteen. By sixteen they're getting too old. The younger they are, the more money they make; it's what the johns want. Young stuff."

"Men are such perverts," Carla said, and Lucas laughed.

"What do you want to do, go fishing or go inside and fool around?" he asked.

"I've already been fishing," she said, wrinkling her nose at him.

CHAPTER
— 13 —

The maddog's secretary served as the office's rumor-central. That might have helped him in office politics—if he had taken part in office politics—but he did not relate well to his secretary. He dealt with her with his eyes averted. He was aware of the habit and struggled to correct it, to look straight at her. He was unsuccessful and had taken to staring at the bridge of her nose. She knew that he was not looking into her eyes.

The situation was made more difficult by her appearance. She was far too pretty for the maddog. She had made it clear soon after his arrival that she would not welcome an approach. In his own way, he was grateful. If she had snared him, if she had been Chosen, she would have to die and that would violate one of the principal rules: Never kill anyone you know.

When he came into the office, three other women were clustered around her, talking.

"Did you hear, Louis?" One of the women in the cluster was speaking to him. Margaret Wilson was her name. She was an attorney who specialized in personal-injury law, and though she was not yet thirty, was rumored to be one of the best-paid attorneys in the office. She had hazel eyes, large breasts, and heavy thighs. She laughed too much, the maddog thought; actually, she frightened him a bit. He stopped.

"Hear what?" he asked.

"That gay guy they arrested, that they thought was the maddog killer? He's not the one."

"Yes. I saw it on the news last night. That's too bad. I

thought they had him," the maddog said, struggling to keep his voice level. The police press conference, the portions he'd seen on TV3, had delighted him. He took another step toward his office.

"They say he can't get it up," said Wilson.

He stopped again, confused. "Pardon?"

"Channel Eight, Annie McGowan? The reporter with the short dark hair-bob like the ice skater What's-her-name? She talked to somebody in the police. They say he's impotent and that's what's driving him to do it," she said. Was she taunting him? There seemed to be an element of challenge in her tone.

"Well, they were wrong about the homosexual . . ." the maddog started tentatively.

"It's all that pop psychology," the maddog's secretary said scornfully. "Everybody else says he rapes them. If he can't get it up, how does he. . . ?"

"They never found any semen," said Wilson. "They think he uses something."

All the women looked at each other, and the maddog said, "Well," and went into his office and shut the door. He stood there, just for a second, suffused with rage. Impotence? Uses something? What were they talking about?

There was a burst of laughter from outside, and he knew they were laughing about him. Uses something. Probably like old Louis there, I wonder what Louis uses? they were saying. They didn't know who he was, what he was; they didn't know the power. And they were laughing at him.

He walked to his desk, dropped his briefcase, sat down, and stared at the duck print on the wall. Three mallards coming into a cattail swamp at dusk. The maddog stared at it without seeing it, the rage growing. There was another burst of laughter from beyond the door. If he'd had a pistol with him, he would have stepped into the hallway and killed them all.

He left the office at eleven-thirty and drove home to watch the noon news. He watched TV3 by preference, believing that what little dignity was allotted to news coverage by television could best be found there.

But he might have to change channels if this McGowan had special sources. He left his car in the driveway and hurried inside. He was a little early and had time to make a cup of hot soup before the news came on. He sat in the overstuffed chair in the living room sipping the salty hot concoction, and when the news came up, McGowan's was the lead story. It was apparently a rehash of the night before, with tape of McGowan interviewing the homosexual on the steps of the county jail and later repeating the impotence story. Her pretty, clear face was intent with the seriousness of her information; as the camera closed in on her face for the last shot, the maddog felt himself stir, even as the anger began to rekindle. He controlled it, breathing hard, and punched off the television. Annie McGowan. Her face hung in the bright afterimage of the television screen. She was an interesting one. Better than the blonde on TV3.

The morning copy of the *Star-Tribune* was still on the kitchen table. He checked it again. There was a large story on the release of Smithe, but there was no reference to the impotence allegations.

Why would the police tell McGowan that he was impotent? They must know he was not. They must know that it was wrong. Could it be an attempt to draw him out? Something to deliberately anger him? But that was . . . crazy. They would do anything to avoid angering him. Wouldn't they?

He went back to work, the anger still roiling his mind. There was a temptation to find Heather, to take her immediately. But not yet, he decided as he sat with his books and his yellow pads. He could feel the strength building, but it had not reached the urgency that guaranteed the kind of transcendent experience he had come to require. To kill Heather now was to strike at the cops, but it would do something . . . unpleasant to his need for her. It would be, he thought, premature, and therefore disappointing. He would wait.

The maddog worked through the weekend, feeling the need for the girl developing, blossoming within him.

He enjoyed himself. The office was empty on Saturday afternoon and Sunday, leaving him alone, as he preferred to be. And he'd found an interesting case. Since it would go to trial, he would not handle it, but the senior trial attorney had passed it down through the assignment system, asking for research.

The defendant was named Emil Gant. He had been harassing his ex-wife and her current boyfriends. He followed them, exchanged words with them, finally threatened violence. The threats were believable. Gant was on parole, having served thirty months of a forty-five-month prison term on a conviction of aggravated assault. The woman was worried.

The current charge came after Gant was caught in his ex-wife's garage. The woman was in her house alone, at night. A neighbor saw Gant sneak in through an open door. The neighbor called the woman, the woman called 911, and the cops arrived in less than a minute. Gant was found hiding behind a car.

Once he would have been charged with lurking. That charge no longer existed. He couldn't be charged with assault because he hadn't assaulted anyone. He couldn't be charged with breaking and entering, because he hadn't broken into the garage. He was finally charged with trespassing.

Actually, the prosecutors didn't much care what he was charged with. A conviction on any charge would send Gant back to Stillwater State Prison for the remaining fifteen months of his original forty-five-month term.

But the maddog, studying the state trespassing law, found a tidy little loophole. The law had been designed to deal with hunters who were trespassing on farms without permission, not with criminal harassment. Nobody wanted to arrest thousands of hunters every fall. Most of them were voters. So the trespass laws had some special provisions.

Most important, the trespasser had to be warned and given a chance to leave—and refuse, or substantially delay—before the act of trespass was complete. The maddog looked over the police reports. Nobody had said anything to the man before the cops arrived. He was never given a chance to leave.

The maddog smiled and started writing the brief. This would never go to trial: Gant had not completed the basic elements of the crime under Minnesota law. So he had been caught hiding in a private garage just before midnight? So what? Nobody told him to go away. . . .

The maddog left the brief on his secretary's desk before he left the office Sunday afternoon. On Monday morning he happened to get on an elevator with the chief trial attorney and his assistant. They nodded to the maddog and turned their backs on him, watching the numbers change.

Halfway up the assistant cleared his throat. "Got something for you on that Gant case," he said.

"Oh yeah?" Olson was a sharp dresser. Gray suits, paisley ties, big white teeth in an easy grin. "I thought I already put a stamp on that turkey and mailed him back to Stillwater."

"Not quite, O wise one," the assistant said. "I got to thinking about the state trespass law and came in over the weekend to look it up. Sure enough. There's a provision in there . . ."

The assistant then related, paragraph by paragraph, the maddog's research. Olson was laughing by the time they got to the skyway level and he slapped the assistant on the back and crowed, "God damn, Billy, I knew there was a reason I hired you."

The maddog stood thunderstruck at the back of the car. Neither of the others noticed. In a half-hour, he was in a rage. He couldn't go to Olson and claim the work as his own. That would seem petty. The assistant would claim he simply had similar ideas.

It had always been like this. He had always been ignored. The rage fed the need for the girl. It built like a thunderhead, and he went home, the need crawling in his blood.

Heather Brown was back on the block. She wore a short leather skirt and a turquoise blouse open to her belt. Glass beads dangled over her thin freckled chest; a headband pinned back her hair.

The maddog walked down the sidewalk toward her, his

eyes running over her body. He was most carefully dressed; more carefully dressed than for any of the other killings, because this pickup would be in public and might well be witnessed.

The maddog wore jeans and boots, a red nylon athletic jacket, and a billed John Deere hat. He was slightly out of place on Hennepin. Not enough to be outrageous, but enough that his clothes might stick in somebody's mind. He was a farmer, clear and simple. In a crowd of farmers, he would fit without the slightest wrinkle, he thought, as long as he kept his mouth shut.

He had cut a hole through the back seam of the jacket pocket and a long wicked blade from Chicago Cutlery nestled in the lining.

"Heather," he said as he approached. He glanced around. The nearest person was a black man sitting on a bus bench across the street. He turned away from the man. Heather had been looking past him and her eyes snapped back.

"How are you, honey?"

"I talked to you the other night . . ."

"I don't remember you."

"I offered fifty for a half-'n'-half . . ."

"Oh, yeah." She tipped her head in bemusement. "You look a lot different."

The maddog looked down at himself, nodded, and changed the subject. "You said you might come up with something more exciting, if I could get the money."

"You get the money?"

"I got a hundred."

"So what you got in mind, cowboy?"

The motel was pleasingly decrepit. Heather went into the office, got a key, and returned a minute later. Inside, the maddog looked around the room, sniffed. Disinfectant. They must spray the place, he decided. The bathroom was tiny, the floor was missing tiles, the bedspread was thin and badly worn.

"Why don't we get the money out of the way first?" Heather Brown asked.

"Oh, yes. A hundred?" The maddog took the bills out of his pants pockets and tossed them on the dresser. Five twenties. "And if we can really do . . . you know . . . I've got another fifty."

"Hey, I like you, guy," she said with a bright smile. "Why don't we just go in here and discuss it while we take a little shower."

"Start it, I'll be right there," he said. He started taking off his jacket, and when she stepped into the bathroom, took the knife out of his pocket and slipped it under the bed.

The shower was agonizing. She carefully washed his penis, and when nothing happened, said, "Have a little trouble there?" She frowned, a wrinkle between her eyes. The impotent ones weren't the worst of the trade, but certainly slowed down the turnover.

"No, no, no, not if we can . . ."

She had silk scarves in her handbag, four of them, one for each wrist and ankle.

"Don't tie them too tight," she said. "Just looping them is enough."

"I can do this," he said through his teeth. He tied her feet first, one out to each corner at the foot of the bed, then her hands, out to the sides, tied to the sideboards.

"How we doing, honey?"

"Fine," he said, turning toward her. He had a half-erection now, his penis standing away from his body.

"If you want to bring it up here for a minute, I can help you out," she offered.

"No, no, I'm fine; but I want to use a rubber . . . I'm sorry . . ."

"No, that's good," she said encouragingly. He turned and picked his jacket up off the floor, found a rubber, ripped it out of the package, and unrolled it on himself. Then he took the Kotex from the same pocket and lay down beside her.

"Open wide," he said.

Sensing that something was wrong, she tried to sit up,

opened her mouth, perhaps to scream, and the maddog grabbed her by the sides of the throat and squeezed and pushed her down on the bed. She flopped, twisting her shoulders, struggling against the binding scarves. As he squeezed and squeezed, her mouth opened wider, and she managed to force out a moan, not loud enough to attract attention in a motel like this, and then he forced the Kotex into her mouth, stuffing it in.

When it was in, he covered her mouth with one hand and fished in the pocket of the jacket with the other, found his gloves and slipped them on, one at a time. The girl watched him, still bucking against the scarves, her eyes wide and terrified now. When the gloves were on, he took his tape from the other pocket and wrapped it twice around her head and across the gag. Next he checked the bonds again; they were holding nicely.

"Look at it now," he said to the girl, kneeling over her. "That's the real thing. And they tried to say I was impotent."

She had stopped struggling and shrank back on the bed, watching him.

"So now we'll have a little fun," he said. He found the knife under the bed, took it out, and showed it to her, the steel blade shimmering in the lamplight. "It won't hurt too much; I'm very good at this," he said. "Try to keep your eyes open when it goes in; I like to watch the eyes," he said.

She looked away, and there was suddenly a smell in the room and he looked down at her pelvis and realized that she had wet herself.

"Oh, for Christ's sake," he said. But he was delighted. She'd wet herself in fear. She knew the power.

But he wouldn't rape her now. The thought of lying in cold urine was distasteful. And rape wasn't necessary, anyway. The maddog stretched out beside her, reached over and kissed her gently on the cheek as she strained away from him. "It'll just take a second," he said. She began frantically jerking her arms against the bonds. He laid the point of the knife just below her breastbone and felt the orgasm rising up within him as he pressed the knife up and in. The girl's eyes opened, straining, straining, and then the light went out and it all stopped for her. The maddog peered into her eyes as the light faded, felt the waves of the orgasm receding and the pressure lifting off his mind.

It had gone very well, he thought. Very well.

He stepped back from the bed and looked at her. Not pretty, he thought, but there was something beautiful in her attitude. He stripped off the rubber and tossed it in the toilet and flushed and began to get dressed, stopping frequently to look at his work. Inside, he rejoiced.

When he was dressed, he took a last long look, reaching out to stroke her cooling leg, and started toward the door.

"Whoops," he said aloud. "Can't forget the note." He fished it out of his jacket pocket and dropped it on her body.

Outside, it was a beautiful crisp fall night. He walked across the blacktopped parking lot, risking a quick glance toward the motel office. The clerk was visible inside the window, the blue light of a television bathing his face. He didn't look out. Keeping his head carefully averted, the maddog walked down the sidewalk and around the corner, where he pulled off the jacket and hat. He rolled the jacket with the hat inside and tucked it under his arm. He turned another corner and was at his car. He climbed inside and tossed the jacket on the floor of the car. If anybody had seen him get in the car, it would not have been a man in a red jacket wearing a billed hat.

He drove six blocks back toward the loop and stopped at a bar. A police car, flashing red lights but without a siren, sped past down Hennepin while he had the first drink. He nursed it, then nodded at the bartender for a refill. When he came out, an hour had passed since he'd left the motel room.

"Another unnecessary risk," he told himself. "I won't drive by, though. Only close enough to watch."

From a traffic signal a block away, he could see at least four police cars at the motel. As he waited for the light to change, a television truck rolled up to the motel and a dark-haired girl got out of the passenger side. He recognized her at once, Annie McGowan, the woman who said he was impotent.

A car horn sounded from behind and he glanced in the rearview mirror and then at the traffic signal, which had turned green. He turned the corner and pulled over to the curb. McGowan was talking to a cop and the cop was shaking his head. A group of people walked down the sidewalk past the maddog's car, attracted by the police lights and the television truck.

The maddog was tempted to join them, but decided against it. Too risky; he'd taken risks enough. Besides, there was enough of a glow from the killing that he should go home where he could relax and enjoy it. A long hot bath, close the eyes, and rerun the part where the light went out in Heather Brown.

CHAPTER
— 14 —

It had been one of the best weekends of the year, with warm days and crisp, cold nights. Brilliant color lingered in the woods, and the faint scent of burning birch logs hung in the air.

"We've got at least another week for the leaves. Maybe two," Carla said. A stand of maples on the north end of the lake was a flaming orange. "Too bad you don't have more maples."

"I thought about that when I bought the place," Lucas said. "I didn't want maples. They're pretty, but I wanted the pines. They give the place a North Woods feel. A little further south, down in the maples and oaks, it feels like farm country."

They drifted along the shoreline, working the bucktail lures around emergent weeds, docks, and fallen timber. "There are some people who'd say it's already too late for bucktails, but I don't hold with that. And they're more fun to throw," Lucas said.

In three hours of casting they caught five northern pike and had two musky follows.

"Bad day for musky, huh?" Carla said as they headed back to the dock.

"Hate to tell you this, but that was a good day. Two follows is all right. Lots of days, you don't see any."

"Great sport."

"Don't have to fool around with cleaning any fish, anyway," he said with a grin.

"When do I have to leave here?" she asked.

"What do you mean, *have to leave*?"

"I assume that the hot pursuit by the television people will have tapered off by now. I could go back. But jeez, you know, I've been living in that studio with a hot plate. I hate to go."

"Hey, stay a month if you want," Lucas said. "I've got to come up in two or three weeks and pull the dock out. After that, there won't be much to do until the freeze and the snow comes in."

"I accept," Carla said, laughing. "Maybe not a month, but for a couple of more weeks. You don't know how much of a break this is for me. I brought up a couple of drawing pads and some pastels and I'm having a great time."

"Good. That's what the place is for."

She looked over at him. "I'm glad you could stay an extra day. It's quiet here all the time, but on Saturday and Sunday there are a few people around. Today we had it to ourselves. It's kind of special on the weekdays."

After dinner, Lucas started a fire in the fireplace, dragging in birch logs cut the previous fall. When the fire was going, they sat on the couch and talked and watched television and then a rental movie, *The Big Chill*.

Toward the end of the movie Lucas started working on her blouse buttons. When the phone rang, he had her blouse off and she was straddling his hips, tickling him. He looked up at her and said, suddenly somber, "I don't want to answer. He's killed somebody else."

Carla stopped giggling and half-turned and reached out to grab the receiver and thrust it at him. He looked at it for a second and then reluctantly took it.

"Davenport," he said, sitting up.

"Lucas," said Anderson, "we've got another one."

"Shit." He looked at Carla and nodded.

"You better get down here."

"Who is it?"

"A hooker. We've got a street name, that's all. Heather Brown. Maybe fifteen. Knife, just like the others. The note's there."

"I don't know her. You check on Smithe?"

"Yeah, he's up at the family farm. We figure she was done around seven o'clock. A TV crew followed him up to the farm. They did some film at six. He's still up there. He's out of it."

"How about the girl's pimp?"

"We're looking for him. That's one reason we need you down here—we need you to look at her, see if you recognize her, shake down some of her people."

"Vice working it?"

"Yeah. They know her, but they haven't come up with anything yet."

"Where was it?"

"Down on South Hennepin. Randy's."

"Yeah, I know it. Okay, I'll be down as soon as I can."

He hung up and turned to Carla, who was slipping into her blouse. He reached out and pressed a palm against one of her breasts.

"I've got to go," he said.

"Who was it?" Her voice was low, depressed.

"A hooker. In a hot-bed hotel. It's the guy, all right, but it's kind of . . . weird. It sounds almost spontaneous. And it's the first time he's gone near a hooker." He hesitated. "I've got a favor to ask you, but I don't want you to take it the wrong way."

She wrinkled her forehead and shrugged. "So ask."

"Could you take a walk down to the dock for a few minutes?"

"Sure . . ."

"I've got to make a phone call, and . . ." He gestured helplessly. "It's not that I don't trust you, but it would be best if I was talking in private. Sometimes I do things that are considered mildly outside the law. If there were ever a grand jury . . . I wouldn't want you to perjure yourself or even think you had to."

She smiled uncertainly. "Sure. So I take a walk. No problem."

"It feels like a problem," Lucas said, running his hands

through his hair. "Every time I get into this situation with a woman, they think I don't trust them."

"You've been in it a lot?" she asked.

"A couple of times. Drives me crazy."

"Okay. So you're a cop."

She picked up one of his long-sleeved flannel shirts that she'd been wearing in the cool evenings and smiled at him. "Don't worry about it, for God's sake. I'll be down at the dock, just call when you're done."

He watched her go down the steps and along the path through the front yard, and a moment later saw her silhouette against the dark water as she stepped out on the dock. He picked up the phone and dialed.

"I need to talk to Annie McGowan immediately. This is an emergency."

"Can I tell her who's calling please?"

"Tell her Red Horse."

A moment later McGowan was on the line. "Red Horse?"

"Annie, there's been another killing. Have you heard yet?"

"No." Her voice was quick, excited. "Where's it at?"

"It's a hooker at Randy's Motel, down on Hennepin. Young girl. Her street name was Heather Brown. We've got people on the scene right now, you better get a crew up there. And let me give you one more piece of information about him, that our shrinks worked out. The chief and the other detectives will probably try to deny it, because they don't want this kind of sensitive information getting out, but we were expecting him to kill a hooker."

"Jeez, why?"

"Our shrinks think the guy is probably so ugly, so unattractive to women that not only can't he get it up, he can't get a woman on his own, either. One probably contributes to the other. We don't know that it's appearance, though. Maybe it's body chemistry or something. You know, maybe he's got like world-class body odor."

"Wow."

"Yeah, you get the idea. Really repellent, like a human lizard. I wouldn't give this to anybody, but I liked the way you blended my last tip, about the impotence, into your story. Now that he's killed the hooker, I think maybe this last piece of information will give the Now Report viewers some exclusive insight into the mind of a serial murderer, you know.''

''This is really heavy, Luca . . . uh, Red Horse. Let me get this stuff going and I'll get back to you. Are you at home?''

''No. I'm way up north, three hours away. I'm about to start back, I'll get there just before midnight. I'll be at my house, probably, sometime after one o'clock, and I'll be up until three or so. If you have to call, call then.''

''Okay. Thanks, Red Horse.''

Carla was on the dock, wrapped in the flannel shirt.
''You going?''
''Yeah.''
''I'll walk you up to your car.''
''I wanted to spend more time,'' he said.
''So come back.''
''If I can.'' He wrapped his arms around her and kissed her and she clung to him for a moment, then broke away and turned to the cabin. Lucas dropped into the Porsche, brought it around in a circle, and headed back to the Cities.

Driving at speed on the narrow roads of the North Woods thrilled him, but he usually did it in the daytime. At night the roadside timber seemed to step in, to press closer to the road. He overran his headlights, brush and phone poles flicking in and out of his vision without leaving time for thought.

Thirty miles out, just across the Minnesota border, he passed a roadside rest and the red lights came up behind him as a highway-patrol car burst onto the road.

Lucas wrenched the car to the shoulder and climbed out with his badge case in his hand. The patrolman was already on the road, one hand on his weapon, the other holding a long steel flashlight.

''I'm a Minneapolis cop making an emergency run back to the Cities,'' Lucas said as he walked toward the patrolman, extending the badge case. "Lieutenant Lucas Davenport. The maddog killer just ripped a hooker, a little girl. I'm trying to get back."

"Uh-huh," the patrolman said. He looked at the badge case and ID card with his light, then flashed it momentarily in Lucas' face.

"If you can call your dispatcher and have them patch you through to our dispatch—"

"I've seen you on TV," the patrolman said. He handed the badge case back. "I'm not going to give you a ticket, but a word to the wise, okay? I clocked you at eighty-three miles an hour. If you drive from here to the Interstate at fifty-five instead of eighty-three, it'll cost you an extra two minutes. If you drive at eighty-three and you hit a deer or a bear, you'll be dead. You're lucky you haven't hit one already. They're really moving right now. You hit a big old sow-bear broadside with that car, it'd be like hitting a brick wall."

"Right. I'm just sort of freaked out."

"Well, cool off," said the patrolman. "I'll call up ahead, tell the guys on the Interstate that you're trying to make up a little extra time. Keep it under a hundred and they won't hassle you, once you get on the Interstate."

"Thanks, man." Lucas headed back to his car.

"Hey, Davenport."

Lucas stopped with the door half-open. "Yeah?"

"Get that cocksucker."

The motel was a shabby single-story L-shaped building with a permanent hand-painted vacancy sign. There were a half-dozen squad cars and four television trucks parked in front when Lucas rolled in. He saw Jennifer and, further down the street, Annie McGowan, both with cameramen. Lucas squeezed the Porsche between two squad cars, got out, locked it, and started toward the yellow tape that blocked the motel driveway.

"Lucas."

"Hey, Jennifer . . ."

"You son of a bitch, you fed her another one."

"Who?"

"You know who. McGowan." Jennifer turned her head to glare down the street at the other woman.

"I did not," Lucas lied. "I was up north at my cabin, for Christ's sake."

"Well, somebody's feeding her select stuff. She's laughing up her sleeve at the rest of us."

"That's the way it goes in the news biz, huh?" He crouched and slipped under the tape. "Give me a call tomorrow, I'll see if I can get something for you."

"Hey, Lucas, you're not still angry? About the Smithe thing?"

"We have to talk," he said. "We have to figure out some kind of arrangement. You off tomorrow night?"

"Yeah, sure."

"So I'll take you to dinner somewhere private. We'll work something out."

"Great." She smiled and he turned and saw Anderson standing in a crowd outside the motel manager's office.

"So what?" he asked, taking Anderson by the sleeve.

"Come on down and take a look." He led the way toward the rear of the motel.

"Who found her?"

"The night clerk," Anderson said, glancing back. "The girl'd stop by and rap on the window when she was coming and going. She rapped going in, but never came back out. After a while, he kind of stuck his head out and says he saw this crack of light around her door. The killer apparently didn't pull it all the way shut when he left. That made the clerk curious and he walked down and knocked. And there she was."

"Did he see the killer? The clerk?"

"Uh-uh. He says he didn't see anybody."

"This clerk, is it Vinnie Short?"

"I don't know his name," Anderson said. "He's short, though."

Heather Brown was bound like the others, but unlike the others, her arms were stretched out at right angles to her body, as though she'd been crucified. The handle of the knife protruded from her chest under her breastbone. Her head was turned to one side, her eyes and mouth open. Her tongue stuck out, obscenely pale. She had long narrow scars on her thighs, white against her too-even machine tan.

"I don't know her," Lucas said. A vice officer walked in. "You know her?" Lucas asked.

"Seen her around a few times, she's been on the street a couple years," the vice cop said. "She used to be over on University, in St. Paul, but her old man OD'd on crank and she disappeared for a while."

"You're talking about Louis the White?"

"Yeah. See the scars on her legs? That was Louis' trademark. Used to beat them with coat hangers. Said it never took more than twice."

"But he's dead," said Lucas.

"Eight months ago. Good riddance. But I'll tell you something. His girls did the specialty tricks. Golden showers, bondage, spanking, like that. So this guy may have known her. The way she's tied up . . . it'd be hard to tie somebody up like that if she wasn't cooperating."

"You guys don't know who's running her now?"

"Nope. Haven't seen her around for a while," said the vice cop.

"We've talked to the night clerk but he claims he doesn't know anything about her," Anderson said. "Said she's been around two, three weeks. She'd come into the office, pay for the room, leave. She'd take a room for the night, bring two or three guys back, knock on the window when she was coming and going. She'd remake the bed herself."

"How much did she pay for the room?"

"I don't know," the vice cop said. "I could check."

"Usually it's one guy, one rent. They don't usually take them for the night. Not if the motel knows what's going on."

"This guy knows," said the vice cop.

"It's Vinnie Short?"

"Yeah."

"We have a long relationship. I'll go talk to him," Lucas said. He looked around the room again. "Nothing, huh?"

"Not much. The note."

"What'd it say?"

" 'Never carry a weapon after it has been used.' "

"Son of a bitch. He's not leaving us much."

Anderson wandered out. Lucas looked at the body again, then picked up Brown's bag and looked through it. A cheap plastic billfold contained fifteen dollars, a driver's license, a social-security card, and a half-dozen photos. He pulled the clearest one out of the billfold and let it fall to the bottom of the bag. In a side pocket he found two twists of plastic. Cocaine.

"Got a couple quarter-grams here," he said to the vice cop. "You inventoried her purse yet?"

"Not yet."

"Stick your head out the door and call Anderson, will you?"

When the cop stepped outside, Lucas pocketed the photograph from the billfold and snapped the billfold shut.

"Yeah?" Anderson stepped back inside.

"Got some toot. Better get a property bag around this purse before it goes away."

Vincent Short was short. He also had long, thinning red hair and thought he looked like Woody Allen. He didn't know nothing. He scratched his head and shook it, and scratched his head some more. The dandruff flakes fell like snow on his black turtleneck shirt. Two vice cops were standing around looking at him when Lucas came in. Short looked up and paled.

"Lieutenant," he said nervously.

"Vincent, my friend, we need to talk," Lucas said cheerfully. He looked around at the vice cops. "Could I have a private talk with this guy? We're old pals."

"No problem," said one of the cops.

"Say, you find the girl's registration card?"

"Yeah, right here."

One of the vice cops handed it to him and Lucas glanced at the total charge. Thirty dollars. "Thanks. See you around."

When they were gone, Lucas turned to Short, who was shrinking back in his chair.

"Maybe we ought to go back in the office where we can talk," he suggested.

"You fuck, Davenport—" Short started to cry.

Lucas leaned over his chair and spoke in kindly tones. "Vincent, you know who the girl's pimp is. Now, you've got to decide, are you more scared of him? Or more scared of me? And let me give you a hint. We're working on a multiple killer here. My ass is on the line. So you should definitely be more scared of me."

"You fuck—"

"And maybe you should think about what the boss is going to say when he finds out you rented a room to a hooker, all night, for thirty bucks. You must have been getting a little on the side, huh? Maybe a little pussy, maybe a little kickback? Huh, Vincent?"

"You fuck . . ."

Lucas glanced out the windows toward the street. Nobody was looking in. He reached down and grabbed the flesh between Short's nostrils between a thumb and forefinger and drove his thumbnail into it. Short arched his head as though he were being electrocuted and dragged at Lucas' hand with his, but Lucas hung on and pressed his other thumb into Short's throat below his Adam's apple so he couldn't scream. They struggled for a few seconds and then Lucas let go and backed off, and Short doubled up in the chair, his face buried in his hands, a long groan squeezing from his mouth.

Lucas leaned over him and wiped his fingers on Short's shirt, his face close to Short's.

"Who's her pimp?" Lucas asked quietly.

"Aw, c'mon, Davenport."

"If you think that hurt, I've got a couple more in places you wouldn't even believe," Lucas said. "Don't show, either."

"Sparks," he mumbled. His voice was almost inaudible. "Don't tell him I told you."

"Who?"

"Jefferson Sparks. She works for Sparks."

"Sparky. God damn." Lucas patted Short on the shoulder. "Thanks, Vincent. The police appreciate the cooperation of our citizens."

Short looked up at him, his eyes rimmed with red, tears running down his cheeks.

"Get out of here, you fuck."

"If this isn't right, if it's not Sparky, I'll be back," Lucas promised. He smiled at Short. "Have a nice day."

Outside, they were moving the body, wheeling it out into the flaring lights of the TV cameras. The vice cops were standing in a small group by the sidewalk, watching, when Lucas walked up.

"Your old pal tell you anything?"

"She worked for Jefferson Sparks," Lucas said.

"Sparky," one of the cops said enthusiastically. "I do believe I know where he's staying."

"Pick him up," said Lucas. "Soliciting or something. We'll talk to him downtown tomorrow morning."

"Sure."

Anderson was talking to the medical examiner. When he finished, he walked over to Lucas, shaking his head.

"Nothing?" asked Lucas.

"Not a thing."

"You're dragging the neighborhood for witnesses?"

"Got guys all over the place. Won't know anything until tomorrow."

"We got a name on the pimp," Lucas said. "Vice is going to look for him. Probably have him tomorrow."

"I hope he's got something," Anderson said. "This is getting old."

Lucas worked on his game for half an hour, editing the scenarios. It was the worst part of the job. The finishing touches were never done. With the murder of Heather Brown, he couldn't focus on the work.

He quit at two o'clock, ate a cup of strawberry yogurt, checked the doors, and turned out the lights. He had been in bed for ten minutes when the doorbell rang. Crawling out of bed, he tiptoed into the workroom so he could look out a window down the length of the house to the front door.

The doorbell rang again as he peeked out. Annie Mc-Gowan, alone in the streetlight, self-conscious as she waited by the door. Lucas sat down with his back to the wall, staring into the dark room. Jennifer was pregnant. Carla was waiting at the cabin. Lucas loved women, new women, different women. Loved to talk to them, send them flowers, roll around in the night. Annie McGowan was stunning, a woman with the face of Helen and what promised to be an exquisite body, pink nipples, pale, solid flesh.

And she was dumb as a stump. Lucas thought about it, pinching the bridge of his nose.

Outside, Annie McGowan waited, and after another minute turned away from the house and started back toward her car. Lucas stood up and peered through a crack between the curtain and the wall as she opened the car door, hesitated, looked back at the house. The window opened vertically, with a crank. His hand was on the crank and it would take only a second to open it, call out to her before she got away. He didn't move. She slid into the driver's seat, pulled the door shut, and backed out of the drive.

In another second she was gone. Lucas walked back to the bedroom, lay down, and tried to sleep.

Visions of Annie . . .

CHAPTER
— 15 —

Lucas' office door was open and the vice cop ambled in and plopped down in one of the extra chairs.

"Sparky's gone," he said.

"Damn. Nothing's coming easy," Lucas said.

"We found his place, down on Dupont, but he split last night," the vice cop said. "The guy who lives upstairs said Sparky came home about midnight, threw his shit in the car, and took off with one of his ladies. Said it didn't look like he was coming back."

"He knew about Brown," said Lucas, leaning back and planting his feet on the desktop.

"Yeah. Looks like."

"So where'd he go?"

The vice cop shrugged. "We're asking around. He's got a couple of other women. We've heard they're working a sauna out on Lake Street. Used to work at a place called the Iron Butterfly, but that's closed now. So we're looking."

"Relatives?"

"Don't know."

"When did we last have him in?" Lucas asked.

" 'Bout a year ago, I guess. Gross misdemeanor, soliciting for prostitution."

"He do time?"

"Three months in the workhouse."

"File upstairs?"

"Yeah. I could get it."

"Never mind," Lucas said. "I'm not doing anything. I'll walk over and take a look."

"We'll keep looking for him," the vice cop said. "Daniel's all over our backs."

Lucas flipped the lock on his office door and was pulling it closed when the phone rang. He stepped back inside and picked it up.

"Lucas? This is Jennifer. Are we going out tonight?"

"Sure. Seven o'clock?" An image of Carla flashed into his mind, her back arched, her breasts flattened, her mouth half-open.

Carla Ruiz.

Jennifer Carey, pregnant. "Yeah, that'd be fine. Pick me up here?"

"See you at seven."

The maddog was waiting for files in the clerk's office when Lucas walked in. The maddog recognized him immediately and forced himself to look back at the file he was holding. Lucas paid no attention to him. He walked through the swinging gate, behind the service counter, and across the room to the supervisor's cubicle. He stuck his head in the door and said something the maddog couldn't quite make out. The supervisor looked up from her desk and laughed and Lucas went in and perched on the edge of her desk.

The detective had an easy way about him. The maddog recognized and envied it. The files supervisor was an iron-girdled courthouse veteran who had seen one of everything, and Davenport had her fluttering like a teenage girl. As he watched, Lucas suddenly turned and looked at him and their eyes touched briefly. The maddog recovered and looked down at the file again.

"Who's the dude at the counter?" Lucas asked.

The supervisor looked around him at the maddog, who dropped the file in the return basket and headed for the door. "Attorney. Can't remember the firm, but he's been around a lot lately. He had that Barin kid, you know, that rich kid who drove into the crowd . . ."

"Yeah." The maddog disappeared through the door and

Lucas dismissed him. "Jefferson Sparks. Bad guy. Pimp. I need the latest on him."

"I'll get it. You can use Lori's desk. She's out sick," the supervisor said, pointing at an empty desk behind the business counter.

Sparks had three recent files, each with a slender sheaf of flimsies. Lucas read through them and found a half-dozen references to the Silk Hat Health Club. He picked up the phone, called vice, and asked for the detective he had talked to that morning.

"Is the Silk Hat still run by Shirley Jensen?" he asked when the detective came on the line.

"Yup."

"I find the name in a couple of places in Sparky's file. Could that be where his women are working?"

"Could be. Come to think of it, Shirley used to do the books on the Butterfly."

"Thanks. I'll run out there."

"Stay in touch."

Lucas hung up, tossed the files in the return basket, and glanced at his watch. Just after noon. Shirley should be working.

The Silk Hat was a black-painted storefront squeezed between a used-clothing store and a furniture-rental agency. The neon sign in the window said "Si k Hat t ealth Club" and the glass in both the window and door had been painted as black as the siding. There was a small wrought-iron door light over the door and a wise guy had spray-painted it red. Or maybe not a wise guy, Lucas thought. Maybe the owner.

Lucas pushed through the door into a small waiting room. Two plastic chairs sat on a red shag carpet behind a coffee table. A fish tank full of guppies perched on the sill of the blacked-out window. There were a half-dozen well-thumbed copies of *Penthouse* magazine on the coffee table. The chairs were facing a six-foot-long business counter that looked like it might have been stolen from a doctor's office. A door beside the counter led into the back of the store.

As Lucas stepped into the waiting room, he heard a buzzer

sound in the back, and a few seconds later, a young woman in a low-cut black dress stepped up behind the counter. She was chewing gum, and a june-bug tattoo was just visible on the swell of her left breast. She looked like Betty Boop but smelled like Juicy Fruit.

"Yah?"

"I want to talk to Shirley," Lucas said.

"I don't know if she's here."

"Tell her Lucas Davenport is waiting and if she doesn't get her fat ass out here, I'm going to fuck the place up."

The woman looked at him for a second, working her jaw until the gum snapped. She was not impressed. "Pretty tough," she said laconically. "I got a guy here you might want to talk to. Before you fuck the place up."

"Who?"

She looked him over and decided he might recognize the name. "Bald Peterson."

"Bald? Yeah. Tell him to get his ass out here too," Lucas said enthusiastically. He reached under his jacket and took out the P7 and the woman's eyes widened and she put up her hands as though to fend off a bullet. Lucas grinned at her and kicked the front panel of the counter and it splintered and he kicked it again and the woman turned and started running toward the back.

"Bald, you cocksucker, come out here," Lucas shouted into the back. He reached across the counter, grabbed the bottom side of the top sheet and pulled and it came up with a groan and he let it go and he kicked the front panel again and a piece of board broke off. "Bald, you motherfucker . . ."

Bald Peterson was six and a half feet tall and weighed two hundred and seventy pounds. He had had a minor career as a boxer, a slightly bigger one on the pro wrestling tour. Some people on Lake Street were sure he was psychotic. Lucas was sure he was not. Bald had attacked Lucas once, years before, when Lucas was still on patrol. It happened in a parking lot outside a nightclub, one-on-one. Bald used his fists. Lucas used a nine-inch lead-weighted sap wrapped in bull leather. Bald went down in six seconds of the first round. And after he went down, Lucas used his feet and a heavy steel flashlight and broke several of the bones in Bald's arms, most of the bones in his hands, the lower bones in both legs, the bones in the arches of his feet, his jaw, his nose, and several ribs. He a!so kicked him in the balls a half-dozen times.

While they were waiting for the ambulance, Bald woke up and Lucas gripped him by the shirt and told him that if he ever had any more trouble with him, he would cut off his nose, his tongue, and his dick. Lucas was suspended for investigation of possible use of excessive force. Bald was in the hospital for four months and a wheelchair for another six.

If Bald had been psychotic, Lucas thought, he would have come after Lucas with a gun, a knife, or, if he was really crazy, with his fists, as soon as he could walk. He didn't. He never looked at Lucas again, and walked wide around him.

"Bald, you dickhead . . ." Lucas shouted. He kicked the front panel of the desk and it caved in. There was a clattering on a back stairs and he stopped kicking and Shirley Jensen hurried up the hallway toward the counter. Lucas put the P7 away.

"You asshole," Jensen yelled.

"Shut up, Shirley," Lucas said. "Where's Bald?"

"He's not here."

"The other cunt said he was."

"He's not, Davenport, I mean, Jesus Christ on a crutch, look at this mess . . ." Jensen was in her late forties, her face lined from years of sunlamps, bourbon, cigarettes, and potatoes. She was a hundred pounds overweight. The fat bobbled under her chin, on her shoulders and upper arms, and quivered like jelly beneath her gold lamé belt. Her face crinkled and Lucas thought she might cry.

"I want to know where Sparky went."

"I didn't know he was gone," she said, still looking at the wreckage of the counter.

Lucas leaned forward until his face was only four inches from her nose. Her Pan-Cake makeup was cracking like a dried-out Dakota lake bed. "Shirley, I'm going to tear this place up. My neck is on the line with this maddog killer, and

Sparky might have some information I need. I'm going to wait here . . ." He looked at his watch, as though timing her. "Five minutes. Then I'm coming over the counter. You go find out where he is."

"Sparky knows something about the maddog?" The idea startled her.

"That was one of his girls who got ripped last night. The maddog's starting on hookers. It's a lot easier than scouting out the straights."

"Don't kick my counter no more," Shirley said, and she turned and waddled down the hallway and out of sight.

A few seconds later the front door opened and Lucas stepped back and away from it. A narrow man with a gray face, thin shoulders, and a seventy-dollar suit stepped inside, blinked at the ruined counter, and looked at Lucas.

"Jeez, what happened?"

"There's a police raid going on," Lucas said cheerfully. "But if you just want to exercise, you know, like push-ups, and drink some fruit juice, that's okay. Go on back."

The narrow man's Adam's apple bobbed twice and he said, "That's okay," and disappeared out the door. Lucas shrugged and dropped into one of the plastic chairs and picked up a *Penthouse*. *"I didn't believe things like this really happened,"* he read, *"but before I tell you about it, maybe I should describe myself. I'm a junior at a big midwestern university and the coeds around here say I'm pretty well-equipped. A girlfriend once measured me out at nine inches of rock-hard—"*

"Davenport . . ." Shirley emerged from the back.

"Yeah." He dropped the magazine on the table.

"Don't know where he is exactly, what hotel," she said, "but it's like in Cedar Rapids, some downtown hotel—"

"Iowa?"

"Yeah. He trolls through there a couple of times a year, Sioux City, Des Moines, Waterloo, Cedar Rapids. So one of his girls says he's down there, she don't know exactly the place, but she says it's a hotel downtown."

"Okay." Lucas nodded. "But if he's not there . . ."

"Fuck you, Davenport, you broke my desk."

Jennifer liked the flowers. Each table had two carnations, one red and one white, in a long-necked vase. The restaurant was run by a Vietnamese family, refugees who left a French restaurant behind in Saigon. The old man and his wife financed it, their kids ran the place and cooked, the in-laws worked the tables and bar and cash register, the ten-year-old grandchildren bused the tables and washed up.

"The big problem with this place," Jennifer said, "is that it's about to be discovered."

"That's okay," Lucas said. "They deserve it."

"I suppose." Jennifer looked at the red wine in her glass, watching the light reflections thrown through the venetian blinds from the street. "What are we going to do?" she asked after a moment of silence.

Lucas leaned back in his chair and crossed his legs. "We can't go on like this. You've really hammered me. Daniel knows about our relationship, and every time something breaks in the press, he's looking at me. Even if it's Channel Eight."

"I'm done reporting, at least for now," she answered. She tilted her head and let her hair fall away from her face, and Lucas' eyes traveled around the soft curve of her chin and he thought he was in love.

"Yeah, but if you get a lead . . . tell me you won't feed it to one of your pals," he said.

Jennifer sipped the wine, set the glass on the table, ran her finger around its rim, and suddenly looked up into his eyes. "Did you sleep with McGowan?"

"Goddammit, Jennifer," Lucas said in exasperation. "I did not. Have not."

"Okay. But I'm not sure about you," she said. "Somebody's feeding stuff to her, and whoever he is, he's tight with the investigation."

"It's not me," Lucas said. He leaned forward and said, "Besides, the stuff she's getting . . ." He stopped, bit his lip. "I could tell you something, but I'm afraid you'd quote me and really louse me up."

"Is it a story?" she asked.

Lucas considered. "It could be, maybe. It'd be pretty unusual. You'd be cutting on McGowan."

Jennifer shook her head. "I wouldn't do that. Nobody in TV does that. It's too dangerous, you'd set off a war. So tell me. If it's like you say, I swear nobody will hear it from me."

Lucas looked at her a minute. "Really?"

"Really."

"You know," he said casually, as though it were of no importance, "I've threatened to stop talking to you in the past, but there were always reasons to get together again. I could always find a way to excuse what you did."

"That's big of you."

"Wait a minute. Let me finish. This time, you've made a direct promise. No ifs, ands, or buts. If it gets out, I'll know where it had to come from. And I'll know that we won't have any basis to trust each other. Ever. Even with the kid. I'm not playing a game now. This is real life."

Jennifer leaned back, looked up at the ceiling, then dropped her eyes to him. "When I was a teenager, I made a deal with my father," she said slowly. She looked up. "If something was really important and he had to know the truth of it, I would tell him the truth and then say 'Girl Scout's honor.' And if he wanted to tell me something and emphasize that it was important and he wasn't kidding or fibbing, he'd say 'Boy Scout's honor' and give me the Boy Scout sign. I know it sounds silly, but we never broke it. We never lied."

"And you won't tell . . ."

"Girl Scout's honor," she said, giving the three-finger sign. "Jesus, we must look ridiculous."

"All right," Lucas said. "What I was going to tell you is this. I don't know where McGowan's information is coming from, but most of it is completely wrong. She says we think the guy is impotent or smells bad or looks weird, and we don't think any of that. It's all courthouse rumor. We think she's probably getting it from some uniform out on the periphery of the investigation.''

"It's all bull?'' Jennifer asked, not believing.

"Yep. It's amazing, but that's the truth of the matter. She's had all these great scoops and it's all bullshit. As far as I know, she's making it up.''

"You wouldn't be fibbing, would you, Davenport?'' She watched him closely and he stared straight back.

"I'm not,'' he said.

"Did you sleep with McGowan?''

"No, I did not,'' he said. He lifted his hand in the three-fingered Scout sign. "Boy Scout's honor,'' he said.

She toyed with the stem of her wineglass, watching the wine roll around inside. "I've got to do some thinking about you, Davenport. I've had some . . . passions before, for other men. This is turning into something different.''

They slept in the next morning. Jennifer was reading the *Pioneer Press* and Lucas was cooking breakfast when the phone rang.

"This is Anderson.''

"Yeah.''

"A cop from Cedar Rapids called. They busted Sparky for conspiracy to commit prostitution, and they've got—''

"Conspiracy to what?''

"Some kind of horseshit charge. He said their county attorney will kick their ass when he finds out. They'll have to tell him this afternoon, before the end of business hours. We got you on a plane at ten. Which gives you an hour to get out to the airport. Ticket's waiting.''

"How long does it take to drive?''

"Five, six hours. You'd never make it, not before they have to tell the county attorney. Then they'll probably have to turn Sparky loose.''

"All right, all right, give me the airline.'' Lucas wrote the details on a scratch pad, hung up, and went to tell Jennifer.

"I won't ask,'' she said, grinning at him.

"I'll tell you if you want. But I'd need the Girl Scout's oath that you won't tell."

"Nah. I can live without knowing," she said. She was still grinning at him. "And if you're going to fly, you might want to break out the bourbon."

The airline that flew between Twin Cities International and Cedar Rapids was perfectly reliable. Never had a fatal crash. Said so right in its ads. Lucas held both seat arms with a death grip. The elderly woman in the next seat watched him curiously.

"This can't be your first time," she said ten minutes into the flight.

"No. Unfortunately," Lucas said.

"This is much safer than driving," the old woman said. "It's safer than walking across the street."

"Yes, I know." He was staring straight ahead. He wished a stroke on the old woman. Anything that would shut her up.

"This airline has a wonderful safety record. They've never had a crash."

Lucas nodded and said, "Um."

"Well, don't worry, we'll be there in an hour."

Lucas cranked his head toward her. He felt as though his spine had rusted. "An hour? We've been up pretty long now."

"Only ten minutes," she said cheerfully.

"Oh, God."

The police psychologist had told him that he feared the loss of control.

"You can't deal with the idea that your life is in somebody else's hands, no matter how competent they are. What you have to remember is, your life is always in somebody else's hands. You could step into the street and get mowed down by a drunk in a Cadillac. Much more chance of that than a plane wreck."

"Yeah, but with a drunk, I could see him coming, maybe. I could sense it. I could jump. I could get lucky. Something.

But when a plane quits flying . . .'' Lucas mimed a plane plowing nose-down into his lap. "Schmuck. Dead meat."

"That's irrational," the shrink said.

"I know that," Lucas said. "I want to know what to do about it."

The shrink shook his head. "Well, there's hypnotism. And there are some books that are supposed to help. But if I were you, I'd just have a couple of drinks. And try not to fly."

"How about chemicals?"

"You could try some downers, but they'll mess up your head. I wouldn't do it if you have to be sharp when you get where you're going."

The flight to Cedar Rapids didn't offer alcohol. He didn't have pills. When the wheels came down, his heart stopped.

"It's only the wheels coming down," the old woman said helpfully.

"I know that," Lucas grated.

Lucas cashed the return portion of the plane ticket.

"You'll take a loss," the clerk warned.

"That's the least of my problems," Lucas said. He rented a car that he could drop back in Minneapolis and got directions to the police station. The station was an older building, four-square concrete, function over form. Kind of like Iowa, he thought. A cop named MacElreney was waiting for him.

"Carroll MacElreney," he said. He had wide teeth and an RAF mustache. He was wearing a green plaid sport coat, brown slacks, and brown-and-white saddle shoes.

"Lucas Davenport." They shook hands. "We appreciate this. We're in a bind."

"I've been reading about it. Sergeant Anderson said you don't think Sparks did it, but might know something? That right?"

"Yeah. Maybe."

"Let's go see." MacElreney led the way to an interview room. "Mr. Sparks is unhappy with us. He thinks he's been treated unfairly."

"He's an asshole," Lucas said. "You find his girl?"

"Yeah. Kinda young."

"Aren't they all?"

Sparks was sitting on one of three metal office chairs when Lucas followed the Cedar Rapids cop into the room. He's getting old, Lucas thought, looking at the other man. He had first seen Sparks on the streets in the early seventies. His hair then had been a faultless shiny black, worn in a long Afro. Now it was gray, and deep furrows ran down Sparks' forehead to the inside tips of his eyebrows. His nose was a flattened mess, his teeth nicotine yellow and crooked. He looked worried.

"Davenport," he said without inflection. His eyes were almost as yellow as his teeth.

"Sparky. Sorry to see you in trouble again."

"Whyn't you cut the crap and tell me what you want?"

"We want to know why you left town fifteen minutes after one of your ladies got her heart cut out."

Sparks winced. "Is that what—"

"Don't give me any shit, Sparky. We just want to know where you dumped the knife." Lucas suddenly stopped and looked at MacElreney. "You gave him his rights?"

"Just on the prostitution charge."

"Jesus, I better do it again, let me get my card . . ." Lucas reached for his billfold and Sparks interrupted.

"Now, wait a minute, Davenport," Sparks said, even more worried. "God damn, I got witnesses that I didn't do nothin' like that. I loved that girl."

Lucas eased his billfold back in his pocket.

"You see who did it?"

"Well, I don't know . . ."

Lucas leaned forward. "I personally don't think you did it, Sparky. But you gotta give me something to work with. Something I can take back. These guys from vice want to hang you. You know what they're saying? They're saying, sure, he might not be guilty of this. But he's guilty of everything else and we can get him for this. Dump old Sparky in Stillwater, it'd solve a lot of problems. That's what they're saying. They found some coke in your lady's purse, and that doesn't go down too well either . . .''

Sparks licked his lips. "I knew that bitch was holding out."

"I don't care about that, Sparky. What'd you see?"

"I seen this guy . . ."

"Let me get my recorder going," Lucas said.

Sparks had a crack habit that was hard to stay ahead of. On the night Heather Brown was killed, he had been sitting on a bus bench across the street, waiting for her to produce some money. He had seen her last date approach her.

"Wasn't it pretty dark?"

"Yeah, but they got all them big blue lights down there."

"Okay."

There was nothing particularly distinctive about the mad-dog. Average height. White. Regular features, roundish face. Yeah, maybe a little heavy. Went right to her, there didn't seem to be much negotiation.

"You think she knew him?"

"Yeah, maybe. But I don't know. I never saw him before, and she was on the street for a while. Wasn't a regular. At least, not while she was with me."

"She still doing the rough trade?"

"Yeah, there was a few boys would come around." He held his hands up defensively. "I didn't make her. She liked it. Get spanked a little. Good money, too."

"So this guy. How was he dressed? Sharp?"

"No. Not sharp," Sparks said. "He looked kind of like a farmer."

"A farmer?"

"Yeah. He had one of them billed hats on, you know, that got shit wrote on the front? And he was wearing one of those cheap jackets like you get at gas stations. Baseball jackets."

"You sure this was her last date?"

"Yeah. Had to be. She went to the motel and I went off to get a beer. The next thing I knew was the sirens coming down the street."

"Farmer doesn't sound right," Lucas said.

"Well . . ." Sparks scratched his head. "He didn't look right, either. There was something about him . . ."

"What?"

"I don't know. But there was something." He scratched his head again.

"You see his car?"

"Nope."

Lucas pressed, but there wasn't anything more.

"You think you'd recognize him?"

"Mmm." Sparks looked at the floor between his feet, thinking it over. "I don't think so. Maybe. I mean, maybe if I saw him walking down the street in the night with the same clothes, I'd say, there, that's the motherfucker right there. But if you put him in a lineup, I don't think so. I was way across the street. All there was, was those streetlights."

"Okay." Lucas turned off his recorder. "We want you back in the Cities, Sparky. You can run your girls. Nobody will hassle you until we get this turkey. When we locate him, we'd like you around to take a look. Just in case."

"You ain't gonna roust me?"

"Not if you stay cool."

"All right. How about this bullshit charge here?"

MacElreney shook his head. "We can process you out in ten minutes if Minneapolis doesn't want you."

"We don't want him," Lucas said. He turned back to Sparks. "But we do want you back in the Cities. If you start trolling the other Iowa cities on your route, we'll roust you out of every one of them. Get back up to Minneapolis."

"Sure. Be a relief. Too much corn down here for the likes of me." He glanced at MacElreney. "No offense."

MacElreney looked offended.

Lucas had unlocked the door of the rental car when MacElreney shouted at him from the steps of the police station. Sparks was right behind him and they walked down the sidewalk together.

"I thought of what was weird about that dude," Sparks said. "It was his haircut."

"His haircut?"

"Yeah. Like, when they walked away from me toward the motel, he took his hat off. I couldn't see his face or anything, only the back of his head. But I remember thinking he didn't have a farmer haircut. You know how farmers always got their ears stickin' out? Either that, or it looks like their old lady cut their hair with a bowl? Well, this guy's hair was like *styled*. Like yours, or like a businessman or a lawyer or doctor or something. Slick. Not like a farmer. Never seen a farmer like that."

Lucas nodded. "Okay. Blond guy, right?"

Spárks' forehead wrinkled. "Why, no. No, he was a dark-haired dude."

Lucas leaned closer. "Sparky, are you sure? Could you make a mistake?"

"No, no. Dark-haired dude."

"Shit." Lucas thought it over. It didn't fit. "Anything else?" he asked finally.

Sparks shook his head. "Nothin' except you're getting old. I remember when I first knew you, when you beat up Bald Peterson. You had this nice smooth face like a baby's ass. You gettin' some heavy miles."

"Thanks, Sparks," Lucas said. "I needed that."

"We all be gettin' old."

"Sure. And I'm sorry about your lady, by the way."

Sparks shrugged. "Women do get killed. And it ain't like there's no shortage of whores."

The drive back took the rest of the day. After a stop near the Iowa line for a cheeseburger and fries, Lucas put the cruise control on seventy-five and rolled across the Minnesota River into Minneapolis a little after eight o'clock. He dropped the rental car at the airport and took a taxi home, feeling grimy and tight from the trip. A scalding shower straightened out his bent back. When he was dressed again, he got beer from the refrigerator, went down to the spare bedroom, put the beer can on the floor next to the bed, and lay back, looking at the five charts pinned to the wall.

Bell, Morris, Ruiz, and Lewis. The maddog. The dates. Personal characteristics. He read through them, sighed, got up, pinned a sixth sheet of paper to the wall, and wrote "Brown" at the top with his Magic Marker.

Hooker. Young. Dark hair and eyes. The physical description was right. But she was killed in a motel, after being picked up on the street. All the others had been attacked in private places, their homes or apartments, or, in Lewis' case, the empty house she was trying to sell.

He reviewed the other features of the Brown murder, including her appearance in court. Could the maddog be a lawyer? Or even a judge? A court reporter? How about a bailiff or one of the other court personnel? There were dozens of them. And he noted the knife. The maddog brought it with him for this killing. Chicago Cutlery was an expensive brand, and it was widely sold around the Twin Cities in the best department and specialty stores. Could he be some kind of gourmet? A cooking freak? Was it possible that he bought the knife recently and that a check of stores would turn up somebody who'd sold a single blade to a pudgy white guy?

Lucas looked at the notes on the maddog chart. That he was well-off, that he could be new to the area. Up from the Southwest. Office job. Sparks had confirmed that he was fair-skinned. The business about the dark hair was a problem; Carla was sure that he was very fair, and that suggested lighter hair. There were some black-haired Irish, and some Finns would fit the bill, but that seemed to be stretching. Lucas shook his head, added "dark hair?" At the end of the list he wrote "Expensive haircut. Dark hair? Wig? Wears disguises (farmer). Gourmet?"

He lay back again, his head propped up on a pillow, took a sip of beer, held the can on his chest, and read through the lists again.

Rich man, poor man, beggar man, thief, doctor, lawyer, Indian chief. Cop.

He glanced at his watch. Nine-forty-five. He got off the bed, the beer still in his hand, walked back to the workroom, and picked up the telephone. After a moment's hesitation he punched in the number for Channel Eight.

"Tell her it's Red Horse," he said. McGowan was on the line fifteen seconds later.

"Red Horse?"

"Yeah. Listen, Annie, this is exclusive. There was a witness on the street near the Brown killing. He actually saw the maddog. Says he looked like a farmer. He was wearing one of those hats with the bills on them, like seed hats? So it's possible that he's driving in from the countryside."

"A commuter killer?"

"Yeah, you could say that."

"Like he commutes to the Twin Cities to murder these women, then goes back home, where he's just another farmer picking potatoes or whatever?"

"Well, uh, we think maybe he's a pig farmer. This guy, the witness, brushed past him, wondered what this farmer-looking dude was doing with a chick like Brown. Anyway, he said there was a kind of odor hanging about him, you know?"

"You mean . . . pig shit?"

"Uh, pig manure, yes. That kind of confirms what we thought before."

"That's good, Red Horse. Is there any chance we can get this guy on camera?"

"No. No chance. If something happens to change that, we'll let you know, but we're keeping his identity a secret for now. If the maddog found out who he is, he might go after him."

"Okay. Let me know if that changes. Anything else?"

"No. That's it."

"Thanks, Red Horse. I mean, I really, really appreciate this."

There was a moment of silence, of pressure. Lucas fought it.

"Uh, yeah," he said. "See you."

CHAPTER
— 16 —

A pig farmer?

The maddog raged through his apartment. They said he was a pig farmer. They said he smelled like pig shit.

He had trouble focusing.

The real issue. He had to remember the real issue: somebody had seen him and remembered the way he dressed. Had they seen his face? Was an artist working on circulars? Would they be plastered around the courthouse in the morning? He gnawed on a thumbnail, pacing. Pain flashed through his hand. He looked down and found he had ripped a chunk of nail out, peeling it away from the lobster-pink underskin. Blood surged into the tear. Cursing, he stumbled to the bathroom, found a clipper, tried to trim the nail, his hand shaking. When it was done, his thumb still throbbing, he wrapped it with a plastic bandage and went back to the television.

Sports. He ran the videotape back and watched Annie McGowan deliver her scoop. Pig farmer, she said. Commuter killer. Smells of pig manure, may explain his inability to attract women. He punched the sound and watched only the picture, her black hair with the bangs curled over her forehead, her deep, dark eyes.

Now she stirred him. She looked like . . . who? Somebody a long time ago. He stopped the tape, rewound it, ran it again, with the sound muted. She was Chosen.

McGowan.

Research would be needed, but he had time. She was a

good choice for several reasons. She would be satisfying; and she would teach a lesson. He was not One to laugh at. He was not One to be called a pig farmer. The Cities would be horrified; nobody would laugh. They would know the power. Everybody: they would know it. He paced rapidly, circling the living room, watching McGowan's face, running the tape back, watching again. A fantasy. A lesson.

A lesson for later. There was another Chosen. She moved through his sleep and his waking vision. She *moved*; she did not walk. She lived less than two long blocks from the maddog. He had seen her several times, rolling down the sidewalk in her wheelchair. An auto accident, he learned. She was an undergraduate at the university when it happened. She had been streaking through the night with a fraternity boy in his overpowered sports car. His neck snapped with the impact when they hit the overpass abutment, her back was shattered by a seat frame. Took an hour to get her out of the car. Both newspapers reported the accident.

But she came back, and both newspapers did feature stories about her return.

Graduated from the school of business, started law. A woman in law; they were all over the place now. She had a backpack hung from the side of her machine to carry her books. She rolled the chair with her own arms, so she'd be strong. Lived by herself in an apartment on the back of a crumbling house six blocks from the law school.

The maddog had already scouted the apartment. It was owned by an old woman, a widow, who lived in the front with a half-dozen calico cats. A student couple lived upstairs. The cripple lived in back. A ground-level ramp allowed her to roll right into the kitchen of the three-room unit. The news clips said she valued her singleness, her independence. She wore a steel ring on a chain around her neck; it had belonged to the boy killed in the wreck. She said she had to live for both of them now. More clips.

The maddog had done his research in the library, finding

her name in the indexes, reading the stories on microfilm. In the end, he was certain. She was Chosen.

If he had the chance to take her. But he had been seen. Recognized. What would the morning bring? He paced for an hour, round and round the apartment, then threw on a coat and walked outside. Cold. A hard frost for sure. Winter coming.

He walked down the block, down the next, past the cripple's house. The upper apartment was lit up. The lower one, the old lady's, was dark. He continued past and looked back at the side of the house; the cripple's window was also dark. He glanced at his watch. One o'clock. She was top of the class, the news clips said. He licked his lips, felt the sting of the wind against his wet mouth. He needed her. He really did.

He continued his walk, across the street, down another block, and another. The vision of the cripple rolling through his mind. He had been seen. Would his face be in the papers the next day? Would the police get a call? Might they be getting a call now? They could be driving to his apartment now, looking for him. He shivered, walked. The cripple floated up again. Sometime later, he found himself standing in front of a university dormitory. A new building, red brick. There was a phone inside. Davenport.

The maddog walked into the dormitory in a virtual trance. A blonde coed in a white ski-team sweatshirt glanced at him as she went through the door into the inner lobby, past the check-in desk. The phone was mounted on a wall opposite the rest rooms. He pressed his forehead against the cool brick. He shouldn't do it. He groped in his pocket for a quarter.

"Hello?"

"Davenport?" He sensed a sudden tension on the other end.

"Yeah."

"What is this game? What is this pig thing?"

"Ah, could you—?"

"You know who this is; and let me warn you. I've chosen the next one. And when you play games, you anger the One; and the Chosen will pay. I'm going to go look at her now. I'm that close. I am looking." The words, in his own ears, sounded pleasantly formal. Dignified.

He dropped the receiver back on the hook and walked back through the empty outer lobby, pushed through the glass doors. Pig farmer. His eyes teared and he bent his head and trudged toward home.

The walk was lost in alternating visions of the Chosen and McGowan and quick cuts of Davenport in the clerk's office, his face turning toward him, looking at him. The maddog paid no attention to where he was going, until he unexpectedly found himself standing outside his apartment. His feet had found their own way; it was like waking from a dream. He went in, began to take off his coat, hesitated, picked up the phone book, found the number, and dialed the *Star-Tribune*.

"City desk." The voice was gruff, hurried.

"When do the papers come out?"

"Should be on the street now. Anytime."

"Thanks." The phone on the other end hit the hook before the word was fully out of his mouth.

The maddog went out to his car, started it, drove across the Washington Street bridge into the downtown. There were two green newspaper boxes outside the *Star-Tribune* building. He pulled over, deposited his quarters, and looked at the front page: MADDOG A HOG FARMER? TV STORY SAYS "YES."

The story was taken directly from McGowan's news broadcast. A brief telephone interview with the chief of police was appended: "I don't know where she got the information, but I don't know anything about it," Daniel said. He did not, however, deny the possibility that the killer was a farmer. "Anything is possible at this point," he added.

There was no sketch. There was no description.

He went back to his car, sat in the driver's seat, and paged quickly through the paper. There was another story about the killings on page three, comparing them to a similar string of killings in Utah. Nothing more. He turned back to the front page.

Hog farmer, it said.

He would not permit it.

CHAPTER

— 17 —

Daniel leaned far back in his chair, the eraser end of a yellow pencil pressed against his lower teeth, watching Sloan. Anderson and Lester slumped in adjacent chairs. Lucas paced.

"What you're saying is, we got nothing," Daniel said when the detective finished.

"Nothing we can use to bag the guy," Sloan said. "When we find him, we've got information we can use to pin him down. We could even run him by Jefferson Sparks, see if he rings a bell. But we don't have anything to point at him."

"What about driver's licenses? Did we get that?"

Anderson shook his head. "They don't track incoming state licenses by individual names."

Lucas paced at the perimeter of the room. "What about those post offices?"

"We're getting some returns. Too many of them. We've had a hundred and thirty-six moves so far, covering the past two years, and we've only heard from post offices covering maybe a tenth of the population we're looking at. If that rate holds up, we'll get about fourteen hundred names. We're also finding out that the most likely moves are young single males. Probably a third of them in that category. That's something like five hundred suspects. And all of it rests on the idea that the guy's maybe got an accent."

"And if he moved here three years ago, instead of in the last two, we're fucked anyway," said Daniel.

"But it's something," Lucas insisted. "How many of the ones that you have so far are single males? Assuming that's what we want to look at?"

''Thirty-eight of the hundred and thirty-six. But some of those apparently moved here with women or moved in with a woman after they got here, or are old. We've had a couple of guys doing a quick scan of the names, and there are about twenty-two that fit all the basic criteria: young, single, male, unattached.''

''White-collar?'' asked Lucas.

''All but two. People don't move here for blue-collar jobs. There are more jobs in Texas, and less cold,'' Anderson said.

''So what are we talking about?'' Daniel asked.

''Well, we're talking about checking these twenty-two. We should be able to eliminate half or better, just walking around. Then we'll focus tighter on the rest of them. 'Course, we'll have new names coming in all the time.''

''Lucas? Anything else?''

Lucas took another turn at the back of the room. He had talked to Daniel the night before about the phone call from the maddog, and told the others at the start of the meeting. He'd taped the call. He was taping all calls now. First thing in the morning, he'd taken a copy of the tape to the university and tracked down a couple of linguists to listen to it.

They had called Daniel during the meeting: Texas, one of them said. The other was not quite so certain. Texas, or some other limited sections of the Southwest. The eastern corner of New Mexico, maybe, around White Sands. Oklahoma and Arkansas were out.

''His accent has a strong overlay of the Midwest,'' the second linguist said. ''There's this one line, 'I'm going to go look at her now.' If you listen closely, break it down, what he really says is 'I'm-unna go look at her now.' That's a midwesternism. Upper Midwest, north central. So I think he's been here awhile. Not so long that he's completely lost his southwestern accent, but long enough to get an overlay.''

''Ah,'' Lucas said. The detectives were looking at him curiously. ''Last night, I was watching Channel Eight. McGowan comes on and she has this piece about the pig farmer. So the maddog calls forty-five minutes later. I checked with the *Pioneer Press* and the *Star-Tribune* to see

what time the first editions came out—they both carried follows on the McGowan story. None of them were out when
the maddog called.''

"So he saw it on TV," Anderson said.

"And I've been thinking about McGowan," Lucas said.
"She fits the type the maddog's been going after . . ."

"Ah, Jesus Christ," Daniel blurted.

"There was something about that call. There's something
special about this 'chosen' one he talks about. I feel it.''

"You think he might go after McGowan?"

"He's watching her on TV. And physically, she fits his
type. And she's had all these weird stories. The guy seems
to want the attention, but from his point of view, everything
she's been saying is negative. He talks about being the 'one'
and she says he's impotent and smells bad and farms pigs.
Last night, he was pissed.''

"That's it," Daniel said, his face flushed. "I want a watch
on McGowan, twenty-four hours.''

"Jesus, chief—" Anderson started.

"I don't care how many guys it takes. Break some of them
out of uniform if you have to. I want guys on her during the
day and I want a watch on her house at night.''

"But delicately," Lucas said.

"What?"

"She's our chance to grab him," Lucas said. He put up
his hands to stop interruptions. "I know, I know, we've got
to be careful. Not take any chances with her. I know all that.
But she might be our best shot.''

"If you're right, he might be looking at her right now,"
Lester said. "Right this minute.''

"I don't think he'll try during the day. She's always around
people. If he tries, it'll be at night. When she's on her way
home or at her home. He could break into her house during
the day and wait for her. We should cover that possibility.''

"You've thought about this," Daniel said, his eyes narrowing.

Lucas shrugged. "Yeah. Maybe I've got my head up my

ass. But it seems like a chance, just like when you put a watch on me."

"Okay," Daniel said. He turned and pressed an intercom lever. "Linda, call Channel Eight and tell them I want to talk to the station manager urgently." He let the intercom go and said, "Lucas, stay a minute. Everybody else, let's get going on the basics. Start processing the list of guys who moved in. It won't do any good if he's really been here for a while, but we've got to check. Anderson, I want you to go back over every note we've got, see if we're missing anything we should have covered."

As the others drifted out of the room, Lucas slouched against a wall, staring at the rug.

"What?" Daniel said.

"This guy is nuts in a different way than I thought. He's not a straight, cold killer. There's something else wrong with his head. The way he was talking about the 'one' and the 'chosen.' "

"What difference does it make?"

"I don't know. Could make it harder to outguess him. He might not react like we expect him to."

"Whatever," Daniel said dismissively. "I wanted to ask you about something else. Where is McGowan getting this crap she's putting on the air?"

Lucas shook his head. "Probably a uniform who's just close enough to the investigation to pick up some stuff, but not close enough to get it right."

"So you're in Cedar Rapids yesterday and it's the first time anybody said the word 'farmer' in the whole investigation. The next thing I know, she's on the air saying the maddog is a farmer."

"Saying *pig farmer*. There's a difference. Whoever's feeding her is cutting the killer up. Sparks doesn't even think the maddog is a farmer. I don't either. I stopped on the way back and called in what Sparks said, so Anderson could get it in the data base. After that? Who knows. There's a leak, but it's all twisted up."

"Okay," said Daniel. He was suspicious, Lucas thought.

More than suspicious. He knew, and was talking for the record. "I'm not going to ask you anything else about this coincidence. But I would remark that if somebody is playing a game, it could be a dangerous one."

"We're already playing a dangerous game," Lucas said. "The maddog's not giving us any choice."

Lucas spent the afternoon on the street, touching informants, friends, contacts, letting them know he was alive. A Colombian had been in town, supposedly to negotiate a four-way cocaine wholesaling net to cover the metro area. It would be run by three men and a woman, each with separate territories and responsibilities. If any of them tried to make a move on somebody else's territory, the Colombian would cut off the troublemaker's supply.

Lucas was interested. Most of the cocaine in the Twin Cities was in weights of three ounces or less, bought on the subwholesale level from Detroit and Chicago, and, to a lesser extent, Los Angeles. There had been rumors of direct Colombian connections before, but they never materialized. This had a different feel to it. He pushed his informants for names, promising money and immunity in return.

There were more rumors of gang activity, recruitments of local chapters out of Chicago and Los Angeles. Gang growth was slow in the Cities. Members were systematically harassed by the gang squads in both towns and were sent to prison so often, and for so long, that any kid with an IQ above ninety stayed away from them.

Indians on Franklin Avenue were talking about a woman who either jumped or was thrown off the Franklin Avenue bridge. No body had shown up. Lucas made a note to call the sheriff's river patrol.

He was back at his desk late in the afternoon when McGowan called.

"Lucas? Isn't it wonderful?" she bubbled.

"What?"

"You know about this thing with the maddog? They're setting up surveillance around me?"

"Yeah, I knew the chief was going to get in touch."

"Well, I agreed to the surveillance, but only if we could tape parts of it. You know, we'll cooperate and everything, but once in a while, when it's natural, we'll get a camera in the house and get some tape of me cooking or sewing or something. They're going to set up a surveillance post across the street and another one behind the house. They'll let a camera come up and shoot the cops watching my house with their binoculars and stuff." She was more than excited, Lucas thought. She was ecstatic.

"Jesus, Annie, this isn't a sporting event. You'll be covered, of course, but this guy is a maniac."

"I don't care," she said firmly. "If he comes after me, the story will go network. I'll be on every network news show in the country, and I'll tell you what—if I get a chance like that and I handle it right, I'll be out of here. I'll be in New York in six weeks."

"It's a nice idea, but death would be a nasty setback," Lucas said.

"Won't happen," she said confidently. "I've got eight cops, twenty-four hours a day. No way he'll get to me."

Or if he got to her, there was no way he'd escape, Lucas thought. "I hope they're setting you up with some sort of emergency alarm."

"Oh, sure. We're working that out right now. It's like a beeper and I wear it on my belt. I never take it off. As soon as I hit it, everybody comes running."

"Don't get overconfident. Carla Ruiz never saw him coming, you know. If she hadn't been worried about going out on the street alone and if she hadn't been carrying that Mace, she'd be dead."

"Don't worry, Lucas. I'll be fine." McGowan's voice dropped a notch. "I'd like to see you, you know, outside of work. I was going to mention something, but now, with twenty-four-hour surveillance . . ."

"Sure," he said hastily. "It wouldn't be good if the chief or even your people found out how close we are."

"Great," she said. "I'll see you, good old Red Horse."

"Take care of yourself."

Detectives from narcotics, vice, and sex set up the direct surveillance, backed by out-of-uniform patrolmen who were assigned unmarked cars on streets adjacent to McGowan's. Lucas stayed away the first night, when the posts were established. Too many cops, too much coming and going, would draw attention from the neighborhood. The second night he went out with a vice cop named Henley.

"You ever seen her place?" Henley asked.

"No. Pretty nice?"

"Not bad. Small older house across the street from Minnehaha Creek. Two stories. Lot and a half. There's a big side yard on the east with a couple of apple trees in it. There's another house on the west, maybe thirty feet between them, all open. Must have set her back a hundred thou."

"She's got some bucks," Lucas said.

"Face like hers on TV, I believe it."

"She said you're on both sides?"

"Yeah. We've got a place directly across the street in front and one across the alley in back," Henley said. "We're watching from the attics in both places."

"We renting?"

"The guy on the Minnehaha side didn't want any money, said he'd be happy to do it. We told him we could be there a couple months, he said no problem."

"Nice guy."

"Old guy. Retired architect. I think he likes the company. Lets us put stuff in the refrigerator, use the kitchen."

"How about in back?"

"That's an old couple. They were going to give us the space, but they looked like they were hurting for money, so we rented. Couple hundred bucks a month, gave them two months. They were happy to get it."

"Funny. That's a pretty rich neighborhood," Lucas said.

"I was talking to them, they're not doing so good. The old man said they lived too long. They retired back in the sixties, both had pensions, they figured they were set for life. Then the inflation came along. Everything went up. Taxes, everything. They're barely keeping their heads above water.''

"Hmmp. Which one are we going to?"

"The architect's. We park on the other side of the creek and walk across a bridge. We come up behind a row of houses along the water, then into the back of his house. Keeps us off the street in front of the place.''

The architect's house was large and well-kept, polished wood and Oriental rugs, artifacts of steel and bronze, beautifully executed black-and-white etchings and drypoints hung on the eggshell walls. The vice cop led the way up four flights of stairs into a dimly lit, unfinished attic space. Two cops sat on soft chairs, a telephone by their feet, binoculars and a spotting scope between them. A mattress lay on the floor to one side of the room. Beside it, a boombox played easy-listening music.

"How you doing?" one of the cops asked. The other one nodded.

"Anything going on?" Lucas asked.

"Guy walked his dog."

Lucas walked up to the window and looked out. The window had been covered from the inside with a thin, shiny plastic film. From the street, the window would appear to be transparent, the space behind it unoccupied.

"She home?"

"Not yet. She does the ten-o'clock news, cleans up, usually goes out for something to eat. Then she comes home, unless she has a date. For the next couple of weeks, she's coming straight home."

Lucas sat down on the mattress. "I think—I'm not sure—but I think if he hits her, he'll come after dark but before midnight. He's careful. He won't want to walk around at a time when people will notice him, but he'll want the dark to hide his face. I expect he'll try to get in the house while she's gone and jump her when she comes back. That's the way he did it with Ruiz. The other possibility would be to catch her right at the door as she's going in. Sap her, push her right inside. If he did it right, it would look like he was meeting her at the door.''

"We thought he might try some kind of con," said one of the surveillance cops. "You know, go up to the door, say he's a messenger from the station or something. Get her to open the door."

"It's a possibility," Lucas said. "I still like the idea—"

"Here she comes," said the cop at the window.

Lucas got up and half-crawled, half-walked to the window and looked out. A red Toyota sports car pulled up to the curb directly in front of McGowan's house, and a moment later she got out, carrying a shopping bag. She self-consciously didn't look around and marched stiffly up to the house, unlocked the door, and went inside.

"In," said the first surveillance cop. The second shone a miniature flashlight on his wristwatch and counted. Thirty seconds. A minute. A minute and a half. A minute forty-five.

The phone rang and the first surveillance cop picked it up.

"Miss McGowan? Okay? Good. But keep the beeper on until you go to bed, okay? Have a good night."

"You coming up every night?" Henley asked casually.

"Most nights, midweek. For three hours or so, nine to midnight or one o'clock, like that," Lucas said.

"You do it for too long, you wind up brain dead."

"And if the surveillance doesn't do it, this fuckin' elevator music will," Lucas said. The easy-listening music still oozed from the boombox.

One of the surveillance cops grinned and nodded at his partner. "Compromise," he said. "I like rock, he can't stand it. He likes country and I won't listen to all that hayseed hillbilly tub-thumping. So we compromised."

"Could be worse," Henley chipped in.

"Not possible," Lucas said.

"Ever listen to New Age?"

"You win," Lucas conceded. "It could be worse."

• • •

"Oh, God damn, folks, she's doing it again."

"What?" Lucas crawled off the mattress toward the window.

"We thought maybe she didn't realize there's a crack in the curtains," the cop said. His partner had his binoculars fixed on McGowan's house and said, "C'mon, babee." Lucas nudged the first cop away from the spotting scope and peered through it. The scope was focused on a space in the curtains on a second-story window. There was nothing to see at first, then McGowan walked through a shaft of light coming from what Lucas supposed was a bathroom. She was brushing her hair, her arms crossed behind her head. She was wearing a pair of white cotton underpants. Nothing else.

"Look at that," whispered the cop with the binoculars.

"Give me the fuckin' things," said Henley, trying to wrench them away.

"Goddamn one-hundred-percent all-American TV-reporter pussy," the surveillance cop said reverently, passing the binoculars to the vice cop. "You think she knows we're watching?"

She knows, Lucas thought, watching her face. It was flushed. Annie McGowan was turned on. "Probably not," he said aloud.

Five days of surveillance produced nothing. No suspicious cars checked her home, no approaches on the street. Nothing but falling leaves and cold winds rattling the tiles on the architect's roof. The curtain never closed.

"Red Horse?" It was midday and Lucas was calling from his home.

"Yeah, Annie. This is no hot tip, but I was out in the neighborhoods and noticed something you might be interested in. One of the women's business clubs is going to hear a lecture from a university shrink about—I'm reading this from a flier—'the relationship between sexual-social inadequacy and antisocial activity, with comments about the serial killer now terrorizing the Twin Cities.' That sounds like it could be good. Maybe you'd want to get a camera over to see this guy before he gives his speech.''

"That sounds pretty relevant. What's the name?''

"Lucas?'' It was Jennifer, a little breathless.

"Jennifer. I was going to call. How are you feeling?''

"I'm getting a little queasy in the morning.''

"Have you seen a doctor?''

"Jesus, Lucas, I'm okay. It's only morning sickness. I just hope it doesn't get much worse. I almost lost my breakfast.''

"With the breakfasts you eat, I believe it. You've got to get off that eggs-and-sausage and butter-toast bullshit. It'll kill you even if it doesn't give you morning sickness. Your cholesterol is probably six hundred and eight. Buy some oatmeal or some Malt-O-Meal. Get some vitamins. I can't figure out why you don't weigh two hundred pounds. For Christ's sakes, will you—?''

"Yeah, yeah, yeah. Listen, I didn't call you for culinary advice. This is an official call. I've been hearing strange rumors. That something heavy is happening with the maddog. That you know who he is and that you're watching him.''

"Absolutely wrong,'' Lucas said flatly. "I can't prove it, obviously, but it's not true.''

"I won't ask you for Boys Scout's honor, because that's personal and this is an official call.''

"Okay, listen, as the woman who is carrying my kid, I don't want you to run around and get exhausted, okay? So on a purely personal basis, I tell you, Boy Scout's honor, we've got no idea who he is.''

"But you're doing something?''

"That's an official question. I can start lying again.''

Jennifer laughed and Lucas felt cheered. "I read you like an open book,'' she said. "I bet I find out what's going on within, say, a week.''

"Good luck, fat lady.''

• • •

Anderson and Lucas were talking in Lucas' office when Daniel edged in. He had never seen Lucas' office before. "Not bad," he said. "It's almost as big as my closet."

"There's a trick wall and it opens into a full-size executive suite, but I only do it when I'm alone," Lucas said. "Don't want to make the peons jealous."

"We were going over the case," Anderson said, looking up at the chief. "It's been ten days since the maddog's last hit. If the shrinks are right, he should be coming up on another one. Probably next week."

"Christ, we gotta do something," Daniel said. He was wringing his hands and Lucas thought he had lost weight. His hair was uncharacteristically mussed, as though he had forgotten to brush it before he left home. The maddog was bearing him down.

"Nothing on the McGowan thing?" he asked.

"Nope."

"Lucas. Tell me something."

"I don't have anything specific. We might be able to cool the media. I'm thinking that we should release some information about him. Something that would make it harder for him to pick up his victims."

Daniel paused. "Like what?"

"A flier listing the type of woman he goes after—dark hair, dark eyes, young to middle-aged, attractive. Then maybe a few hints about him. That he's light-complected, dark-haired, a little heavy, maybe recently moved in from the Southwest. That he dressed like a farmer at least once, but that we believe him to be a white-collar worker. Appeal to women who fit the type, and who feel approaches from men like that, and ask them to call us."

"Christ, you know how many calls we'd get?" Anderson asked.

"Can't be helped," Lucas said. "But we're not getting anywhere, and if he takes another one next week . . . We'd be better off if the press thought we were doing something about it."

Daniel pursed his lips, staring blankly at the pebbled plaster on Lucas' office wall. Eventually he nodded. "Yes. Let's do it. At least we're doing something."

"And maybe call an alert for next week," Lucas suggested. "Put a lot of extra cops on the street. Let the media know about it, but ask them not to publish. They won't, and it'll make them feel like they're in on something."

"Not bad," Daniel admitted with a wintry smile. "And after it's over, we can all go on television and debate media ethics, whether they should have cooperated with the cops."

"You got it," said Lucas. "They love that shit."

Lucas called her from a street phone.

"Red Horse?"

"Listen, Annie, Daniel has ordered Anderson—you know, from robbery-homicide?—he's ordered him to make up a list of characteristics for both the victims and the maddog killer and release it to the media. Probably sometime this afternoon. Some of them are already well-known, but some of them were confidential up to this time."

"If I can get it in ten minutes, I can make the noon report."

"I can't give you all of it, but we think he's fairly new to the area. We don't think he's been here more than a few years and that he moved in from the Southwest."

"You mean like Worthington, Marshall, down there?"

"No, no, not southwest Minnesota, the southwestern United States. Texas, probably. Maybe New Mexico. Like that. Daniel will make it official that he was seen in farmer clothes, just like you had it. But now they think it might be a disguise and that he's really white-collar."

"Great. Really great, Red Horse. What else?"

"There'll be more on the list, but that's the best stuff. And listen, before you put it on the air, call Anderson and ask him about it. He'll tell you. He's in his office now." He gave her Anderson's direct line. "Thanks. I'll see you on the air in fifteen minutes."

• • •

Midafternoon. Lucas was suffering post-luncheon *tristesse*, and sluggishly picked up the phone.

"Lucas?"

"How're you feeling, Jennifer?"

"What's going on with McGowan?"

"Jennifer, goddammit—"

"No, no, no. I'm not asking you if you screwed her. You already gave me Boy Scout's honor on that. What I want to know is, what's going on with McGowan and the surveillance? Why are the cops watching her?"

Lucas hesitated before answering, and instantly knew he had made a mistake.

"Ah. You *are* watching her," Jennifer crowed.

"Jennifer, remember when I asked you to talk to the chief before you did anything on Carla Ruiz? I'm asking you to talk to him again."

Evening. The sun went down noticeably early now. The summer was gone. Lucas waited outside the door of Daniel's office. He had been waiting fifteen minutes when Daniel came in from the outside.

"Come in," he said. He pulled off his topcoat and tossed it on the couch. "I'm asking you straight out. Did you tip Jennifer Carey on the surveillance?"

"Absolutely not. She's got her own sources. She called me and I sent her to you."

Daniel poked a finger at him. "If I find out otherwise, I'll kick your ass."

"It wasn't me. What happened when she called?"

"I called the station manager, got him with Carey in a meeting, and read them the riot act. Carey started on this media-ethics trip and the station manager told her to shut up. Said he wasn't going to have his station blamed if a star from another station was murdered by the maddog."

"So that's it?"

"They wanted equal access with Channel Eight. They're going to take a camera into her house over the weekend, when nothing's happening, shoot some film of McGowan ironing shirts or something. We'll let them in the surveillance post for a few minutes. Just the once.''

"And they hold the film until we catch him?''

"That's the deal.''

"Not a bad deal,'' Lucas said approvingly. "What did Jennifer have to say about it?''

"She was unhappy, but she'll go along. She'll produce the McGowan interview. Some kid's reporting it,'' Daniel said. "To tell you the truth, I think she's a little jealous. I think she wishes it were her, not McGowan.''

"Do you remember that awful poem you wrote to me when we first started going out? About having my baby?''

"That wasn't so awful,'' Lucas said, propping himself on one elbow. There was a little edge to his voice. "I thought it was rather intricate.''

"Intricate? It sounded like a bad teenage rock-'n'-roll song from 1959.''

"Look, I know you don't particularly like my—''

"No, no, no. I loved it. I kept it. I have it taped to the pull-out typewriter tray on my desk, and about once a week I open it and read it. I just read it today, and I was thinking: Well, I really am having his baby.''

Lucas pressed his ear to Jennifer's bare midriff.

"Am I supposed to be hearing anything yet?''

"Are you listening really closely?''

"Yeah.'' He pressed down harder.

"Well, if you listen very closely . . .''

"Yeah?''

"You can probably hear that Budweiser I had before bed.''

Lucas arrived at the lake in time to watch the sun go down Saturday evening. Carla was gone on the bike, but arrived a half-hour later with a small bag of groceries and a bottle of red wine. Lucas spent Saturday night and Sunday, and most of Sunday night at the cabin. At two in the morning he kissed Carla on the lips and drove back to the Cities, hitting his own bed a little after five. He was late for the project meeting again.

"Whatever happened to the list of people we got from the Rice woman?" Lucas asked. Monday morning in the chief's office. Half the detectives looked out of focus, tired from another weekend's overtime. "You know, when we were checking about the maddog's gun and who bought it from her husband?"

"Well, we checked everybody she could remember," said Sloan, who had done the Rice interview.

"Nothing?"

"We didn't actually interview everybody. We checked them. If they were way off the profile, we let it go. You know, women, old men, boys, we let them go. We did interviews with everybody that might come close to the profile, and came up dry. We were going to go back to the rest, but everything slowed down when Jimmy Smithe started to look good. Everything got thrown on that."

"We should go back for interviews with everybody," Lucas said, turning to Daniel. "We know that goddamn gun is critical. Maybe somebody bought it and resold it. I say we check women, boys, old men, everybody."

"Get on it," Daniel told Anderson. "I assumed it was done."

"Well . . ."

"Just get it done."

Lucas sat on the attic floor.

"Wednesday. I didn't think we'd make it to Wednesday," said the surveillance man. "He's overdue."

"Cold in here," Lucas said. "You can feel the wind coming through."

"Yeah. We keep the door open but there aren't any heating vents. We're thinking about bringing up a space heater."

"Good idea."

"Thing is, downtown doesn't want to pay for it. And we don't want to get stuck for the money."

"I'll talk to Daniel," Lucas said.

"Car coming," said the second surveillance man.

The car rolled slowly down the street, paused beneath them, and then kept going, around the corner.

"Get the plate?"

"Guy at the end of the street's doing that, one of the cars. He's got a starlight scope."

A radio sitting beside the mattress suddenly burped.

"Get him?" the surveillance man asked.

"Yeah. Neighbor."

"He slowed down outside her house."

"Guy's sixty-six, but I'll note it," said the radio voice.

"How's it going?"

"Cold," the car man said.

They went back to waiting.

"Action stations," the surveillance man said twenty minutes later. "I get the scope."

Lucas watched through binoculars. McGowan was wearing a frothy pink negligee and tiny matching bikini pants. She moved back and forth behind the eight-inch gap in the curtain, more tantalizing than any professional stripper.

"She's gotta know," the surveillance cop said.

"I don't think so," Lucas said. "I think she's just so used to that gap in the curtains that she doesn't notice—"

"Bullshit. Look at that, when she stretches. She's showing it off. But she never shows all of it. She walks around without a bra, but you never catch her without her pants, even when she's been in taking a shower. She's teasing us. I say she knows . . ."

They were still arguing about it when the maddog did the cripple.

CHAPTER
— 18 —

The maddog got a flier at the county clerk's office, a piece of pink paper handed to him as he walked out the door. He read it as he stood in front of the bank of elevators.

There was no attempt at a drawing and no real description. They said he was white-collar, possibly connected with the Hennepin County Government Center or Minneapolis City Hall. Fair-skinned. Southwestern accent, possibly Texas. Once seen dressed as farmer, but that was probably a disguise.

The maddog folded the paper and stood watching the lights on the elevator indicator. When it came, he stepped inside, nodded to the other two occupants, turned, and stared at the door. He hadn't thought that he might have an accent. Did he? In his own ears, he sounded like everybody else. He *knew* talking to Davenport would be a mistake. Now he might pay for it.

The maddog's mind slipped easily into the legal mode. What could they make of it? So he had an accent. Hundreds of people did. He was white-collar. So was most of Minneapolis. He frequently passed through the Government Center. So did ten thousand people a day, some with business in the Center, some passing through in the skyways. A conviction? No chance. Or little chance, anyway. Some leeway must be given for the vagaries of juries. But would he take a jury? *That* was something to be contemplated. If they got him, he could ask for a nonjury trial. No judge would convict him on what they had on the flier. But what else did they have? The maddog bit his lip.

What else?

As he worried, the need for another was growing. The law student's face floated before him, against the stainless-steel doors. He was so taken with the vision of her that when the doors opened, he started, and the woman standing beside him glanced at him curiously. The maddog hurried off the elevator, through the skyways, and back to his office. His secretary was out somewhere. As he passed her desk, he saw the corner of a pink slip of paper under a file folder. He paused, glanced around quickly, and pulled it out. A flier. He pushed it back in place. Where was she?

He went inside his office, dropped his briefcase beside the desk, sat down, and cupped his face in his hands. He was still sitting like that when there was a tentative knock at the door. He looked up and saw his secretary watching him through the vertical glass panel beside the door. He waved her in.

"Are you okay? I saw you sitting like that . . ."

"Bad day," the maddog said. "I'm just about done here. I'm going to head out home."

"Okay. Mr. Wexler sent around the file on the Carlson divorce, but it looks pretty routine," she said. "You won't have to do anything on it before the end of the week anyway."

"Thanks. If you don't have anything to do, you might as well take the rest of the day," he said.

"Oh. Okay," she said brightly.

On the way out to his car, he thought about the innocent conversation. He had said, "Bad day." He had said, "I'm just about done here, I'm going to head out home." That's what he thought he had said. Had his secretary heard, "Bayed day-ee"? Had she heard "Ah'm" instead of "I'm"? Was "head out" a Texas expression, or did they use that here?

Did he sound like Lyndon Johnson?

At his apartment, the maddog looked in the freezer, took out a microwave dinner, set the timer on the oven, and punched the Start button. His face was reflected in the window of the microwave. Lips like red worms. His hand slipped into his coat pocket and encountered the flier. He took it out and read through it again.

The victims, it said, were a type. Dark eyes, dark hair. Attractive. Young to middle-aged.

He thought about it. They were right, of course. Maybe he should take a blonde. But blondes didn't appeal. The pale skin, the pale hair. Cold-blooded people. And he didn't want anyone old. That was distasteful. Old women would know too much about their own deaths. His women should be confronting the prospect for the first time.

I won't change, he thought. No need to, really. There were better than a million women in the Twin Cities. Probably a quarter of a million fit his "type." A quarter-million prospective Chosen women. From that point of view, the description of a "type" was meaningless. The police wouldn't have a chance. He felt a surge of confidence: the whole thing was meaningless. Having been fought off by one woman, having been seen at the Brown killing by another witness, he realized the police had less than he had expected. If they were telling everything.

The microwave beeped at him and he took the dinner out and carried it to the table. If they catch me, he thought as he ate the lonely meal, I could use the microwave defense. Like the guy who claimed he was driven crazy by excess sugar from an overdose of Twinkies. The Twinkie defense; his would be the Tater-Tot defense. He speared one of the potato nubbins and peered at it, popped it in his mouth.

Tonight, he thought. I can't wait any longer.

He called the cripple's house a little after six but there was no answer. He called again at seven. No answer. At eight there was an answer.

"Phyllis?" he asked in his highest-pitched voice.

"You must have the wrong number." It was the first time he'd heard her voice. It was low and musical.

"Oh, dear," he said. He sounded dainty in his own ears;

like anything but a killer. He gave her a number with one digit different from her own.

"That's the wrong number," she said. "I'm five-*four*-seven-six."

"Oh. I'm sorry," he said, and hung up. She was home.

He prepared carefully, the excitement growing but under control. A hunter's excitement, a hunter's joy. He would wear his best tweed sport coat, the black cashmere overcoat, with black loafers. Snap-brim felt hat.

The overcoat had big pockets. They would take the potato—the potato had worked so well last time. He went to the closet, took a Kotex pad out of the box he'd bought three months before. Tape. Latex gloves under his leather driver's gloves. A scarf would partially cover the bottom of his face, giving him more protection against recognition: this was new, after all, a collection in his own neighborhood. Had to be ready to abort, he thought. If anyone sees me outside her door, forget it.

Knife? No. She'd have one.

When he was ready, he went through the side door into the attached garage, got in the car, punched the button on the remote garage-door opener, backed into the street, closed the garage, drove two blocks, and parked the car. He reached into the back seat and got a brown business envelope, opened the flap, and looked inside. A half-dozen forms, procured from a bin on the first floor of the Government Center. Applications for employment.

As he walked down to the door, the excitement became almost unbearable. I am coming, he prayed, I am coming for the Chosen; the One is coming. He felt the cold wind on his face and exulted in it, the smell of the Northwest, the expectant winter.

He walked briskly to her house, a businessman on business, and without breaking step turned down her sidewalk. The door had four small panes set in the center, just at head height, partly covered by a small curtain. He looked into her kitchen. She was not in sight. The maddog rapped on the door.

And waited. Rapped again. A noise? Then he saw her, rolling down the linoleum floor in her wheelchair. Not a wealthy woman, but such a face; such a fresh face, for one who had been so badly injured. An optimist.

She half-opened the inner door, left the outer one closed. "Yes?"

"Miss Wheatcroft? I am Louis Vullion, an attorney with Felsen-Gore. I'm on the Minnesota Bar Association scholarship committee." He reached under his coat, took out a business card, opened the outer door, and handed it to her. She looked at it and said, curiously, "Yes?"

He held up the brown envelope. "I was just talking to Dean Jensen at the law school. Actually, I was over there picking up applications for the Felsen Legal Residencies and Dean Jensen said you must have neglected to submit yours. Either that, or it was lost?" He waved the brown envelope at her, started to fumble out the white application forms.

"I don't know about that," she said. "I never heard of them."

"Never heard of them?" The maddog was puzzled. How could she not have heard of them? "I'm sorry, I assumed all the top students knew about the residencies. They pay so well, and, you know, you probably get more experience in top-level personal injury and tort. They're at least as sought after as the clerkships, especially since they pay so well."

She hesitated, looked at his face, his clothes, the brown envelope, the business card. "Maybe you better come in, Mr. . . . ."

"Vullion," he said, stepping inside. "Louis Vullion. Nasty night, isn't it?"

This one was different. Comfortable, almost. He took almost twenty minutes to kill her, lying nude beside her on her bed, the rubber firmly protecting him from seminal disclosures. He needed it. He came once as he worked on her and again when he finally slipped the knife under her breastbone and her back arched and she left him.

And he felt sleepy, looking at her, and laid his head upon her breast.

Cold. Stiff. He sat up, looked around. My God, he had been asleep. Panic gripped him and he looked down at her cooling body and then wildly around the room. How long? How long? He glanced at his watch. Nine-forty-five.

He stood, tore off the rubber, flushed it. His body was covered with blood. He stepped into the tiny bathroom, turned on the shower, and rinsed himself. He kept the latex gloves on; he didn't want to leave prints. Not now. Not in his finest hour so far.

When he'd cleaned off most of the blood, he stepped out of the shower but left it to run. If he'd lost any hair in the shower, the water might wash it down the drain. He picked up a towel, then put it down. Hair again. He dried himself with his undershirt, and when he was reasonably dry, he stuffed the shirt in his coat pocket. Thinking about hair had made him paranoid. He had continued shaving his pubic hair, but he feared the loss of hair from his chest or head. He got his roll of tape, made a loop around his hand, and blotted the bed where he'd been lying. When he was finished, he looked at the tape; there were small hairlike filaments stuck to it, and what might have been one or two black pubic hairs, the woman's. Nothing red, nothing of his. He stuffed the tape in his coat pocket with the damp shirt, stepped into the bathroom, turned off the shower, and dressed.

When he was ready, he looked around, took stock. Still wearing the latex gloves. Sport coat, overcoat, hat, scarf, driving gloves. Was he forgetting anything? The business card. He found it on the floor. That was everything. Leave the sock and potato on the floor. Drop the note on her chest: *Isolate yourself from random discovery.* Ready. He patted her on the tummy and left.

He stepped out, walked down the sidewalk and around the house, stripping off the latex gloves as he walked. The old woman's apartment was dark. There was a light upstairs, in the third apartment, but nobody at the window. He walked briskly down the sidewalk, and, as he passed under a street-light, noticed a dark stain on the back of one hand. He hesitated, looking at it. Blood? He touched it to his tongue. Blood. Sweet. He passed no one on the street on the way to his car. He opened it, climbed in, and drove.

Out to I-94. Pressure behind his eyes. He was going to do it. Telephone on a pole, outside a Laundromat. One guy inside, reading a newspaper while his clothes went around in the dryer. It was a mistake before, it would be a mistake again. But he needed it. He needed it like he needed the women. Someone to talk to. Someone who might understand. The maddog pulled in to the Laundromat phone, dialed Davenport's house.

And got an answering machine. "Leave a message," Davenport's voice said tersely, without identifying itself. There was a beep. The maddog was disappointed. It was not the same as human contact. He touched his tongue to the spot of blood on the back of his hand, savored it, then said, "I did another one."

The line stayed open and he wet his lips.

"It was lovely," he said.

CHAPTER
— 19 —

"It was lovely."

Lucas listened a second time, the despair growing in his chest.

"Motherfucker," he whispered.

He ran the tape back and played it again.

"It was lovely."

"Motherfucker." He sank down beside the desk, put his elbow on it, propped his forehead up with his hand. He sat for three minutes, unable to think. The house huddled around him, dim, protective, quiet. A car rolled by in the street, its lights tracking across the wall. Rousing himself, he called Minneapolis and asked for the watch commander.

"Nothing here," he was told. St. Paul said the same. Nothing in Bloomington. There were too many suburbs to check them all. And Lucas thought it likely that the maddog had killed one in Lucas' own jurisdiction. It was a contest now. Explicitly.

"Lucas?" Daniel's voice had an ugly edge to it.

"I got a call. He's says he's done another one."

"Sweet bleedin' Jesus," Daniel said. In the background Lucas heard Daniel's wife ask if there had been another one, and where.

"I don't know where," Lucas said. "He didn't tell me. He just said it was lovely."

They found the law student two days later, in the late afternoon. She rarely missed class. When she was gone the first day, her absence was noted, but not investigated. When she missed the second day with no word from her, no excuse, a friend called her apartment but got no answer. At dinnertime the friend stopped and saw the light in the back. She knocked, peered through the window, saw a rubber grip handle of the wheelchair protruding from the bedroom doorway. Worried, she went to the old woman, who brought her keys. Together they found the Chosen.

"I was afraid the maddog had killed her," the friend wept when the first cops arrived. "I thought of it on the way over. What if the maddog's taken her?"

"Red Horse?"

"Annie, there's another one," Lucas said. He gave her the name and address. "Over by the university. A law student, crippled. Name Cheryl—"

"Spell it."

"Wheatcroft, C-h-e-r-y-l W-h-e-a-t-c-r-o-f-t. There have been a bunch of newspaper stories about her, I think, in the *Strib*."

"I can look. We've got an on-line library."

"Look in the *Pioneer Press* too. She was a senior, right at the top of her class. Her folks are here; they live over on the east side of St. Paul. Nobody else knows about it yet, but everybody's going to find out pretty soon. There are about a million cops in the street, going in and out. And the medical examiner. We're attracting neighbors and students. But if you get a crew over here fast, you should catch the parents coming out."

"Five minutes," she said, and hung up.

"Cheryl Wheatcroft," Daniel said. He stood in the kitchen, hatless, coatless, angry. "What did she do to deserve this, Davenport? Did she sin? Did she fornicate in the nighttime? Did she miss Mass on Sunday? What did she fuckin' do, Davenport?"

Lucas looked away from the outburst, tried to deflect it with a question. "What'd they show her folks?"

"Her face. That's all. Her mother wanted to see the rest

of her, but I told her old man to get her out of here. He was almost as bad as the old lady, but he knew what we were talking about, he got her out. That TV camera was right in their faces. Jesus Christ, those people are animals, the fuckin' TV people are as bad as the fuckin' maddog.''

The homicide detectives moved around the apartment with their heads down, as though with poor posture they might somehow avoid Daniel's wrath. The talk was in whispers. It continued in whispers after Daniel left. When he went out the door, the TV cameras across the street caught his face and held it. For the next week, his profile, frozen in anguish like a block of Lake Superior ice, was used to promo the nightly news on Channel Eight.

Lucas stayed at the scene while the technicians processed it. ''Is there anything out of the pattern?'' he asked the medical examiner.

The chief examiner was on the scene in person. He turned his eyes on Lucas and gave him a tiny nod. ''Yeah. He butchered her. The other ones, it was surgical. Go in, kill. This one, he cut apart. She was alive for most of it.''

''Sex?''

''You mean did he rape her? No. Doesn't look like it. She has numerous stab wounds over the pelvic area, up into the vaginal opening, the rectum, then across the anterior aspect of the pelvis—''

''The what?''

''The front, the front, right up her front. It looks like . . . Mother of God . . .'' The medical examiner ran his hands through his graying hair.

''Sam . . .''

''It looks like he was trying to find where the pain started. She has a case full of medical records, and from what I can tell, the spinal event that crippled her was relatively high. Above the hip, below the breasts. She would have lost the superficial . . . Jesus, Lucas, this is freaking me out. Can't you wait for the reports?''

''No. I want to hear it.''

''Well, when you have a spinal accident, you lose varying

amounts of muscular control and the super . . . the feeling in your lower body. The loss ranges from minor disability to total paralysis, where you lose everything. That's what happened to her. But depending on where the damage happens to the spine, you lose superficial sensory . . . you lose the feeling over different areas. We're talking about the pain. And it looks like he was systematically working up her body, trying to find where it began.''

''What about all the stab wounds in the vaginal area?''

''I was about to say, that doesn't fit with the other pattern of wounds. That appears to be sexual. And it's not uncommon when there's a sexual motivation behind a murder. There was also substantial flensing of the breasts—''

''What? Flensing?''

''He was skinning her. I think he stopped when he realized she was dying. That's when he finally put the knife in, so he could do it himself. Kill her.''

''Jesus God.''

The technicians tramped in and out. Lucas poked through the cripple's possessions, found a small collection of graduation pictures tucked in the top drawer of her chest. She was wearing a black gown and mortarboard, tassel to the left. He slipped the picture in his pocket and left.

Lucas was awake when the newspaper hit his screen door. He lay with his eyes closed for a moment, then gave up and walked out to retrieve it.

A double-deck headline spread across the page. Beneath it a four-column color photograph dominated the page, a shot of the covered body being rolled out to the medical examiner's wagon on a gurney. The photographer had used a superwide lens that distorted the faces of the men pushing the gurney. HANDICAPPED, the headline said. TORTURE, it said. Lucas closed his eyes and leaned against the wall.

The meeting started angry and stayed that way.

''So there's nothing substantial?'' They were gathered in

Daniel's office—Lucas, Anderson, Lester, a dozen of the lead detectives.

"It's just like the others. He left us nothing," said Anderson.

"I'm not going to take this kind of answer anymore," Daniel suddenly shouted, smashing the top of his desk with his hand, staring at Anderson. "I don't want to hear this bullshit about—"

"It's not bullshit," Anderson shouted back. "It's what we got. We got nothing. And I don't want to hear any shit from you or Davenport about any fuckin' media firestorms—that's the first fuckin' thing you said when we came in: what about the fuckin' media? Fuck the fuckin' media. We're doing the best we fuckin' can and I don't want to hear any fuckin' shit about it. . . ." He turned and stomped out of the room.

Daniel, caught in mid-explosion by Anderson's outburst, slumped back in his chair. "Somebody go get him back," he said after a minute.

When Anderson came back, Daniel nodded at him. "Sorry," he said, rubbing his eyes. "I'm losing it. We've got to stop this dirtbag. We gotta get him. Ideas. Somebody give me ideas."

"Don't cut the surveillance on McGowan," Lucas said. "I still think that's a shot."

"She was all over the place out at the Wheatcroft scene," one of the detectives said. "How'd she know? She was there a half-hour before the rest of the media."

"Don't worry about it," Daniel snapped. "And I want the surveillance on her so tight that an ant couldn't get to her on his hands and knees. Okay? What else? Anything? Anybody? What's happening with the follow-up on the people who might have gotten the gun from Rice?"

"Uh, we got an odd one on that," said Sloan. "Rice was over in Japan right after World War II and he brought back these souvenirs, these little ivory-doll kind of things? Netsoo-kees? Anyway, he told some guy about them, a neighbor, and the neighbor told him about this gallery that deals in Oriental art. This guy from the gallery comes over and he buys these things. Gave Rice five hundred dollars for fifteen of them. We got the receipt. I went over to talk to the guy, Alan Nester's his name, he's over on Nicollet.''

"I've seen his place," said Anderson. "Alan Nester Objets d'Art Orientaux. Ground floor of the Balmoral Building.''

''Pretty fancy address,'' said Lucas.

"That's him,'' said Sloan. "Anyway, the guy wouldn't give me the time of day. Said he didn't know anything, that he only talked to Mr. Rice for a minute and left. Never saw any gun, doesn't know about the gun.''

"So?'' asked Daniel. "You think he might be the guy?''

"No, no, he's too tall, must be six-five, and he's real skinny. And he's too old for the profile. Must be fifty. One of those really snotty assholes who wear those scarves instead of ties?''

''Ascots?''

"Whatever, yeah. I don't think he's the guy, but he was nervous and he was lying to me. He probably doesn't know anything about the maddog, but there's something he's nervous about.''

"Look around, see what you can find out,'' Daniel said. "What about the other people?''

"We've got six more to do,'' he said. "They're the least likely ones.''

"Do them first. Who knows, maybe somebody'll jump up and bite you on the ass.'' He looked around. "Anything else?''

"I've got nothing,'' Lucas said. "I can't think. I'm going out on the street this afternoon, catch up out there, then I'm going up north. I'm not doing any good here.''

"Hang around for a minute, will you?'' Daniel asked. "Okay, everybody. And I'm sorry, Andy. Didn't mean to yell.''

"Didn't mean to myself,'' Anderson said, smiling ruefully. "The maddog is killing us all.''

"Anderson doesn't want to talk about the media,'' Daniel said, rapping the pile of newspapers on his desk. "But we've got to do something. And I'm not talking about saving our jobs. We could see some panic out there. This might be routine in Los Angeles, but the people here . . . It just doesn't happen. They're getting scared."

"What do you mean by *panic*? People running in the streets? That won't happen. They'll just hunker down—"

"I'm talking about people carrying guns in public. I'm talking about a college kid coming home from the U when his parents don't expect him, in the middle of the night, and having the old man take off his head with the family Colt. That's what I'm talking about. You're probably too young to remember when Charlie Starkweather was killing people out in Nebraska, but there were people walking around in the streets of Lincoln carrying shotguns. We don't need that. And we don't need the National Rifle Association cranking up its scare campaign, a gun in every house and a tank in every garage."

"We should talk to the publishers and the station managers or the station owners," Lucas said after a moment's reflection. "They can *order* the heat turned down."

"Think they'll do it?"

Lucas considered for another moment. "If we do it right. Media people are generally despised, but they're like anybody else: they want to be loved. Give them a chance to show that they're really good guys, they'll lick your shoes. But it's got to come from you. Like, top guy to top guy. And maybe you ought to take the deputy chiefs with you. Maybe the mayor. That'll flatter them, show them that you respect them. They're going to ask some stuff like, 'You want us to censor ourselves?' You've got to say, 'No, we don't. We just want to *apprise* you of the dangers of public panic; we want you to be *sensitive* to it.' "

"Do I have to *share* those thoughts with them?" Daniel asked sarcastically.

Lucas pointed a finger at him. "Quit that," he said harshly. "No humor. You're dealing with the press. And yeah, say *share*. They talk like that. 'Let me share this with you.' "

"And they'll buy it?"

"I think so. It gives the newspapers a chance to be responsible. They can do that because they aren't making any money off the deal anyway. You don't get more advertisers because you're carrying murder stories. And they don't care much about short-term circulation gains. They can't sell those, either."

"What about the TV?"

"That's a bigger problem, because their ratings *do* shift, and that *does* count. Christ, I think I read in the paper last week that the sweeps are coming up. If we don't cut some kind of a deal with TV, they'll go nuts with the maddog stuff."

Daniel groaned. "The sweeps. I forgot about the sweeps. Jesus, this is supposed to be a police department. We're supposed to catch crooks, and I sit here sweating about the ratings sweeps."

"I'll get the names of everybody you want to talk to," Lucas said. "I'll give them to Linda in an hour. With phone numbers. Best to call them directly. Then they think you know who they are."

"Okay. One meeting? Or two? One for the papers and one for the TV?"

"One, I think. The TV people like to be in the same discussions with the newspaper guys. Makes them feel like journalists."

"What about radio?" Daniel asked.

"Fuck radio."

Anderson propped himself in Lucas' office doorway.

"Something?"

"He may drive a dark-colored Thunderbird, new, probably midnight blue," he said with just the mildest air of satisfaction.

"Where'd that come from?" Lucas asked.

"Okay. The medical examiner figured she was killed sometime Wednesday night or Thursday morning. We know she was alive at seven o'clock because she talked on the telephone with a friend. Then a guy who lives across the street works on the night shift, he got home at eleven-twenty and noticed that her light was still on. He noticed because she usually went to bed early.''

"How's he know that?''

"I'm getting to it. This guy works a rotating shift out at 3-M. When he was working the day shift, seven to three, he used to see her going down the sidewalk when he left for work. One time he asked her why she got up so early, and she said she always did, it was the best time of day. She couldn't work at night. So he noticed the light. Thought maybe she had a big test.''

"And . . .''

"So we think she was dead then. Or dying. Then, about ten o'clock—we're not exact on this time, but within fifteen minutes either way—this kid was walking up toward his apartment and he noticed this guy walking down the sidewalk on the other side of the street. Going the same way. Middle height. Dark coat. Hat. This is the street that runs alongside Wheatcroft's house. Anyway, they walk along for a couple of blocks, the kid not paying attention. But you know how you keep track of people when you're out at night on foot?''

"Yeah.''

"It was like that. They walk for a couple of blocks and the guy stops beside this car, this Thunderbird. The kid noticed it because he likes the car. So the guy unlocks it, climbs in, and drives away. When the kid hears about Wheatcroft, he thinks back and it occurs to him that this guy was kind of odd. There were a million parking places on the street around there, and it was cold, so why park at least two or three blocks from wherever you're coming from?''

"Smart kid.''

"Yeah.''

"So did you look at him?'' Lucas asked.

"Yeah. He's okay. Engineering student at the U. He's got a full-time live-in. The guy across the street looks okay too.''

"Hmph.'' Lucas rubbed his lip.

Anderson shrugged. "It's not a major clue, but it's something. We're checking insurance records on Thunderbirds, going back three years, against people who transferred policies up here from somewhere else. Like Texas.''

"Luck.''

The meeting was held the next day at midmorning in a *Star-Tribune* conference room. Everybody wore a suit. Even the women. Most of them had leather folders with yellow legal pads inside. They called the mayor and Daniel by their first names. They called Lucas "lieutenant.''

"You're asking us to censor ourselves,'' said the head of the *Star-Tribune* editorial board.

"No, we actually aren't, and we wouldn't, because we know you wouldn't do it,'' Daniel said with a treacly smile. "We're just trying to *share* some concerns with you, point out the possibility of general panic. This man, this killer, is insane. We're doing everything we can to identify and arrest him, and I don't want to minimize the . . . the horribleness— is that a word?—of these crimes. But I would like to point out that he has now killed exactly five people out of a population of almost three million in the metropolitan area. In other words, your chances of dying in a fire, being murdered by a member of your own family, being hit by a car, to say nothing of your chances of dying from a sudden heart attack, are much more significant than your chances of encountering this killer. The point being, news coverage that produces panic is irresponsible and even counterproductive—''

"Counterproductive to what? You keeping your job?'' asked a *Star-Tribune* editorialist.

"I resent that,'' snapped Daniel.

"I don't think it was entirely appropriate,'' the paper's publisher commented mildly.

"He doesn't have to worry about it anyway,'' said the Minneapolis mayor, who was sitting at the foot of the table. "Chief Daniel is doing an excellent job and I intend to reappoint him to another term, whatever the outcome of this investigation.''

Daniel glanced at the mayor and nodded.

"We have a problem here," said the station manager for TV3. "This is the most intensely interesting story in the area right now. I've never seen anything like it. If we deliberately deemphasize the coverage and our colleagues over at Channel Eight and Channel Six and Channel Twelve don't, we could get hurt in terms of ratings. We don't have newspaper circulation counts to go by, the ratings are our lifeblood. And since we're the top-rated station—"

"Only at ten; not at six," interjected the Channel Eight manager.

"And since we're the overall top-rated station," the TV3 manager continued, "we have the most to lose. Frankly, I doubt our ability to work out any kind of agreement that everybody would hold to. There's too much in the balance."

"How about if me and a bunch of other cops went through the force man by man and told them how a particular station was hurting us with their coverage? How about if we asked each and every cop, from the watch commanders on down, not to talk to that station? In other words, shut down one station's contacts with the police force. Froze you out. Would that have an impact on ratings?" asked Lucas.

"Now, that's a dangerous proposition," said the representative from the St. Paul papers.

"If we get some media-generated panic, *that*'s a dangerous proposition," Lucas said. "If some kid who's living in the dorm comes home from the university at night unexpectedly, and his old man blows him away because he thinks it's the maddog, whose fault is that going to be? Whose fault for building up the fear?"

"That's not fair," said the TV3 manager.

"Sure it is. You just don't want it to be," Lucas said.

"Calm down, lieutenant," the mayor said after a moment of silence. He looked down the table. "Look, all we're asking you to do is not to hammer so hard. I timed Channel Eight last night, and you gave more than seven minutes to this case in four separate segments. In terms of television news, I think that's overkill. There almost *weren't* any other stories. I'm just suggesting that everybody look at every piece of coverage and ask, 'Is this necessary? Will this really build ratings? And what if Chief Daniel and the mayor and the City Council and the state legislators get really angry and start talking about the irresponsible press and mentioning names? Will that help ratings?' ''

"Bottom line, then, you're saying don't make us mad," said the news director from Channel Twelve.

"Bottom line, I'm saying, 'Be responsible.' If you're not, you could pay for it."

"That sounds like a threat," said the news director.

The mayor shrugged. "You take a dramatic view of things."

As they went through the lobby on the way to the street, Daniel looked at the mayor.

"I appreciate that thing about the reappointment," he said.

"Don't go out and celebrate yet," the mayor said through his teeth. "I could change my mind if you don't catch this asshole."

CHAPTER
— 20 —

The two days between the taking and the discovery of the body had been days of delicious anticipation. The maddog relaxed; he smiled. His secretary thought him almost charming. Almost. Except for the lips.

The maddog ran the tapes over and over, watching McGowan report from the Wheatcroft scene.

"This is Annie McGowan reporting from the scene of the latest in the series of killings by the man called maddog," she said, her lips making sensual O's. "Minneapolis Police Chief Quentin Daniel himself is inside this house just three blocks from the University of Minnesota campus. It was here that a crippled law student, Cheryl Wheatcroft, celebrated as one of the best minds of her law-school class, was tortured, stabbed to death, and sexually mutilated by a man police say is little better than a wild beast . . ."

He liked it. He even liked the "wild beast." The "pig farmer" was gone, forgotten. He reveled in the papers, read the stories over and over, lay on his bed and reran the memory of Wheatcroft dying. He masturbated, the face of Annie McGowan growing prominent in his visions.

The media reaction built through the weekend, culminating in three pages of coverage in the Minneapolis Sunday paper, a smaller but more analytical spread in the St. Paul paper. On Monday, the coverage died. There was almost nothing, which puzzled him. Burnt out already?

That afternoon, he went to the county recorder's office and politely introduced himself as a lawyer doing real-estate-tax research. He showed them his card and they instructed him in the use of computerized tax files. McGowan? The names ran up the computer monitor: McGowan, Adam, Aileen, Alexis, Annie. There she was. A sole owner. Nice neighborhood.

The computer gave him square footages, prices. He would need more research. He went from the computer files to the plat books and looked at the neighborhood maps.

"If you need aerial photos, you'll find them in those cases over there," said the clerk, smiling pleasantly. "They're filed the same way."

Aerial photos? Fine. He looked them over, picking out McGowan's house, noting its relationship to the neighboring houses, the garden sheds, the detached garage. He traced the alley behind the house with a fingertip. If he walked in from the north side, he could approach from the alley and go straight to the back door, pop it, and go in. If he came in early enough, when he knew McGowan was on the air, he would have a chance to explore it. What if there was another occupant? Easy enough to find out; that was what the telephone was for. He would call night and day, while she was working, looking for a different voice; he knew hers so well now. Maybe she had a roommate. He thought about that, closed his eyes. He could do a double. Two at the same time.

But that didn't feel right. A taking was personal, one-to-one. It was to be shared, not multiplied. Three's a crowd.

The maddog left the recorder's office and walked through another glorious fall day to the library, to the crime section, and began pulling out confessional books by burglars. They were intended, their authors said, to help homeowners protect their property.

From a different perspective, they were also a short course in burglary. He had studied a couple of them before he went into Carla Ruiz' studio. They helped. The maddog believed in libraries.

He thumbed through the books, picked the four best that he hadn't read. As he walked out of the stacks, past rows of books on crime and criminals, the name "Sam" caught his eye. Son of Sam. He had read about Sam, but not this particular book. He took it.

Outside in the sunshine, the maddog took a deep breath and watched the people scurrying by. Ants, he thought. But it was hard to take the thought too seriously. The day was too good for that. Like early spring in Texas. The maddog was not unaffected.

The burglary books gave him material for contemplation; the Sam book, even more.

Sam should not have been caught, not when he was.

On his last mission, as the maddog thought of it, he had shot a young couple, killing one, wounding and blinding the other. He had parked some distance away, near a fire hydrant. His car had been ticketed.

A woman out walking her dog had seen both the ticketing and, later, a man running to the car and driving away. When the latest Sam murders hit the press, she called the police. There had been only a few tickets given in the area at that time of night, and only one for parking at a hydrant. The police were able to read the car's license number off the carbon of the ticket. Sam was caught.

The maddog was reading in bed. He dropped the book on his chest and stared at the ceiling. He had known this story, but had forgotten it. He thought about his last note, the one dropped on Wheatcroft. *Isolate yourself from random discovery,* it said. He thought about his car. All it would take was a ticket. Now that he thought about it, it was a certainty that police were checking tickets issued near the killings.

He tossed the book on the bed and padded out to the kitchen, heated water in a teakettle, and made a cup of instant cocoa. Cocoa was one of his favorites. As soon as the hot bittersweet chocolate hit his tongue, he was back at the ranch, standing in the kitchen with . . . Whom? He shook it off and went back to the bedroom.

He had done it right with Wheatcroft. He had driven so that he wouldn't be seen leaving his house on foot. He had parked and walked in to the killing so that his car wouldn't be spotted at the crime scene.

Walk in to the killing. Keep the car out of the way. Make sure, make doubly sure, that the car was legally parked. And get it close enough to the house that he could reach it in a minute or so, at a run, but far enough away that it would not be immediately remembered as being a strange car near the site of a killing.

Five blocks? What would five blocks be? He got out a sheet of paper and drew streets and blocks. All right, if he parked five blocks away, the cops would have to check some fifty blocks before they got as far out as his car.

If he parked six blocks out from McGowan's house, they'd have to check seventy-two blocks. It would be double that if it weren't for that damned creek across the street.

He looked at his map and figured. If he parked north of her house, he could get six blocks out along the end blocks, which were narrow. He would also have access to alleys that came out of the end blocks, good places to hide, if hiding became critical.

The plat books had indicated that the lots were seventy feet deep, with a fifteen-foot alley. The streets were thirty feet. He figured on his piece of paper. A little over two hundred yards. He should be able to run that in less than a minute. He got up, went back into the kitchen, found a city map in a drawer, and counted up six blocks.

Not six blocks, he thought. Five blocks would be better. If he parked five blocks up, he'd be on a street that had access to Interstate 35. Once in the car, he could be on the highway in less than a minute, even driving at the speed limit.

He closed his eyes and visualized it. At a dead run, panic situation, it was two minutes from her house to the highway. Once on the highway, eight minutes to his garage. He would have to think.

The maddog got McGowan's phone number from a city cross-reference directory. Called her at home, spoke to her: "Phyllis? . . . Sorry, I must have misdialed," he said. Called back. Called back again. An answering machine, but never a strange voice.

The maddog did one reconnaissance. He did it in his midnight-blue Thunderbird.

Sunday afternoon. Annie McGowan was visiting her parents in Brookings, South Dakota. She was due back to work on Monday. There were still cops watching her house, one in front, from the architect's, one in back, from the retired couple's house. The cops out on the wings, in cars, had been temporarily withdrawn while McGowan was out of town.

With McGowan gone, it was hard to take the surveillance seriously. The cop at the post in back was reading through a stack of 1950's comic books he'd found in the attic, wondering about the possibility of stealing them. God only knew what they were worth, and the old couple certainly didn't seem to care about them or even remember they were there. Every two or three minutes the cop would glance out the window at the back of McGowan's house. But everyone knew the maddog never attacked on a weekend. He wasn't paying much attention.

He was reading a *Superman* when the maddog rolled past in front. If the maddog had driven down the alley behind the house, the cop would have seen him for sure—would have heard the car going by—and might have caught him or identified him right there. But a garbage can had fallen over at the far end of the alley. When the maddog started to turn in, he saw it, considered it, and backed out. No point in being seen outside the car, in daylight, fooling around with somebody else's garbage can.

The cop in the architect's house, across the street from McGowan's, should have seen him go by in front. He knew the maddog might be driving a dark-colored Thunderbird. But when the maddog went past, he was downstairs, his head in the refrigerator, deciding between a yogurt and a banana to go with the caffeine-free Diet Coke. He was in no hurry to get back to the attic. The attic was boring.

All told, he was away from the window for twenty minutes, although it seemed like only four or five. When he got back, he opened the yogurt and looked out the window. A kid up the street was washing his old man's car. A dog was watching him work. Nothing else. The maddog had come and gone.

And the maddog thought to himself: Tomorrow night.

CHAPTER
— 21 —

When Lucas pulled in, Carla was sitting in the yard, wrapped in an old cardigan sweater with a drawing pad in her lap. He got out of the car, walked through the dry leaves, deep-breathing the crystalline North Woods air.

"Great day," he said. He dropped beside her and looked at the pad. She was drawing the forms of the fallen leaves with sepia chalk on blue-tinted paper. "And that's nice."

"I think—I'm not sure—but I think I'm going to get the best weavings I ever did out of this stuff," Carla said. She frowned. "One of the problems with the form is that the best of it is symbolic but the best art is antisymbolic."

"Right," Lucas said. He flopped back in the leaves and looked up at the faultless blue sky. A light south wind rippled the surface of the lake.

"Sounds like baloney, doesn't it?" she asked, smiling, her face crinkling at the corners of her eyes.

"Sounds like business," he said. He turned his head and saw a cluster of small green plants pushing up through the dead leaves. He reached out and picked a few of the shiny green leaves.

"Close your eyes," he said, holding his hand out toward her and crumbling the leaves in his fingertips. She closed her eyes and he held the crumbled leaves beneath her nose. "Now, sniff."

She sniffed and smiled and opened her eyes. "It's the candy," she said in delight. "Wintergreen?"

"Yeah. It grows all over the place." She took the crumbled

leaves from him and sniffed again. "God, it smells like the outdoors."

"You still want to go back?"

"Yes," she said, a note of regret strong in her voice. "I have to work. I've got a hundred drawings and I have to start doing something with them. And I called my gallery in Minneapolis and I've sold a couple of good pieces. I've got money waiting."

"You could almost start making a living at this," Lucas said wryly.

"Almost. They tell me a man from Chicago, a gallery owner, saw some of my pieces. He wants to talk to me about a deal. So I've got to get going."

"You can come back. Anytime."

Carla stopped drawing for a minute and patted his leg. "Thanks. I'd like to come back in the spring, maybe. You've no idea what this month has done for me. God, I've got so much work, I can't even fathom it. I needed this."

"Go back Tuesday night?"

"Fine."

Lucas rolled to his feet and walked down to the dock, looked at his boat. It was a fourteen-foot fiberglass tri-hull with a twenty-five-horsepower Johnson outboard mounted on the back. A small boat, wide open, just right for fishing musky. There was a scum line around the hull. The boat had not been used enough during the fall.

He walked back up the bank. "I'm going to have to take the boat out before we leave," he said. "It hasn't been getting much use. The maddog has killed the fall."

"And I've been too busy walking in the woods to go out on the water," Carla said simply.

"Want to go fishing? Now?"

"Sure. Give me ten minutes to finish this." She looked up and across the lake. "God, what a day."

In the afternoon, after lunch, they walked back into the woods. Carla carried the pistol on her belt. At the base of the hill, firing at the cutbank from twenty yards, she put eighteen consecutive shots into an area the size of a large man's hand. They were dead center on the silhouette she'd sketched in the sand. When she fired the last round, she put the muzzle of the pistol to her lips and nonchalantly blew off the nonexistent smoke.

"That's decent," Lucas said.

"Decent? I thought it was pretty great."

"Nope. Just decent," Lucas repeated. "If you ever have to use it, you'll have to make the decision in a second or so, maybe in the dark, maybe with the guy rushing you. It'll be different."

"Jeez. What's the use?"

"Wait a minute," Lucas said hastily. "I don't mean to put you down. That's really pretty good. But don't get a big head."

"Like I said, pretty great." She grinned up at him. "What do you think of the holster? Pretty neat, huh?" She had sewn a rose into the black nylon flap.

Much later that night she blew in his navel and looked up and said, "This could be the best vacation I ever had. Including the next couple of days. I want to ask you a question, but I don't want to ruin it."

"It won't. I can't think of any question that would ruin it."

"Well. First we have a preamble."

"I love preambles; I hope you finish with a postscript. Even an index would be okay, or maybe—"

"Shut up. Listen. Besides being a vacation, I've gotten an enormous amount of work done up here. I think I've broken through. I think I'm going to be an artist like I've never been an artist before. But I've met men like you . . . there's a painter in St. Paul who's an awful lot like you in some ways . . . and you're going to move on to other women. I know it, that's okay. The thing is, when you do, can we still be friends? Can I still come up here?"

Lucas laughed. "Nothing like a little honesty to destroy an incipient hard-on."

"We can get it back," she said. "But I want to know—"

"Listen. I don't know what's going to happen to us. I have had . . . a number of relationships over the years and a lot of the women are still friends of mine. A couple of them come up here, in fact. Not like this, for a month at a time, but for weekends. Sometimes we sleep together. Sometimes we don't, if the relationship has changed. We just come up and hang out. So. . ."

"Good," she said. "I'm not going to fall apart when we break it off. In fact, I'm going to be so busy I don't know if I could keep a relationship together. But I would like to come back."

"Of course you would. That's why my friends call it a pussy trap—ouch, ouch, let go, goddammit. . . ."

"You got a minute?" Sloan leaned in the doorway. He was sucking on a plastic cigarette substitute.

"Sure."

Lucas had gotten back to Minneapolis so relaxed that he felt as though his spine had been removed. The feeling lasted for fifteen sour minutes at police headquarters, talking to Anderson, getting his notebook updated. He had wandered down to his office, the North Woods mood falling apart. As he put the key in his door, Sloan appeared up the hallway, saw him, and walked down.

"Remember me talking about this Oriental-art guy?" Sloan asked as he lowered himself into Lucas' spare chair.

"Yeah. Something there?"

"Something. I don't know what. I wonder if you might have a few words with him."

"If it'll help."

"I think it might," Sloan said. "I'm mostly good at sweet talk. This guy needs something a little harder."

Lucas glanced at his watch. "Now?"

"Sure. If you've got time."

Alan Nester was crouched over a tiny porcelain dish, his back to the door, when they walked in. Lucas glanced around.

An Oriental carpet covered a parquet floor. A very few objects in porcelain, ceramics, and jade were displayed in blond oak cabinetry. The very sparsity of offerings hinted at a storehouse of art elsewhere. Nester pivoted at the sound of the door chimes and a frown creased his lean pale face.

"Sergeant Sloan," he said crossly. "I told you quite clearly that I have nothing to contribute."

"I thought you should talk to Lieutenant Davenport here," Sloan said. "I thought maybe he could explain things more clearly."

"You know what we're investigating, and Sergeant Sloan has the feeling that you're holding something back," Lucas said. He picked up a delicate china vase and squinted at it. "We really can't permit that . . . Ah, I'm sorry, I didn't mean to make that sound so severe. But the thing is, we need every word we can get. Everything. If you're holding back something, it must have some importance or you wouldn't hold it back. You see where we're coming from?"

"But I'm not holding back," Nester cried in exasperation. He stood up, a tall man, but thin, like a blue heron, and stepped across the rug and took the vase from Lucas' hand. "Please don't touch anything. This is delicate material."

"Yeah?" Lucas said. As Nester replaced the vase, he picked up a small ceramic bowl.

"All we want to know," he said, "is everything that happened at the Rice house. And then we'll go away. No sweat."

Nester's eyes narrowed as he watched Lucas holding the small bowl by its rim.

"Excuse me for a second." He crossed to a glass case at the end of the room, picked up a telephone, and dialed.

"Yes, this is Alan Nester. Let me speak to Paul, please. Quickly." He looked across the room at Lucas as he waited. "Paul? This is Alan. The police officers came back, and one of them is holding a S'ung Dynasty bowl worth seventeen thousand dollars by its very rim, obviously threatening to drop it. I have nothing to tell them, but they won't believe me. Could you come down? . . . Oh? That would be fine. You have the number."

Nester put the receiver back on the hook. "That was my attorney," he said. "If you wait here a moment, you can expect a phone call either from your chief or from the deputy mayor."

"Hmph," Lucas said. He smiled, showing his eyeteeth. "I guess we're really not welcome, are we?" He carefully set the bowl back on its shelf and turned to Sloan. "Let's go," he said.

Outside, Sloan glanced sideways at him. "That wasn't much."

"We'll be back," Lucas said contentedly. "You're absolutely right. The motherfucker is hiding something. That's good news. Somebody has something to hide in the maddog case, and we know it."

They called Mary Rice from a street phone. She agreed to talk to them. Sloan led the way up to the house and knocked.

"Mrs. Rice?"

"You're the policemen."

"Yes. How are you feeling?" Mary Rice's face had gotten old, her skin a ruddy yellow and brown, tight and hard, like an orange left too long in a refrigerator.

"Come in, don't let the cold in," she said. It wasn't quite a moan. The house was intolerably hot, but Mary Rice was wrapped in a heavy Orlon cardigan and wore wool slacks. Her nose was red and swollen.

"We talked to the man who bought the ivory carvings from your husband," Sloan said as they settled around the kitchen table. "And we're wondering about him. Did your—"

"You think he's the killer?" she asked, her eyes round.

"No, no, we're just trying to get a better reading on him," Sloan said. "Did your husband say anything about him that you thought was unusual or interesting?"

Her forehead wrinkled in concentration. "No . . . no, just that he bought them little carvings and asked if Larry had any other things. You know, old swords and stuff. Larry didn't."

"Did they talk about anything else?"

"No, I don't know . . . Larry said this man was kind of in a hurry and didn't want any coffee or anything. Just gave him the money and left."

Sloan looked at Lucas. Lucas thought a minute and asked, "What did these carvings look like, anyway?"

"I still got one," she offered. "It's the last one. Larry gave it to me as a keepsake when we were married. You could look at that."

"If you could."

Rice tottered off to the back of the house. She returned a few minutes later and held her hand out to Lucas. Nestled in her palm was a tiny ivory mouse. Lucas picked it up, looked at it, and caught his breath.

"Okay," he said after a minute. "Can we borrow this, Mrs. Rice? We can give you a receipt."

"Sure. But I don't need no receipt. You're cops."

"Okay. We'll get it back to you."

Outside, Sloan said, "What?"

"I think we've got our friend Alan Nester by the short and curlies, but I also think I know what he's lying about. And it isn't the maddog," Lucas said gloomily. He opened his hand to look at the mouse. "Everything I know about art you could write on the back of a postage stamp. But look at this thing. Nester bought fifteen of them for five hundred bucks. I bet this thing is worth five hundred bucks by itself. I've never seen anything like it. Look at the expression on the mouse's face. If this isn't worth five hundred bucks, I'll kiss your ass on the courthouse lawn."

They were both peering into Lucas' hand. The mouse was exquisite, its tiny front and back legs clenching a straw, so that a hole ran between the legs from front to back. "They must have used it for something, a button or something," Lucas said.

Sloan looked up and Lucas turned to follow his gaze. A patrol car was in the street, almost at a stop, the two cops peering out the driver's-side window at them.

"They think we're doing a dope deal," Sloan laughed. He pulled his badge and walked toward the car. The cops rolled down the window and Lucas called, "Want to see a great-lookin' mouse?"

The Institute of Art was closed by the time they left Rice's house, and Lucas took the mouse home overnight. It sat on a stack of books in his workroom, watching him as he finished the last of the hit tables on the Everwhen game.

"God damn, I'd like to have you," Lucas said just before he went to bed. Early the next morning he got up and looked at it first thing. He thought it might have moved in the night.

It took a while to find out about it. Lucas picked up Sloan at his house. Sloan's wife came out with him and said, "I've heard so much about you I feel like I know you."

"It's all good, I expect."

She laughed and Lucas liked her. She said, "Take care of Sloan," and went back inside.

"Even my wife calls me Sloan," Sloan said as they drove away.

A curator at the art institute took one look at the mouse, whistled, and said, "That's a good one. Let's get the books."

"How do you know it's a good one?" Lucas asked as he tagged along behind.

"Because it looks like it might walk around at night," the curator said.

The search took time. Sloan was wandering through the photo gallery when Lucas returned.

"What?" he said, looking up.

"Eight thousand," Lucas said to him.

"For what? For the mouse or for all fifteen?"

"For the mouse. That's his low estimate. He said it could be twice as much at an auction. So if it's eight thousand and the others are as good, Nester paid a man dying of cancer five hundred dollars for netsukes worth something between a hundred and twenty thousand dollars and a quarter-million." He said "net-skis."

"Whoa." Sloan was nonplussed. The amounts were too big. "That's what they are? Net-skis?"

"I guess. That's what the curator was saying."

"I didn't know."

"I bet Alan Nester does."

They stopped at Rice's house.

"Eight thousand dollars?" she said in wonderment. A tear trickled down one cheek. "But he bought fifteen of them . . ."

"Mrs. Rice, I expect that when your husband asked Mr. Nester to come over here, all he really wanted was an evaluation so he could sell them later, isn't that what you told us?" Lucas asked.

"Well, I don't really remember . . ."

"I remember your saying that in the first interview," Sloan said insistently.

"Well, maybe," she said doubtfully.

"Because if he did, then he cheated you," Lucas said insistently. "He committed a fraud, and you could recover them."

"Well, that's what he come over for, to valuate them," Mary Rice said, nodding her head vigorously, her memory suddenly clearing up. She picked up the mouse, handling it tenderly. "Eight thousand dollars."

"Now what? Get a warrant?" Sloan asked. They were on the walk outside Rice's house again.

"Not yet," Lucas said. "I don't know if we have enough. Let's hit Nester first. Tell him what we've got, ask him to cooperate on the gun thing. Tell him if he cooperates, we'll let it go as a civil matter between his attorney and Rice's attorney. If he doesn't, we get a warrant, bust him, and put it in the press. How he ripped off a man who was dying of cancer and was trying to leave something for his wife."

"Oooh, that's ugly." Sloan smiled. "I like it."

"Where's Nester?"

The man behind the counter was small, dark, and much younger than Nester.

"He's not here," the man said. There was a chill in the

air; Lucas and Sloan didn't look like customers. "Might I ask who is inquiring?"

"Police. We need to talk to him."

"I'm afraid you can't," the young man said, raising his eyebrows. "He left for Chicago at noon. He'll already be there and I have no idea where he's staying."

"Shit," Sloan said.

"When's he due back?" Lucas asked.

"Tuesday morning. He should be in by noon."

"Do you have any netsukes?" Sloan asked.

The young man's eyebrows went up again. "I believe we do, but you'd have to ask Alan. He handles all the more expensive items."

CHAPTER
— 22 —

Lucas took off his coat and tossed it on the mattress. The two surveillance cops, one tall, one short, were sitting on folding chairs, facing each other, with another chair between them. They were playing gin, the cards laid out on the seat of the middle chair. One of the cops watched the window while the other surveyed his hand. They were good at it. Their shift covered the prime time.

"Nothing?" asked Lucas.

"Nothing," said the tall cop.

"Anything from the cars?"

"Not a thing."

"Who's in them?"

"Davey Johnson and York, up north, behind McGowan's. Sally Johnson and Sickles, out east. Blaney is over on the west side with a new guy, Cochrane. I don't know him."

"Cochrane's that tall blond kid, plays basketball in the league," the short cop chipped in. He fanned his cards, dropped them on the seat of the chair between them, and said, "Gin."

A radio against one wall played golden-oldie rock. A police radio sat silently next to it.

"He's about due," Lucas said, peering out into the street.

"This week," the short one agreed. "Which is odd, when you think about it."

"What's odd?"

"Well, one of the notes he left said something about 'Don't set a pattern.' So what does he do? He kills somebody every two weeks. That's a pattern if I ever saw one."

"He kills when he needs to," Lucas said. "The need builds up, and eventually he can't stand it."

"Takes two weeks to build up?"

"Looks like it."

The police radio burped and all three of them turned to look at it. "Car," it said. And a moment later, "This is Cochrane. It's a red Pontiac Bonneville."

The tall cop leaned back, picked up a microphone, and said, "Watch it. It's the right size, even if it's the wrong color."

"Coming your way," Cochrane said. "We got the tag, we'll run it."

Lucas and the surveillance cop watched the car roll down the street and ease to the curb two houses down. It sat with its lights on for one minute, two, and Lucas said, "I'm going down there."

He was at the stairs when the tall cop said, "Hold it."

"What?"

"It's the girl."

"High-school girl down the street," said the short cop. "She's going up to the house now. Must be a date."

Lucas walked back in time to see her going through the porch door. The car left.

"Could be something going on with her phones," the short cop said a while later. The phone-monitoring station was at the other surveillance post, behind McGowan's house.

"What? You mean McGowan's?" asked Lucas.

"There were a bunch of calls last week and over the weekend. There'd be a whole group, a half-hour apart, more or less. But whoever it is doesn't leave a message on the answering machine. The machine answers and they hang up."

"Everybody does that—hangs up on machines," Lucas said.

"Yeah, but this is a little different. It's the first time it's happened, for one thing, a bunch of calls. And she has an unlisted number. If it was a friend, you'd think he'd leave a message instead of calling over and over."

"It's like somebody's checking on her," said the tall cop.

"Can't trace them?"

"It's two rings and click, he's gone."

"Maybe we ought to change the machine," said Lucas.

"Maybe. She's due home in, what, an hour and a half?"

"Something like that."

"We could do it then. Set it for five rings."

Lucas went back to the mattress and the two cops started the gin game again.

"What do I owe you?" asked the tall cop.

"Hundred and fifty thousand," said the short one.

"One game, double or nothing?"

Lucas grinned, closed his eyes, and tried to think about Alan Nester. Something there. Probably the fear that the netsuke purchase would be discovered and questioned. The purchase bordered on fraud. That was almost certainly it. Damn. What else was there?

Half an hour later, the cop radio burped again.

"This is Davey," a voice said, carrying an edge of excitement. "It's showtime, folks."

Lucas rolled to his feet and the tall cop reached back and grabbed the microphone.

"What do you got, Davey?"

"We got a single white male dressed in dark slacks, dark jacket, dark gloves, watch cap, dark shoes, on foot," Davey Johnson said. Johnson had been on the street for years. He didn't get excited without reason, and his voice was crackling with intensity. "He's heading your way, coming right down the street toward you guys. If he's heading for McGowan's, he'll be in sight of the side of the back-lot house in one minute. This dude's up to something, man, he ain't out for no country stroll."

"York with you?"

"He's gone on foot, behind this guy, staying out of sight. I'm staying with the unit. God damn, he's walking right along, he's crossing the street, you other guys out on the wings, start moving up, goddam—"

"We see him out the side windows of our house," said a new voice.

"That's Kennedy at the other post," the tall cop said to Lucas.

Lucas turned and headed for the stairs. "I'm going."

"He's going in the alley," he heard Kennedy call as he ran down the first few steps. "He's in her yard. You guys move . . ."

Lucas ran down the three flights of steps to the front door and brushed past the white-haired architect who stood in the hallway with a newspaper and a pipe, and ran out into the yard.

The maddog parked five blocks from McGowan's house, facing the Interstate. Checked the street signs. Parking was okay. Lots of cars on the same side of the street.

The weather had turned bad early in the morning. A cold rain fell for a while in the afternoon, died away, started again, stopped. Now it felt like snow. The maddog left the car door unlocked. Not much of a risk in this neighborhood.

The sidewalk was still damp, and he walked along briskly, one arm swinging, the other holding a short, wide pry bar next to his side. Just the thing for a back door.

Down one block, another, three, four, onto McGowan's block. A car started somewhere and the maddog turned his head in that direction, slowed. Nothing more. He glanced quickly around, just once, knowing that furtiveness attracts attention all by itself. His groin began to tingle with the preentry excitement. This would be a masterpiece. This would set the town on its ear. This would make him more famous than Sam, more famous than Manson.

Maybe not Manson, he thought.

He turned into the alley. Another car engine. Two cars? He walked down the alley, reached McGowan's yard, glanced around again, took a half-dozen steps into the yard. A car's wheel squealed in deceleration a block away, the other end of the alley.

Cops.

In that instant, when the turning wheels squealed against the blacktop, he knew he had been suckered.

Knew it. Cops.

He ran back the way he had come.

Another car, down the block. A tremendous clatter behind him; one of the cars had hit something. More cops. A door slammed. Across the street. Another one, behind Mc-Gowan's.

He turned out of the alley, the pry bar slipping from beneath his jacket and falling to the grass, and he ran across the yard one house down from McGowan's, through bridal wreath, running in the night, hit a lilac bush, fell, people shouting, "Hold it hold it hold it . . ."

The maddog ran.

The rookie Cochrane was at the wheel, and tires squealed as he slowed and cranked left into the alley, an unintended squeal, and his partner blurted "Jesus!" and quick as a turning rat, they saw the maddog run into the alley ahead of them. Cochrane wrenched the car straight in the alley, smashed through two empty garbage cans, and went after him.

The maddog was running between houses when the other wing car burst into the alley toward them and Cochrane almost hit it. The other car's doors flew open and the two cops inside leapt out and went after the maddog. Cochrane's partner, Blaney, yelled, "Go round, go round into the street . . ." and Cochrane swung the car past the other unit toward the street at the end of the alley.

Sally Johnson jumped out of her car and saw Lucas coming from across the street, running in a white shirt, and she turned and ran after her partner, Sickles, between houses as Cochrane's car cranked around her car and went out toward the street.

The maddog had already crossed the next street, and Sally Johnson snatched her radio from her belt carrier and tried to transmit, but couldn't find words as she ran fifteen feet behind Sickles, Sickles with his gun out. Another cop, York, came in from the side and behind her, gun out, and Sally Johnson tried to get her gun out and saw the maddog go over a board fence across the street and dead ahead.

The maddog, fear and adrenaline blinding him to anything but the tunnel of space in front of him, space with no cops, sprinted across the street, as fast as he had ever run, hit the board fence, and vaulted it in a single motion. He could never have done it if he'd thought about it, the fence four feet high, as high as his chest, but he took it like an Olympian and landed in a yard with an empty swimming pool, a small boat wrapped in canvas, and a dog kennel.

The dog kennel had two separate compartments with rugs for doors and inside each compartment was a black-and-tan Doberman pinscher, one named July and the other named August.

August heard the commotion and pricked up his ears and poked his head out and just then the maddog came sailing over the fence, staggered, sprinted across the yard, and went over the back fence. Either dog could have taken him, if they'd had the slightest idea he was coming. As it was, July, exploding from her kennel, got his leg for an instant, raked it, and then the man was gone. But there was more business coming. July had no more than lost the one over the back fence than another came over the front.

The maddog never saw the Doberman until it was closing in from the side. And a good thing, because he might have hesitated. He saw it just as he hit the fence, a dark shadow at his feet, and felt the ripping pain in his calf as he went over the back fence.

Carl Werschel and his wife, Lois, were almost ready for bed when the dogs went crazy in the backyard.

"What's that?" Lois asked. She was a nervous woman. She worried about being raped on a remote North Woods highway by gangs of black biker rapists, though neither she nor anyone else had seen a black biker gang in the North Woods. Nevertheless, it was clear in her dreams, the bikers hunched over her, ravens circling overhead, as they did the foul deed on what seemed to be the hood of a '47 Cadillac. "It sounds like . . ."

"Wait here," Carl said. He was a very fat man who worried about black biker gangs himself and had stockpiled both ammo and plenty of camouflage clothing against the day. He got the Remington twelve-gauge pump from beneath the headboard and hustled for the back door, jacking a shell into the chamber as he went.

Just for an instant, Sickles, who was forty-five, felt a little kick of joy as he cleared the board fence. He was forty feet and one fence behind the maddog and he was in good shape, and with any luck, with the other guys coming in from the side . . .

The dogs hit him like a hurricane and he went down, clenching his gun but losing the flashlight he'd had in the other hand. The dogs were at his shoulders, his back, going crazy, barking, snarling, ripping his hands, the back of his neck . . .

Sally Johnson cleared the fence and almost landed in the tight ball of fury around Sickles, and one of the dogs turned toward her, slavering, coming, and Sally Johnson shot the dog twice and then the other one was coming and she turned and aimed the pistol, aware of Sickles on his hands and knees off to the left, enough clearance, and she pulled the trigger once, twice . . .

Carl Werschel ran out his side door with the twelve-gauge and saw the young punk in jeans and black jacket shooting his dogs, shooting them down. He yelled "Stop!" but he didn't really mean "Stop," he meant "Die," and with an atavistic Prussian-warrior joy he fired the shotgun at a thirty-foot range into Sally Johnson's young head. The last thing

Sally Johnson saw was the long muzzle of the gun coming up, and she wished she could say something on the radio to stop it from happening. . . .

Sickles felt the dogs go, and he started to roll out, when the long finger of fire reached out and knocked back the partner who had just saved him from the dogs. He knew that much, that he'd been saved. The finger of fire flashed again and Sally went down. Sickles had been around long enough to think, "Shotgun," and the cops' tone poem muttered somewhere in his unconscious as he rolled half-blind with blood: "Two in the belly, one in the head, knocks a man down and kills him dead." He fired three times, one shot piercing Werschel's belly, wiping out his liver, knocking him backward, the second shot ruining his heart. Werschel was dead before he hit the ground, though his mind ticked over for a few more seconds. Sickles' third shot went through the wall of the house, into the dining room, through a china cabinet and a stack of plates inside it, through the opposite wall, and, as far as cops investigating later could prove, into outer space. The slug was never found.

When Werschel opened up with the shotgun, the maddog had crossed the street and had fallen into a trench being dug to replace a storm sewer. It was full of wet, yellow clay. He clambered out the far side, a mud ball, not understanding why he had not yet been caught.

And he would have been, except that the north car, with Davey Johnson on board, had closed onto the block when the shotgun blast lit up the neighborhood. Johnson dumped the unit and headed into the fight. His partner, York, on foot, had been caught in mid-block when the maddog changed direction, hadn't seen it happen, and wound up running behind Sickles and Sally Johnson and just ahead of Lucas, who had cut across McGowan's yard.

Cochrane and Blaney had driven out of the alley intending to turn north, in the direction the maddog was running, when the firefight started. The firefight took all priority. They assumed Sickles and Sally Johnson had cornered the maddog, found him armed, and shot it out. And when the bad guy's shooting a shotgun . . . Like Davey Johnson, they dumped their car and went in on foot.

Lucas had just crossed the fence, gun in hand, screaming for someone to call for ambulances and backup, when the maddog got out of the ditch and ran through another blacked-out yard, across an alley, another yard, and on. In forty seconds he reached his car. In another minute he was nearing the Interstate. No lights behind him. Something had happened, but what?

In the Werschels' yard, Lucas was packing his shirt into a gaping hole in Sally Johnson's neck, knowing it was pointless, and Sickles was chanting *Oh my God, oh my God* and Cochrane came over the fence with his gun in his fist and shouted *What happened, what happened* and pointed at the dead Werschel and shouted *Is that him?*

Lois Werschel came out the side door of her house and called, "Carl?"

Blaney called for backup within a few seconds of the firefight. The radio tape later released to the media showed that it was six minutes later when Lucas called in with Cochrane's handset to request that all dark late-model Thunderbirds in South Minneapolis be frozen and the occupants checked.

The dispatcher momentarily lost it when she heard that a cop was down, and started calling for identity and condition and routing the ambulances and the backup into the neighborhood. She did not rebroadcast the request that all Thunderbirds be frozen for another two minutes, assuming that it was a lower priority than the other traffic. By that time, the maddog was passing downtown Minneapolis. Two minutes later he was at his exit, and less than a minute after that, waiting in the driveway as the automatic opener rolled up his garage door.

The paramedics got to the Werschels' house before the maddog got home, but it was too late for Sally Johnson and

Carl Werschel. The paramedics took one look at Werschel and wrote him off, but Sally still had a thin thready heartbeat and they started saline and tried to compress the neck wound and there was nothing to do about the head wound and they got her in the ambulance, where they lost the heartbeat, injected a stimulant, and started toward Hennepin Medical Center, but her pupils were fixed and dilated and they kept trying but they knew she was gone. . . .

Lucas knew she was gone. When they took her out, he stood on the boulevard outside the Werschel house and watched the flashers until they disappeared. Then he headed back to the fenced yard, where two more paramedics were working with Lois Werschel and Sickles, who were both descending into shock. Carl Werschel, looking like a beached whale, lay belly-up in a bed of brown, frost-killed marigolds.

"Who was that in the car, squealed the tires?" Lucas asked quietly. Blaney glanced at Cochrane and Lucas caught the glance and Cochrane opened his mouth to explain and Lucas hit him squarely in the nose. Cochrane went down and then the light hit them and Lucas grabbed Cochrane by the shirt and lifted him halfway to his feet and hit him again in the mouth with his other hand and York wrapped Lucas up from behind and wrestled him away.

"You motherfucker, you killed Sally, you ignorant shit-head," Lucas screamed and the light blinded him and York was hollering "Hold it hold it" and Cochrane was covering his broken nose and teeth with one hand and trying to push up off the ground with the other, his face cranked toward Lucas, his eyes wide with fear. Lucas struggled against York for a few seconds and finally slumped, relaxed, and York pushed him away and Lucas turned and saw the TV camera and lights over the fence, focused on the group in the yard. The figures behind the lights were unrecognizable and he started toward them, intending to pull down the lights, when Annie McGowan emerged from them and said, "Lucas? Did you get him?"

• • •

Daylight was leaking in the office windows when the meeting convened. Daniel's face look stretched, almost gaunt. He had not shaved, was not wearing a tie. Lucas had never seen him in the office without a tie. The two deputy chiefs looked stunned and fidgeted nervously in their chairs.

". . . don't understand why we didn't have automatic stop on all Thunderbirds the instant something started happening," Daniel was saying.

"We should have, but nobody decided who was going to call. When it went down and the fight started and Blaney started hollering for backup and then for the ambulances, we just lost it," said the surveillance crew's supervisor. "Lucas was on the air pretty quick, six minutes—"

"Six minutes, Jesus," said Daniel, leaning back in his chair, his eyes closed. He was talking calmly, but his voice was shaky. "If one of the surveillance crews had called the instant it started going down, it would have been rebroadcast and we'd have had cars on the way before Blaney got on the air. That would have eliminated the foul-up by the dispatcher. We'd have been eight minutes or nine minutes faster. If Lucas is right and he was parked up near the entrance to the Interstate, he was downtown having a drink by the time we started looking for his car."

There was a long silence.

"What about this Werschel guy?" asked one of the deputy chiefs.

Daniel opened an eye and looked at an assistant city attorney who sat at the back of the room, a briefcase between his feet.

"We haven't figured it out yet," the attorney said. "There's going to be some kind of lawsuit, but we were clearly within our rights to go into his yard in pursuit of the killer. Technically, his dogs should have been restrained, no matter how high the fence was. And when he came out and opened fire, Sickles was clearly within his rights to defend himself and his partner. He did right."

"So we got no problem there," said one of the deputy chiefs.

"A jury might give the wife a few bucks, but I wouldn't worry about it," the attorney said.

"Our problem," Daniel said in his remote voice, "is that this killer is still running around loose, and we look like a bunch of clowns running around killing civilians and each other. To say nothing of beating each other up afterward."

There was another silence. "Let's get back to work," Daniel said finally. "Lucas? I want to talk to you."

"What else you got?" he asked when they were alone.

"Not a thing. I had . . . a feeling about the McGowan thing—"

"Bullshit, Lucas, you set her up and you know it and I know it, and God help me, if we could do it again I'd say go ahead. It should have worked. Motherfucker. Motherfucker." Daniel pounded the top of his desk. "We had him in the palm of our hand. We had the fucker."

"I blew it," Lucas said moodily. "That gunfight went up and I came across the fence and saw Werschel lying there and I knew he wasn't the maddog because the maddog was all dressed in black. And Sally was down and still pumping some blood and Sickles was there to help her, and the other guys, and I should have kept going. I should have gone over the back fence after the maddog and left Sally to the other guys. I thought that. I had this impulse to keep going, but Sally was pumping blood and nobody else was moving . . ."

"You did all right," Daniel said, stopping the litany. "Hey, a cop got blown up right in front of you. It's only human to stop."

"I fucked up," Lucas said. "And now I don't have a thing to go on."

"Nails," Daniel said.

"What?"

"I can hear the media getting out the nails. We're going to be crucified."

"It's pretty hard to give a shit anymore," Lucas said.

"Wait for a couple days. You'll start giving a shit." He hesitated. "You say Channel Eight got some film of you and Cochrane?"

"Yeah. God damn, I'm sorry about that. He's a rookie. I just lost it."

"From what I hear, it's going to be pretty hard to take back what you said. Most of the cops out there think you're right. And Sally had some years in. If Cochrane had just taken it easy, he'd have been right down that alley before the maddog knew you were coming. You'd have squeezed him between you and nobody would ever have gone into the yard with those fuckin' dogs."

"Doesn't make it better to know how close we came," Lucas said.

"Get some sleep and get back here in the afternoon," Daniel said. "This thing should start shaking out by then. We'll know what to expect from the media. And we can start figuring out what to do next."

"I can't tell you what to do," Lucas said. "I'm running on empty."

CHAPTER
— 23 —

They didn't come for him.

Somewhere, in the back of his head, he couldn't believe it, that they didn't come for him.

He staggered through the connecting door from the garage into his apartment, took a step into the front room, realized that he was tracking sticky yellow clay onto the carpet, and stopped. He stood for a minute, breathing, reorganizing, then carefully stepped back onto the kitchen's tile floor and stripped. He took off everything, including his underwear, and left it in a pile on the floor.

His leg was bleeding and he sat on the edge of the bathtub and looked at it. The bites were not too deep, but they were ragged. In other circumstances, he would go to an emergency room and get stitches. He couldn't now. He washed the wounds carefully, with soap and hot water, ignoring the pain. When he had cleaned them as well as he could, he pulled the shower curtain around the tub and did the rest of his body. He washed carefully, his hands, his hair, his face. He paid special attention to his fingernails, where some of the clay might have lodged.

Halfway through the shower, he broke down and began to gag. He leaned against the wall, choking with adrenaline and fear. But he couldn't let himself go. He didn't have the luxury of it. Nor did he have the luxury of contemplating his situation. He must act.

The maddog fought to control himself. He finished washing, dried with a rough towel, and bandaged the leg wounds with gauze and adhesive tape. Then he went into the bedroom, dressed in clean clothes, and returned to the kitchen.

All of the clothing he'd worn that night was commonly available: Levi's, an ordinary turtleneck shirt, a black ski jacket purchased from an outdoor store. Jockey underwear. An unmarked synthetic watch cap. Running shoes. He emptied the pockets of the jacket. The Kotex pad, the gloves, the tape, the sock and potato, the pack of rubbers, all went into a pile on the floor. He'd lost the pry bar when he was running, but it should be clean; the cops wouldn't get anything from it. He carried the pile of clothing and shoes to the laundry room and dumped it in the washing machine.

With the clothes washing, he got a small vacuum cleaner, went out to the garage, and cleaned the car. Some of the clay was still damp and stuck tenaciously to the carpet. He went back in the house, got a bottle of dishwashing liquid and a pan, went back out, and carefully shampooed each area that showed a sign of the clay. If the cops sent the car to a crime laboratory, they might still find some particles of the stuff. He would have to think about it. And he would, for sure, vacuum it again after the damp carpet had dried.

When he was finished with the car, the maddog went back inside and checked the washing machine—the wash cycle was done—and transferred the clothing and shoes to the dryer. Then he found the box of surgeon's gloves he used in his attacks and pulled on a pair. From under the kitchen sink he got a roll of black plastic garbage bags, opened one, took the dust bag out of the vacuum, and threw it inside. Next he threw in the equipment he'd taken from his clothing, along with the box of remaining Kotex pads that he'd kept in a back closet.

Anything else? The potatoes. But that was ridiculous. Everyone had potatoes in the house. On the other hand, maybe there was some kind of genetic examination that could show they came from the same place. The potatoes went in the garbage bag.

The clothes were still in the dryer, and the maddog went back to the bedroom and pulled out the file of newspaper

clippings. SERIAL KILLER STALKS TWIN CITIES WOMEN said
the first. He slipped it out and read through it quickly, one
last time, as he carried the file to the bathroom. Removing
the clips one by one, he tore them into confetti and flushed
them down the toilet.

The clothes, when they were dry, went in another bag. By
eleven o'clock he had finished collecting all of his equipment
and the clothing he'd worn to McGowan's. He phoned a car-
rental agency at the airport and was told that it would be
open for another hour. He reserved a car on his Visa card,
called for a cab, rode out to the airport, signed for a car, and
brought it back. It would be best, he thought, to keep his car
off the streets for a while. There had been so much commotion back at McGowan's, the gunfire, the whole neighborhood must have waked up. If somebody had noticed his car
leaving . . . And the cops just might be desperate enough to
stop any Thunderbird they found on the highway, taking
names and running checks.

Back at the apartment, he loaded the garbage bags of clothing and equipment into the rental car. A few minutes after
midnight he drove onto Interstate 94, driving east, through
St. Paul and into Wisconsin. He stopped at each rest area
between St. Paul and Eau Claire, disposing of different pieces
of equipment and clothing in separate trashcans.

He'd paid a hundred and sixty dollars for the ski jacket and
hated to see it go. But it must go. It could have microscopic
particles of the yellow clay inextricably impressed in the fab-
ric. He couldn't throw it in a trashcan. It was too expensive.
Somebody might wonder why it had been discarded, and
publicity about the attempt on McGowan by a black-clad
maddog would be intense. He finally left the jacket hanging
on a hook in a rest room at an all-night truck stop, as though
it had been forgotten. With any luck, it would wind up in
Boise.

He had the same problem with the shoes. They were new
Reeboks, a fashionable mat black. He liked them. He pitched
them separately out the car window into the roadside ditch,
a mile or so apart. He would have to buy a new pair, to

replace his aging Nike Airs. He'd better stick with the Airs, he thought, just in case the cops found prints in that muddy ditch and matched them to Reeboks.

At Eau Claire the maddog checked into an out-of-the-way motel and paid with his Visa card. The receipt had no time stamp. Should the police someday come after him, the sleepy clerk almost certainly wouldn't remember him, much less what time he had arrived. And he would have a receipt to prove that he was in Eau Claire the night of the McGowan attack.

In his room, he stripped, showered again, and put a new dressing on the dog bites. By three in the morning it was all done and he was in bed, the lights out, the blankets pulled up under his chin.

Time to think. He lay awake in the dark and mentally retraced his steps from the car to McGowan's house. Down the dark side streets. The car starting. Where was he? The maddog had not yet turned into the alley. Then the second car starting.

They'd had McGowan's house under surveillance, he realized. They had ambushed him, and the ambush should have worked. Davenport? Almost certainly. He had been manipulated into an attack, probably with the woman's cooperation.

The maddog knew that he might someday be caught. He had no illusions about that. But he had supposed that if he were caught, it would be through a combination of uncontrollable and unforeseeable circumstances. He had imagined, in waking nightmares, the struggle with a woman, perhaps like the struggle with Carla Ruiz. And the intervention of another man, or maybe even a crowd; a lynch mob. Somehow, in these visions, the mob seemed to pursue him through a department store, with women's clothing racks flying helter-skelter and shoppers screaming and glass cases breaking. It was ludicrous, but felt real, the endless aisles of clothing through which he fled, with the crowd only a rack or two behind and closing on the flanks.

He had not imagined being manipulated, being tricked,

being suckered. He had not imagined *losing the game through inferior play.*

But he nearly had.

In the back of his head he still couldn't believe that they hadn't come for him. That they didn't now know who he was.

He reviewed in his mind the destruction of the evidence at his apartment. He had done a good job, he concluded, but was there a telling trace of mud somewhere? Was it possible that somebody had seen his car license?

The videotape. Damn. He had forgotten the videotape with the news broadcasts on it. But wait: he had never known when the news broadcasts would carry stories about the mad-dog, so he'd carefully taped whole broadcasts. Some carried nothing at all about the maddog . . . not that there had been many of those these last few weeks. So the tape should be okay. It wasn't as specific to the maddog as individual news-paper clips.

He felt a twinge of regret about the destruction of the clips. Maybe he could have kept them, maybe he should have car-ried them out to the car, and in Eau Claire tomorrow he could have rented a safe-deposit box. Too late. And probably fool-ish. When he was done with the women, when he was leaving the Twin Cities—maybe it was time—he could get copies from the library.

With the evening's events rattling through his mind like a pachinko ball, the maddog pulled the blankets a little higher, his calf now burning like fire, and waited for dawn.

CHAPTER
— 24 —

Before he went home, Lucas returned to McGowan's. There were a half-dozen squad cars, three city cars, and a technician's van at the Werschel house. Two more squads were parked in the street at McGowan's. A Channel Eight truck with a microwave remote dish mounted on top had backed into her yard and a half-dozen black cables snaked out of the back of the truck to the house and disappeared inside.

A patrol lieutenant saw Lucas coming down the sidewalk and got out of his car.

"Lucas. Thought you'd gone home," the lieutenant said.

"On my way. How's it look?"

"We're covering everything. We got some footprints out of that ditch, looks like he fell right in it. Could have hurt himself."

"Any blood?"

"No. But we put out a general alert to the hospitals with the description on the fliers and added some stuff about the clay. They should have an eye out for him."

"Good. Have you found anybody who saw him after he got out of the ditch? Further north?"

"Nobody so far. We're going to knock on doors six or seven blocks up—"

"Concentrate on the street that leads out to the expressway. I'd bet my left nut that's where he parked."

The lieutenant nodded. "We've already done that. Started while it was still dark, getting people out of bed. Nothing."

"How about the footprints? Anything clear?"

"Yeah. They're pretty good. He was wearing—"

"Nike Airs," Lucas interjected.

"No," the lieutenant said, his forehead wrinkling. "They were Reeboks. When we called in, we told the tech we had some prints and he brought along a reference book. They're making molds, so they can look at them back at the lab, but there's no doubt. They were brand-new Reeboks. No sign of wear on the soles."

Lucas scratched his head. "Reeboks?"

Annie McGowan was sparkling. Seven o'clock in the morning and she looked as though she'd been up for hours.

"Lucas," she called when she caught sight of him by the door. "Come on in."

"Big show tonight?"

"Noon, afternoon, and night is more like it. Right now we're setting up for a remote for the *Good-Morning Show*." She glanced at her watch. "Fifteen minutes."

A producer came out of the living room, saw Lucas, and hurried over. "Lieutenant, what's the chance of getting a few minutes of tape with you?"

"On what?"

"On the whole setup. How it worked, what went wrong."

Lucas shrugged. "We fucked up. You want to put that on the air?"

"With this case, if you want to say it, I think we could get it on," the producer said.

"You going to use your tape of the fight?"

The producer's eyes narrowed. "It's an incredible piece of action," he said.

"I won't comment if you're going to use it," Lucas said. "Hold it back and I'll talk."

"I can't promise you that," the producer said. "But I can talk to the news director about it."

"Okay," Lucas said wearily. "I'll do a couple of minutes. But I want to know what questions are coming and I don't want any tricky stuff."

"Great."

"And you'll see about holding the fight tape?"

"Yeah, sure."

The taping took almost an hour, with a break for McGowan's remote. When he got home, Lucas unplugged the telephones and fell facedown on the bed, not bothering to undress. He woke to a pounding noise, sat up, looked at the clock. It was a little before one in the afternoon.

The pounding stopped and he put his feet on the floor, rubbed the back of his neck, and stood up. A sharp rapping sound came from the bedroom window and he frowned and pulled back the venetian blind. Jennifer Carey, out on the lawn.

"Open the door," she shouted. He nodded and dropped the blind and went out to the door.

"I figured it out," she said angrily. "I don't know why I didn't see it, but as soon as we heard about the attack, I figured it out." She didn't take off her coat, and instead of walking through to the kitchen as she usually did, she stood in the hallway.

"Figured what out?" Lucas asked sleepily.

"You set McGowan up. Deliberately. You were feeding her those weird tips to make the maddog angry and attract him to McGowan."

"Ah, Jesus, Jennifer."

"I'm right, aren't I?"

He waved her off and started back to the living room.

"Well, she sure as hell paid you back," Jennifer said.

Lucas turned. "What do you mean?"

"That awful tape of you confessing. You know, saying it was all your fault. And then the tape of the fight, with you beating up that poor kid."

"They weren't going to show that," Lucas said hollowly. "We had a deal."

"What?"

"I gave them the interview and the producer said he'd call the news director about not using the tape of the fight."

Jennifer shook her head. "My God, Lucas, sometimes you are so *naive*. You're supposed to know all about this media stuff, right? But there was no way they wouldn't use that tape. Man, that's terrific action. Big gunfight and two people dead and a police lieutenant beating the crap out of his brother cop who caused it? That tape will probably make the network news tonight.''

''Ah, fuck.'' He slumped on the couch and ran his fingers through his hair.

Jennifer softened and touched him on the crown of the head.

''So I came over here to see if we could use you one more time. And I do mean *use*.''

''What?''

''We'd like to get a joint interview with you and Carla Ruiz. You talking about what you know about the killer, with Ruiz chipping in about the attack. Ellie Carlson will do the interview. I'm producing.''

''Why now?''

''The truth? Because if we don't have something heavy to promo for tonight, McGowan and Channel Eight are going to kick us so bad that we'll hurt for weeks. They'll do it anyway, but with a joint interview we might keep a respectable piece of the audience, for at least one of the news shows. Especially if we promo it right.''

''Is this sweeps week?''

''You got it.''

''I'll have to talk to the chief.''

Daniel was gloomy, withdrawn. He gestured Lucas to a chair and turned his own chair, staring out his office window at the street.

''I saw the interview tape on Channel Eight. Taking the blame. Nice try.''

''I thought it might help.''

''Fat chance. I gave Cochrane two weeks' administrative leave with pay, told him to stay away from the media, get his face fixed up. You really clobbered him.''

''I'll try to find him, talk to him,'' Lucas said.

"I don't know," Daniel said. "Maybe it'd be better if you just stayed away for a while."

Lucas shifted uncomfortably. "This is a bad time to talk about it, but Jennifer Carey wants a joint interview with me and Carla Ruiz. She's up-front about it. It's because of the sweeps this week. But she thinks if they can get some tape, promo it, it might cut down on Channel Eight's impact. At least we'd get something positive out there."

"Go ahead, if you want," Daniel said. He didn't seem to care much, and continued staring out at the street.

"Did the guys out at the scene get anything we can use?"

"Not that they told me about," Daniel said. They sat in silence for a moment, then Daniel sighed and swung his chair around.

"Homicide isn't going to catch the guy, unless it's by accident," he said. "With this close call, we might scare him off for a week, or two weeks, but he'll be back. Or maybe he'll leave town and start somewhere else. You know something? I don't want him to do that. I want to nail him here. And you're going to have to do it. The McGowan thing was a disaster, all right, but I keep thinking, not a total disaster. I keep thinking that Davenport figured the guy out. And if he did it once, maybe he can do it again. Maybe . . . I don't know."

"I don't have an idea in my fuckin' head," Lucas said.

"You're messed up," Daniel said. "But it'll go away. Your head will start working again."

"You're wrong about the way we'll break it," Lucas said. "It won't happen because I figured him out, because I haven't. When we get him, we'll get him on a piece of luck."

"I hate to depend on luck; I'd hoped we could come up with something a little more reliable."

"There isn't anything reliable, not in this world," Lucas said. "The maddog's had a fantastic game. Ruiz should have been able to tell us more than she did—I mean, she actually had her hands on him. If she'd pulled away his mask . . . We should have gotten a better description out of the attack on Brown. I keep thinking: If only Sparks had been on the other side of the street. He might have seen him full-face. I keep thinking: If only Lewis had written the guy's name on her calendar. Or if she had written *anything* about him. We should have nailed him at McGowan's; when he got away, we should have been able to freeze his car, if it really is a Thunderbird. He's been incredibly lucky. But there's one certainty in the world of game-playing: luck will turn. It always does. When we get him, we'll get him on a piece of luck.''

"Christ knows it's our turn for some," Daniel said.

Jennifer had already talked to Carla about an interview, and when Lucas called to agree, she told him that Carla was ready. They would shoot it at three o'clock and run an early, tight version at six o'clock. A longer version would be pro-moed for the ten-o'clock news, which the station had decided to expand to accommodate the interview.

Wear a suit, she said, and a blue shirt.

Shave again.

The interview lasted an hour, Lucas cool and distracted, Carla warm and insistent. With a proper cut, it would look good. Jennifer watched the interviewer talking with them, and halfway through, realized that Lucas and Carla were sleeping together. Or had slept together.

When the interview was over, she left with Lucas, trailing behind the cameraman and sound technician, who were carrying gear down to the van. Alone in the elevator she said, "I thought you might have been sleeping with McGowan. I see I was wrong. It was Carla Ruiz."

"Ah, man, Jennifer, I can't deal with this today," Lucas said, staring at the elevator floor.

"I don't mind so much," she said sadly. "I knew it was going to happen. I was hoping it wouldn't be this soon."

"I think it's done with," Lucas said dispiritedly.

"Just slam-bam-thank-you-ma'am?"

Lucas shook his head. "She gave me a little talk a few days ago. She likes me okay, but she's ready to cut me off when I conflict with her work."

"Oh, my, that hasn't happened before, has it?" Jennifer

asked. Her tone was light, even sarcastic, but a tear rolled down her cheek. Lucas reached out and thumbed it away. "Don't do that, for Christ's sake."

"Why not? You can't tolerate real emotion?"

He looked at the floor between his feet, then cocked his head at her. "Sometimes people don't know each other as well as they think they do. You're giving me shit and I'm supposed to take it like a man, right? You know what I feel like? I feel like going home and sticking my forty-five in my mouth and blowing my brains out. I've been beat up by a madman. I might recover. I might not. But I'll never forget it. Not in this life."

The elevator door opened and he walked away and never looked back.

Elle watched him across the expansive game board. The bookie and attorney had gone together, the two students followed a few minutes later. The grocer was still staring at the map, figuring.

Meade was no dummy. After a day's fighting, in which the South controlled most of the heights south of Gettysburg, he cautiously withdrew to the south, toward Washington. There were prepared positions waiting. Now the ball was in Lee's court. Lee—Elle, with advice from Lucas, as Longstreet—could continue his invasion of the North. That looked increasingly untenable. Or he could go after Meade's army to the south. That army would have to be destroyed in any case. But if Lee went after Meade, it would mean the kind of Napoleonic attack that failed at the real Gettysburg. Once he got down to close-quarters fighting around Washington, with the mountains to his west and a flooding Potomac to his south, it would be kill or be killed. Lucas' game could end the Civil War two years early . . .

"You can't keep thinking about it," Elle said.

"What?" Lucas had been balancing on the back two legs of his chair, staring at the ceiling.

"You can't keep brooding about the tragedy out at the reporter's house. It's pointless. And you almost had him. You drew him in. If you'd stop feeling sorry for yourself, you'd come up with something new.''

Lucas dropped the chair to the floor and stood up.

"My problem is, I can't think of anything. My head is frozen. I think he's gone.''

"No. Something is going to happen," Elle said. "You know how there's a rhythm to these games? When we all know something is about to happen, even when it doesn't have to? I feel the same kind of rhythm here. The rhythm says this whole thing is about to resolve itself.''

"The problem is, how?" the grocer interjected.

"That is the problem," Lucas said, snapping a finger at the grocer. "Exactly. Suppose the guy resolves it by leaving? He could start all over somewhere else, and we wouldn't even know it. And we've really got nothing to go on. Not a real clue in the bunch. If he wants to leave, he can walk.''

"He won't," Elle said positively. "This thing is rushing to a conclusion. I can feel the wheels.''

"I hope so," Lucas said. "I don't think I can take much more of it.''

"We're praying for you," Elle said, and Lucas realized the second nun was also watching him. She nodded. "Every night. God will answer. You've got to get him.''

CHAPTER
— 25 —

The maddog called in sick from Eau Claire. He lay in bed watching cable television from the Cities and finally left the motel just before the noon checkout time. He got back to his apartment in the early afternoon, cleaned up, drove down to his office, and said he was feeling better. He tried to work. He failed.

The fiasco at the McGowan house was the big news. The entire office was talking about it. The maddog took no pleasure in the talk, felt no power flowing from it. He had been mousetrapped. Davenport had done it, had lured him to McGowan. Davenport understood him that well. Had stalked him. Had failed only through a set of circumstances so bizarre that they could never be repeated.

The maddog knew he had been lucky. So lucky. It was time to reconsider the game. Perhaps he should stop. He was far ahead. He had the points. But could he stop? He wasn't sure. If he couldn't, perhaps he could move somewhere else. Back to Texas. Get away from the cold. Rethink the game.

It took him until well after five to clear his desk, finish the routine real-estate and probate work. When he left, a television was flickering in one of the associates' offices, an indulgence not permitted during the regular workday. Lucas Davenport's face was on the screen, the camera tight on his features. There were dark marks under his eyes, but he was well-controlled. The picture froze momentarily and then the cameras switched to the anchorwoman.

He stepped closer to listen. ''. . . the complete interview with the survivor Carla Ruiz and Lieutenant Lucas Davenport tonight on an expanded edition of TV3's Ten-O'Clock Report.''

He was torn between Channel Eight and TV3. Channel Eight had been breaking all the most interesting news during the game, but the interview on TV3 might tell him more about the man who mousetrapped him. He finally decided, after consulting his video recorder's instruction book, that he could tape TV3 while he watched Channel Eight. He tried it with a network comedy. It worked.

McGowan, so beautiful, led the evening news, dominated it. She recounted the surveillance, showed off the alert beeper she'd worn on her belt. Told of sitting in her bedroom alone at night, listening to every sound, wondering if the maddog was coming. She was taped as she made a single woman's portion of stir-fry. Unused copper skillets hung from the walls. An old-fashioned pendulum clock ticked in the background.

With the scene set, she recounted the attack, running through the night with a camera bouncing behind her, ending with a camera-activated reenactment of the shootings, McGowan playing all parts. Then across the final fence to the sewer ditch, where she pointed out the maddog's footprints in the yellow clay.

It was brilliant theater, and like all brilliant theater, ended with a punch: the fight in the harsh light, Davenport destroying the rookie cop, his hands moving so fast they could barely be seen. Then Davenport starting toward the cameras, murder in his eye, until stopped by McGowan's voice.

Brutal. Davenport was not just a player. He was an animal.

When the show ended, the maddog stared at the television for a few moments, then punched up the tape of the TV3 interview.

Davenport again, but a different one. Cooler. Calculating. A hunter, not a fighter. The maddog recognized the quality instinctively, had seen it in the ranchers around his father's place, the men who talked about *my deer* and *my antelope*.

Ruiz still drew him, her face, her dark eyes. The connection was not essential, was not the connection he felt with a Chosen—she had passed beyond that privilege. But there was an undeniable residue of their previous relationship, and the maddog felt it and thought about it.

Was he being manipulated again? Was this another Davenport trick? He thought not.

The maddog had never had a two-sided relationship with a woman, but he was acutely sensitive to the relationships between others. Halfway through the interview, he realized that Davenport and Carla Ruiz were somehow involved with each other. Sexually? Yes. The more he watched, the more he was convinced that he was right.

Interesting.

CHAPTER
— 26 —

"Come on. Let's do it." Sloan was leaning in the doorway.

"No fuckin' point, man," Lucas said. He felt lethargic, emotionally frozen. "We know what he's hiding. He's worried about his reputation. He ripped off the Rices and he's afraid somebody will find out."

"How do you feel?"

"What?"

"How do you feel? Since the Fuckup?"

Lucas grinned in spite of himself. The disaster at McGowan's had been dubbed the Fuckup. Everybody from the mayor to the janitors was using it. Lucas suspected everybody in town was. "I feel like shit."

"So come on," Sloan urged. "We'll go over and jack that mother *up*. That ought to clear out your glands."

It was better than sitting in the office. Lucas lurched to his feet. "All right. But I'll drive. Afterward we can go out and get something decent to eat."

"You buying?"

The shop assistant went into the back room to get Nester, who was not happy to see them.

"I thought you understood my position," he said, heading for the telephone. "This has now become harassment. I'm going to call my attorney first thing, rather than listen to you at all."

"That's up to you, Nester," Lucas said, baring his teeth. "It might not be a bad idea, in fact. We're trying to decide whether to bust you on felony fraud or to let Mrs. Rice's attorney handle it as a civil matter. You want to be stubborn, we'll put the cuffs on and drag you downtown and book you right now.''

The shop assistant's head was swinging back and forth like a spectator's at a tennis match. Nester glanced at him, his hand on the telephone, and said, ''I have no idea what you're speaking of.''

''Sure you do,'' Lucas said. ''We're talking about netsukes that might be worth a quarter-million dollars, that you were asked to valuate for insurance purposes. You told the owner that they were virtually worthless and bought them for a song.''

''I never,'' Nester sputtered. ''I was never asked to valuate those netsukes. They were offered for sale and I paid the asking price. That is all.''

''That's not what Mrs. Rice says. She's willing to take it to court.''

''Do you think a jury would believe some . . . some *washerwoman* instead of me? It is my word against hers—''

''You wouldn't have a chance,'' Sloan said in his soapiest voice. ''Not a chance. Here's a guy who fought for his country and brought home some souvenirs, not knowing what he had. Then he goes through life, a good guy, pushing a broom, and finally dies of cancer that slowly eats its way up his body, killing him inch by inch. He wants to sell whatever personal possessions he can, to help his wife after he's dead. She's aging herself and they're living hand to mouth. Probably eating dog food—I can guarantee they will be, by the time their lawyer gets done with it.''

''Maybe cat food. Tuna parts,'' Lucas chipped in.

''And they've got this treasure trove, without knowing it,'' Sloan continued. ''Could be a happy ending, just like in a TV movie. But what happens? Along comes this slick-greaser dealer in objets d'art who gives them five hundred dollars for a quarter-million bucks' worth of art. Do you really think a jury would side with you?''

''If you do, you're living in a dream world,'' Lucas said. ''I've got some friends in the press, you know? When I feed them this story, you'll be more famous than the maddog killer.''

''That's not a bad idea, you know?'' Sloan said, looking sideways at Lucas as he picked up the hint. ''We haul him in, book him for fraud, and put out the story. It could take some of the heat off—''

''You better come back to my office,'' said Nester, now deathly pale.

They followed him through a narrow doorway into the back. A storeroom protected with a steel-mesh fence took up most of the space, with a small but elegantly appointed office tucked away to one side. Nester lowered himself behind the desk, fussed with calendar pages for a moment, then said, ''What can we do about this?''

''We could arrest you for fraud, but we don't really want to. We're worried about other things,'' Lucas said, lowering himself into an antique chair. ''If you just tell us what we want to know, we'll suggest that Mrs. Rice get a lawyer and work this out in civil court. Or perhaps you could negotiate a settlement.''

''I *talked* to this person,'' Nester protested, nodding at Sloan. ''I told him everything that happened between Mr. Rice and myself.''

''I had a very strong feeling that you were holding back,'' Sloan said. ''I'm not usually wrong.''

''Well. Frankly, I thought if you learned about the price paid for the netsukes, which was the price Mr. Rice asked—let the seller beware—that you might feel it was . . . inappropriate. I was not hiding it, I was merely being discreet.''

Lucas grimaced. ''If you had told us that, or even suggested it, we wouldn't have hassled you,'' he said. ''We're trying to trace the gun Rice had. We're running down everybody who talked to him while he had it.''

''I never saw a gun and he never mentioned a gun or offered to sell one,'' Nester said. ''I didn't see anyone else while I was there, not even Mrs. Rice. We didn't talk. I went in and said I would be interested in looking at the netsukes. He backed his wheelchair up, got them from a box and gave them to me, and went back to his reading. I asked how much, he said five hundred dollars. I gave him a check and left. We didn't exchange more than fifty words.''

''That doesn't sound like Rice,'' Sloan said. ''He was supposed to be quite a talker.''

''Not with me,'' Nester said.

Lucas looked at Sloan and shook his head.

''I think because he was so involved with his will,'' Nester continued. ''He had to read it and sign it before his attorney picked it up.''

''His attorney?'' Lucas asked. He turned to Sloan. ''His attorney?''

Sloan started paging through his workbook.

''He said his attorney was on his way,'' Nester said, looking from one to the other. ''Does that help?''

''We don't show any attorney,'' Sloan said.

Lucas felt his throat tighten. ''Did he say what his attorney's name was?''

''No, nothing like that. Or I don't remember,'' Nester said.

''We may want to talk to you some more,'' Lucas said, standing up. ''Come on, Sloan.''

Sloan pumped a quarter into the pay phone. Mary Rice picked it up on the first ring.

''Your husband's will, Mrs. Rice, do you have a copy of it there? Could you get it? I'll wait.''

Lucas stood beside him, looking up and down the street, bouncing on the balls of his feet, calculating. A lawyer. It would fit. But this was ridiculous. This would be too easy. Sloan shifted from foot to foot, waiting.

''Did you look in the top drawer of your dresser?'' Sloan said finally. ''Remember you told me once you'd put stuff there . . . Yeah, I can wait.''

''What is she doing?'' Lucas blurted. He wanted to rip the phone away from Sloan and shout the woman into abject obedience.

''Can't find it,'' Sloan said.

''Let's run down there and shake down the house or—''

Sloan put up a hand and went back to the phone. "You did? Good. Look at the last page. Is the lawyer's name there? No, not the firm, the lawyer. There should be a signed name with the same name typed underneath. . . . Okay, spell it for me. L-o-u-i-s V-u-l-l-i-o-n. Thank you. Thank you."

He wrote the name in his book, Lucas looking over his shoulder. "Never heard of him," Lucas said, shaking his head.

"Another call," Sloan said. He took a small black book from his shirt pocket, opened it, found a number, and dug in his pocket for a quarter. He came up empty.

"Got a quarter?" he asked Lucas.

Lucas groped in his pockets. "No."

"Shit, we gotta get change . . ."

"Wait, wait, we can use my calling card, just dial zero. Here, give me the phone. Who is this, anyway?"

"Chick I know up at the state Public Safety."

Lucas dialed the number and passed the receiver to Sloan when it started to ring. Sloan asked for Shirley.

"This is Sloan," he said, "over at Minneapolis PD. How are you? . . . Yeah. Yeah. Great. Listen, I got a hot one, could you run it for me? . . . Right now? . . . Thanks. It's Louis Vullion." He spelled it for her. He waited a moment, then said, "Yeah, give me the whole thing."

He listened, said, "Aw, shit," and, "Whoa," and, "Hey, thanks, honey." He hung up the phone and turned to Lucas. "Yeah?"

"Louis Vullion. White male. Twenty-seven. Five ten, one ninety, blue eyes. And some good news and some bad news. What do you want first?"

"The bad news," Lucas said quickly.

"Sparks is positive he had dark hair. He doesn't. He's a fuckin' redhead."

Lucas stared at Sloan for a moment, licked his lips. "Red hair?"

"That's what his license says."

"That's fuckin' wonderful," Lucas whispered, his face like stone.

"What?" Sloan was puzzled.

"Carla was sure he was light-complexioned. She was positive. You don't get anybody lighter than a redhead. Sparky was sure he had dark hair. I couldn't figure it out. But you put a redhead under those mercury-vapor lights down on Hennepin at night . . ." He pointed a finger at Sloan's chest, prompting him.

"Son of a bitch. It might look dark," Sloan said, suddenly excited.

"Fuck *might*," Lucas said. "It *would* look dark. Especially from a distance. It fits; it's like a poem." He licked his lips again. "If that was the bad news, what's the good news?"

Sloan put up a finger. "Registered owner," he said, "of a midnight-blue Ford Thunderbird. He bought it three months ago."

Daniel's door was closed. His secretary, Linda, was typing letters.

"Who's in there?" Lucas asked, pointing at the door. Sloan was standing on his heels.

"Pettinger from accounting," Linda said. "Lucas, wait, you can't go in there . . ."

Lucas pushed into the office, with Sloan trailing self-consciously behind. Daniel, startled, looked up in surprise, saw their faces, and turned to the accountant.

"I'm going to have to throw you out, Dan," he said. "I'll get back this afternoon."

"Uh, sure." The accountant picked up a stack of computer printouts, looked curiously at Lucas and Sloan, and walked out.

Daniel pushed the door shut. "Who is he?" he rasped.

"A lawyer," said Lucas. "A lawyer named Louis Vullion."

CHAPTER
— 27 —

"Where is he?" Lucas spoke into a handset as he pulled to the curb a block from the maddog's apartment. The five-year-old Ford Escort fit seamlessly into the neighborhood.

"Crossing the bridge, headed south. Looks like he might be on his way to the Burnsville Mall. We're just north of there now."

There was a six-unit net around the maddog, twelve cops, seven women, five men. They followed him from his apartment to a parking garage not far from his office. They watched him into the office, through a solitary lunch at a downtown deli. He was limping a bit, they said, and was favoring one leg. From the fall into the ditch? They watched him back to the office, through a trip to the courthouse, up to the clerk's office, back to his office.

While he worked through the afternoon, an electronics technician fastened a small but powerful radio transmitter under the bumper of his car. When the maddog left the office at night, the watchers followed him back to his car. He returned to his apartment, apparently ate dinner, and then left again. Heading south.

"He's gone into the mall parking lot."

Lucas glanced at his watch. If the maddog turned around and drove back to his apartment as quickly as he could, it would still take twenty minutes. That was almost enough time.

"Out of his car, going inside," the radio burped. The net would be on the ground now, moving around him.

Lucas turned the radio off and stuck it in his jacket pocket.

He did not want police calls burping out of his pocket at an inopportune moment. The power lockpick and a disposable flashlight were under the seat. He retrieved them, shoved the flashlight in another pocket, and slipped the pick beneath his coat, under his arm.

He got out of the car, turned his collar up, and hurried along the sidewalk, his back to the wind, the last dry leaves of fall scurrying along by his ankles.

The maddog lived in a fourplex, each unit two stories with an attic, each occupying one vertical corner of what otherwise looked like a Victorian mansion. Each of the four apartments had a small one-car attached garage and a tiny front porch with a short railing for the display of petunias and geraniums. The flowerpots stood empty and cold.

Lucas walked directly to the maddog's apartment, turned in at his entry walk, and hurried up the steps. He pressed the doorbell, once, twice, listened for the phone. It was still ringing. He glanced around, took out the power pick, and pushed it into the lock. The pick made an ungodly loud clatter, but it was efficient. The door popped open, then stopped as it hit the end of a safety chain. The maddog had gone out through the garage, and that door would be automatically locked.

Lucas swore, groped in his pocket, and pulled out a board full of thumbtacks and a couple of rubber bands. Glancing around again, he saw nothing but empty street, and he pushed the door open until it hit the end of the chain. Reaching in as far as he could, he pushed a thumbtack into the wood on the back of the door, with the rubber band beneath it. Then he stretched the rubber band until he could loop it over the knob on the door chain. When he eased the door shut, the rubber band contracted and pulled the chain-knob to the end of its channel. With a couple of shakes, it fell out.

"Hey, Louis, what's happening?" Lucas called as he pushed the door open. There was no response. He whistled for a dog. Nothing. He pushed the door shut, turned on the hall light, and pried the thumbtack out of the door. The hole was imperceptible. He took out the handset, turned it on, and called the surveillance crew.

''Where is he?''

''Just went into a sporting-goods store. He's looking at jackets.''

Lucas thumbed the set to the monitor position and quickly checked the apartment for any obvious indications that Vullion was the maddog. As he passed the ringing telephone, he lifted it off the hook and then dropped it back on, silencing it.

In a quick survey of the first floor he found a utility room with the water heater, washer and dryer, and a small built-in workbench with a drawer half-full of inexpensive tools. A door in the utility room led out to the garage. He opened it, turned on the light, and looked around. A small snow-blower, a couple of snow shovels, and a stack of newspapers packaged for disposal in brown shopping bags. If he had time, he would stop back and go through the papers. With luck, he might find one that had been cut to make the messages left on the maddog's victims' bodies. There was nothing else of interest.

He shut the garage door, walked through the tiny kitchen, opening and closing cabinet doors as he passed through, poked his head into the living room, checked a small half-bath and a slightly larger office space with an IBM computer and a few lawbooks.

The second floor was divided between two bedrooms and a large bathroom. One of the bedrooms was furnished; the other was used as storage space. In the storage room he found the maddog's luggage, empty, an electronic keyboard which looked practically unused, and an inexpensive weight bench with a set of amateur weights. He checked the edges of the weights. Like the keyboard, they appeared practically untouched. Vullion was a man with unconsummated interests . . .

A battered couch sat in one corner, along with three boxes full of magazines, a *Playboy* collection that appeared to go back a dozen years or more. He left the storeroom and walked to the other bedroom.

In the ceiling of the hallway between the two bedrooms was an entry panel for the attic, with a steel handle attached to it. Lucas pulled down on the handle, and a lightweight ladder folded down into the hallway. He walked up a few steps, stuck his head into the attic, and flashed the light around. The attic was divided among the four apartments with thin sheets of plywood. Vullion's space was empty. He backed out, pushed the ladder with its attached door back into place, and took out the handset.

"Where is he?"

"Still in the store."

Time to work.

Lucas put the radio back in his pocket, took a miniature tape recorder from the other, thumbed it on, and went into the bedroom.

"Bedroom," he said. "Closet. Sport coat, forty-two regular. Suit, forty-two regular. Pants, waist thirty-six. Shoes. Nike Airs, blue, bubble along outer sole. No Reeboks. . . .

"Bedroom dresser . . . lubricated Trojan prophylactics, box of twelve, seven missing. . . .

"Office," he said. "Bill from University of Minnesota Law Alumni Association. Federal tax returns, eight years. Minnesota, Minnesota, Minnesota, Minnesota, Minnesota, Texas, Texas, Texas. Shows address in Houston, Texas, under name Louis Vullion.

"Computer files, all law stuff and correspondence, opening correspondence, all business. . . .

"Kitchen. Under sink. Bag of onions, no potatoes . . ."

Lucas went methodically through the apartment looking for anything that would directly associate Vullion with the killings. Except for the Nike Airs, there was nothing. But the indirect evidence piled up: the life in Texas before the year at the University of Minnesota law school, the clothes that said his size was right, the prophylactics . . .

"Where is he?"

"Looking at shoes."

The lack of direct evidence was infuriating. If Vullion had kept souvenirs of the kills, if Lucas had found a box of surgeon's gloves in association with a box of Kotex, with a roll of tape next to them . . . or if the kitchen table had been littered with the shreds of a newspaper that one of his messages had been cut from . . .

If he had kept those things, they could find a way to get a warrant and take him. But there was none of it. Standing arms akimbo, Lucas looked around the unnaturally neat living room, and then realized: it was unnaturally neat.

"We scared the cocksucker and he cleaned the place out," Lucas said aloud. If they had talked to Nester the previous week, before the incident at McGowan's . . . No point in thinking about it. He started to turn out of the living room, when the videocassette recorder caught his eye. There were no tapes in evidence, but an empty tape carton sat beside the television. He reached down, turned the machine on, and punched the eject button. After a minute's churning, the VCR produced a tape.

"Where is he?"

"Leaving the shoe store."

Lucas turned on the television and started the tape. It was blank. He stopped it, backed it up, ran it again, and was startled when his own face popped up on the screen.

"God damn, the interview," Lucas muttered to himself. The camera cut to Carla. He watched the interview through to the end, waited until the screen went blank, and turned off the recorder and the television.

What little doubt he had had disappeared with the video recording. He walked back to the bedroom, lifted the bedspread, and pushed his arm between the mattress and box springs. Nothing.

He dipped back in his jacket pocket and took out an envelope and shook out the pictures. Lewis, Brown, Wheatcroft, the others. Handling the photos by their edges, he pushed them under the mattress as far as he could reach. A thorough search would find them.

When it was done, he straightened the bedspread and began moving out of the apartment, working as methodically on his way out as he had on the way in. Everything in place. Everything checked. All lights out. He peered out at the sidewalk. Nobody there. He put the chain back on the front door and went into the garage. He took ten minutes to check the newspapers. None were shredded. He restacked the bundles as he'd found them, and let himself out through the garage door.

Back on the sidewalk, he walked briskly away. He had almost reached the Ford Escort when the monitor beeped.

"He's out of the mall, headed toward his car. Three and five stay on the ground, lead cars saddle up now. . . ."

Lucas and Daniel sat alone in Daniel's dimly lit office, looking at each other through a yellow pool of light cast by a desk lamp. "So even if we got in, we wouldn't find anything," Daniel concluded.

"I couldn't swear to that, but it looks to me like he cleaned the place out. He may have hidden something—I didn't have enough time to really tear the place apart," Lucas said. "But I didn't find anything conclusive. The Nikes are right, the rubbers are right, his size is right, the car is right. But you know and I know that we could find that combination in fifty people out there."

"Fifty people who are also lawyers and hang around the courthouse and have a Texas accent and would get a gun from Rice?"

"But we've got no direct evidence that he got the gun from Rice. And all the other stuff is real thin. You've got to believe that he'd get the best attorney around, and a good attorney would cut us to pieces."

"How about voice analysis on the tapes?"

"You know what the courts think of that."

"But it's another thing."

"Yeah. I know. It's tempting . . ."

"But?"

"But if we keep watching him, we should get him. He didn't get his kill. He's scared now, but if he's compelled to kill, he'll be going back out. Sooner or later. I'd bet in the next week. This time, we won't lose him. We'll get him entering some place and he'll have all that shit with him, the Kotex and the potato and the gloves. We'll have him cold."

"I'll talk to the county attorney. I'll tell him what we have now and what we might get. See what he says. But basically, I think you're right. It's too thin to risk."

Surveillance posts were set up in an apartment across the street from the maddog's and one house down; and behind and two houses down.

"It was the best we could do, and it ain't bad," the surveillance chief said. "We can see both doors and all windows. With the freeway on the south, he can only get out of the neighborhood to the north, and we're north of him. And he ain't going to see us anyway."

"What's that glow? Is he reading in bed?"

"Night-light, we think," the surveillance chief said.

Lucas nodded. He recalled seeing one in the bedroom but couldn't say so. "He's trying to keep away the nightmares," he said instead.

"He'd have them if anybody did," said the surveillance chief. "Are you going to work a regular schedule with us?"

"I'll be here every night," Lucas said. "If he breaks off his regular work pattern during the day, I want you to beep me. I'll come running. He hasn't ever hit anybody in the early morning, so I'll head home after he goes to bed. Get some sleep. I'll check with the surveillance team first thing in the morning."

"Stay close. When it goes down, it could go fast."

"Yeah. I was at the Fuckup, remember?"

Lucas looked out the window at the maddog's apartment, at the steady dim glow from the second floor. This time there wouldn't be a fuckup.

CHAPTER
— 28 —

The maddog should never have spotted the surveillance. It was purely an accident.

He left a late-afternoon real-estate closing at a bank in the Mississippi River town of Hastings, twenty-odd miles south of the Twin Cities. It was dark. He crossed the Mississippi at the Hastings bridge and drove north on Highway 61, through the suburban towns of Cottage Grove, St. Paul Park, and Newport. As he passed through St. Paul Park he found himself behind an uncovered gravel truck. Pieces of gravel bounced out of the back of the truck and along the highway. A big one could star a windshield.

The maddog, thinking of the shiny finish on his new Thunderbird, moved into the left lane and accelerated around the truck. The close-surveillance car behind him caught the truck a moment later. Since the maddog appeared to be in no particular hurry, intent only on staying ahead of the truck, the surveillance car fell in behind it.

Gravel bounced around the surveillance car, but the cops inside didn't care. The car was mechanically sound, but, like most surveillance cars, was not much to look at, just a plain vanilla Dodge. A few dings more or less wouldn't make any difference. And the gravel truck made excellent cover.

None of it would have mattered if one particularly large rock hadn't bounced off the highway and knocked half the plastic lens off the amber left-turn light. The cops inside heard the thump, but couldn't see the broken lens.

"We oughta give this asshole a ticket," one of the surveillance cops said as the rock bounced off.

"Right," the driver answered. "Go ahead and stick the light on the roof."

"Could you see Daniel's face? We say, 'Well, we was following him when we ran into this incredible asshole with a truck full of rocks . . .' "

"He'd put us in prison," the first cop said. "He'd find a way."

The maddog decided to stop at a fast-food restaurant off the Interstate loop highway, I-494. The loop intersected with Highway 61 just north of the town of Newport. When the maddog pulled onto the circular entrance ramp for I-494, he glanced into the rearview mirror and noted, with no particular interest, the unusual turn signal on a car a hundred yards back. The signal flashed a peculiar combination of amber and unshielded white.

The close-surveillance car was tighter on the maddog's tail than it normally would have been. The lead car had continued up Highway 61 through the I-494 interchange and would now have to find a place to turn around and catch up from behind. In the meantime, until one of the trailing surveillance cars could move up into the lead position, the cops in the close-surveillance car couldn't take chances. They stuck close.

They were still close when the maddog turned off on the Robert Street exit, heading for one of the restaurants just north of the interchange. As he came down the ramp and slowed to a stop at the bottom, the maddog again noticed the car with the odd turn light. Something was wrong with it, he thought. A broken lens or something. The car was slow in coming down the ramp behind him.

When the traffic signal turned green, the maddog forgot about it and took a left, went up the hill, and pulled into a restaurant parking lot. Outside the entrance, he got a copy of *USA Today* and carried it inside.

While the maddog ate and read his newspaper, the surveillance cops took turns stocking up on burgers and Cokes at a McDonald's a half-mile away. Two teams always stayed on the maddog.

When he left the restaurant, the maddog decided to drive

into St. Paul on Robert Street. It was a crowded, tricky street, but there were two movie theaters not far ahead. A movie would go down well.

He saw the shattered turn light halfway up Robert Street. It was three cars back. At first he wasn't certain, but then he saw it again, more clearly. And again.

They were on him.

He knew it.

He sat halfway through a green light, staring blindly at the street ahead, until the cars behind him started to honk. Should he run for it?

No. If he was being watched, it would tip them off that he knew. He needed time to think. Besides, maybe he was wrong. He wasn't certain about the light. It could be a coincidence.

But it didn't feel like a coincidence.

He passed a shopping center, took a right turn, and drove down to the high-speed Highway 3, which went north to intersect with Interstate 94. Coming off the exit ramp, he watched the mirror. A car followed him down the ramp, but far enough away that he couldn't see the turn light.

He thought about pulling over, feigning car trouble; but that could precipitate something, force their hands. He was not sure that he wanted to do that. He did a mental catalog. There was nothing at the apartment. Nothing. Nothing in the car. There was nothing to hang him with. If they were really watching, they must be waiting for an attack.

Approaching the I-94 interchange across the LaFayette Bridge, the maddog let his speed drop sharply. The cars behind began to close up, and he picked up the surveillance car in an adjacent lane. He still couldn't see it clearly, but there was something definitely wrong with its turn signal.

Two cops in a trailing surveillance car had moved up and finally passed the maddog as they all drove north on Highway 3. As they approached I-94, the two women cops in the new lead car made the logical decision that the maddog was heading back to Minneapolis on the Interstate. They committed to the ramp. Behind them, the maddog drove through the interchange and into the dark warren of streets in St. Paul's Lowertown. The net spread out around him on parallel streets, staying in touch. Again, with the lead car out of it, the close-surveillance car moved in a bit tighter. Tight enough that when they turned a corner and found the maddog at a dead stop, backing into a parking place, they had to drive by.

And the maddog, who was watching for them, clearly caught the broken lens on the turn signal.

He was being watched. Coincidence was one thing. To believe all these sightings were coincidences was to believe in fairy tales.

The maddog locked his car and walked briskly into a downtown shopping mall and went up two floors. The net was thinner, but still in place. The drivers of the trailing units had been alerted by the close-surveillance car that the maddog was parking. The passenger-cops were on the street before the maddog had fully gotten into his parking place.

They followed him into the theater. The theater was a place to think. How had they gotten onto him? Perhaps, as part of their surveillance of McGowan's house, they had routinely noted the license plates of all cars in the neighborhood. Perhaps somebody had heard the shots, seen him drive away, and noted the tag number. Maybe they had nothing at all but a number that didn't quite fit in the neighborhood. Perhaps he should start preparing an alibi for being there. He couldn't think of any offhand, but something might occur to him if he considered the problem.

If they were following him, there was little he could do about it. He didn't dare try to dodge the surveillance. That would confirm that he was guilty. He had disposed of all evidence that would put him at the crime scene. As far as he knew, there was no conclusive evidence against him anywhere.

When the movie ended, the maddog walked down to his car, resisting the almost overwhelming temptation to look around, to search the doorways for watchers. He wouldn't see them, of course. They would be too good for that. He stayed on city streets out to I-94, then turned east toward his own exit. He didn't see the broken turn signal on the way out to the Interstate. That meant nothing, he knew, but he couldn't suppress a tiny surge of hope. Maybe it *had* been coincidence.

The Interstate was crowded, and though he watched, he didn't see any cars with broken turn signals. He sighed, felt the tension seeping out. When he reached his exit, he ran the car up the ramp to the traffic signal and waited. Another car came off behind. Coasted up the ramp, slowly. Too slowly.

The traffic light changed to green. The maddog waited. The other car eased up. The left-front turn signal was broken, the white light shining brightly past the amber. The maddog looked up, saw the green, and took a right.

"Jeez, you don't look so good. You sick?" His secretary seemed concerned.

"No, no. Just had a little insomnia the last few nights. Could you get the papers for the Parker-Olson closing?"

The maddog sat at his desk, the office door closed, a blank yellow pad in front of him. Think.

The news stories of the surveillance on McGowan's house mentioned that the cops set up observation posts both in front and in back. Would they have done the same at his place? Probably. There were empty apartments on the block; he'd seen the signs, but not paid much attention. Nor did he know his neighbors, other than to nod at the others in his fourplex. Could he spot the other surveillance posts?

The maddog stood and stepped over to the window, hands in his jacket pockets, staring sightlessly out at the street.

Maybe. Maybe he could spot them, maybe he could deduce where they were. Where would that get him? If they came for him, he would not resist. That would be pointless. And had he not imagined himself in court, defending himself against his accusers? Had he not dreamed of capturing the jury with his eloquence?

He had. But now the vision of a magnificent defense did not come so easily. Deep in his heart, he knew they were right. He was not a good attorney; not in court, anyway. He'd never taken the fact out and looked at it, but the fact was there, like a stone.

He paced two steps one way, two steps back, tugging at his lip. They were watching. No matter how long he suppressed the urge to take another woman, they would eventually come. They wouldn't wait forever.

He sat down, looked at the yellow pad, and summarized:

They were not sure enough to arrest him yet.

They could not wait forever.

What would they do?

He thought of Davenport, the gamer. What would the gamer do?

A gamer would frame him.

It took him a half-minute on his knees in the garage to find the radio transmitter on the car. It took another hour to find the photographs under the mattress. The beeper he left in place. The photos he stared at, frightened. If the police should come through the door at this instant, he would go to jail for eighteen years, a life sentence in Minnesota.

He took the photographs into the kitchen and, one by one, burned them, the pictures curling and charring in the flames from the stove burner. When they were gone, reduced to charcoal, he crushed the blackened remains to powder and washed them down the kitchen sink.

That night he forced himself to lie in bed for fifteen minutes, then crept to the window and looked down the street. There was a patchwork of lighted windows, and many more that were dark. He watched, and after a while crawled back to his bed, got both pillows and put one on the floor and the other upright against the wall, where he could lean on it. It would be a long night.

After three hours, the maddog dozed, his head falling forward. He jerked it back upright and peered groggily through the window. Everything was about the same, but he couldn't watch much longer. There were only two lights still on, he had noted them, and he was simply too tired to continue.

He got up, carrying the pillows, and flopped facedown on the bed. Paradoxically, as soon as he was willing to allow himself to sleep, he felt more alert. The thoughts ran through his brain like a night train, hard and quick and hardly discernible as independent ideas. A mishmash of images—his women, their eyes, Lucas Davenport, the fight outside McGowan's, the broken turn signal.

From the mishmash there came an idea. The maddog resisted it at first, because it had the quality of a nightmare, requiring a broad-scope action under the most intense stress. Finally he considered it and paraded the objections, one by one. The longer he turned it in his mind, the more substantial it became.

It was a winning stroke. And the surveillance? What better alibi could he find? Would he have the courage to attempt the stroke? Or would he sit there like a frightened rabbit, waiting to have his neck wrung by the hunter?

He bit his lip. He bit so hard that he found blood on the pillow the next morning. But he had decided. He would try.

CHAPTER
– 29 –

Lucas sat on a tall three-legged stool, hunched over his work-bench, manipulating pieces of white two-inch polyvinyl-chloride pipe, wing nuts, bolts, aluminum tubes, and lengths of the Thinsulate batting normally used as insulation in winter coats.

He had hoped to settle the maddog himself. Instead, the investigation was moving into a tedious rook-pawn endgame. The outcome would probably be determined by laborious maneuver rather than a *coup de maître*.

Nevertheless, he would prepare for the *coup*, should one unexpectedly present itself.

His first attempt at building a silencer cost him blood.

"I don't know," he said aloud. It should work, but it looked awful. A foot-long length of PVC pipe split length-wise, screwed back together with wing nuts but with gaps down the split. Through the gaps, the tightly wound batting protruded in soft puffs. Deep inside, the aluminum pipe was pierced with dozens of hand-drilled holes.

He attached the assembly to the barrel of one of his cold street weapons, a Smith & Wesson Model 39 in nine-millimeter parabellum. He turned on a miniature tape recorder, jacked a round into the chamber, pointed the weapon at a stack of St. Paul Yellow Pages, and pulled the trigger. There was very little noise from the shot, but there was a mechanical clank as the telephone books jumped and simultaneously the silencer twisted in his hands and came half apart. A sharp edge on the PVC pipe sliced into the side of his middle finger.

"Son of a bitch," he said. He turned off the tape recorder and went upstairs, looked at the cut, which was superficial, washed it, bandaged it, and went back down the stairs.

The tape recorder had picked up the sound of the shot, along with the clank when the silencer pulled apart, but he would not have identified either of the noises as a shot.

The silencer was a mess. The internal tube had been knocked out of alignment with the gun's barrel, either by the blast of gases ahead of the slug or by the slug itself. It hadn't changed the slug's trajectory much. He made some mental notes on alterations to the silencer. The main requirement was that it had to be easily detached from the gun and just as easily disassembled. Accuracy counted not at all.

When he had finished examining the silencer and decided on the alterations he would make, he dug the slug out of the telephone books and looked at it. It was a handgun hunter's hollow-point and was so deformed that it would take an expert to identify its exact caliber.

Lucas nodded. He had the right ammunition, but he needed time to work on the silencer.

He had yet to make the blank.

Midmorning. Gray light filtered in through the kitchen window as he tried to wake up with coffee and an aging bagel. The Smith, with silencer modified and reattached, was in a disreputable-looking gym bag he'd found in a back closet. The gun/silencer combination was grossly illegal. If, somehow, it was found in his car, he would claim that he'd taken it off the street.

A car door slammed close by and he picked up the cup of coffee and stepped into the hallway and peered out the front windows. Carla Ruiz coming up the driveway, a taxi pulling away. He stuffed the gym bag under the kitchen sink, walked back to the bedroom, and pulled on a pair of sweatpants. The doorbell rang and he pulled a sweatshirt over his head, went out to the door, and let her in.

"Hi," she said softly, her face down, looking at him only in brief lateral glances.

"What's wrong?"

"I thought we should have some coffee."

"Sure," he said curiously. "I've got some hot water." He led her into the kitchen, dumped a heaping teaspoon of instant coffee into an oversize ceramic cup, and handed it to her.

"Jennifer Carey came over last night," she said as she sat down. She unbuttoned her coat but left it on.

"Oh." Lucas sat down across the table.

"We had a talk."

Lucas looked away from her into the front room. "And did you decide my future? Between the two of you?"

Carla smiled a very small smile. "Yeah," she said. She took a sip of coffee.

"Good of you to let me know," Lucas said sourly.

"We thought it was the polite thing to do," Carla said, and Lucas had to laugh in spite of himself.

"What did you decide?"

"She gets custody," Carla said.

"You don't mind?"

"I mind, kind of. It makes me angry that you were sleeping with us alternately, one down here, one up in the North Woods. But I figured our relationship wasn't long for the world. We live in different places. I weave, you shoot people. And it seemed like she had a better prior claim, with the baby and all."

"What about what I want?"

"We decided that didn't matter too much. Jennifer said you'd wiggle and squirm, but eventually you'd come around."

"Now, *that* pisses me off," Lucas said, no longer smiling.

"Tough," Carla said.

They stared at each other across the table. Lucas flinched first. "I may tell Jennifer to take a hike," he said.

"Not with her being pregnant," Carla said, shaking her head. "No chance. That's Jennifer's judgment, and I agree. I asked her what she'd do if you went with somebody else. She said she'd go over and have another talk with the somebody else."

"Jesus," Lucas said. He closed his eyes and tilted his head back and massaged the back of his neck. "What'd I do to deserve this?"

"Slept with one too many women," Carla said. "It's actually pretty flattering, when you think about it. She's good-looking and smart. And in her own screwed-up way, she's in love with you. In my own screwed-up way, I'm not—though I'd still like to use the cabin a couple of times a year. Until I can afford my own."

"Anytime," Lucas said wistfully. He wanted to say more, but couldn't think of anything.

Carla took a last sip of coffee, pushed the cup, still half-full, into the middle of the table, and stood up.

"I better get going," she said. "The cab should be back."

Lucas sat where he was. "Well, it was real."

"What's that supposed to mean?" she asked as she retrieved her purse.

"That's what you say when you can't think of anything to say."

"Okay." She buttoned her coat. "See you."

"How come Jennifer didn't deliver the message?"

"We talked about that and decided I should do it. That'd make a clean break between us. Besides, she said you'd spend about a half-hour on some kind of Catholic guilt trip, then you'd go into a rage and kick stuff, then you'd try to call her on the telephone so you could yell at her. Then in about two hours you'd start laughing about it. She said she'd rather skip the preliminaries." Carla glanced at her watch. "She'll be over in two hours."

"Motherfucker," Lucas said in disbelief.

"You got that right," Carla said as she went out the door. A yellow cab was waiting. She stopped with the screen door still open. "Call you next spring. About the cabin."

It was more like three hours. When Jennifer arrived, she wasn't embarrassed in the slightest.

"Hi," she said when he opened the door. She walked past

him, took off her coat, and tossed it on the couch. "Carla called, said the talk went okay."

"I'm pretty unhappy—" Lucas started, but she waved him off.

"Spare me. McGowan's going to network, by the way. It's all over town."

"Fuck McGowan."

"Better hurry," Jennifer said. "She'll be gone in a month. But I still think what you did was awful. McGowan's just too dumb to recognize it."

"Goddammit, Jennifer . . ."

"If you're going to yell, we could have this talk some other time."

"I'm not going to yell," he said grimly. He thought he might strangle.

"Okay. So I thought I might give you my position. That is, if you'd like to hear it."

"Sure. I mean, why not? You're running the rest of my life."

"My position is, I'm pregnant and the daddy shouldn't screw anybody else until the baby is born, and maybe" — she paused, as though considering the fairness of her proposition— "maybe a year old. Maybe two years old. That way, I can kind of pretend like I'm married and talk to you about the baby and what we did during the day and his first words and how he's walking and I won't have to worry about you fooling around. And then, when you can't stand it and start fooling around again, I can just pretend like I'm divorced."

She smiled brightly. Lucas was appalled.

"That's the coldest goddamn thing I ever heard," he said.

"It's not exactly an extemporaneous speech," she said. "I rewrote it about twelve times. I thought it was rather cogently expressed, but with enough emotion to make it convincing."

Lucas laughed, then stopped laughing and sat down. He looked haggard, she thought. Or harried. "All right. I give up," he said.

"All right to all of it?"

"Yeah. All of it."

"Scout's honor?"

"Sure." He held up the three fingers. "Scout's honor."

Late in the evening, Lucas lay on the surveillance team's mattress and thought about it. He could live with it, he thought. For two years? Maybe.

"That's weird. You see that?" said the first surveillance cop.

"I didn't see anything," said his partner.

"What?" asked Lucas.

"I don't know. It's like there's some movement over there. Just a little bit, at the edge of the window."

Lucas crawled over and looked out. The maddog's apartment was dark except for the faint glow from the night-light.

"I don't see anything," he said. "You think he's doing something?"

"I don't know. Probably nothing. It's just every once in a while . . . it's like he's watching *us.*"

CHAPTER
— 30 —

It was the winning stroke. If he had the nerve, he could pull it off. He imagined Davenport's face. Davenport would *know*, but he wouldn't know how, and there wouldn't be a damn thing he could do about it.

In some ways, of course, it would be his most intellectual mission. He didn't *need* this particular woman, but he would take her anyway. To the police—not Davenport, but the others—there would be a logic to it. A logic they could understand.

In the meantime, the *other* pressure had begun to build. There was a woman who lived in the town of Richfield, a schoolteacher with almond eyes and rich sable hair, wide teeth like a Russian girl's. He had seen her with a troop of her children in the basement level of the Government Center, installing an elementary-school art show . . .

No. He put her out of his mind. The need would grow, but he could control it. It was a matter of will. And his mind had to be clear to deal with the *stroke*.

He first had to break free, if only for two hours. He didn't see them, but they were there, he was sure, a web of watchers escorting him through the city's streets and skyways. His night watches and his explorations in the attic had been fruitful. He knew, he thought, where two of their surveillance posts were. The lighting patterns were wrong for families or individuals, and he saw car lights coming and going at odd hours of the night, always from the same two houses. One of the houses, he was sure, had been empty until recently.

They were waiting for him to move. Before he could, he

had to break free. Just for two hours. He thought he had a way.

The law firm of Woodley, Gage & Whole occupied three floors of an office building two blocks from his own. He had twice encountered one of their attorneys in real-estate closings, a man named Kenneth Hart. After each of the closings, they'd had lunch. If someone had ever asked the maddog who his friends were, he would have mentioned Hart. Now he hoped that Hart remembered him.

At Woodley, Gage, status was signified by floor assignment. The main reception area was on the third floor, the floor shared by the partners. The lesser lights were on the fourth. The smallest lights of all were on the fifth. With a less-affluent firm, a client arriving at the third-floor reception area in search of a fourth- or fifth-floor attorney would be routed back down the hall to the elevators. With this firm, no such side trip was necessary. There was an internal elevator and an internal stairway.

Best of all, there were exits to the parking garage on all of the first eight floors. If he could go into Woodley, Gage on the third floor, and the cops didn't know about the internal elevator, he could slip out on five.

Before he could use Woodley, Gage, a preliminary excursion would be necessary, and it would have to take place under the noses of his watchers.

The maddog left the office early, drove his bugged Thunderbird south to Lake Street, found a place to park, got out, and walked along the row of dilapidated shops. He passed a dealer in antiques, peered through the dark glass, and breathed a sigh of relief. The fishing lures were still in the window.

He walked on another half-block to a computer-supply store, where he bought a carton of computer paper and headed slowly back to the car, still window-shopping. He paused at the antiques dealer's again, pretending to debate whether or not to enter. He should not overplay it, he thought; the watchers would be professionals and might sense something. He went inside.

"Can I help you?"

A woman emerged from the back of the shop. She had iron-colored hair tied back in a bun, her hands clasped in front of her. If she'd been wearing a shawl, she'd have looked like a phony grandmother on a package of chocolate-chip cookies. As it happened, she was wearing a cheap blue suit with a red tie and had the strained rheumy look of a longtime alcoholic.

"Those fishing lures in the window; are they expensive?" asked the maddog.

"Some are, some aren't," the woman said. She maneuvered around him toward the display, keeping her feet wide apart for balance. She's drunk, the maddog thought.

"How about the bluegill one?" he asked.

"That's hand-carved, hand-painted up at Winnibigoshish. There are a lot of fakes around, you know, but this is the real thing. I bought the whole bunch from an old resort owner last summer, he was cleaning out his cellar."

"So how much?"

She looked him over speculatively. "Twenty?"

"Sold."

She looked like she wished she'd asked for more. "Plus tax," she said. He left the store with the lure in a brown paper bag and went to the bank, where he wrote a check for two thousand dollars.

The bluegill was carved from a solid piece of pine and had three rusty treble hooks dangling from it. An early pike lure, the woman said, probably carved back in the thirties. The maddog knew nothing about fishing lures, but this one had the rustic rightness of real folk art. If he collected anything, he thought, he might collect this stuff, like Hart did. He would call Kenneth Hart tomorrow, just after lunch.

He rethought the entire project during the night and decided to call it off. At dawn, groggy, he staggered to the bathroom and took half a pill. Just before it carried him away, he changed his mind again, and decided to go ahead.

"Hello, Ken?"

"This is Ken Hart . . ." A little wary.

"This is Louis Vullion, down at Felsen . . ."

"Sure. What's up?" Friendly now.

"You going to be in for a few minutes?"

"I've got a meeting at two . . ."

"Just want to see you for a minute. Got something for you, actually."

"Come on over."

The invisible net, he supposed, spread around him as he moved through the skyways. He tried not to look, but couldn't help himself. A lot of the watchers would be women, he knew. They were the best tails. At least, the books said so.

The maddog left his regular wool overcoat in his office and went to Hart's office wearing a suit coat and carrying a briefcase. An inexpensive tan trench coat was rolled and stuffed inside the briefcase, along with a crushable tweed hat.

The maddog went directly to the third-floor reception area of Hart's firm.

"I'm here to see Ken Hart," he told the receptionist.

"Do you have an appointment, Mr. . . . ?"

"Vullion. I'm an attorney from Felsen-Gore. I called Ken a few minutes ago to tell him I was running over."

"Okay." She smiled at him. "Go down the hall . . ."

He smiled back as pleasantly as he could. "I know the way."

He went down the hall and punched the private elevator for the fifth floor. The net, he hoped, was fixed on the third-floor reception area.

"Ken?" The other attorney was paging through a brief, and looked up at the maddog.

"Hey. Louis. Come on in, sit down."

"Uh, I really can't, I'm in a rush," the maddog said, glancing at his wristwatch. "I wanted to drop something off. Remember when we ate lunch, you mentioned you collected old fishing lures? I was up north a couple weeks ago . . ."

He dumped the lure out of the paper bag onto Hart's desk.

"Whoa. That's a good one," Hart said, looking pleased. "Thanks, man. How much do I owe you?"

"I virtually stole the thing," the maddog said, shaking his head. "I'd be embarrassed to tell you. Of course, if you want to buy the cheeseburgers after the next closing . . ."

"You got a deal," Hart said enthusiastically. "Damn, this is really a good one."

"I've got to get out of here. Can I get out on this floor, or do I have to run back down . . . ?"

"No, no, just down the hall," Hart said. He came with him to his office door and pointed. "And jeez, Louis, thanks a lot."

Thank *you*, the maddog thought as he left. The whole charade had been an excuse to walk through the door on the fifth floor. He hesitated before he pushed through. This was critical. If there were people outside in the hallway, and if one of them happened to wander along behind as he went out through the parking ramp, he would have to call it off. He took a breath and pushed through the door. The hallway was empty.

The maddog walked the width of the building to the parking ramp, stopped before the steel fire door, took out the coat and hat, put them on, and stepped outside. The ramp had its own elevator, but the maddog took the stairs, looking down each flight before he took it. At the ground floor he kept his head down and strode out onto the sidewalk a full block from the entrance to Hart's building. He crossed the street, jaywalking, walked into another office building, up one floor, and into one of the remotest skyways in the system. He walked for two minutes and glanced back. There was nobody behind him.

He was alone.

The maddog called for a cab and took it directly to a used-car lot on University Avenue, a mile from his apartment.

He looked over the row of cars and picked out a brown Chevrolet Cavalier. "$1,695" was written on the windshield in poster paint. He peered through the driver's-side window.

The odometer said 94651. A salesman approached him crab-like through the lot, rubbing his hands as though they were pincers.

"How do you like this weather, really something, huh?" the salesman said.

The maddog ignored the gambit. The car was right. "I'm looking for something cheap for my wife. Something to get through the winter," he said.

"This'll do 'er, you betcha," the salesman said. "Good little car. Uses a little oil, but not—"

"I'll give you fourteen hundred for it and you pick up the tax," the maddog said.

The salesman looked him over. "Fifteen hundred and *you* pick up the tax."

"Fifteen hundred flat," said the maddog.

"Fifteen and we split the tax."

"Have you got the title here?" the maddog asked.

"Sure do."

"Get somebody to clean the paint off the windshield and take the consumer notice off the side window," the maddog said. He showed the salesman a sheaf of fifties. "I'll take it with me."

He told them his name was Harry Barber. With the stack of fifties sitting there, nobody asked for identification. He signed a statement that said he had insurance.

On the way back to his apartment, the maddog stopped at a salvage store and bought a two-foot length of automobile heating hose, a bag of cat litter, a roll of silver duct tape, and a pair of work gloves. As he was going past the cash register he saw a display of tear-gas canisters like the one Carla Ruiz had used on him.

"Those things work?" he asked the clerk.

"Sure. Works great."

"Give me one."

In the car, he wrapped the open end of the heating tube with the duct tape until it was sealed, then poured the tube full of cat litter and sealed the other end. When he was done, he had a slightly flexible two-foot-long weighted rubber club.

He put the club under the seat and the tape in the bag with the cat litter.

Then, if he remembered right from his university days . . .

The motel vending machines were all gathered in a separate alcove. He dropped in the coins and got the single-pack Kotex and stuffed it in his pocket. A few more coins bought two slim roles of medical adhesive tape.

He dumped the sack of kitty litter and the duct tape in a motel garbage can, locked everything else in the trunk of the car, and drove quickly but carefully back to his own neighborhood. He parked on a side street three blocks from his apartment, carefully checking to make sure he was in a legal space. The car should be fine for a few days. With any luck, and if his nerve held, it wouldn't have to wait for more than a few hours.

He glanced at his watch. He'd been out of Hart's office for an hour and a half. If he wanted to attempt the pinnacle of gaming elegance, he would go back to Hart's office on the fifth floor, walk down the stairs, and exit past the receptionist. There was a chance—even a good chance—that the cops would never have made inquiries about where he was.

But if they had, and knew he had left Hart's office, then a faked return would tip them off. They would know that he *knew*. They would move on him, if they could, and he didn't want to spring any traps prematurely.

On the other hand, if he innocently walked back past the third-floor law office in the well-used main skyway, right past the watchers, wearing only his suit, without a coat or hat . . .

They'd almost certainly assume that however he'd gotten out, he had been on an innocent trip of some kind. Lunch.

He hoped they'd think that.

The *stroke* depended on it.

The maddog walked over to a university dormitory to call a cab.

CHAPTER
— 31 —

"You lost him?" Lucas' eyes were black with rage.

"For at least two hours," the surveillance chief admitted, hangdog. He was remembering Cochrane and the fight after the Fuckup. "We don't know whether he suckered us or just wandered away."

"What happened?" They were in the front seat of Lucas' car on the street outside Vullion's office. The maddog was inside, at work.

"He started out just like he always does, carrying his brief-case, except he wasn't wearing a coat or hat or anything."

"No coat?"

"No coat, and it's cold out. Anyway, he walks over two blocks to another law office. It's a big one. It's got a glassed-in reception area on the third floor of the Hops Exchange."

"Yeah, I know it. Woodley and something-something."

"That's it. So we set up to watch the door and the rest of the third floor, in case he came out the back. We had guys on the skyway level and on the first floor, watching the exits there. After an hour and a half or so, when he didn't come out, we started to get worried. We had Carol call—"

"I hope she had a good excuse."

"It was semihorseshit but it held up okay. She called and said she had an important message for Mr. Vullion and could the receptionist get him. The receptionist called somebody—we're watching this through the glass—and then she comes back on and tells Carol that he'd left a long time ago. Just stopped in to see some guy named Hart for five minutes."

"So where'd he go?"

"I'm getting to that," the surveillance man said defensively. "So Carol says this message is important, and asks, like girl-to-girl, did she see him leave? He's so absentminded, she says, you know how lawyers are. The receptionist says no, she didn't see him leave, but she assumed he left through the fifth-floor exits. See, you can only get in through the reception area, but there are three floors, and you can get out on any of them. They've got an internal elevator, and we didn't know."

"He could have known that," Lucas said. "He probably did. Was it deliberate? Do you think he spotted you?"

"I don't think so. I talked to the people, they all think we're clean."

"Christ, what a mess," said Lucas.

"You think we ought to take him?"

"I don't know. How'd you get him back?"

"Well, we were freaking out and I was talking to everybody to see if there was *anything*, any trace. And then here he comes, bigger'n shit, right through the skyway. He's got his briefcase and a rolled-up *Wall Street Journal* and he goes motoring past the skyway man like he's in a hurry."

"He went right back to his office?"

"Straight back."

"So what do you think?"

The surveillance man nibbled his lip and considered the problem. "I don't know," he said finally. "The thing is, if he was deliberately trying to lose us, he could have gone out through the parking ramp from the fifth floor. But the other thing . . ."

"Yeah?" Lucas prompted.

"I hate to admit it, but he might have gotten by the skyway guy. Completely innocently. We had a lot of spots to block, in case he got by us, somehow. We had a guy in the skyway, watching both the elevators and the stairs. If the elevators opened at just the right minute, and our guy looked over at them, and Vullion popped out of the stairway just at that minute and turned the other way . . ."

"He could have gotten past?"

"He could have. Without ever knowing we were there."

"Jesus. So we don't know," Lucas said. He peered up at Vullion's office window, which was screened by venetian blinds. The lights were still on.

"I kind of think . . ."

"What?" Lucas prompted.

"There's a bunch of fern-type restaurants down from where he was coming when we picked him up again. And he was carrying that paper all rolled up, like he already looked at it. I wouldn't swear to it in a court, but I think he just might've gone down to have lunch. He hadn't eaten lunch yet."

"Hmph."

"So? What do we do?"

Lucas raked his hair with his fingertips and thought about the Fuckup. It shouldn't influence him, he knew, but it did.

"Leave him," Lucas said. "I just hope no dead bodies show up under a counter in a skyway shop."

"Good," the surveillance chief said in relief. If they'd had to grab Vullion because the surveillance had screwed up, somebody could wind up working the tow-truck detail in February.

The game was done; the final night had been one of discussion, not play. It was deemed a great success. A few touches might be desirable . . .

Lee had been mauled by Meade's well-protected troops dug in along Pipe Creek. Meade himself had taken severe casualties. The three days of fighting were as confusing and bloody as the Wilderness or Shiloh. The worst of it had fallen on Pickett: as the first into Gettysburg, his division had held the high ground just south of town. In the pursuit of the Union forces as they retreated on Washington, Pickett's division had been last in the route of march. On the final day at Pipe Creek, Lee had thrown Pickett's relatively fresh division into the center of the line. It died there. The Union held the ground and the Confederates reeled toward a hasty recrossing of the Potomac. The southern tide was going out.

"Something's changed," Elle said to Lucas. They were standing near the exit, away from the others. Elle spoke in a low voice.

Lucas nodded, his voice dropping to match hers. "We think we know who he is. Maybe it was your prayers: a gift from God. An accident. Fate. Whatever."

"Why haven't you arrested him?"

Lucas shrugged. "We know who he is, but we can't prove it. Not quite. We're waiting for him to make a move."

"Is he a man of intelligence?"

"I really don't know." He glanced around the room, dropped his voice another notch. "A lawyer."

"Be careful," Elle said. "This is galloping to a conclusion. He's been playing a game, and if he's a real player, I'm sure he feels it too. He may go for a *coup de maître*."

"I don't see that one's available to him. We'll just grind him down."

"Perhaps," she said, touching his coat sleeve. "But remember, his idea of a win may not be a matter of avoiding capture. He's a lawyer: perhaps he sees himself winning in court. Walking off the board with impunity after an acquittal. This is a very tricky position all the way around."

Lucas left St. Anne's at eight o'clock, drove restlessly home, punched up his word processor, sat in a pool of light, and tried to put the finishing touches on the Everwhen scenario. The opening prose must be lush, must hint of bare-breasted maidens with great asses, sword fights in dark tunnels, long trips, and hale-and-hearty good friends—everything a fifteen-year-old suburban computer freak doesn't have and yearns for. And it had to do all that while scrupulously avoiding pornography or anything else that would offend the kid's mother.

Lucas didn't have it in him. He sighed and shut down the computer, tossed the word-processing disk into his software file, and walked down to the library and sat in the dark to think.

The missing two hours worried him. It *could* have been an

accident. And if the maddog had slipped away deliberately, why had he done it? Where had he gone? How and when did he spot the watchers? He hadn't gone out to kill—he wouldn't have his equipment, unless he carried it around in his brief-case, and he wasn't that stupid.

The trip to the antiques shop on the previous day was also worrisome. True, the maddog had stopped first at the computer store and picked up a case of paper. But Lucas remembered a half-case of paper sitting under the printer. He really didn't need any more. Not badly enough to make a special trip for it. Then he'd gone into the antiques shop, and one of the watchers, who had been passing on the opposite side of the street, saw the shop owner take the fishing lure out of the window. That had been confirmed after the maddog left, when Sloan had been sent in to pump the woman.

An antique fishing lure. Why? The maddog's apartment was virtually bare of ornament, so Lucas couldn't believe he'd bought it for himself.

A gift? But for whom? As far as they could tell, he had no friends. He made no phone calls, except on business, and got none at home. His mail consisted of bills and ad-vertisements.

What was the lure for?

Sitting in the dark, his eyes closed, he turned the problem in his mind, manipulated it like a Rubik's Cube, and always came up with mismatched sides.

No point in sitting here, he thought. He looked at his watch. Nine o'clock. He got up, put on a jacket, and went out to the car. The nights were getting very cold now, and the wind on his face triggered a memory of skiing. Time to get his downhill skis tuned and the cross-country skis scraped and hot-waxed. He was always tired of winter by the time it ended, but he kind of liked the beginning.

The maddog's apartment was five miles from Lucas' house. Lucas stopped at a newsstand to buy copies of *Powder* and *Skiing*.

"Nothing," the surveillance cop said when he came up the stairs. "He's watching television."

Lucas peered out the window at the maddog's apartment. He could see nothing but the blue glow of a television through the living-room curtains. "Move, you motherfucker," he said.

CHAPTER

— 32 —

The maddog forced himself to eat dinner, to clean up. Everything as usual. At seven o'clock he turned on the television. All drapes pulled. He glanced around. Now or never.

The maddog had never had a use for many tools, but this would not be a sophisticated job. He got a long-handled screwdriver, a clawhammer, a pair of pliers, and an electric lantern from the workroom and carried them upstairs. In his bedroom he put on two pairs of athletic socks to muffle his footsteps. When he was ready, he pulled down the attic stairs.

The attic was little better than a crawl space under the eaves of the apartment house, partitioned among the four apartments with quarter-inch plywood. Since the apartment's insulation was laid in the attic floor and the attic itself was unheated, it was cold, and suitable only for the storage of items that wouldn't be damaged by Minnesota's winter cold. The maddog had been in it only twice before: once when he rented the apartment, and again on the day when he conceived the *stroke*, to examine the plywood partitions.

Padding silently across the attic floor, the maddog crossed to the partition for the apartment that was beside his, facing the street. The plywood paneling between his part of the attic and the opposite side had been nailed in place from his side. The work was sloppy and he was able to slip the end of the screwdriver under the edge of the panel and carefully pry it up. It took twenty minutes to loosen the panel enough that he could draw the nails out with the clawhammer and the pliers. Again, the work had been sloppy: no more than a dozen nails held the plywood panel in place.

When the panel was loose, he pulled it back enough that he could slip into the opposite side of the attic. The other side was almost as empty as his, with only a few jigsaw puzzles stacked near the folded stairs. Silence was now critical, and he took his time with the next job. He had plenty of time, he thought. He wouldn't move until the police spies thought he was in bed. Working quietly and doggedly in the light of the electric lantern, he loosened the plywood panels between his neighbor's attic and the attic of the woman who lived in the apartment diagonally opposite his.

That was his goal. The owner was a surgical nurse, recently divorced, who, ever since moving into the apartment, had worked the overnight shift in the trauma-care unit of St. Paul Ramsey Medical Center. He had called the hospital from his office, asked for her, and been told that she would be on at eleven o'clock.

It took a cold half-hour to get into her side of the attic. When the access was clear, he quietly propped the panels back in place so a casual inspection wouldn't reveal the missing nails. He stole back down the stairs to his bedroom, leaving the flashlight, tools, and nails at the top of the steps. When he got back, he would push the nails as best he could into their holes. Tomorrow morning, when the people opposite had gone to work, and before the maddog's last victim was found, he would go back and hammer them in place.

Downstairs again, he considered a quick trip to a neighborhood convenience store. A walking trip. It might be an undue provocation, but he thought not. He turned off the television, put on his jacket, checked his wallet, and went out the front door. He tried to goof along, two blocks, obviously not in a hurry. He crossed the blacktopped parking area of the convenience store, went inside, bought some bakery goods, some instant hot cereal, a jug of milk, and a copy of *Penthouse*. Back outside, he bit into a bismarck, savored the cherry filling that squirted into his mouth, and sauntered back home.

That should do it. That should prepare them psychologically for the idea that he would be in for the rest of the evening. He crossed his porch, pushed inside, locked the door behind him, put the cereal and milk away, and turned on the football game.

It was just starting. The Cowboys and the Giants. He watched the first half, staring blankly at the screen, not much caring what happened; caring less when the Giants started to roll. At halftime he slipped the tape of Davenport into the videocassette recorder and watched the interview. Davenport, the player. Carla Ruiz, the once-and-never Chosen. He ran it a second time and turned it off and deliberately walked around the apartment. Out to the kitchen. Look in the silverware drawer. Open refrigerator, drink milk, put glass on cupboard. Ten-forty-five. Pick up phone, call nurse. Twenty rings. Thirty rings. Forty. Fifty. He was tempted to call the hospital and ask for her, but better not. The phone could be tapped. A risk, but he would have to live with it.

He turned out the lights and went upstairs, where he undressed, dropped his clothes in a heap, and began to dress again. Dark turtleneck. Jeans. Nike Airs, with laces tied together and looped around his neck. New ski jacket, navy blue with a dark turquoise flash on the breast. Gloves. Watch cap. He turned out the bedroom light.

He went down the hallway and up the attic stairs on stocking feet, guiding himself through the dark with a hand on the wall. At the top of the steps he found the light, switched it on, and eased into the opposite quadrant of the attic, then into the nurse's quadrant. He pushed down on the release for the stairs, opening the hallway hatch just an inch, and listened. Not a sound. No lights.

Her apartment was laid out like a left-handed version of his own. He checked the bedroom first, flashing the light through the open door. The bed was neatly made and empty. He went down through the kitchen, saw the phone, paused, and thought: Why not? He checked the phone book, called the hospital, and asked for her.

"This is Sylvia." He hung up, clicking the hook rapidly, as though there had been line trouble. She was there, at the hospital.

He went through the kitchen, into the utility room, and cracked the door to the garage. Empty. Given the landscaping—the hedge across the back of the lot—he should be able to open the garage door a foot or more without being seen. He checked to make sure the garage wasn't locked, and lifted it, slowly, slowly. When it was up a foot, he slid out on his back.

It was a dark night, cloudy, and he lay for a moment in the door inset, invisible from the street, gathering his courage. When he had controlled himself, he eased the door most of the way down, leaving a gap of an inch or so. When he returned, it would be easier to lift.

Now for the bad part, he thought. On his hands and knees, he crossed to the base of the hedge and followed it out to the sidewalk. He looked both ways. The houses around him were all occupied by families. The two surveillance houses, which would cover the sides of his own apartment, were behind him now. His only problem would come if there were wing cars out on the street, out of sight of his apartment. That wouldn't make much sense, from the police point of view, stationing men where they couldn't see the target's apartment, but who knew what they might be doing?

Steeling himself, he made his move. Stepped out on the sidewalk and walked along, his head bobbing, straight away from the house. He tried not to be obvious about it, but he checked parked cars. Nobody. If there were surveillance cars, they should be out on the wings. It was unlikely that they would be parked back by the Interstate: there was no way out that way.

It was three blocks down to the car. He unlocked it, slipped inside, and took stock. He was loose, he was sure of it. It all *felt* right. He sat for a moment, *feeling* the environment around him, extending himself into the night. He was free. He turned on the light, cranked the engine, and headed out. He had thought about this, and hadn't made up his mind. Now he did. Davenport drove a Porsche, the papers said. Would it be parked at one of the surveillance houses? If they were surveillance houses? He took the street one back from his own, cruising by the house he suspected. Two cars, non-descript Ford sedans. Like cops might drive. How about the other house? He took a left, two blocks, his headlights raking an oncoming car. A Porsche, in fact. He caught a quick glimpse of Davenport's face as he rounded the corner. The maddog slowed, did a U-turn, and went back. Davenport's car had stopped outside the second surveillance house. He was getting out with a white rectangular box of some kind . . . A pizza.

A pizza.

It answered the next question for him. He had not decided how to get into Ruiz' apartment. He had thought of pulling the fire alarm. He would hit her when she stepped into the hallway. But when the janitor learned that it was a false alarm, he might check the building's occupants to see if anybody had a problem. And there was the possibility that somebody else would come into the hallway before Ruiz. He had thought of imitating Lucas' voice—but what if the door was on a chain and she peeked out and a stranger was there? She would *know*.

But a pizza . . .

He stopped and got a pizza, waiting impatiently as the slow-moving pizza-maker kneaded the dough, tossed it around, pounded it out, and pushed it into the oven. Cooking took another ten minutes. The maddog glanced at his watch. Eleven-thirty-five. He'd have to hurry. The janitor usually locked Ruiz' building at midnight.

It was another ten minutes to the squat old St. Paul ware-house; he could see it from the Interstate as he started into the exit ramp. He parked near the building's main door and got his equipment out of the trunk: the hose full of cat litter, the can of Mace, the roll of tape, the work gloves. Everything but the hose went in his pockets.

He went in the door and up the stairs; the janitor, who doubled as the elevator operator, usually hung out by the elevator door where he could listen to his boombox. The first two floors were silent. Somebody on the third floor was playing a radio, and a faint laugh trickled down the concrete hallways. The fourth floor was quiet, as was the fifth.

Down four doors. Light under her door. He breathed a sigh of relief. She was in. He had been prepared to abort, to do it over again if he had to. Now he wouldn't. The *stroke* would happen.

He pulled on the yellow cotton gloves, took a breath, let it out, rapped on the door, and called, "Pizza." She had never seen his face.

He heard her footsteps crossing the floor. "I didn't order a pizza," she said from the other side of the door.

"Well, I got a pizza for this studio for Lucas Davenport. I'm supposed to say the wine is on the way, if it isn't already here."

There was a moment of silence, then a soft, "Oh, no."

What? What was wrong? The maddog tensed, ready to flee, but the door was opening. There was a chain. Ruiz seemed to be alone. She peeked out, saw the box.

"Just a minute," she said with a note of resignation in her voice. There was something going on that he didn't understand. She pushed the door shut and he heard the chain come off. He had the pizza balanced on the hand that held the hose. The Mace was in the other. Ruiz opened the door, nobody behind her. The maddog thrust the pizza at her and stepped forward. She stepped back, looking up at him as the pizza came at her so unexpectedly hard, she saw the gloves, and then, in an instant, she *knew*, but the can was up and he hit her in the mouth and eyes with the spray and she dropped the pizza and tried to cover her face and choked and staggered backward. The maddog pressed into the apartment and swung the hose. She had one arm up and it glanced off. Gagging, she half-turned and stumbled toward a bookshelf with her hands outstretched, and the maddog stopped just for an instant and kicked the door shut and went after her. She was pawing the bookshelf, still blind, looking for something, looking, and the maddog was on her and she had one hand on a small chrome-steel pistol and he hit her with the hose and she went down and still had the weapon and with a vision as acute and clear and sharp as water crystal he saw that she had it by the butt only, that her fingers were not fitted through the trigger guard and he took just an extra fragment of a second to get the right backswing and he hit her again on the back of the head and then again, bouncing off her shoulder, and again, straight into her face . . . she stopped moving, curled into a fetal position . . .

The maddog, breathing hard, dropped the hose and fell on her like a tiger on a staked goat. Pulling her head back, he thrust the Kotex into her mouth, wrapped her head with tape. She was dazed and unresisting. He worried for a moment that he had killed her and thought, absurdly: This is not a Chosen, this is a raid, it makes no difference when she dies . . .

The pistol was lying on the floor and he pushed it away, stood up, grabbed her by the shirt collar, and dragged her into the bedroom and used the tape to bind her to the bed. She was wearing a man's flannel shirt and he ripped it open, a button popping off and clicking against the wall, the maddog's hearing now supernaturally keen, the sensory high coming with a rush. He snatched the side of her bra and wrenched the back strap, breaking it, and the shoulder straps. Unfastened her jeans, pulled them halfway down her legs. Ripped the crotch out of her underpants and pulled them up her belly.

Stood back, surveyed the prisoner. Just right. She wasn't a Chosen, but she could be fun. He reached out, rubbed her patch of pubic hair.

"Don't go away," he said in sweet sarcasm. "I'll need something sharp for the rest of this."

CHAPTER

— 33 —

"Has he gone to bed?" Lucas asked.

"Yeah," said the first watcher, the tall one.

"Shit." Lucas looked at the ceiling, brooding. Maybe he'd spotted them. "He's got to move soon. He's *got* to."

"My stomach's moving now," said the second surveillance cop. "I need something to eat."

"Three more hours," said the first one.

"Christ." The second cop looked at Lucas. "So. What're you doing?"

Lucas had been lying on the surveillance mattress, reading the copy of *Powder*.

"Uh . . ."

"I don't suppose you'd be interested in a pizza?"

"Sure. I guess." Lucas rolled to his feet.

"There's a place over by the university. Pretty good," said the hungry cop. "I'll call, they'll have it ready when you get there."

"You got your handset?" asked the first cop.

"Yeah."

"I'll holler if anything happens."

The pizza wasn't ready when he got there, but it was ready five minutes later. He took it out to the car and headed back, letting the Porsche run a bit, cutting dangerously close to an oncoming car as he turned into the street that led to the surveillance house. Can't do this, he thought as the other car's lights raked over him. The last thing he needed was a fistfight with some outstate redneck who didn't like being cut off.

He hustled the hot pizza up three flights of steps to the surveillance post on the top floor.

"Nothing," said the first cop.

"Quiet as a fuckin' bunny rabbit," said the hungry one. He pried the top off the pizza box. "If this thing has anchovies on it, you're a dead man."

Lucas took a piece of the pizza and went back to the magazine.

"Night-light must have burned out," the first cop said after a while.

"Hmmph?"

"No night-light tonight."

Lucas crawled to the window and looked out. The maddog's bedroom window was a flat black rectangle. Not a glimmer of light. That was odd, Lucas thought. If a guy slept with a night-light, he usually needed it . . .

"Dammit," he said, pivoting and sitting with his back against the wall, his knees bent in front of him.

"What?"

"I don't know." He turned his head and stared over the windowsill. "That freaks me out. That's not right."

"Just a fuckin' night-light," the hungry cop said as he finished the last of the pizza and licked his fingers.

"It's not right," Lucas said. He smelled the wrongness. Watching him now for almost two weeks, a night-light every night. But there was no other way out of the house. Not unless he poked a hole in the walls.

The attic, he thought. That fuckin' attic.

Lucas crawled to the telephone. "What's his number?" he asked the first surveillance cop, snapping his fingers.

"Jesus, are you gonna—?"

"Give me the goddamn number," Lucas said, his voice cold.

The first cop glanced at his no-longer-hungry companion, who shrugged and took a small notebook from his pocket and read the number. Lucas punched it in.

"If he answers, it's just a wrong number," he said, glancing at the others. "I'll ask for Louise." The maddog's phone rang. Fifteen times. Thirty. Fifty. No light in the window. Nothing.

"Son of a gun," said the first cop.

"Give me the number again. Maybe I misdialed," Lucas said. The cop read him the number and he punched it in again. "You sure it's the right number?"

"It's right," said the cop. The phone rang. And rang. No answer.

"Let it ring," Lucas said, running for the door. "I'm going over there."

"Jesus . . ."

Lucas banged out the front door of the surveillance house, ran across the street to the maddog's porch. He could hear the phone ringing and he pushed the doorbell and kept it down. Five seconds, ten. No light. He wrenched open the storm door and tried the interior door. Locked. No time for subtlety. He backed off a step and kicked the door at the lock with all of his strength, smashing it open.

Inside, he ran to the base of the stairs.

"Vullion?" He was carrying the Heckler & Koch P7, and had it in his fist as he went up the stairs. "Vullion?"

A light went on in the living room, and Lucas' head snapped back and he saw the first surveillance cop following him with his pistol drawn. Lucas went the rest of the way up the stairs and saw the steps from the attic. They had been pulled down into the hallway.

"Motherfucker's gone," he yelled at the cop behind him. "Kill that phone, will you?" Lucas checked the bedroom, then climbed the steps into the attic. The partitions separating the attic quadrants were loose. The phone stopped ringing as Lucas backed down the steps.

"He went through the attic into one of the other apartments and out that way," he shouted to the cop. "Get everybody on the street, look for a guy on foot. Bust him. We got him for housebreaking, if nothing else."

The surveillance cop ran out the front door. Lucas moved through the front room, turned once, and looked at it. Nothing. Not a thing. His eyes narrowed and he went back up to the bedroom, slid his hand under the mattress. Then swept it around. The pictures were gone.

He went back down and headed for the telephone. Call Daniel, he thought. Get some help out here. As he picked up the phone, his eye caught the tiny rectangular red light on the VCR. Vullion had been watching a tape. Lucas dropped the phone, turned on the television, ran the tape back a few numbers, and punched the On button. Carla. Lucas looked up, his eyes gone blank. The interview. Carla.

He ran, his mind sifting the possibilities, his body already doing what his mind would eventually decide. Vullion was going after Carla. He wouldn't take a bus, so he must, somehow, have gotten wheels. Lucas had a handset. He could call the St. Paul cops and have somebody at Carla's apartment in three or four minutes. That's what it would take for the cops to understand what he was saying, to get together, and get over to Carla's warehouse.

But he was only six miles away. All of it Interstate. The Porsche could be there in five minutes, six at the outside. Would the extra minutes kill her? If they would not, he might make the *coup*.

Lucas dove into the Porsche, cranked it, and hammered the accelerator, slid through the first turn, hit the second at forty-five, braked to fifty to get onto the Interstate ramp. A Honda Civic was ahead of him on the ramp and Lucas put two wheels on the grass and blew past the Honda at seventy, the other driver's frightened face a half-moon on the periphery of his vision. He was doing eighty-five coming off the ramp, and floored it, the speedometer climbing without hesitation through the hundred mark, one ten, one twenty. He left it there, sweeping past the cars on the highway, the exits clicking past like heartbeats.

Two minutes. Lexington Avenue. Three minutes. Dale. Three minutes, twenty seconds, sweeping into the Tenth Street exit, downshifting, the machine clawing through the first intersection, the warehouse looming in front of him. He wrenched the car to the side of the street, took the gym bag with the silenced pistol from behind the seat, and ran toward the building's side door.

As he approached, the janitor appeared with keys in his hands.

"No," Lucas shouted, and the janitor paused. Lucas groped in his shirt pocket, found his identification, and flashed it as he pushed through the door.

"You stay right here," he told the janitor, who stood with his mouth hanging open. "Some St. Paul cops are going to come here, and you take them up in the elevator. You wait right here, you got it?"

The janitor nodded. "Wait right here," he said.

"Right." Lucas patted him on the shoulder and dashed up the stairs.

Carla's door had better locks, he thought breathlessly as he came up the last few steps, but it was still a crappy door. No time to think about it really. Christ, if the maddog wasn't here, this was going to be embarrassing. He hurried down to the doorway, saw the light coming from beneath it. He dropped the gym bag, took a step back, and kicked the door in. Lucas exploded into the room, his pistol in a two-handed grip.

The studio was empty.

CHAPTER
— 34 —

There was a quiet sound from the left, like a cat dropping from a bookcase. But it was no cat. Lucas pivoted and extended the gun. There was a small room, dark, cavelike. A groan. He stepped forward. Couldn't see. Stepped forward, still couldn't see. Another step, three feet from the door. A white shape, trussed, arched, on the bed, another groan, nothing else. . . .

Another step, and suddenly Vullion was there, his eyes wide and hard like boiled eggs, his hands covered with fuzzy yellow gloves, a pipe of some kind in one hand, the pipe sweeping down, and Lucas twisted the last three inches he needed to fire and the pipe smashed into the back of his hand and the gun went down on the floor. Lucas felt the bones in his right hand go and he pushed the pipe sideways with his left and Vullion's other hand was coming up in a long sweeping thrust and in it the knife was glittering like a short-sword toward Lucas' bowels. Lucas pivoted and caught the thrust with his broken hand and felt the hand flex and he screamed but the blade passed clear, under his arm, and he caught Vullion's knife hand with his left hand and smashed his right elbow into Vullion's eye socket. The impact lifted Vullion back, and they staggered together back into the tiny bedroom and Vullion's legs folded beneath him as he hit the bed and they fell together on top of Carla and Lucas pounded Vullion's face with his forearm once, twice, three times, the pain from his broken hand like lightning in his brain.

And then Vullion stopped. Then Lucas twisted the knife arm, and the knife fell to the floor. Vullion was stunned, not out. Lucas hit him twice with his left hand, pounding Vullion's ear, then rolled him off Carla into the narrow space between the bed and the wall and knelt on his head and shoulders.

"Motherfucker," Lucas groaned. His own breath was harsh and ragged in his ears. He reached awkwardly into his pocket with his good hand and took out his key ring. A miniature Tekna knife dangled from the ring. He pulled the knife out of its plastic sheath and gently slipped the blade under the tape that circled Carla's head, holding the gag in place. When he pulled the Kotex from her mouth, she gasped and then whimpered, an animal cry, like a rabbit's. She was alive.

"Hurt me," Vullion moaned from beneath Lucas' knees. "I'm hurt."

"Shut up, motherfucker," Lucas said. He hit him on the head with his closed left fist and Vullion twitched and moaned again.

Lucas reached forward and cut the tape that bound Carla's arms to the bed, then freed her legs.

"It's me, Lucas," he said next to her ear. "You're going to be okay. The ambulance is coming, just stay here."

He levered himself up off the bed, grabbed Vullion by the back of his shirt and physically lifted him from the floor and half-dragged, half-led him into the studio. Lucas' pistol was lying against the wall. With a sweeping kick he knocked Vullion's legs out from beneath him, and guided his upper body down to the floor, protecting his head. He didn't want him unconscious. Vullion went down like a rag man.

While he was down, Lucas picked up the pistol and walked quickly backward to the hallway, got the gym bag, and brought it inside. He pushed the door closed with his foot.

Vullion, on his stomach, brought his hands to his ears.

"Get up," Lucas said to Vullion. Vullion made no response, and Lucas kicked him in the hip. "Get up. Come on, get up."

Vullion struggled up, fell back to his stomach, then pushed up to one knee. Blood was running from his nose into his mouth. The pupil of one eye was dilated. The other eye was closed, the lid and flesh around the socket bloody and swollen.

"On your feet, asshole, or I swear to Christ I'll kick you to death."

Vullion was watching him as best he could, still dazed. With an exhausted heave he got to his feet and swayed.

"Now, back up. Five steps." Lucas thrust the pistol at Vullion's chest. Vullion stepped back carefully, but looked as though he might be recovering.

"Now, you just stand there," Lucas said as he stepped toward the telephone.

"I knew about the surveillance," Vullion said through broken teeth.

"I figured that out about ten minutes ago," Lucas said. He gestured with his left hand.

"Is your hand broken?"

"Shut up," said Lucas. He lifted the receiver from the phone.

"Did you deliberately lure me here? With your friend? Like you did with McGowan?"

"Not this time. McGowan was bait, though," Lucas said.

"You're worse than I am in some ways," Vullion said. Blood dribbled down his chin. He swayed again, and he reached out to Carla's sink to brace himself. "I was taking people who were . . . chips. You set up a friend. If I had a friend, I would never do that."

"Like I told the papers, you're not that much of a player," Lucas said quietly in a voice just above a whisper.

"We'll see about that," the maddog said. He was growing stronger, and Lucas was impressed in spite of himself. "I have defenses. You won't be able to prove any of the murders. After all, I did not kill Miss Ruiz. And you'll notice that my method is different this time. You won't find a note. I was going to make it here, afterward. If it comes to negotiations, I'll get an insanity plea. A few years at the state hospital and I'm out. And even if worse comes to worst, and I get a first-degree, well, it's eighteen years at Stillwater. I can do it."

Lucas nodded. "I thought of that. It would be like losing,

seeing you get away alive. I really couldn't stand that. Not with an inferior player.''

''What?''

Lucas ignored him. He groped in his pants pocket and took a single nine-millimeter shell from his pocket. Watching Vullion carefully, he braced the pistol against his armpit and punched the magazine out of the pistol butt. This was when Vullion would act, if he was going to, but he did not; he stood still, puzzled, as Lucas pushed the blank into the top slot, slammed the magazine back into the butt, and jacked the shell into the chamber.

''What are you doing?'' Vullion asked. Something was happening. Something not right.

''First, I'm going to call the cops,'' Lucas said. He stepped to Carla's wall phone and dialed 911. When he got the dispatcher, he identified himself and asked for an ambulance and backup. The operator asked that he leave the line open and Lucas said he would. That was standard operating procedure. Lucas let the phone dangle and stepped away from it.

Vullion was still watching him, frowning. When Lucas stepped away from the phone, the maddog stepped back from the sink. Lucas pointed his pistol at the ceiling, fired once, his eyes tracking the ejected shell, the maddog's eyes involuntarily widening at the sharp explosion. He was still reacting when Lucas fired two more shots. One hit Vullion in the right lung, one in the left.

The three shots were in a quick musical rhythm, a bang; bang-bang.

Vullion was swatted back a step, two, and then he fell, going straight down as though his bones had melted. His mouth worked a few times and he rolled onto his back. The shots were killing shots, but not too good; not too aimed. It was supposed to have been a gunfight. Lucas stepped over to look down at the dying man.

''What happened?''

The voice might have come from an animal. Lucas turned, and Carla stood in the doorway to the bedroom. She was no longer bleeding, but had been battered, her nose broken, her face cut. She tottered over to Lucas.

"You've got to go back and lie down," Lucas said.

A witness could kill him.

"Wait," Carla said as he gripped her arm. She looked down at Vullion. "Is he dead?"

"Yeah. He's gone."

But Vullion was not quite gone. His eyes moved fractionally toward the dark-haired woman who stood over him, and a tiny spate of blood trickled out of the corner of his mouth as his lips spasmed and opened.

"Mom?" he asked.

"What?" said Carla. Vullion's legs spasmed.

"Forget it," Lucas said. He moved her physically back toward the bedroom, pushed her onto the bed. "Stay here. You're hurt." She nodded dumbly and let her body fall back.

There was almost no time now. The St. Paul cops would be here in seconds. He stepped quickly back out of the room, over to Vullion. Vullion was dead. Lucas nodded, retrieved the gym bag, and lifted out the silenced pistol. He fitted it to Vullion's gloved hand, pointed it at Carla's shelf of art books, and pulled the trigger. There was a *phut* and *pop*! as the slug hit a three-inch-thick copy of *The Great Book of French Impressionism*. Lucas pulled the silencer off the muzzle and laid the weapon on the floor a few feet from Vullion's outstretched hand. He looked around on the floor, found the shell casing from the blank he'd fired, and pocketed it.

The elevators started up and Lucas pulled the silencer apart as he reviewed the scene.

There would be powder residue, nitrites, on Vullion's glove, on his bare wrist, on the sleeve of his coat and his face. The slug in the bookshelf, if it could be salvaged at all, would match test shots from the Smith found on the floor next to Vullion's body. Both the Smith and Lucas' P7 were nine-millimeters, so that would account for the fact that the shots would sound the same on the 911 tape. And the shots were sequenced so closely that no one would doubt that Lucas had fired in self-defense.

It would hold up, he thought with satisfaction. He would have to work on his story a bit. He and Vullion fought in the bedroom. He dragged Vullion out, not wanting to endanger Carla, and outside the room, Vullion had pulled the pistol, which had been tucked into his waistband. That would do it. Nobody would want to know too much, anyway.

He walked to a window, pulled it open, and threw out the two big plastic pieces of the silencer. Just more street junk. The Thinsulate wrapping and the internal tube he tossed among Carla's stock of weaving materials. He would retrieve it later, get rid of it.

He slipped his own pistol into its holster and walked back to Carla's bedroom. She lay unmoving on the bed, but her chest was rising and falling regularly.

"It's Lucas again," he told her, gripping her leg with his good hand. "Everything's going to be okay. It's Lucas."

He heard the first St. Paul cop enter the room, and yelled, "Back here, Minneapolis police, Lucas Davenport, we need an ambulance quick . . ."

As he called out, Vullion's stunned and dying face flashed through the back of Lucas' mind.

He thought, "That's six."

CHAPTER
— 35 —

Two days after Christmas, his hand still in a cast six weeks after the surgery, Lucas walked across an empty campus, through a driving snowstorm, to Elle Kruger's office in Fat Albert Hall. Her office was on the third floor. He took the worn concrete steps, unzipping his parka and brushing snow from his shoulders as he climbed. The third-floor hallway was dark. At the far end, one office showed a lighted pane of frosted glass. His footsteps echoed as he walked down and knocked.

"Come in, Lucas."

He pushed open the door. Elle was reading in an armchair that sat to one side of the desk, facing a small couch. An inexpensive stereo played "The Great Gate of Kiev" from *Pictures at an Exhibition*. Lucas handed her a package he'd carried in his coat pocket.

"A gift." She smiled happily, her face lighted, weighing the package in her hand. "I hope it wasn't expensive."

Lucas hung his parka on a coatrack and dropped onto the couch. "Tell you the truth, it cost an arm and a leg."

Her smile diminished slightly. "You know we seek poverty."

"This won't make you any richer," Lucas said. "If you ever sell it, I'll come over and strangle you."

"Ah. Then I suppose . . ." She shook her head and began to unwrap the box. "My biggest problem, the cause of my most grievous sin, is curiosity."

"I'll never understand the Church," Lucas said.

The nun opened the small red box and fished out a medallion of yellow gold on a long gold chain. "Lucas," she said.

"Read it," he said.

She turned it in her hands and read, " *'Agnus Dei: qui tollis peccata mundi, miserere nobis'* . . . it's from the Missal. 'O Lamb of God, who takest away the sins of the world, have mercy on us.' "

"That's certainly pious enough."

She sighed. "It's still gold."

"So wear it with disdain. When you start to like it, send it to Mother Teresa."

She laughed. "Mother Teresa," she said. She looked at the medallion again, then looked closer and said, "What's this? On the other side."

"A minor inscription."

"The letters are so small." She held it eight inches from her nose, peering at it.

> *Necessity has no law*
> *As Augustine descries her,*
> *So the maddog's brought to earth*
> *With the help of Nun the Wiser.*

She gasped, then started to laugh, throwing her head back and letting it roll out. "This is *terrible*," she said at last. "Augustine is whirling in his grave."

"It's not *that* bad," Lucas said with a bit of frost. "In fact . . ."

"Lucas, it's *awful*." She started laughing again, and finally Lucas began laughing with her. When she stopped, she brushed tears from her eyes and said, "I'll treasure it forever. I don't know what my sisters will think when they find it on my body . . ."

"*They* can send it to Mother Teresa," Lucas suggested.

They talked as old friends: of phony fainting spells during the rosary after school, of the boy who admitted in fourth grade that he didn't believe in God. His name was Gene, that's all they could remember.

"Are you okay?" she asked after a while.

"I think so."

"And your relationship . . ."

"Is doing well, thank you. I want to marry her, but she won't."

"Officially, I'm appalled. Unofficially, I suspect she must be quite an intelligent woman. You are definitely a high-risk proposition. . . . What about Carla Ruiz?"

"Gone to Chicago. She has a new friend."

"The nightmares?"

"Getting worse."

"Oh, no."

"She's seeing a counselor."

And later still.

"You feel no qualms about Louis Vullion's death?"

"None. Should I?"

"I had wondered at the circumstances," she said.

Lucas pondered for a moment. "Elle. If you want to know everything, I'll tell you everything."

It was her turn to ponder. She turned to the big window, a black silhouette against the snow that drove against the glass.

Finally she shook her head, and he noticed she was clutching the medallion. "No. I don't want to know everything. I'm not a confessor. And I will pray for you and for Louis Vullion. But as for knowing . . ."

She turned back, a tiny, grim smile on her face. ". . . I'm content to be Nun the Wiser."

If you enjoyed RULES OF PREY,

then don't miss John Sandford's

bestseller . . .

SHADOW PREY

Available in paperback from

Berkley Books.

Here is a sample of this explosive

novel of shattering suspense . . .

•   •   •

Ray Cuervo sat in his office and counted his money. He counted his money every Friday afternoon between five and six o'clock. He made no secret of it.

Cuervo owned six apartment buildings scattered around Indian country south of the Minneapolis loop. The cheapest apartment went for thirty-nine dollars a week. The most expensive was seventy-five. When he collected his rent, Cuervo took neither checks nor excuses. If you didn't have the cash by two o'clock Friday, you slept on the sidewalk. Bidness, as Ray Cuervo told any number of broken-ass indigents, was bidness.

Dangerous business, sometimes. Cuervo carried a chrome-plated Charter Arms .38 Special tucked in his pants while he collected his money. The gun was old. The barrel was pitted and the butt was unfashionably small. But it worked, and the shells were always fresh. You could see the shiny brass winking out at the edge of the cylinder. Not a flashgun, his renters said. It was a shooter. When Cuervo counted the week's take, he kept the pistol on the desktop near his right hand.

Cuervo's office was a one-room cubicle at the top of three flights of stairs. The furnishings were sparse and cheap: a black dial telephone, a metal desk, a wooden file cabinet, and an oak swivel chair on casters. A four-year-old *Sports Illustrated* swimsuit calendar hung on the left-hand wall. Cuervo never changed it past April, the month where you could see the broad's brown nipples through the wet T-shirt. Opposite the calendar was a corkboard. A dozen business cards were tacked to the corkboard along with two fading bumper stickers. One said SHIT HAPPENS and the other said HOW'S MY DRIVING? DIAL 1-800-EAT-SHIT. Cuervo's wife, a Kentucky sharecropper girl with a mouth like barbed wire, called the office a hellhole. Ray Cuervo paid no attention. He *was* a slumlord, after all.

Cuervo counted the cash out in neat piles—ones, fives, and tens. The odd twenty he put in his pocket. Coins he counted, noted, and dumped in a Maxwell House coffee can. Cuervo was a fat man with small black eyes. When he lifted his heavy chin, three rolls of fat popped out on the back of his red neck. When he leaned forward, three more rolls popped out on his side, under his armpits. And when he farted, which was often, he unconsciously eased one obese cheek off the chair to reduce the compression. He didn't think the movement either impolite or impolitic. If a woman was in the room, he said, "Oops." If the company was all male, he said nothing. Farting was something men did.

A few minutes after five o'clock on October third, an unseasonably warm day, the door slammed at the bottom of the stairs and a man started up. Cuervo put his fingertips on the Charter Arms .38 and half stood so he could see the visitor. The man on the stairs turned his face up and Cuervo relaxed.

Leo Clark. An old customer. Like most of the Indians who rented Cuervo's apartments, Leo was always back and forth from the reservations. He never had trouble with him.

Leo paused at the second landing, catching his breath, then came up the last flight. He was a Sioux, in his forties, a loner, dark from the summer sun. Long black braids trailed down his back and a piece of Navaho silver flashed from his belt. He came from the West somewhere: Rosebud, Standing Rock, someplace like that.

"Leo, how are you?" Cuervo said without looking up. He had money in both hands, counting. "Need a place?"

"Put your hands in your lap, Ray," Leo said. Cuervo looked up. Leo was pointing a pistol at him.

"Aw, man, don't do this," Cuervo groaned, straightening

up. He didn't look at his pistol, but he was thinking about it. "If you need a few bucks, I'll loan it to you."

"Sure you will," Leo said. "Two for one." Cuervo did a little loan-sharking on the side. Bidness was bidness.

"Come on, Leo." Cuervo casually dropped the stack of bills on the desktop, freeing his gun hand. "You wanna spend your old age in the joint?"

"If you move again I'll shoot holes in your head. I mean it, Ray," Leo said. Cuervo checked the other man's face. It was as cold and dark as a Mayan statue's. Cuervo stopped moving.

Leo edged around the desk. No more than three feet separated them, but the hole at the end of Leo's pistol pointed unwaveringly at Ray Cuervo's nose.

"Just sit still. Take it easy," Leo said. When he was behind the chair, he said, "I'm going to put a pair of handcuffs on you, Ray. I want your hands behind the chair."

Cuervo followed instructions, turning his head to see what Bluebird was doing.

"Look straight ahead," Leo said, tapping him behind the ear with the gun barrel. Cuervo looked straight ahead. Leo stepped back, pushed the pistol into the waistband of his slacks, and took an obsidian knife from his front pants pocket. The knife was seven inches of beautifully crafted black volcanic glass taken from an obsidian cliff at Yellowstone National Park. Its edge was fluted and it was as sharp as a surgeon's scalpel.

"Hey, Ray?" Leo said, stepping up closer to the slumlord. Cuervo had farted, either in fear or exasperation, and the fetid smell filled the room. He hadn't bothered to say "Oops."

"Yeah?" Cuervo looked straight ahead. Calculating. His legs were in the kneehole under the desktop—it'd be hard to move in a hurry. Let it ride, he thought, just a couple more minutes. When Leo was putting on the cuffs, maybe the right move . . . the gun glittered on the desk a foot-and-a-half from his eyes.

"I lied about the handcuffs, Ray," Leo said. He grabbed

Ray Cuervo by the hair above his forehead and jerked his head back. With a single powerful slash, Leo cut Ray Cuervo's throat from ear to ear.

Cuervo half stood and twisted free and groped helplessly at his neck with one hand while the other hand crawled frantically across his desk toward the Charter Arms .38. He knew even as he tried that he wouldn't make it. Blood spurted from his severed carotid artery as though from a garden hose, spraying the leaves of green dollars on the desk, the *Sports Illustrated* broad with the tits, the brown linoleum floor.

Ray Cuervo twisted and turned and fell, batting the Maxwell House coffee can off the desk. Coins pitched and clattered and rolled around the office and a few bounced down the stairs. Cuervo lay faceup on the floor, his vision narrowing to a dim and closing hole that finally settled around Leo Clark, whose face remained impassively centered in the growing darkness. And then Ray Cuervo was dead.

Leo turned away as Cuervo's bladder and sphincter control went. There was two thousand and thirty-five dollars on the desktop. Leo paid it no attention. He wiped the obsidian knife on his pants, put it back in his pocket and pulled his shirt out to cover the gun. Then he walked down the stairs and six blocks back to his apartment. He was splattered with Cuervo's blood, but nobody on the sidewalk seemed to notice.

The cops got only a very slender description. An Indian male with braids. There were five thousand Indian males with braids in Minneapolis.

A large number of them were delighted to hear the news about Ray Cuervo.

Fuckin' Indians.

John Lee Benton hated them. They were worse than the niggers. You tell a nigger to show up, and if he doesn't, he has an excuse. A reason. Even if it is bullshit.

Indians were different. You tell a guy to come in at two o'clock and he doesn't show. Then he comes in at two the next day and thinks that's good enough. He doesn't *pretend* to think so. He *really* thinks so.

The shrinks at the joint called it a cultural anomaly. John Lee Benton called it a pain in the ass. The shrinks said the only answer was education. John Lee Benton had developed another approach, all on his own.

Benton had seven Indians on his caseload. If they didn't report on schedule, he'd spend the time normally used for an interview to write the papers that would start them back to Stillwater. In two years, he'd sent back nine men. Now he had a reputation. The fuckin' Indians walked wide around him. If you're going out on parole, they told each other, you didn't want to be on John Lee Benton's caseload. That was a sure ride back inside.

Benton enjoyed the rep.

John Lee Benton was a small man with a strong nose and mousy hair combed forward over watery blue eyes. He wore a straw-colored mustache, cut square. When he looked at himself in the bathroom mirror in the morning, he thought he looked like somebody, but he couldn't think who. Somebody famous. He'd think of it sooner or later.

John Lee Benton hated blacks, Indians, Mexicans, Jews, and Asians, more or less in that order. His hate for blacks was a family heritage, passed down from his daddy as Benton grew up in St. Louis in a sprawling blue-collar slum. He developed his animus for Indians, Mexicans, Jews, and Asians on his own.

Every Monday afternoon Benton sat in a stifling office in the back of the Indian Center off Franklin Avenue and talked to his assholes. He was supposed to call them clients, but fuck that. They were criminals and assholes, every single one.

"Mr. Benton?"

Benton looked up. Betty Sails stood in the doorway. A tentative, gray-faced Indian woman with a beehive hairdo, she was the office's shared receptionist.

"Is he here?" John Lee spoke sharply, impatiently. He was a man who sweated hate.

"No, he's not," Betty Sails said. "But there's another man to see you. Another Indian man."

Benton frowned. "I didn't have any more appointments today."

"He said it was about Mr. Cloud."

Glory be, an actual excuse. "All right. Give me a couple of minutes, then send him in," Benton said. Betty Sails went away and Benton looked through Cloud's file again. He didn't need to review it, but liked the idea of keeping the Indian waiting. Two minutes later, Tony Bluebird appeared at the door. Benton had never seen him before.

"Mr. Benton?" Bluebird was a stocky man with close-set eyes and short-cropped hair. He wore a gingham shirt over a rawhide thong. A black obsidian knife dangled from the thong and Bluebird could feel it ticking against the skin below his breastbone.

"Yes." Benton let his anger leak into his face.

Bluebird showed him the gun. "Put your hands in your lap, Mr. Benton."